a stolen suit

ANGELA CASELLA

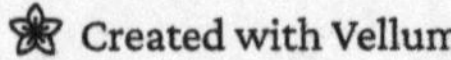 Created with Vellum

Babes of Brewing

Best Served Cold

Worst Nanny Ever

Unlucky in Love

The Love Fixers

The Love Bandits

The Love Losers

The Love Destroyers

The Thief Who Saved Christmas

Finding You

You're so Extra

You're so Bad

You're so Basic

You're so Vain

Fairy Godmother Agency

A Borrowed Boyfriend

A Stolen Suit

A Brooding Bodyguard

A Reluctant Roommate

Bringing Down the House (Nicole and Damien's story)

Highland Hills

(co-written with Denise Grover Swank)

Matchmaking a Billionaire

Matchmaking a Single Dad

Matchmaking a Grump

Matchmaking a Roommate

Bad Luck Club

(co-written with Denise Grover Swank)

Love at First Hate

Jingle Bell Hell

Fraudulently Ever After

Matchmaking Mischief

Asheville Brewing

(co-written with Denise Grover Swank)

Any Luck at All

Better Luck Next Time

Getting Lucky

Bad Luck Club

Luck of the Draw (novella)

All the Luck You Need (prequel novella) by Angela Casella

May we all find friends like Nicole to do our dirty work for us.

one

GRACE

I DON'T USUALLY dislike people. I'm the kind of person who prefers to think the best of everyone—right up until the moment they screw me over. Even then, I might make excuses for them. Maybe they have childhood trauma or a parent straight out of a fairy tale. I do. Maybe they just woke up on the wrong side of the bed.

I'm a sucker for puppies and flowers and the beauty of a good sunrise, and I read romance novels as if they're Halloween candy I've hidden under my mattress.

But if there's one truth I hold at the core of my being, it's this: I *hate* Enoch Laskin.

And now he's infiltrated my life like a worm burrows into a crunchy apple.

"Grace, are you quite all right?" my boss, Vera, says, sounding put out.

Maybe because I've been gaping at Enoch for at least twenty seconds without responding to her "introduction" to her new brand manager.

Enoch smirks back at me like he considers this some kind of victory, and contrary soul that he is, he probably does. He's wearing a charcoal-gray suit, because he *always* wears a suit, even

1

when we were in business school together and only a few other people bothered. His black hair is perfectly trimmed, as if he has a hairdresser on call, and his light green eyes look like they're laughing at me. He thinks he pulled one over on me, and he's right.

I hoped I'd never have to see him again after business school, but he showed up at my friend's bar a couple of weeks ago. I thought it was an anomaly, a piece of bad luck, because Enoch is supposed to live two hours away, in Charlotte.

I left the bar without speaking to him that day, but he had the nerve to give his card to my friend, who gave it to me. I figured that was that.

Now here he is again, popping up like a bad penny. Only this time the penny has gum on it, and it's going to stick to my shoe.

For weeks, Vera has been talking about her new inspiration. She's a famous romance author, and most of her heroes are based on real men, however abstractly. *He's so handsome,* she said, *strong and alpha, but there are layers of complexity to him. He'll do nicely. Very nicely.*

I was surprised she hadn't brought him around, since her muses usually spend time around her house, but it turns out her muse isn't a lover this time, unless Enoch is pulling double duty, a thought that fills me with fresh horror. He's her new brand manager, and Parker Brand Management moved him to Asheville to work with her.

The irony is that Enoch was *my* muse too. My novel, newly finished, sitting unread on Vera's Kindle, was inspired by *him*, and if he finds out...

I'll die of embarrassment.

I'll change my name and move to Alaska.

I'll crumple into a ball and die.

I'll...

"Grace," Vera says sharply. "You're being rude."

Enoch's eyes sparkle some more.

"I already know Enoch." I swallow dryly. "We went to business school together."

He works for my father's company. He betrayed me.

She beams at me and then him. Her hair is dyed a shade of red never seen in nature, her signature style since she first began writing, and she's wearing a colorful kaftan that makes her look like she's on vacation in a tropical place, rather than enduring the end of a relatively mild winter in the mountains of Western North Carolina. Her office looks a little like that too. Colorful scarves and shawls drape the furniture, some of which was chosen by me, and her chair is so delightfully impractical and plush I wonder how she ever summons the will to get out of it.

It's the kind of place that invites you to linger. To dream.

Right now, I feel unpleasantly awake.

Vera *does* spend some winters in warmer places, and I usually get to come with her, but this year she chose to stay home. Maybe it was because she was working on her deal with Enoch.

Am I so low in her estimation that she didn't think to tell me before now?

Unless...does she know I am...was...*the* Grace Parker? Has Enoch told her?

No, she asked me to snake the hair out of her drain yesterday, saying her housekeeping service never did it right. She wouldn't have done that if she knew.

"What a delightful coincidence," Vera says, clapping her hands.

I eye Enoch, because I don't find it delightful and I struggle to believe it's a coincidence. Did my father put him up to this?

He gives me a cool look that tells me nothing.

"I always forget you went to business school," Vera continues. "Say, Grace, it's about time for you to bring Pumpkin for her haircut. The appointment's in half an hour. Remember to tell the stylist that I want her hair no shorter than an inch and a quarter on top. But she should make sure to cut the hair around Pumpkin's butt short enough. Last time she didn't, and the poor thing kept getting poop stuck in her hair."

I know. I was asked to clean it.

I feel Enoch eyeing me. Probably with that telltale smirk that reminds me he's here as Vera's brand manager, as someone *important*, and I'm her personal assistant.

I can feel the message oozing from him. He and I went to the same program, and my GPA was point one higher than his, yet I'm a nobody.

It's what my father believes. Why should his disciple think any differently?

"Of course," I say blankly.

"Away with you," she says, giving me a dismissive hand gesture. "Enoch and I have some real work to do."

Her words are a slap to the face.

When I took this job, I felt like I'd won the lottery. Vera Valence was my *hero*, the person whose beautiful love stories had inspired me to write, something I'd always done on the sly, without daring to whisper to myself or anyone else that it was something I wanted to do *for real*.

I only revealed my secret to one person in my old life, and my gaze shifts to him. He's eyeing me with open disdain.

"Yes, Pumpkin and I will see you both later," I say, averting my gaze.

I leave the room to search for Pumpkin, Vera's ill-tempered bichon frise. She's bitten me no fewer than twenty times since she was brought on board last spring, and since she's not a fan of haircuts, I'm guessing today will make twenty-one. I head down the long hallway to the great room, where Pumpkin likes to soak in the sunshine, and am not surprised to find her chowing down on a Vera Wang shoe on Vera's Aubusson rug.

"Pumpkin, no," I hiss.

She ignores me.

Sighing, I reach into my purse for the dog treats I carry around with me. Yes, I carry around treats for someone else's dog.

Before I can pull one out, I hear footfalls moving toward me. I don't need to look to know it's him—they have just the right tone of officiousness and confidence.

Without looking up, I tug the treats out of my purse.

"I *did* ask you to get in touch with me," Enoch says, his voice a low purr. "I gave your friend my card."

"Yeah, your business card for Parker Brand Management. I threw it in the trash."

His laugh finally gets me to turn toward him. "I thought maybe you would."

"Did you know I worked for her?"

He tilts his head. "Maybe."

"Did my father put you up to taking this position?"

"It's a big job," he says, raising his brows. "It's going to bring in a lot of revenue for the company, and I'm going to bring in a lot of revenue for Vera."

That's a nonanswer if I've ever heard one.

"Good for you. And Vera. This can't be your only job. You're not the kind of man who likes to stay idle."

"Thank you for noticing." His smile is smug; my regret is immediate. "We have big plans for Vera, but yes, I'll keep some other clients. A couple of guys already work down here. We've formed a satellite office. I already picked out the sofa."

Dread beats into me. "Let me guess: it's pitch black, like your soul. I've got to go. Pumpkin and I have a date with disaster."

"I'd like to talk to you, Grace," Enoch says.

I gesture between us. "Isn't that what we're doing now?"

"You know what I mean." He takes another step toward me.

I flatten my hand in the universal *stop* gesture. "Stay put, or I'll sic Pumpkin on you."

Then the bastard does something truly unforgivable. He

crouches down, puts out a hand, and calls her name. He doesn't even have one of the smelly, crumbling bacon bits from my purse, but she leaves the half-chewed shoe and goes to him.

"You always did have a way with women," I say darkly as I pick up the shoe and stuff it into my bag. I'll take a look at it later to determine whether it's salvageable. If not, I'll be having an uncomfortable conversation with Vera.

"At one time, I had my way with you," he replies, that half-amused smirk back on his face.

I feel a weird lurch as I watch Pumpkin lean into Enoch's touch, smitten with him. It gives me some comfort to think he might get dog hair on that expensive dark gray suit. "Yes, and I see you're still sleeping your way to the top."

"That's not what happened between us," he growls.

"You have your story, and I have mine. Say hello to my father, will you?"

It would have been a good note to end on, but I'm in an unfortunate position. I need Pumpkin, and Pumpkin is currently making love to his hand. "Pumpkin," I say, flourishing one of the smelly treats.

She yips and stays put.

Enoch smirks at me. He picks up Pumpkin, and no joke, she snuggles into his chest like she's a newborn. Maybe she senses evil and thrives on it.

"Need some help, Gracie?" Enoch asks.

There's another thing to hate about him. Ever since we first met, he's persisted in calling me Gracie, even though that's a privilege I only allow my friends. He is *not* my friend. He never was, even if I let myself think differently for a short, deluded time.

"No," I say, although a glance at the clock on the wall informs me that time is not on my side. Pumpkin's stylist sees herself as an artist, and she considers any amount of tardiness a betrayal. I'm pretty sure the overly long hair on Pumpkin's rear end was a form of revenge since I was two and a half minutes late last time. I do not want to spend the next month picking feces out of her fur.

From the slight tipping of his lips, Enoch seems to know he has me in a corner.

Damn him.

"Would you like me to hand her over to you, *Gracie*?" He says it again like he knows it annoys me.

"Fine." I walk cautiously toward him.

He doesn't hand her over.

"I have a condition."

"Of course you do," I say, trying to sound bored. My heart thumps in my chest. My friend Marnie has this theory that she and I are both prey animals, and our third best friend, Andy, is a predator. The fight-or-flight response that's taken over my body suggests she's right.

Enoch is a predator.

How am I supposed to one-up a predator?

I feel a surge of longing for my friends. We're all gathering tonight for a party Marnie's throwing for her sister, but tonight feels very far away right now, pinned as I am by Enoch's gaze.

"Lunch. Tomorrow," he says.

"I don't usually take a lunch break."

He glowers at me. "I see you haven't changed. You let everyone walk all over you." He gestures to Pumpkin, cuddled against his chest. "Even this dog walks all over you."

I don't want it to hurt, but it does. It has the peculiar sharpness of an unwelcome truth.

I firm my chin. "You'd like to join them, I suppose."

"Lunch," he insists, giving Pumpkin a pet that speaks of no real affection. "You work on Vera's social media accounts, which is part of her brand. I need to meet with you for professional reasons. I'll make the arrangements with her."

"No, you won't," I say, furious. He thinks he can stroll into my place of employment and start interfering with my job? No, thank you. "We can have *coffee*. Saturday morning. Fifteen minutes. We'll go to Bear's Buns."

"Are you going to time it?" Enoch asks. He's watching me carefully, looking for some kind of reaction, although I couldn't say what.

"Absolutely."

"I'd expect nothing less." He swallows, and my eyes track his Adam's apple as it bobs in his throat. "Your phone number?"

"You don't need it. I'll meet you there at nine."

He hands Pumpkin over, and I take her, hoping the treat in my hand will ensure the transition is made with minimal damage to my person. She nips me anyway and gobbles up the bacon bite in an instant. There are moments when I'm fond of the little beast, terrible behavior aside. This is not one of them.

"Did she hurt you?" Enoch asks, reaching to take the dog from me. His expression is severe, displeased, the set of his jaw hard. "Vera needs to train her dog. I'll have a talk with her."

"No," I say as I pull away from him. Pumpkin whines but doesn't nip me again. "I'm fine. I've *been* fine, thank you very much. If you mention anything to Vera, I can guarantee you it's going to come back and bite me in the ass. So stay out of my way, kindly, and I'll do the same."

"We'll see." He straightens his tie, which wasn't remotely out of alignment. "Saturday, coffee. Bear's Buns." He makes a face. "What kind of a place is that?"

"One where they make coffee. I trust you know how to use Google."

"I've been known to refer to it from time to time."

"Goodbye, Enoch."

"You look different, Gracie," he says, holding my gaze. The words needle into me because I know he doesn't mean them as a compliment. The Grace he knew wore pencil skirts and collared shirts, or tailored dresses. Heels. I'm wearing a pair of old jeans and a flannel shirt, and I wear glasses half the time because writing on a computer gives me eyestrain.

"You look exactly the same," I retort.

I know he'll understand that's not a compliment either.

I leave the room, but I feel his eyes watching me.

two

GRACE

BY THE TIME I return with Pumpkin, I'm covered in hair clippings and I have a new welt on my arm. In my head, Enoch whispers that I let everyone walk all over me, even Pumpkin.

I'd like to dismiss the accusation, but Vera hasn't kept her promises. Maybe this makes me sound naïve, but despite what happened with Enoch and my father, I'm still inclined to take people at their word, and she's promised multiple times to help launch my career "when the time comes." She's treated it as something that *will* happen, not might, and up until now I've believed her. Sometimes she's difficult, but I figured I was paying my dues.

There's no sign of Vera or Enoch, thank God. I take a few photos of Pumpkin with the red ribbon in her hair, knowing it'll be shredded by the time Vera gets home, and get her settled in her room. Yes, she has her own room. Before I leave, I head into Vera's office to straighten up.

I notice her Kindle, sitting on her desk with a charger plugged into it.

My heart starts thumping faster. Should I look?

No, Grace, it's an invasion of privacy.

I was raised to be a rule follower. My mother died when I was young, and I was raised by a progression of nannies. My father made it known to them that I wasn't allowed to set foot in his home office or bedroom, and for years those rooms felt as off-limits as the west wing in *Beauty and the Beast*. The mystery built up in my mind, fed by a steady diet of mysteries and romances and adventures. Something important was hidden in one of those rooms, maybe something related to the mother I barely remembered.

When I was fourteen, I finally broke his rule out of curiosity, knowing he was at dinner with a client. I wasn't sure what I expected to find, but his office was a room like any other, with a desk and chair and a filing cabinet. There was no wilting rose under a glass dome, no scandalous secrets hidden in the cabinet. No file with my name on it. Nothing related to me at all, not even a framed picture of me, although he did have one of my mother.

He hadn't wanted me to stay away because there was anything important in there...he just hadn't wanted me in his space.

I feel like I'm on the cusp of another hurtful revelation, but I can't help myself.

I need to see if she's even started it. Something deep inside of me needs to know.

I turn the Kindle on and gasp. It's on the menu screen, and I can see my book—*Between the Stacks*—at the edge of the screen. It says *READ*, which means she's paged through the entire thing, start to finish.

Shock turns me into a human statue. She hasn't said *anything*. Why wouldn't she tell me?

Because she thinks it sucks, a voice in my head supplies. *She's trying to spare your feelings.*

My friends Marnie and Andy both liked the book—actually, they said they loved it—but they're partial. Vera's the real judge. She's been writing romances for as long as I've been alive. Reading her books helped me feel less alone in my father's sterile house. Reading them made me want to be an author too.

My heart sinks to my feet.

My dream seems foolish and small now, the fantasy of a little girl who never grew up. I imagine Vera and Enoch sipping cocktails somewhere fabulous, laughing at my sad attempt to be somebody.

She left it all behind for this, he'd say.

Then she'd call me up so she could ask me to buy some grapes and peel them for her.

My mind is full of buzzing bees as I make my way to Summer Nights, the bar where my friends have gathered.

I probably shouldn't go in. Marnie is having a celebration for her sister, and I'm definitely not in a party mood, but she and Andy are my chosen family.

When I first moved to Asheville six years ago, I didn't know anyone other than Vera, so I wrote a Meetup ad for a book club. Only two people showed up: Marnie and Andy. They were already best friends, but they accepted me without hesitation.

Right now, I need them.

I need to vent, or all of this will choke me.

I step into the bar, steeling myself and trying to control my expression. I must do a shit job of it, because as soon as I walk in, my friends hurry toward me. I distantly register the other people who are present. Marnie's boyfriend, Griffin. Her friends, Nicole and Damien. The old guy who hangs out at the bar all the time whose name I can't remember.

"Gracie? Are you okay?" Marnie asks. She looks like she's spent the last three weeks in a day spa, but that's what being in love can do to a woman.

Love is transformative.

It's like candy you can eat without getting breakouts and sugar lows.

It's like feeling the sun rise inside your chest.

I've seen it happen for other people, and it never ceases to amaze me. If there's one thing I believe in wholeheartedly, it's love. I want to soak it in like a sponge, even if it belongs to other people. It makes me genuinely happy.

I mean...a contact high is better than nothing, right?

In any case, if anyone deserves love, it's Marnie, who went through hell for months. Her ex-fiancé left her at the altar, and if that weren't bad enough, her mother stole footage of her fleeing the ceremony from *my* phone and posted it online. The gif and memes were insanely popular, and for a while Marnie was getting recognized almost as much as her famous sister, Sinclair Jones.

Andy and I were worried about her, and then Andy heard about the Fairy Godmother Agency from a friend who'd been helped by them. Nicole and Damien are a husband-and-wife PI team who give back by helping one pro-bono client at a time. They chose women who have been screwed over—usually by men—and are in need of a boost.

Nicole and Damien helped Marnie figure out who'd distributed the video, and as a very motivating bonus, they got her a boyfriend. At first glance, Griffin is a bit intimidating, muscular and tattooed like one of the bad boys in the romances I read, but he's actually really nice, and—

And Marnie's staring at me with a crease in her forehead. It all comes back to me in a rush of crap. Enoch. Pumpkin. That *READ* on Vera's Kindle.

"You won't believe it," I say. "*I* don't believe it. It's Enoch." I hiss his name out through clenched teeth. It's as if even my mouth is allergic to him. Distantly, I register the decorations around us—the mannequins dressed in caps and gowns. The pennants. The keg. Marnie's sister, Sinclair, is on an extended visit to Asheville. She just quit her big Netflix show, which is about a bunch of eternal college students, so Marnie's throwing her a graduation party. They closed down the bar for it because she's trying to keep a low profile—wearing wigs and makeup supplied by Nicole for her jaunts around town, and renting her penthouse under a pseudonym.

Am I wrecking her night by being here?

Nicole edges toward us. Under the low lights of the bar, she actually looks like a fairy godmother, her pink hair glowing with a slight halo, golden specks glistening in her eyes. The *I'm with Stupid. You're Stupid.* T-shirt slightly damages the effect, but it fits her personality. She looks mildly interested in the situation.

"Who's a eunuch?" she asks.

The thought of Enoch as a eunuch is laughable. There's always been something primal about him, if he's a lion in man's clothes.

It's mesmerizing, and he knows it.

"*Ee-nak*," I pronounce. Then I let out a harsh laugh. "I *wish* he were a eunuch."

Griffin, who's both the manager and principal bartender of this establishment, slides a drink to me from across the bar. I must look like I need one, because he didn't even ask.

"Thanks, Griffin."

"What did he do?" Marnie asks tightly. "Did you call him? I was wondering if you'd kept his card."

A sound escapes my throat. "I didn't call him. I saw him at work. He's Vera's new muse. He's her *new muse*!"

"Enoch's having a fling with the dragon lady?" Andy asks, sweeping her long black curls over her shoulder. Usually, I'd ask her not to call Vera that, but it feels accurate right now.

In my mind, I see the screen of her Kindle. *READ*.

"No," I say, my heart beating faster in my chest. I hate him so much that I also hate the thought of him touching her...or anyone. "Maybe. I don't know. She hired my dad's company to be her brand managers. Enoch fucking moved here to manage her account. He *lives* here now."

"Who exactly is this guy?" Nicole asks, a spark lighting in her eyes.

"He made nice with her in business school so he could get an in with her dad," Marnie says in an undertone, as if she's worried about upsetting me.

"He more than 'made nice' with me," I say, feeling rage unfurl from me, spilling out of my mouth like bile. "He took my V-card."

Andy gives my arm a *no way* shove. "What the hell? Seriously?"

"Why didn't you tell us?" Marnie asks with wide eyes.

It's a good question. I've told them everything else. I guess it's because I'm ashamed that I let him fool me into feeling something for him, however temporary.

"I don't know." I tug at the ends of my bob. "It's embarrassing. You're right. I wrote him into my book, and now I'm stuck with him in my life *and* my book, and if he finds out, I'm just going to die."

Nicole says something to Marnie, but there's blood rushing in my ears and I don't really register what she said. But I definitely hear what she says next.

"Welcome to the rest of your life, Grace. We're going to make that son of a bitch regret he was ever born."

ENOCH

I'M IN A BLACK MOOD.

I don't like how things went down with Gracie earlier. Truthfully, I'm not sure what a good outcome would have been. She wasn't receptive at the bar a couple of weeks ago, not that I'd expected otherwise. The last time we saw each other before that, I'd told her that I'd accepted a job with her father.

Right after convincing her to refuse to work for him.

I couldn't tell you why I kept riling her up earlier, only it's always come easily to me, and part of me likes knowing that I can still slip under her skin. At least I can do that.

Remi's picking at his spaghetti. I don't cook—never have, never will—and my father's right hand was so badly damaged in the accident that he can't do much around the kitchen despite pretending otherwise. He's a stubborn bastard. Like he says, takes one to know one.

Remi's the only one of us who bothers to prepare food, but he hasn't been eating much lately. I should probably talk to him about that. I'm the one who's responsible for him now, a thought that makes me want to grind my teeth.

"When do I get to meet her?" Remi asks, looking up at me. His eyes are light brown, but they're the same shape as mine, as my half sister's, and his hair is a mass of black curls.

"Gracie?" I respond, caught off guard. "You want to meet her?" My mind conjures an image of her from earlier, that stupid dog clutched in her arm, her glasses slipping down her nose a little. She was dressed in flannel and jeans, not exactly a polished look compared to the button-up-shirt-and-pencil-skirt look she favored in business school, and yet...

She seemed more herself in some fundamental way.

One thing hasn't changed: the only person she seems capable of speaking up to is *me*. It's clear from the one interaction I witnessed between her and Vera that she takes so much shit from her boss she'd need a semitruck to haul it all.

Did she shift from one jailer to another? The thought pisses me off on a deep level. Up until recently, I'd hoped she was free. I'd hoped she was finally doing what she wanted, how she wanted.

"He's talking about the famous one, dum-dum," my father says. "The Valence lady."

I snort. "You don't want to meet her."

"Correction," Remi says, setting down his fork, which probably hasn't moved anything from the plate into his mouth. "I *do* want to meet her. I want her to sign my books."

I'm a second away from asking him if his mother lets him read that shit, when I remember.

Truthfully, I don't want Vera anywhere near my nephew. I've seen the way she looks at me, like I'm the last cupcake on the platter, and I don't want to encourage her delusions. The deal between us is a business deal, and that's not a line I'm interested in crossing again, particularly not with a woman old enough to be my mother.

Still. Remi hasn't shown interest in anything lately...

"She's doing a photo shoot at her mansion in two weeks," I say. "You can come and watch."

I'm probably going to regret that. Hell, I *already* regret it, but he's smiling now. Although I can't imagine why anyone would want to watch Vera take glamour shots with that little hell dog, let alone witness the newly arranged open call for cover models—our attempt to push her brand as local—he *does* want to be a photographer someday. In five or ten years, it'll be him taking the photos.

"What about me?" Dad asks, forking up some spaghetti.

A genuine laugh escapes me. "What *about* you, you surly bastard? Are you saying you want to go to Vera Valence's photo shoot?"

He gives me a look that ties contempt with amusement. "Maybe I want to see what all the fuss is about. She must be some bird for you to move here for her."

My mouth firms. "She's one of the highest-selling authors of all time. It's a huge opportunity."

I want to remind him that he didn't need to come to Asheville. That I found him a perfectly nice retirement community in Charlotte. We haven't been close since I was a kid much younger than Remi, and living some bizarre *Odd Couple* life with him isn't likely to change that. We're both far too set in our ways and our opinions of each other. But he insisted he wanted to keep Remi company, and because I knew Remi would be alone a lot if he lived with me, I agreed like someone who's much more of a sucker.

I prefer things the way they used to be—living alone in my clean, crisp loft in Charlotte with no one to take care of but myself and whatever soon-to-die plant my mother had pressed on me.

It's not just the unexpected company. The house isn't to my taste. We needed to find something quickly, and it had to be large enough that we wouldn't be tripping over each other. That narrowed our choices. So we ended up in an old gray arts-and-crafts house, two stories, where nothing is level. The disorder troubles me more than I'd care to admit.

Dad grumbles something I choose not to hear, and Remi rolls his eyes. "You two bicker more than an old married couple."

"You should have heard him and my mother go at it," I say.

My father flinches. It was a shitty thing to say, probably, since my mom threw him out when I was nine.

Grace would have apologized for the remark, but I guess I am the asshole she thinks I am, because I won't.

Turning to Remi, I say, "How's school going?"

He makes a face.

My father grunts. "How do you think it's going? You transferred the kid halfway through the year. I told you they'd make life hell for him."

"It's fine," Remi says as he pushes his plate away. "Can I go do my homework?"

"A kid asking to do his homework," my father says, shaking his head. "Don't know where you two got it from."

"Not you, obviously." Turning to Remi, I say, "Yes. After you bring your plate to the kitchen."

His gaze shoots toward the kitchen. We eat in there sometimes, but my mother always insisted dinner should be eaten in the dining room, and even though our dining room back then was the size of a postage stamp, the lesson stuck.

"I'll clean up the dinner dishes. You cooked."

It's our deal. He cooks, I clean. He gets good grades, I get him that fancy camera he wants.

Negotiation is good for the soul, or so I've always thought. It gives a man something to strive for. Reaching beyond yourself is the only way to get to your goals.

"I'll clean up with you, Uncle Knock," he says, giving me a significant look. It suggests he has something else he wants to say to me, something he'd prefer for my father not to hear.

"Sure, bud." I pick up my plate and my father's, since he's not willing and possibly not able to clean up after himself.

Remi walks with me, but he doesn't start talking until we're in the kitchen, in our stations by the sink and dishwasher.

I scrape Remi's nearly untouched spaghetti into the trash, feeling another pulse of worry about his lack of appetite. Sauce sprays my workout shorts.

"Good thing you changed, huh?" Remi says.

I wipe at it with the dishcloth hanging over the handle of the refrigerator door. "One thing to learn before you start wearing suits, my man. Never wear them when you're eating spaghetti."

He snorts. "Don't hold your breath."

Fair enough. I guess photographers aren't much on formal wear. To me, though, a nice suit has always been a symbol.

"So what's up?" I ask, heading to the sink. I turn the water on, and Remi opens the dishwasher—when we do this together, I rinse, he puts them in. We've done this dance before.

"I'm worried about Pop."

I almost laugh. Leave it to Remi to be worried about someone else when his own life is a shitshow. He's worth twelve of me. He's a bit like Gracie, actually, although he can stomach being in the same room with me.

"Why are you worried about him?" I ask, handing him a rinsed dish. He stows it away, and we repeat the pattern.

"He doesn't go out, Uncle Knock. He stays in this house all day long with the shades drawn. All he does is watch TV. It's not healthy."

I feel a pang of guilt. Dad has friends in Charlotte, buddies he could shoot the shit with. But he couldn't stay at his house anymore, and he didn't want to go to the retirement community I found, so here we are. The last thing I want is to feel responsible for his mental welfare, but I don't want Remi to take on the burden. He's the kid. He should be allowed to feel like one, whenever possible.

"Maybe I'll hire someone to come around."

Remi laughs as he sets a cup in the dishwasher. "There's no way he'll accept that. He'll think you're getting him a babysitter."

I point to my temple. "This is where you can learn from me, kid.

I'll say I'm hiring a housecleaner. He won't object to someone cleaning up after him."

If there's bitterness in my tone, in my heart, I'm the one who put it there.

Remi shakes his head slowly, smiling at me. "Like Machiavelli himself."

I don't like that, but I won't say so. Not to him. So I just nod. "How are things at school? I mean, how are they really?"

"Pop's right," he says with a shrug. "They suck. Especially this one kid, Jeremy. He seems to have a special interest in being a dick to me."

I tousle his curly hair, and he crinkles his nose at me. "I'm not a kid anymore."

"Yes, you're very grown up and important," I say. "Jeremy and the other kids who are assholes to you, it's not because—"

"No. Being gay isn't all that exciting. Most people don't care. They find plenty of other things to give me crap about."

A look of raw pain flashes in his eyes, and fuck, I want to hug him. I want to protect him from the world, especially from his asshole stepfather and my sister, who didn't love her own son enough to choose him over the man she's deemed her second chance.

"Good," I say, swallowing down the emotion. "That's good. I mean, it obviously doesn't solve the problem of them being shits, but it's still good. You want to give me their names? I can talk to the principal. Or maybe write their parents threatening letters."

He smiles at me. "Yeah, that's going to make me popular."

"Fair point. Let me know if there's anything else I can do."

"You've already got me in therapy." His smile widens. "You've done a lot," he adds, sounding more mature than any sixteen-year-old should have to be. "You've done more than most people would."

"I'm your uncle," I say. "Of course I've done more for you than most people would."

"And she's my mother," he says pointedly, "and we both know that doesn't mean jack shit."

I should tell him not to swear. Hell, I should stop swearing around him too, but I'm probably not going to do either of those things.

I clap him on the back instead. I want to tell him that his mother will come around—that his stepfather will hopefully either fuck off or fall down a well. But I'm not confident either of those things will happen, and I don't want to lie to him.

"We'll get through this," I say instead. "You really want to meet Vera Valence?"

He gives me a wry look. "She's an *icon.*"

If he says so.

I haven't found much to like about Vera other than her success, which I can—and will—power higher.

It's because of the way she treats Gracie.

I ignore the voice. After all, there are plenty of other things to dislike about Vera, from her habit of checking out my ass to her insistence on sitting to everyone's left because it gives them her preferred view of her profile.

"Who's Grace?" Remi asks, and I startle. "You mentioned her earlier."

It takes me a solid ten seconds to answer. I haven't told him about her before. Why would I? Our history doesn't exactly paint me in the best light.

"She's someone I used to know. We went to school together, and she just so happens to work for Vera."

He lifts an eyebrow. "Is this a good coincidence or a bad one?"

I answer him as directly as I can. "I guess we'll have to wait and see, won't we?"

It hasn't escaped me that if Remi comes to the photo shoot, Grace will learn about him.

Maybe this is further proof that I'm an asshole, but I don't hate the thought. I want her to think there's more to me than a suit.

I'd like to think that too.

We finish the dishes, and I head to the gym for a long workout before returning to the house. When I get back, Remi's in his room and my father's asleep in his recliner in front of the TV. He looks... old. Vulnerable. His injured hand is splayed out on the arm of the chair, the severed fingers on display, the others warped almost beyond recognition.

When did the rest of his hair turn white? I can't remember it happening, but there's not a single strand of black left.

"Dad," I say, jostling his arm. It takes him a moment to wake up, and his eyes don't immediately focus on mine.

"What time is it?" he asks.

"It's only nine," I say, feeling my pulse pounding in my ears. "You fell asleep out here."

"Nothing wrong with that," he says, gruff. Defensive. "I'm sixty-eight. I can fall asleep wherever I please."

Still, I'm relieved when he gets up and slowly makes his way to his room at the end of the first floor.

I'm left with one thought: *Remi was right.*

I go to my office, sit, and before I do a damn thing for Vera or my other accounts, I write an ad and post it in five different places.

Caretaker wanted: Searching for a caretaker/companion for a stubborn elderly man and occasionally a teenage boy. Will need to do some light household tasks. References required.

There. I did my part.

When I open my email, the first message is from my boss, Grace's father.

I grit my teeth again.

If there's one person I resent more than my sister, it's John Fucking Parker.

I DON'T STAY at the party for long.

Andy and Marnie insist on seeing me home, as if I'm a small child in need of a guardian. I don't fight them. The guest of honor, Marnie's sister, is deep in conversation with their brother and Griffin, and I *want to be with my friends.*

Before we leave, Nicole points two fingers at her eyes, then at me. "Get ready, Grace." She pumps her elbow up and down, her forearm raised. "The revenge train is leaving the station."

I'm meeting her and Damien for lunch tomorrow—Nicole talked about it as a done deal, and I demurred, annoyed by the memory of Enoch telling me that I let everyone walk all over me, satisfied in the knowledge that he won't like it if I get lunch with someone else when I refused to break my normal schedule for him.

Nicole seems to be waiting for a response, so I settle for a wave as we leave.

When we get to my loft—one of my mother's gifts to me, although she'll never know it—Andy points to my bedroom. "Get changed into cozy pajamas. Stat."

"Bossy," I say with a smile, "but I'll take it."

I get changed into soft flannel pants and a long-sleeve shirt that says *I read romance, what's your superpower?*, and when I leave my room, Marnie solemnly hands me a pint of ice cream, while Andy, standing on the other side of the door, offers me a stiff drink. I laugh as I take their offerings. "Look at me, I get four fairy godmothers for the price of nothing."

"Damn straight," Andy says.

Marnie gives me a stern look. "You're not alone, Grace. We've got your backs. Always."

"Yeah, tell us whose ass to kick, and it'll have two feet in it," Andy adds.

I have to choke back emotion. I remember what it felt like to be alone. That's how it was before I knew Enoch. I had friends in elementary school and high school, but they weren't the kind of friends who felt like family, and in business school? I always felt like I had a target on my back, and everyone else had a constant supply of darts.

Now I have a whole crew of people at my back, ensuring that I don't fall apart. It's nice. It's a reminder that I haven't wasted my time here, even if I've possibly wasted it with Vera.

"Sit down," I tell them, pointing to the couch with the spoon. "Actually, get yourselves some spoons first. I need to tell you something."

"A good something or a bad something?" Marnie asks as she gets the extra spoons from the small open kitchen. Andy sits down, and I sit next to her, on the middle cushion—the ideal spot for sharing ice cream.

"Definitely not good," I say, my mind flashing to that Kindle screen. "It's the kind of something that requires ice cream."

"Good thing you had some," Marnie says, sitting and handing Andy her spoon.

And I tell them.

"That bitch," Andy says, her eyes flashing.

"What she said," Marnie agrees around a spoonful of ice cream. She swallows and sets the spoon down on the coffee table with a resounding click. "I can tell from the look on your face that you think it means your book is bad. Don't go there."

"Of course it's not bad." Andy's brow furrows with righteous indignation. "We told you it was incredible. Don't you believe us?"

I set my spoon down beside Marnie's. "You have to admit that you're not impartial."

"We're not good liars," Marnie says. "You would have known immediately."

"Speak for yourself," Andy scoffs. "I'm an exceptional liar when the situation calls for it."

"Not the kind of thing you should brag about," Marnie rebuts, reaching around me to give her a playful shove. "But fine." Turning back to me, she says, "*I'm* not a good liar, and I think your book is amazing. Way better than Vera's last dozen books, at least."

My heart thumps with the desire to believe her, or to think that at least it's not *nothing*. *Please* let it not be nothing.

"The ending needs work," I say blandly, my tongue as dry as if I just inhaled a mouthful of dust.

I'd poured too much of myself and Enoch into the characters, and even though I'm a lifelong romance addict, a devourer of happy endings, I couldn't bear to give one to my characters. It felt like a betrayal of myself and everything I've been through. So instead I ended it with a question mark—a reunion of the characters that might or might not lead somewhere.

Marnie tilts her head a little, and Andy interjects, "Yes, the ending sucks, but the rest is straight-up amazing. You can fix the ending."

Not with Enoch lurking around, reminding me of all my grievances.

"Should I ask her about it?" I ask, even though my heart quails at the thought.

"Yes, absolutely," Marnie says. "Trust me. I tried to hide for months after someone circulated that video of me. Hiding doesn't get you anywhere. Talk to her."

Andy gives me a dubious look, tugging on one of her long dark curls. "Just don't expect her to tell you the truth. I was pretty sure I didn't trust Dragon Lady, and now I *know* I don't. I'm sorry I have to be the one to say it," she begins, and I have to fight a smile, because even though I don't really want to hear what she has to say, I'm pretty sure she *does* want to be the one to say it, "but that woman is jealous of you. She's not going to help you."

I don't believe the first part. What is there to be jealous of? Vera has a gorgeous mansion, three closets full of designer clothes, and an endless stream of hot men who look like they walked off the pages of her books. She even has a poorly paid assistant to do her dirty work. Why would she want *my* life?

I'm perfectly content with it, mind you, but I'm not foolish enough to think it's the kind of thing someone else would covet.

"What about Enoch?" Marnie asks, studying me. "You didn't tell us that—"

I cut her off, knowing how she'll end that sentence. "It's not important. Everyone has to have a first time, right? I was a late bloomer. You've seen him. Being an asshole doesn't make him any less attractive, and one thing led to another. I would never have done it if I'd known how much of a jerk he was. That only became clear later."

"Don't worry," Andy says with a vicious smile. "Nicole and Damien are going to make mincemeat of him."

A girl can hope.

* * *

28

"This is how it's gonna go down," Nicole says with authority.

I'm glad she knows, because I'm still hungover from last night. Although I didn't really drink at the party, I imbibed pretty heavily after Marnie and Andy left.

My condition hasn't been improved by the way I spent my morning. On Vera's orders, I reorganized her book collection into a rainbow of color so I could take a single photo of Pumpkin in front of the display before returning them to alphabetical. The photo turned out really well, actually, and I enjoyed the task for the pure pleasure of seeing a rainbow of books. Pumpkin was in one of her moods, though, and she peed on a priceless copy of *Pride and Prejudice*, which is enough to sour any book lover's day.

Besides, the whole time I felt very aware that Enoch and Vera were shut into her office together, doing God knows what.

In my mind, they were laughing at me again.

He'd tell her about my foolish dreams, she'd tell him about my book, and then they'd, I don't know, copulate on the desk or something.

The last thought makes me cringe, although obviously not because I'm jealous.

If Enoch Laskin had a hold on my heart once, it was only by a paperclip, and he's the one who wrenched it off.

No, it's just...*weird*.

For some reason, I find myself telling Nicole and Damien, who obviously don't give a shit, about the devastation Pumpkin wreaked on *Pride and Prejudice*. I haven't told them Vera's possible contempt for *my* book. I can't really bring myself to, so I've decided it's irrelevant to our work together.

"You look like you could use a hangover cure," Damien tells me, raising his eyebrows.

One of them is scissored through with a scar, like the villain in Vera's book *The Scarred Heart*. The morally gray hero got that scar doing wicked things. I wonder how Damien got his? My mind conjures a dozen different scenarios, from a duel defending Nicole's honor to a hibachi cooking class. I want to ask, but even though I like Damien and Nicole, maybe even love them for what they did for Marnie, I can't deny I'm intimidated by them. This the first time I've been their sole focus, and their focus is *intense*.

Nicole tilts her head and studies me, the restaurant lights glinting off her pink hair. "Yes. Your complexion is the color of oatmeal." She pauses. "That's not a good thing, in case that was unclear."

"I'm not feeling my best," I admit.

"Our friend makes a killer hangover cure," Nicole says, patting her purse. "I brought some if you want it."

Damien's mouth curls with amusement. "This is where you should tell her there's a good chance it'll give her explosive diarrhea all day."

"What?" I ask, edging back in my seat, because two seconds ago, I'd been ready to beg her for it. My headache feels like it's split into two separate headaches that are banging. "No. Why would anyone..."

"Depends how bad that hangover is," Nicole interjects with a shrug. "If you were desperate enough, you'd take it."

"I'm suddenly feeling a whole lot better."

"Suit yourself," she says. "Anyway, we already have a basic plan. *You're welcome.* But we need to know more about what went down with this Enoch guy before we get rolling. Our goal is to tailor your revenge to his person."

The thirst for revenge feels like a dark emotion, one a nice girl wouldn't have, so I suck in a breath and say, "Revenge is secondary. I mostly want him to leave. Soon."

She gives me a long look. "And is he the kind of person who's going to scamper off if you ask nicely?"

"No," I admit.

No. Enoch's the kind of man who takes what he wants or expects it to be given to him.

She waves a hand. "So tell us about him."

I don't want to talk about Enoch, but that's why we're here, so I can hardly deny her. The waiter comes by with our lunch order, which looks about as appetizing as whatever hangover cure Nicole has tucked into her purse. At least I had enough presence of mind to get nothing but dry toast.

I pick at a piece of toast, then say, "Where do you want me to start?"

"The beginning is usually a good approach," Damien says wryly.

I give a slight nod. "We were at business school together, UNC Charlotte. His nickname was the Suit."

"*Cute*," Nicole says in a tone that suggests otherwise.

"We were the top two in our year, in practically all the same classes by the end." My mind conjures an image of him from back then, always dressed in a suit, although he sometimes dispensed with the tie. Pinstripes. Gray. Black. Dark blue. Every time I answered a question, he'd smirk at me. "He was a jerk," I blurted. "Always trying to intimidate me or make me feel like he was better. Half of our classmates worshipped him, and the other half wanted to destroy him."

"We know the type," Damien says with a slight nod.

I take a bite of the toast to buy myself a moment, then immediately regret it when the dry bread gets clogged in my throat. I down some water.

"Quit stalling," Nicole says.

Maybe I'm a glutton for punishment, because I keep playing with the bread. "No one knew anything about him. Not where he was from or what his family was like. He was sort of a legend for it. Anyway, we were supposed to work on this group project together, just the two of us. I think the professor assigned us to work together as a challenge

—or maybe a punishment. It was *not* going well in the beginning. But he caught me at a weak moment, and he...comforted me. We ended up drinking together and talking, and one thing led to another..."

"He popped your cherry," Nicole says. "Did he at least show you a good time?"

My mind flashes to the night of. I try not to think about him that way, believe it or not. Yes, I wrote him—*us*—into my book, but it was my attempt to exorcise it from my mind. "It hurt."

"Obviously," Nicole says. "There's no getting around that, although your romance books might have fooled you into thinking otherwise. Did he at least make you come?"

My gaze shifts to Damien, but if he's embarrassed it doesn't show. Then again, he's married to Nicole—if he were capable of embarrassment, she'd have burned it out of him long ago.

"Yes," I admit. "More than once."

First with his mouth. Then with his hand. He stared up at me the whole time, those light green eyes flashing with lust instead of amusement, for once.

"Did he know it was your first time?"

"Well...once it got to that point—"

This time it's Damien who smiles and says, "There's no getting around *that*."

No doubt he slept with plenty of virgins in his day. He looks like the kind of man who could deflower a woman with a glance.

Nicole shoots him an annoyed look, which he returns with a smug one, and the energy sparking between them stirs something in me. No, not like *that*. I'm not into polyamory or polyanything. All I want is one man to call my own. It's just...their connection is electric, exactly the sort of love I'd like to capture on the page.

Maybe it would be easier if you'd ever been in that kind of relationship yourself...

I shake off the thought because I don't like where it leads. Still, there's no denying that the other stories I've tried to write—the ones that weren't inspired by Enoch—feel flat and listless in comparison.

"And then?" Nicole prompts, dragging me out of my thoughts.

I abandon the decimated toast and tug on the ends of my blond bob. "I was supposed to work for my father after graduation. That was the *plan*. But I confessed to Enoch that I'd always dreamed about becoming an author. He convinced me to tell my father that I didn't want the job. To let him know who I really was...what I wanted. So I did."

There's more. Enoch and I spent the whole weekend together, telling each other things, pulling off the masks we'd worn, but I'm no longer sure what was true and what wasn't, and I've said all I can stomach to say. I push the plate away.

When I look up, Damien's staring at me. His gaze is warm, though. Understanding.

"I think I can guess how he reacted," he says. His tone is soft, like he knows he's intimidating and is trying to atone for it. "My father is a bit like yours. Powerful men think it's their God-given right to control everyone, especially their own children."

"Who's your father?" I ask before I can help myself.

"Edward Mitchell," he says with a smirk, "scion of Mitchell Furniture."

"Oh, I've heard of them," I say. I already knew Nicole and Damien were loaded—that's why they help their Fairy Godmother Agency clients pro bono—and I'm assuming this is why. Mitchell Furniture is a huge conglomerate.

"Yes, but we're not here to talk about Damien's shitty father," Nicole says pointedly. "We're here to talk about yours. What happened next?"

I sigh and push the picked-at toast back onto the plate. It looks like a bird attacked it.

"When he learned I wanted to write, he laughed. When he learned I intended to write *romance*, he disowned me. Said he'd wasted years of investment in me in the form of private schools and business school." I look up at them. "He told me that he'd never allow his name to be connected with a daughter who writes porn, and I said it was a good thing I'd already started going by my mother's maiden name. He told me I would've been an embarrassment to my mother if she were still alive."

Nicole makes an aggrieved sound. "Nothing like a rich white guy speaking for a dead woman."

A laugh bubbles out of me. "To be fair, she was a rich white woman."

My mother took care of me. Most people only have their spouses in their wills—they presume that person will take care of their children. But my mother had a trust fund set up for me. It makes me wonder if she saw his flaws. Was she in love with him anyway?

Would she have stayed if she'd lived?

After she died, my father instantly had her things boxed up. I used to sneak up to the attic to peek inside of those boxes, to get a whiff of her scent—lemon and lavender—and look at all the beautiful things she'd left behind. Butterfly clips and earrings and necklaces. *Books*. Because those things were all I'd ever have of her.

I tug my hair a little again. "But yes, my father enjoys speaking for other people. He always used to say it makes him good at what he does. Brand management, I mean."

It's amusing or at least ironic that he was so blindsided by my interest in creating fiction when he spends his life doing just that. Except he's so invested in the lies he spins, he seems to believe them. He certainly cares about them more than he does any living person.

Pain prickles my skin as I say, "I haven't spoken to him since."

I'd thought he would fold, at first. That he'd at least send me check-in emails to ensure I was okay or try to convince me to change my mind. But maybe he'd been relieved to cut ties with me.

The last words he'd said to me were that he didn't want to hear from me, or even about me, until I came to my senses. He had very clearly meant it.

Nicole tilts her head. "You said Enoch works for your father. He took your job?"

"Yes," I say, the word coming out like a curse. "He brought me out for congratulatory drinks before I talked to my dad, saying I was finally going to be free. The very next day, he accepted the job I'd turned down, so maybe he was congratulating himself for manipulating me."

"That fucker," she says, but there's an edge of glee to it that tells me she's enjoying herself or maybe just enjoying the prospect of bringing him down a few pegs.

"So what are we going to do?" I ask, looking from one of them to the other. I notice with some surprise that they've eaten their lunches, at least somewhat. I've been so spun up in my thoughts, surrounded by them like a fly in a web, that I didn't even notice. "You said you have a plan."

Nicole's grin has a ferocity that makes her look like a wolf in human form. Or maybe I've been reading too many shifter romances. "I think I have an in to his household."

"You're going to break in?" I ask, my heart thumping uneasily. What if he catches them? What if he traces them back to me? "That doesn't seem like a good idea."

Damien laughs, his whole face lighting up with it. "Don't worry, it's nothing like that. She has a *legal* in. Well. Legal-ish." The corners of his mouth hitch higher. "And I have a plan to infiltrate his workplace."

"You mean *my* workplace?" I ask in wonder.

"Yeah," he says with a smirk. "Based on what you've said, Vera likes having Enoch around. You don't want to be blamed if he leaves. We're going to ensure you're not."

I feel a pang as I remember that *READ* on her Kindle screen...and what Andy and Marnie said to me last night. Their words didn't fail to penetrate, but even if they're right about the book—and about Vera—I still need Enoch to leave.

"Aren't you going to tell me what you're planning?" I ask. They're both being purposefully vague, it seems.

"No," Nicole says. "The less you know, the better."

I glance around, decide that no one is paying attention to us, then whisper furiously, "You said you weren't going to do anything illegal."

"I don't believe we said that," Nicole says, glancing at Damien. "Did we say that?"

"No," he says, turning to me. "I said Nicole had a legal *in*. I didn't say she'd only do legal things once she used it."

Then he winks.

What on earth have I gotten myself into?

"What about a makeover?" Nicole says, looking me over doubtfully. I'm dressed in a flannel shirt and black leggings.

"No," I say, adjusting my shirt. "I've spent most of my life dressing for other people. I'm not going back to that."

"While I'm happy you're willing to take a stand about something," Nicole says, "I'm going to have to respectfully tell you no."

"What?" I ask, rubbing my forehead. My headache has only gotten worse.

"Okay, fine, I'm going to have to disrespectfully tell you no." She sighs dramatically. "Look at it this way, Grace. If you want to really torture this dude, you need to make him realize what he's missing. I'm not saying you have to dump the flannel—although you really should—but buy some red lipstick, for fuck's sake. And if you *must* wear glasses so often, get a pair that doesn't look like it was picked up from the five-dollar bin at S-Mart. Get a little glow up. You'll feel more confident. You need to be confident in yourself before you can properly tell someone to go fuck themselves. That's my goal for you. Of course, you'll want at least one really bad-bitch outfit just to mess with him."

She crushes at a crumb on the table, and I imagine it as Enoch, getting crushed under my heel. I think again of the way he looked at me yesterday, when he told me that I let everyone walk all over me. To be honest, I've thought about it a lot. "Okay," I say slowly. "I can see the merit in that."

"Good," she says, pushing back her chair. "Let's go."

"But I have to get back to work!"

She rolls her eyes. "*Pumpkin* can wait."

I'M fifteen minutes early for my meeting with Gracie on Saturday.

Bear's Buns is an aggressively cheerful bakery, and it amuses me that she chose it for our meeting. Add a point to her scoreboard, I guess.

I order an Americano and sit, pulling out my phone. I have to leave town for a few days the week after next to take meetings in Los Angeles, so the timetable for finding a companion for my father and Remi has been pushed up. There have been a sum total of two responses to my ads so far. One is from a woman who later admitted to having a fear of severed fingers, the other from a college kid whose email address includes the handle *bongbongboom*. Amusing, yes. Helpful, no.

I click into my email account, and my back straightens when I see a new response. Thank fuck. Although there's no point in getting enthusiastic until I read it. For all I know, it's from another seventeen-year-old future college dropout hoping to get paid to smoke pot in my bathroom.

I open the email, drumming my foot under the table a little because *I need this to work.*

Dear Mr. Laskin,

I am a housekeeper with ten years of experience in caregiving, having cared for my own father until his death. I know the elderly have their pride, just like all of us, and I am more than happy to clean (and even cook!) and care for your father and nephew without seeming to ;-).
If it works out, I am available to start in a week.

With warm wishes,
Dana Mitchell

She sounds too good to be true, but I'm all about having my expectations exceeded. I email her my phone number, asking to set up a meeting ASAP, and then go back to the rest of my emails.

I'm answering someone else, a social media influencer who's interested in taking things to the next level, when a throat is cleared next to the table. I look up and drop my phone, the screen protector cracking on the table.

"Oops," Gracie says. "You should be more careful with your things, Enoch."

She sits down across from me, and all I can do is stare. She's not wearing anything flashy—black leggings with mesh cutouts and a colorful tunic—but her clothes fit better, and she has on bright red lipstick. Her wire-frame glasses must have been left at home. Although she's always been very liberal about telling me to go fuck myself, both in words and in manner, there's a new confidence in her. I feel an awareness of her as a woman and a memory of her being *my* woman...if only for a brief time.

"You said you didn't take lunch," I tell her, raising my brows. "But apparently you have no compunction about leaving work to get a makeover. Vera told me you came back looking different."

Something tightens in her face, and then she clucks her tongue.

"Haven't you heard? It's gauche to talk about a woman's appearance in the workplace."

I laugh. "Touché."

She lifts a to-go cup of coffee I hadn't noticed she had and takes a sip, her lips leaving a bright red imprint that sends a pulse of blood to my dick. Setting it down, she pulls out her phone, making sure it's within my view, and very pointedly adds fifteen minutes to the timer. I have to laugh. She did warn me, after all.

I *like* this side of her. Part of me also likes that I'm the one who gets to see it—the Gracie Parker...or, I should say, *Donnelly* that isn't all sunshine and romance books and chocolate.

"Well?" she says, lifting her eyebrows. "Didn't you ask me here to complain about how I run Vera's social media accounts?"

She runs them competently, actually. Because she's about two thousand times too qualified to be anyone's assistant, a thought that makes me want to punch a wall. I'm going to prove it to her too, but not today.

Although Vera's social media accounts *do* need to be updated to reflect our new strategies, that's no longer the main purpose of this meeting. No, her father gave me a new objective.

"You know Sinclair Jones's sister," I say. "I need a meeting with Sinclair."

I know this because I did research on Sinclair—and why she's hanging out in Asheville—after I got off the phone with John Parker the other night. Imagine my surprise when I recognized Sinclair's sister as Gracie's friend, the brunette I talked to at that bar a couple of weeks back.

"What?" Gracie squawks, leaning back in her chair. I've managed to surprise her, which gives me some satisfaction.

"You know her. I need a meeting with her."

"So you said," she bites out. "How do you even know she's in town?"

"I didn't," I say, feeling no small amount of satisfaction. "But I do now."

Her red mouth twists to the side. "Oh, fu— You're impossible."

"Thank you."

"It wasn't a compliment."

"If it makes you feel any better, I already knew. People know she's your friend's sister. She's been noticed." John Parker pays people for information, and his network serves him well.

"You really think I'm going to give *you* an in with my friends?"

"I'm good at what I do, *Gracie*. She just quit her headliner show *and* dropped her manager. She needs someone's help." I lift my eyebrows. "We both know you could help her, but you'd prefer to pick up after Pumpkin for some godforsaken reason."

Before leaving Charlotte, Gracie had told me in no uncertain terms to go fuck myself, but I'd set up a Google alert for her name—both Grace Donnelly and Grace Parker. I'd figured it wouldn't be long before I saw something—a book, maybe. A residency. Maybe even a teaching job at a college. She'd shown me one of her short stories, and it was good. She's talented, driven. With wings, I figured she'd soar. But the only Google alerts I found were about Vera Valence, with Gracie mentioned as her personal assistant.

Personal assistant.

I've spent enough time with Vera over the past weeks to know she values Gracie less than she does that damn dog. Vera has her strengths, but discernment isn't one of them. If she had that power, she'd realize how much she's let Gracie take over without even realizing it.

Gracie does her social media accounts.

She's her first reader.

She organizes her calendar and media events.

She manages the rest of her staff.

Without Gracie, her life would be in chaotic disorder.

I wouldn't have encouraged Gracie to speak truth to power if I'd thought *this* was what would come of it. Has she even been writing?

I'd like to ask her, but I know that I'm the last person she'd confide in. If every person on Earth simultaneously keeled over and died and only she and I were left, she probably still wouldn't talk to me.

I can't blame her.

She's fuming at me, her eyes blistering with blue heat, like the burner on a stove, and she's so gorgeous it hurts.

To be honest, I didn't come here thinking she'd arrange a meeting between me and her friend's sister. I might be contemptible, but I'm not stupid. I wanted an excuse to see her. To push some more of her buttons.

Still. I'll get that meeting with Sinclair Jones. It's my job, for one thing, and I'm goddamn good at it. I also think I can really help her, and if I do, maybe Gracie will see that I'm not all talk.

I'm willing to put in the work.

My mother raised me with the knowledge that the things you want most are the ones you have to work for, to wait for.

"You are un-fucking-believable," Gracie seethes.

"Thank you. I think so too," I say with a smirk.

She starts gathering her stuff. I can't have her leaving though, not yet, so I point to her phone.

"You're a woman of your word, Gracie. You gave me fifteen minutes, and I have ten left. Are you really going to compromise your principles just to mess with me?"

She gives me a look that tells me exactly what she thinks of me. I'm probably a sick fuck, because it makes me half-hard.

She stays in her seat. "Sinclair's off the table. What else do you want?"

"Vera's books. What three words would you use to describe them?"

She looks at me, her eyes darting to my lips for a millisecond, like she's remembering what they taste like. I remember what *hers* taste like.

"Sexy," she says, drawing out the word, her red lips the perfect frame for it. "Emotional. *Scandalous*."

Shit. So much for half-hard. I'm all the way there.

"And which of them would be best for a movie adaptation?" I ask, letting none of my feelings seep into my voice.

She laughs. "You think you're going to get Vera a movie? You're a *brand manager*."

"Correction," I say. "I am going to help her film agent get her a movie. I'm going to Los Angeles for a few days the week after next to meet with him and some producers."

"Shouldn't you be asking Vera this question?" she asks, playing with the sleeve on her coffee cup. "She has very firm opinions."

"She does." I fight the urge to squirm, thinking deflating thoughts, but it's not so fucking easy with her sitting across from me. She's cut her hair short, and the ends frame her face in gold. "I'm asking you because your instincts are better than hers."

Surprise radiates from her eyes. "Where's a tape recorder when you need one?"

"You've always been competent. I've made no secret of thinking so. What I don't know is why you're doing *this*."

Her eyes turn contemptuous, the warm waters freezing over. "And you, Enoch? What's it feel like to suck my dad's dick for six years?"

"Dehydrating."

She gives a snort that's not quite a laugh. "Glass houses and all that. So my dad thinks he can poach Sinclair?"

"We're going to help her," I say, meaning it. "She needs rebranding. You can't be a thirty-something teenager forever."

She gives her head a little shake. "I thought you'd have figured it out by now. My father only helps himself."

"I know that," I say. "I've always known that."

Her eyebrows wing up. "And yet you work with him? What does that say about you?"

"Nothing good." I want to press her about Vera, who's no better, or barely so, but instead I ask, "And you, Gracie? Have you been writing?"

She swallows, staring at me with those eyes that go from ice to blue fire and back. "That's none of your damn business. You didn't take that job for me. Don't you dare pretend otherwise."

"I never told you I did," I say. She's not quite right about me, but she's not quite wrong either. "I'd still like to know."

"And you'll go on wondering." Her gaze lingers on me for a long moment. Maybe she's daydreaming about throwing her coffee in my face. Maybe she's thinking about actually giving me an answer about her writing. Then she surprises me by saying, *"The Wind in Her Hair."*

"Pardon?"

"*The Wind in Her Hair*. That's the one that would make the best movie. It's the book that made me want to work with Vera."

It's only after she explains that I place the title. It was published twenty years ago, but it's the book that pushed Vera, then successful but by no means big, to new heights of fame and popularity. There's still two minutes on Gracie's phone timer, but I don't comment when she picks it up and pockets it.

"Thank you, Gracie," I say. "I'll email you about the socials."

She gives me the finger and walks out.

I'm left smiling, watching her ass sway as she steps out into the cold February day.

Once she's gone, no trace of her left except for the scent of her perfume, citrus with a spicy bite, I pull my phone back out. There's already a text from Dana—a request to meet—and I ask her if she can come here, now.

If I can get this sorted before I leave for Los Angeles, all the better.

Absolutely, Mr. Laskin, she texts back. *I can be there in twenty minutes.*

I tell her to look for the guy in the suit.

While I'm waiting, I pull up the e-book for *The Wind in her Hair* —Vera sent her whole library to me, all sixty-nine books—and start reading.

I've already read several of Vera's books, not an exercise I've enjoyed, to be honest, but to properly brand a product or a person, you have to *know* them: inside and out. This is an old book, though, and I started with her more recent ones.

The difference is immediately obvious. There's a raw energy in the writing, a passion that's lacking in the newer books. A *spark.*

In fact, I'm so sucked into it that I jolt when a woman sits down across from me.

"Yes?" I ask, annoyed by the presumption. She's blond and pretty, wearing a dress decorated with little red lollipops. The dress deepens my annoyance.

But then she smiles at me expectantly and says, "You're Enoch, right? You're the only one in here wearing a suit."

I put it on for Gracie. Because she expects it from me. Because she told me once, on that stolen weekend, that she always looked forward to seeing which suit I'd be wearing each morning. That she fantasized about me tying her up with my ties.

I straighten the lapels of my jacket, trying to shake off both Gracie and the book. The last thing I want to do is bring my cock back to half-mast. "Yes, hello, Dana. Would you like anything to drink?"

"No, I'm fine," she says with a wide smile. "What can I tell you about myself?"

"I'd like to hear more about your experience," I say.

Everything she says is perfect. Her father had Parkinson's, and she cared for him as his home nurse for over five years until he passed away last fall. It sounds like she misses him and wants someone to take his place. If she's hoping my father will be good company, she's probably in for a rude awakening, but I don't feel the need to warn her. Remi's a good kid, and she'll have him around too.

"References?" I ask.

She hands over a sheet of paper with a bright smile. There are four of them, listed in alphabetical order. It's a nice touch. So is the paper—she took the trouble of printing it on finer stock.

"I think this is going to work out well, Dana," I say, because I'm already pretty sold on hiring her. It doesn't hurt that I'm on a time crunch and one of the other two applicants would almost certainly sell Remi drugs.

"Oh, so do I," she says, smiling back. There's something a little off about the way she says it, like there's a second meaning layered beneath her words, but I'm pretty sure she's not hitting on me. There's a ring on her ring finger, and I haven't noticed any telltale glances.

So what gives?

"I'll be in touch," I say, a little stiffly, and she beams beatifically at me before leaving.

It doesn't escape me that she and the dark-haired woman behind the counter exchange a significant look. *They know each other.*

I try to process that second of disquiet, then decide I'm only suspicious because the situation seems too perfect. Things usually don't work out this neatly, so when they do, it's natural to expect there's a downside. But why shit on a rainbow?

Still, on my way out, I stop at the counter. The woman behind it gives me a bright, dimpled smile and says, "Anything else for you, sir?"

"That woman," I say. "You know her?"

"You mean Dana? Yes, she's the best. Highly recommend her."

"How do you know I was interviewing her?" I ask, giving her my best blank-slate face.

"Sir," she says with a hint of attitude, "I'm standing right here. I might only be a manager at a bakery, but there's nothing wrong with my powers of observation."

A laugh slips out of me. Maybe because I'm getting told off left and right today, and I have a feeling Gracie would enjoy that.

I order some food to bring home to Remi and Dad, to help soften the news of my father's new companion-slash-maid. On my way to the car, I make the first of the reference calls—to a lawyer who says Dana has cleaned her apartment for years and "makes the floors clean enough that a person could eat off them...although I wouldn't recommend that anyone eat off a floor." I make the second and third calls in the car. The last is to a man named Reggie, who says he was her father's best friend. He actually breaks into tears while telling me about the way she took care of her dad.

It's uncomfortable as hell, trying to comfort a stranger over the phone, but the calls help soothe the unease that popped up at the end of my interview with Dana. Maybe she really is the perfect person for the job. Either way, there's no one else. So my final call is to her, telling her she's hired.

"Oh, goody," she says, which makes me cringe a little. "I can't wait to get started. I have *so* many plans."

six

GRACE

Undisclosed number: *Vera gave me your number. I agree about the book. It's movie material. What's your dream cast?*
Undisclosed number: *This is Enoch.*

"SCREW HIM," I mutter. Leave it to Enoch to text me at a number I never gave him, without disclosing his own number. Of course, I *do* have it, on that card I threw away and then retrieved from the trash after he showed up at the bar last month.

I didn't mean to take it out.

But I was tossing and turning that night, and after I fished it out, placing it on top of the refrigerator, I tumbled into a restful, dreamless sleep.

It's Sunday night, past eight. After my meeting with Enoch yesterday, I avoided my friends and spent the evening brooding at home in my pajamas. I tried to write a short story, but I couldn't get past the first two lines—*She hated him. She hated the way he made her feel most of all.* It felt a little too close to home.

Now I'm sitting in my apartment, drinking a glass of wine while I conduct some research for Vera. Sometimes she hears about sexual fetishes or practices and asks me to study them and write reports for her. It's one of the inappropriate parts of my job that is actually pretty interesting. Today's entry: soaking. The name is a bit of a mystery since apparently the act goes like this: a man will thrust into the woman, stay put, and another person will jump on the bed to create the movement between them. It's supposedly something Mormon kids do as a sex replacement, even though it's...well, sex.

I mean...where did Vera even hear that word?

Did Enoch tell her?

I should ignore him.

Or tell him to go fuck himself.

But I can't help getting swept up by the thought of *The Wind in Her Hair* becoming a movie. He wonders if I have a dream cast in mind? I have a Pinterest board for it I've been working on for years.

I type back: *Don't you have anything better to do than text a woman who has zero interest in you?*

Then: *Unrelated. Are you the one who told Vera about soaking?*

Enoch: *You're the one who answered. Soaking what?*
Me: *Never mind. It's a niche sexual thing she asked me to research.*
Enoch: *It's sexual harassment for her to ask you to do that. Does she have you do this often?*
Me: *It's a legitimate part of my job, asshat. She's a romance writer.*
Enoch: *Disagree. She can do her own sexual research. Sounds like she's done plenty.*

Does that mean he hasn't been part of her research? Despite myself, I'm relieved by the supposition.

Enoch: *What kind of niche sexual thing?*

My mind, the feckless traitor, summons images of Enoch reaching down to stroke himself. He'd do it with the same intensity he takes to everything.

Me: *That's between me and my incognito tab.*
Enoch: *You know I'm going to look this up, don't you?*
Me: *I'm not your net nanny.*
Enoch: *You're feeling saucy tonight. I bring that out in you. ;-)*
Me: *The only thing you bring out in me is abject hatred.*

There's a pause for a few moments, and I put my phone down, annoyed at myself for the way my attention's riveted to the screen. He's probably gone off to do whatever it is he does at night—seduce other virgins, drink battery acid, plan to take over the world. But then he writes, *Any man who can thrust into a woman only once doesn't want her very much.*

Tingles shoot through my body and center between my legs, because I can practically hear him *saying* it. His voice would be a seductive, husky whisper, and...

I hate that he can still affect me this way. I hate it. The sooner Nicole and Damien run him out of town, the better. I'm not sure how much more I can take.

Me: *Or maybe they just have better self-control than you do?*
Enoch: *No, that's definitely not it. Few people have better self-control than I do.*

I harumph out loud, although no one is here to hear it. Maybe I should get a dog—my mind flashes to Pumpkin—or a cat. Except...a cat would probably give me a judgmental look and stalk off instead of sympathizing.

Enoch: *We've gotten off track. Let's go back to the movie. Don't you want to make your mark on a future cinema classic? I figured you'd have at least one vision board. From what I recall, you like vision boards.*

I do. I did. I made one for our shared project in business school, for *all* my projects in business school. He always used to make smug comments about them, but on our weekend he admitted to me that he actually liked them. Looked forward to them even.

Leave it to him to bring that up now.

I can see him in my mind's eye, one side of his mouth lifting above the other, his light eyes glimmering. He's wearing a suit, of course.

What is his game?

What, exactly, does he want from me?

Did he actually read the book?

Did he *like* it?

Feeling a wrinkle form in my brow, I type, *What did Rose do after she caught Eli hiding in her barn?*

Enoch: *She hit him in the head with a frying pan. I think he would have died. Realism doesn't have a place in romance, does it?*
Me: *No, and that's why I like it.*

I can't help it, I like the thought of him reading the book and enjoying it. He sends a photo, and my heart beats a little faster as it downloads—Enoch in workout clothes, with a flat expression.

Enoch: *This is me being unsurprised.*
Me: *Who is this? You can't be Enoch. Enoch only wears suits.*
Enoch: *Funny. I think it would attract the wrong kind of attention if I wore one at the gym. Not to mention the dry cleaning bill. So? Vision board?*

If my heart flutters again as I text him my Pinterest board, it's only because it's nice to feel my ideas are valued. It's been a while since Vera has treated me as someone whose opinions she cares about. *Feel free to plunder my ideas. It's been your favorite pastime since business school.*

It takes him a while to respond this time, and although I don't like the thought that I'm waiting for him, that's exactly what I'm doing. I take a sip of wine. I watch some YouTube. I look at my laptop screen.

Finally, my phone lights up again.

Enoch: *I think of it as more of a vocation. That's who you want for the leading lady, huh? I was thinking Sinclair Jones.*

Something sinks inside of me, and I'm horrified to realize I'm disappointed. Part of me wanted to think he was texting me because he wanted my take, because he wanted to *talk* to me. But of course he was chasing his own ends, the way he always does.

Me: *Why am I not surprised? Feel free to go fuck yourself. For most people it's not as satisfying as sex, but I suspect it's different for narcissists.*

I feel a brief glow, because it's the kind of response Nicole would have made, but a memory cuts into it—Enoch pushing inside me after making me come. The look in his eyes when he realized that he was the first person who'd ever been inside of me. Shock. Warmth. Wanting.

Or at least that's what it seemed like at the time.

Those three telltale dots appear on the screen, then disappear, then reappear.

He never responds.

I toss and turn all night.

* * *

Monday passes. Then Tuesday and Wednesday, none of those days having much to recommend them. Vera doesn't mention the book. I don't either. I don't see or hear from Enoch.

On Thursday, I exit her office and literally run into him. It's the kind of thing that would happen in a romance novel, except it's not nearly as graceful in real life. While he does offer me his hand, I'd never give him the satisfaction of taking it, so I hoist myself up off the floor.

Enoch grins at me, his suit a dark blue today, with a pinstriped tie. "If you wanted to touch me, Gracie, all you had to do was say so."

"Ugh, gross," I say, although he didn't feel gross—more like a brick wall made human. Of course, I can't imagine I'd ever want to lick and touch an actual wall.

"Has Vera asked you to do any more sexual-harassment searches? If she's told you to look up *bukkake*, blink twice."

I repress a smile. "Very funny." I try to pass him, not because I have anything particularly important to do—Vera's tasks have become increasingly pointless over the last few weeks—but because I'm still annoyed by his request about Sinclair. Among other things. I also don't like the way he makes me feel, like part of me wants him and the rest would enjoy nothing better than to dole out a dramatic slap.

"You know, romance is your area of expertise," he says, lifting his brows. "You'd be doing a favor if you watched some movies with me."

"Porn?" I sputter, now leaning more toward wanting to hit him.

He laughs with genuine amusement. "Romance movies. Rom-coms. You know, the popcorn shit that drives the masses to the theater. It would be research."

"You know I'm not going to watch a movie with you."

Some of his bravado drops. "Not even one with your friend in it?"

I can't tell if he's saying it just to spite me, or maybe test me, or if he actually thinks he can bully me into setting up a meeting with her. Whatever his reasoning, it's not happening.

"Why don't you go on in?" I say, with the full knowledge that Vera is in her office listening to an extremely erotic audiobook while she scrolls through nude photos of male models for inspiration.

He wants romance? Have at it.

"What am I going to find when I go in there?" he asks, his lips inching up a bit.

"I have no idea what you're talking about," I snap.

"Is she clipping her toe nails and making pictures with them?"

"*Ex*-cuse me?"

"Giving Pumpkin a colon cleanse?"

"What on *earth* are you talking about?"

"She's obviously doing something objectionable. Your lip curled when you told me to go in."

He says it so knowledgeably, as if he's intimately aware of every feature of my face and where it's supposed to be, and for some reason it infuriates me.

"It did no such thing."

"Okay," he agrees good-naturedly. "So I guess there's no reason for me not to enter that room without knocking."

"None at all," I say, lifting my chin, all bluster. "She doesn't like it when people knock."

True, actually. She told me a long time ago that I could interrupt a pivotal scene by knocking during one of her writing sprints.

Enoch has an obnoxious knowing look on his face as he approaches the door and disappears inside. I should really keep moving—today's pointless task is to go to the sun room and alphabetize Vera's fan mail by return address so she can neglect to open it in a different order, and those letters won't rearrange themselves. But I find myself lingering by the door. There are no screams, not that I think Enoch would let himself scream even if a serial-killing clown knocked on his door. For some reason, I keep waiting. For some reason, my pulse has picked up, just slightly, but enough for me to notice.

Then the door cracks open, and he gives me a wry look through the opening. That's it, but for an instant there, when our eyes connect, we feel almost like friends.

I spend the rest of the day trying to forget about it, pausing only to be impressed and slightly alarmed that there are several red-enveloped letters that are obviously from the same person, unnamed in the return address. When I bring them into Vera's office later, she clucks her tongue but seems unalarmed.

"You know who this is?" I ask.

"Oh, yes, he's written to me before." She meets my eyes and smiles. "We're all the stars of our own stories, Grace. That gives some people an elevated sense of self-importance."

Her words feel a little on point since I poured so much of myself into my book, but I don't want her to know that.

"Yes, I guess we are," I say, tugging at the ends of my hair. "Is this writer not a fan of *your* heroine, i.e., you? Should we be concerned?"

"No, no, I have it well under control."

I leave her office, Pumpkin barks at me, and that's that.

By the time I meet Marnie and Andy for our book club meeting at Summer Nights—Griffin's bar—I've summoned the will to be annoyed at Enoch again.

"I'm sorry to say Enoch has designs on your sister," I announce to Marnie. Honestly, I probably should have told her before now.

"Designs?" she asks. "What...does he want to *date* her?" Her face scrunches up. "That's weird. I mean...not *weird* weird—probably half of the men in the continental United States want to date her—but I thought—"

I laugh. "Oh. No. He thinks he can help her with her career."

Marnie pulls a face, but I can tell it's not a *that arrogant bastard* kind of face. She doesn't think it's a terrible idea. Her sister doesn't have a new gig lined up, and in the meantime she's been hanging out here in Asheville, doing...well, Marnie's not sure. But it sounds like a whole lot of nothing.

"Marnie," I say. "Not *him*."

"No," she agrees, pulling her mouth to the side. "I guess not."

"Strawberry shortcake cocktails, ladies," Griffin says, coming up to our booth with a tray.

"You made us themed drinks?" I say, delighted. We read *The Hating Game* this month, and the hero calls the heroine Shortcake because her family runs a strawberry farm. Funnily enough, I made the selection before I was also pressed into working with a man I hate.

The drinks look fantastic, and judging from previous experience, they'll taste that way too.

Marnie gives Griffin a dreamy look that practically radiates love. "He even read the book."

"Now you're just bragging," Andy says, making us both laugh.

"Absolutely, I am."

"Don't worry," Griffin says. "I'm not angling to join your book club. Yet." He gives us an impish smile. "It's part of my long game."

"Thank you," Marnie says, leaning up to kiss him. "I like your face."

His grin stretches. "Maybe you'll do me a solid and sit on it later."

"Too much. Definitely too much," Andy says. "It was cute at first, but now you two are officially annoying."

Griffin laughs as he steps away and slides back behind the bar. Marnie seems surprisingly unfazed, but maybe that's what happens after your brother has walked in on you naked with your boyfriend. Nothing can quite compare to that on the embarrassment scale. Marnie's brother, Drew, still complains about it regularly.

"So what'd you tell Enoch?" Marnie asks.

"I told him to fuck off, obviously," I say.

They're both giving me sidelong looks.

"What?"

"It's just…you're not like this with anyone else," Marnie says slowly as if she's worried about setting me off.

Me!

Nothing sets me off.

Nothing except…

"No, I'm not," I seethe. "He's constantly tap-dancing on my last nerve. You know, he actually told me the other day that he trusts my opinion more than Vera's. Like…what kind of bullshit is that?"

Andy tilts her head. "I'm not saying he's not an asshole. He shows every appearance of being an asshole, but I have to say I agree with him there."

"Ditto," Marnie says.

I scowl at them. "You guys are just pissed at her because of the manuscript thing."

"*You* should be pissed at her because of the manuscript thing," Andy says, looking at me intently. "Tell us you're going to confront her about it."

I play with the swizzle stick in the drink. A flamingo with its foot dipping down. Part of me wants to bring it home. When I was a kid, I was a pack rat for anything bright and colorful, kind of like a squirrel seeks out shiny things. Our house was always pale and lifeless, like a hollow ruin someone had decided to inhabit. Only, I knew my father too well to display any of my findings openly. I had a little box in my closet, except instead of keeping souvenirs like a serial killer, I collected swizzle sticks and pretty stones and art prints on post cards. I hid my books under my bed or in my mother's boxes.

"Grace," Andy says, her tone all bad cop now.

"I'm going to talk to her about it," I say airily. "Tomorrow. I mean it." I make a face. "Definitely by Monday."

"You've been saying that for days," she says. "We're holding you accountable this time. No sticker on your chart if you don't follow through."

Andy's a daycare teacher. She probably *would* make me a sticker chart, and truthfully, I probably *would* put it up on my refrigerator.

"No," Marnie says, arching her eyebrows. "Nicole and Damien are holding you accountable, and they're not the sticker-chart types."

No, they're not. I feel a prickle of unease at the reminder, because I still don't know what they're up to. I tried texting Nicole about it the other night, but she'd only say that their plan kicks off next week. Every time I sent her a question beyond that, she responded with a picture of her ripping a page out of a book.

I stopped asking.

"Yeah, about that... They refuse to tell me anything."

Marnie makes a face. "They're not over-sharers. I think they get off on keeping people in a constant state of suspense."

"They're succeeding. Can we talk about the book?"

I would have enjoyed it more if I weren't living out my very own hating game right now, but I'd much rather talk about someone else's book than think about my own. Or about the fact that Vera no longer has any interest in conversing with me unless it's about Pumpkin's bowel movements.

She's writing something. Usually she'd ask me to look at the pages, but she hasn't given me anything. I guess that's a blessing since her new book is partially inspired by Enoch, and I might vomit if I had to read about his cock from Vera's perspective.

My friends and I spend the next hour or so pleasantly, discussing the book, drinking the fantastic themed cocktails Griffin made for us, and segueing very smoothly into a discussion of Sinclair. Marnie's worried she's going through some kind of crisis—either a late quarterlife one or an early midlife one. Her behavior has been erratic ever since she came to town. First, she went to several wine-and-paint classes and suggested she might be considering a career change, only to drop painting for a metal-smithing class. She made a few lopsided rings before declaring that pastime defunct and moving on to a gardening class. It only took her a couple of sessions in the greenhouse to remember she doesn't like getting her hands dirty.

Although Andy's expression is pinched, I'm not without sympathy for Sinclair's situation. I know what it's like to be the clay someone tries to mold. I was never very good at holding the shape put to me, but that's not so for her—she became the star her mother had always wanted her to be.

Now that she's fired her momager, she needs to find her own shape.

"It's growing pains," I say.

Andy snorts. "I thought we just had her graduation party. Shouldn't she be past the growing stage?"

Marnie gives her a little shove. "That would imply that we should also be past the growing stage. And I think I've grown a lot over the last couple of months."

Andy sizes her up. "Nope. Still a half-pint."

"Very funny."

"What? You're our Shortcake. Lucy liked it when Josh called her that in the book."

"No, she didn't," I say. "She found it obnoxious and infantilizing."

Kind of like when any man calls you a nickname you didn't ask for.

Gracie.

Andy lifts her hands. "My mistake."

"And I'm with Marnie. I think a person can grow at any age," I say.

Or at least I'd like to believe so. If not, I'll still be picking poop out of Pumpkin's hair by the time I hit forty.

Andy leaves first, on account of she has to be at work at seven thirty, and Marnie and I go sit at the bar. I should probably go home too, but I don't feel up to it yet.

The old timer who's here so much he's left a permanent butt imprint on his favorite bar stool—not an easy feat when you're working with wood—turns to look at us, his eyes surprisingly sharp. He looks like Santa Claus, if Santa Claus made merry with something other than bowls full of jelly.

He winks at me. "I have a good feeling about Nicole getting that job."

Job? What job?

Then it hits me like a brick to the face—this guy knows what Nicole is up to. Better yet, I have the distinct impression he doesn't care about things like secrets.

"Oh," I say slowly, "her interview went well, then?"

He laughs. "With no small thanks to me. Butter would've melted in my mouth. You know, I was an actor myself, back in the day. I had a part on *The Young and the Restless*. One of the actresses left her husband for me."

I'm torn between being impressed and not believing him. Based on Marnie's expression of dubious interest, she's closer to the latter. I want to ask him for his name so I can stop internally calling him Santa Claus, something that makes me feel guilty, but don't want him to realize he's oversharing and shut up.

"So she used you as a reference, huh?"

He nods. "She told me all about the suit first, so I knew how to play it when he made the call. Different roles take different preparation, you know? I made her sound like Mother Teresa."

"And he believed you?" I press, trying not to act to eager. In my peripheral vision, I see Griffin coming up to us. He says something to Marnie from behind the bar, and she steps onto the balance bar and presses a kiss to his nose.

"He bought it hook, line, and sinker," the older guy says with a snort, his craggy face lighting up. Lying to people seems to suit him —he suddenly looks more like Santa's younger brother than the big man in red. "He's going to hire our girl, no question. Although I have no idea what she'll do looking after a kid and an old guy. She's not the warm-and-fuzzy type."

He says it with fondness, as if he considers this a good mark of character, but my mind is stuck on what he just said. *A kid and an old guy.* He *is* talking about Enoch, right?

I mean...he called him the suit and he's telling me all of this, which suggests he thinks it has some relevance to me. Of course, he might just be the kind of person who spouts off random facts to strangers, but the conversation seemed too pointed for that.

Does this mean Enoch has a *child*? And if he has an old guy living with him...is it his father?

I don't know much about his family, but he did tell me that his relationship with his father was strained. His parents broke up when he was a kid, and his mom got primary custody.

Nicole might not be warm and fuzzy, but Enoch isn't either. He's also not the kind of person who believes in forgiveness. So why would his father be living with him?

Maybe it's a different suit. Maybe...

"What'd this guy do to piss you off, anyway?" Santa Claus says, ripping out a burp. "He bang another chick? Or did he jilt you like Marnie's guy?"

"I'm quite happy to have been jilted, Reggie," Marnie tells him, giving me his name. I feel her eyes on me, though. She wants to know how I'm dealing with this information.

I'd tell her if I knew. My mind is reeling. Enoch, living with a child and possibly his father. What does this mean?

Could he have changed?

The man I knew had his heart locked in a hermetically sealed box...if he could be said to have a heart in the first place.

When I get home, I text Nicole.

Me: *Reggie says you interviewed last weekend for a job at Enoch's, as a caretaker for a kid and an older gentleman. Is it true?*

Nicole: *Damn it, I knew Reggie was the weak link. Also, gentleman? What is this? A Victorian tea party? Are you going to start asking me about crumpets next? Because I know a woman who runs a tea shop, and I still don't know what a fucking crumpet is.*

Me: *Who's living with Enoch?*

Nicole: *Don't get cold feet, Gracie. The minivan has left the station.*

Me: *Okay, well, what's Damien going to do?*

Nicole: *Wouldn't you like to know?*

Me: *Yes, that's why I asked.*

Nicole: *His role starts next weekend. Wouldn't want to ruin the surprise. ;-)*

I seriously wish she would.

seven

ON MONDAY MORNING, Dana shows up for her first day of work in a neat black uniform. She has a pleasing air of competence, and I'm proud of myself for having found such a perfect solution to my problem. The house will be clean, and my conscience will be clear.

"Reggie spoke very highly of you," I tell her.

"Yes," she says with a prim smile. "We go way back."

I give her a list of things that need to be done around the house and also what I'd like her to do with my dad. Exercise, which he'll hate. Pleasant conversation, which he'll hate even more.

"He's not going to want to do any of this," I warn her.

"Oh," she says, giving me a sharp-toothed grin, "I'm an expert at getting stubborn men to do things they hate."

It's a bit of a strange response, and I feel a prick of unease again, but it dissipates with what she says next.

"Does he enjoy Parcheesi?" she asks, tilting her head. "I'm a shark at Parcheesi. I used to play it with my husband's grandmother."

"He does." And neither Remi nor I like it, so it's a perfect in with my father. Maybe he won't be opposed to having her around after all. "That'll get you far."

When I introduce her to my dad, he grunts in annoyance. "Seems a little rich to hire a full-time housekeeper for a place this size."

"Don't worry," Dana says with a wink. "Your son already told me that your armchair is off-limits. It could probably use a good scrubbing, but I'll keep my distance. He also tells me you're a mean Parcheesi player, so I'd like to challenge you to a few rounds. Fair warning, I don't let anyone win."

I didn't tell her any such thing about his chair, but it was the perfect thing to say, and I watch in amazement as they fall into easy conversation.

"Remi will be home at around four," I remind Dana before I leave the house.

"I'll be here," she says brightly. "I'll even make him a snack."

He's sixteen, more than old enough to make his own snacks, but I leave that unsaid. The kid could use some spoiling, for one, and I'm relieved to have found someone for this job so quickly. I'm leaving for Los Angeles on Thursday, returning on a red-eye on Sunday so I can get back in time for the photo shoot.

Before I go, I have a meeting with Vera this afternoon to discuss my approach for the meeting with her film agent. Truthfully, it's a little irregular that she's not going with me, but it's not necessarily a bad thing. I like working alone, something Gracie would no doubt blast me for. Working alone, you know what to expect. You have control over all of the elements of a problem, and there's no room for surprise. Surprises can be useful, but they can also be the enemy of success.

I spend my morning at the new office, taking calls with or about other clients—ones we're pursuing, ones whose reputations and careers we're trying to boost.

When I arrive at Vera's house, Gracie's the one who answers

the door, and with a speed that suggests she was waiting for me. Her lips are painted red again—the way they have been since our coffee date a little over a week ago, and the sight of them excites me. Her hair is pushed back behind her ears, efficient. She's wearing a long flannel tunic, but it's over a pair of leggings that'll give me a good view of her ass. Today, she has on a new pair of glasses, square and black-rimmed, making her look like a sexy librarian.

"Excited to see me, huh?" I say. I can't seem to help myself. Just like last week, when I asked her to watch a movie with me, even though I knew it was out of the question.

"Not particularly, no," she says as Pumpkin comes racing toward me. "I didn't want the bell to disturb Pumpkin."

"Yes, we mustn't disturb Pumpkin," I say. And because I want to get a rise out of Gracie—or more of a rise—I lower to the ground to pet the little terror, who instantly turns to butter in my grasp.

"You're such a show-off," Gracie says under her breath, and I laugh as I rise to my feet.

"Is Vera in her office?"

"Yes, she's waiting for you."

I notice the microfiber cloth in her hand, and my back stiffens. "She has you fucking dusting? Doesn't she use a housecleaning service?"

Grace's cheeks pinken, and I feel a rare stirring of guilt, but she keeps her head held high. "She doesn't trust anyone else with her rare books. I'm just dusting the shelf."

"Lucky you."

Her gaze beats into me, those blue eyes like ice, but they burn instead of freeze. I feel a tone-deaf need to sweep her off her feet and carry her away from this godforsaken house, but she wouldn't thank me for it. She doesn't want to be saved, and she particularly doesn't want to be saved by me. She's made that abundantly clear.

"You can go now, Enoch," she says, her voice forceful, and I'm proud of her for standing up for herself with at least one person, even if that person's me.

I *should* leave. I don't. I feel caught in her pull, as if Grace is a magnetic field I can't escape.

"I'm meeting with her about *The Wind in Her Hair*," I say. "I'm going to Los Angeles on Thursday morning."

"Is this another attempt to get me to set up a talk between you and Sinclair?" she snaps. "Because that's not happening. Third time is not the charm." She pauses, considers her words, then adds, "Or second."

"No," I say honestly. The dog whines and paws at my legs, and I lower to give it another pat. It's a miserable little creature, but if I'm petting it, presumably it won't be biting Gracie. "I just... Thank you for recommending the book. It was a good call. I think we can make some magic happen."

She smiles, and I'm gratified to see there's at least a touch of real humor to it. "Well, well, ladies and gentleman, Enoch Laskin thinks he can make some magic happen. That's a true miracle."

"Very funny," I say, feeling the urge to reach for her. Denying it. "Enjoy your dusting." The smile drops, and I instantly feel like an asshole. "Gracie—"

"Do you have roommates?" she asks out of nowhere.

"Why? Do you want to come over?" I wink at her, trying to stifle the weird twist in my chest. "I can sneak you into my bedroom."

"Yeah, no."

I laugh. "So why do you want to know? You taking a census?"

Her cheeks get the slightest bit pink, a sign that at least I'm getting to her, even if it's not the kind of *getting to her* that's good.

"Just curious. Never mind."

I'm not sure why I tell her, but this is the first sign of interest she's shown in me, so I'm not going to squander it. "My dad's living with me," I say, "and my nephew, Remi."

Her eyes widen. "Did your half sister die?"

The laughter that spills out of me is as bitter as bile. "No, she's still very much alive. Do *you* have roommates?"

"No," she says, her brow furrowing. "I live in a loft in that building downtown that used to be a bank. You know the one." She makes a face. "I shouldn't have told you that."

"My stalking plans are complete."

"Your half sister—"

I'd say more. Gracie's talking to me, actually talking, but a throat clears. Vera has emerged from the hallway leading to her office. I didn't notice her, and she's not the kind of woman who likes to go unnoticed. She's wearing a caftan covered in silver sequins—a glamor look, as if she forgot the timing of the photo shoot and thinks it's today instead of this weekend—but I suppose I'm not one to talk. I wore my favorite pinstripe suit today. To be honest, I did it for Gracie.

"Enoch, dear, don't distract Grace from her duties."

Her superior tone makes me want to grind my teeth.

"Isn't it a waste of Grace's talent to have her dusting?" I ask, a harsh edge in my voice. I'm playing my cards, which I shouldn't do, which I normally *wouldn't* do, but talking to Gracie has put me off my game.

The look on Gracie's face says she won't thank me for it—that she thinks this is yet another sign of my overreach.

Vera doesn't seem any more pleased. Giving me a speculative look, she says primly, "Grace is a woman of many talents, and I make use of all of them."

I'll bet. She has her out here working like fucking Cinderella.

"Surely your housecleaner can take care of your special collections?"

If looks could cut, the one Gracie's giving me would lop off my balls.

"I don't trust anyone else as much as I do my dear Grace," Vera says.

Swooping toward me like a bird of prey, she grabs my arm with her hand, her talons practically piercing my suit jacket. "Let's go, dear. There's something I simply *need* to talk to you about."

Gracie glares at me, and I can see what she's not saying. *Look at you, Enoch. You're as much of a patsy as I am; you're just wearing a better outfit.*

She's right, and she's wrong—something that describes so much of our relationship.

I let Vera lead me away, the little nightmare dog trotting along at our feet, but I feel Gracie's eyes on my back.

Once we step into her office, Vera shuts the door behind us.

"Get yourself comfortable," she says, pouring plenty of suggestion into her suggestion. She gestures toward a bright red loveseat in a cluster of furniture by the window. The cushions are shaped like goddamn hearts.

"Thanks, I will." I lower into the furry white armchair across from her desk. I know from experience that the fuzz will attach itself to my suit—an annoyance—but sitting here will force her to sit behind her desk. It'll keep her from pairing her unwelcome insinuations with even more unwelcome advances. Pumpkin lies down at my feet, so I'll probably also wind up with claw marks on my shoes.

At least Dana will be bringing a few of my suits to the dry cleaner's this morning in advance of my trip.

"Suit yourself," Vera says airily, although I sense annoyance behind the words. She's not happy with me for talking to Gracie, whom she'd apparently like to keep as part of the scenery in her little Shangri-la. Too bad.

Vera plays with her bright red hair, probably meant to be a coquettish move, but I ignore it and stick to the subject at hand—my meeting with her film agent.

"The book we want to push to film is *The Wind in Her Hair*," I say. "That's the one that'll get you to the top."

"I *was* at the top," she says, her gaze sharp.

"You were," I say. "Past tense. You need to be again. This will help make that happen."

"It's an old book."

"It's your best book," I say bluntly. "There's an energy in it that's missing from the others." I'm not a romance reader, not even a little, but I believe in being prepared—in doing research and putting in time—and I've done just that. Gracie was right, not that I'm surprised. That book is at the top of its class.

Vera gives me a shrewd look. Maybe a bit pissed too. "And that's the branding you want to do for me? To make me look dated and incapable of living up to past successes?"

"No, I want you to come off as smart. Able to judge what will work best. Besides, we've been talking about playing up your local roots, and what better way? The book is set in Western North Carolina."

She hums under her breath, considering it. I can tell she has natural resistance to the idea, for some reason, but I've gotten to know Vera over the last few weeks, and she's nothing if not shrewd—a businesswoman to her bones. She'll see reason.

"And what led you to that particular book, Enoch?"

I could tell her the truth, but I don't think she'll swallow it well. She's made it clear she doesn't intend to give Gracie credit for anything other than menial tasks.

"Let's call it inspiration." I give her my million-dollar grin, the one that's suckered in hundreds of clients before her. "They do say this place brings it out in people. Isn't it something about the crystals?"

According to *The Wind in Her Hair* and some research I did after reading it, Asheville's built on the largest deposit of white quartz in the state of North Carolina. Artists and the sort of people who enjoy talking about the Universe with a capital *U* say that the crystals make it a special place, full of the fire artists need to make magic happen. I say it just means there's a bunch of colorless rocks buried beneath it.

Vera gives a bawdy laugh. She taps her long French manicure against the table, studying me as if mulling something over.

She must decide I'm worthy of the confidence, whatever it is, because she brightens and then says, "I'm going to let you in on a little secret, Enoch. I assume you're the kind of man who can keep a secret."

"Of course," I say, my tone as smooth as fine scotch, "I thrive on them."

She laughs again, delighted, and says, "I have a book that's better than *The Wind in Her Hair* on my back burner. Would you like to read it?"

"You've been holding out on me, Vera?" I ask. I'm not so sure I believe her. Like I said to Gracie, I value her judgment above Vera's, but there's nothing Vera likes better than a good ego stroking. I'm used to working with narcissists. Some say I am one, but I'm not the kind of shark that plays with its food. No, that honor is reserved for people like Vera and John Parker.

"Only a foolish woman would hold out on you," she says suggestively, making me internally groan. Another tap of her fingernails. "I've been working on a top secret project for years now."

"Something other than the one I inspired?" I ask. She hasn't hesitated to let me know that I'm her most recent inspiration, something I found amusing and a little troubling, to be frank. I don't want Vera sneaking into my house to look through my underwear drawer as inspiration, or spraying me with her hose so she can see what I look like with my shirt wet.

"Yes," she says. "Something that's finished." She makes a face. "Almost finished. The ending is the weak link, but it'll be an easy fix. This is the book you should be pitching to agents."

Tap.

"And it's not published yet?"

This intrigues me more, because if it hasn't yet been published and her film agent manages to sell the rights, it's possible the film could be released soon after publication. That would certainly launch Vera right back up to the top. If we could get the production company to commit to filming locally? Even better. It would be a brand makeover people would weep over. Suddenly I'm eager to read this book, whatever it is. It might be the golden grail I've been looking for.

"No," she confirms. "I'll be sending it to my agent shortly, but maybe I'll let you look at it first, lucky boy, since you're leaving for Los Angeles so soon. It would be a shame for you to waste your meeting with Frank. He's much better at strategizing in person."

Despite the possible advantages, it seems like an ass-backward way to do things—talking film before she talks publication, but when I say so, she waves a hand dismissively.

"There are a few loose ends I need to take care of before I make things official, but I have no doubt my publisher will want it. It's the best work I've done in years."

"Color me intrigued."

"I need to shore up a few details—the ending, like I said, and a few other inconsequential things—but it's going to be a real hit. I'll make sure to get it to you before your flight on Thursday."

I give a nod. "What's it called?"

"*Between the Stacks*."

GRACE

I'M GOING to do it.

I'm going to damn well do it.

Tomorrow.

I meant to talk to Vera today, but she was in a weird mood after Enoch took off. She shut herself into her office and only left once, to ask me to find her some laxatives. It seemed like a bad idea to bring up a serious topic if she was backed up, and after I brought them to her...well, she was going to be busy, right?

I can practically hear Andy in my head telling me, *You're making excuses.*

Actually, I don't need to hear her in my head—she's been bombarding me with texts about it since last Thursday. Consider this conversation from earlier tonight:

Andy: *You said today was the day. Was today the day?*
Me: *No.*
Andy: *No time like the present. Ticktock.*
Me: *It's nine o'clock.*
Andy: *She looks like a night owl.*
Andy: *Do you want me to confront her for you? I'll totally do it.*

The thing is, if there was any chance this conversation would go well, then Vera herself would have brought it up, right? I mean, I'd love to believe she'll sit me down and tell me my book is brilliant and the only reason she's been silent is because she's been planning some sort of cake surprise to celebrate my genius. Actually, I like that scenario so much, I spend a good five minutes visualizing it, but it never hardens around the edges. When Vera wants to say something, she out and says it. She has the confidence of a woman who's used to building universes with her words. The thought gives me an ache, because that's what I want for myself.

So why don't you take it?

I can feel Enoch telling me I'm weak. That I'm letting someone else decide who I am for me...and I accidentally bite my tongue. Crap. It's bleeding.

I don't like that he's right, and not just because I hate it when he's right about anything.

I also don't like that it's come to this. In the beginning, my job was maybe twenty percent personal errands and eighty percent helping Vera with *her* job. I can't pinpoint when that changed—it was one small thing at a time. There's that saying about eating an elephant, how you need to do it one bite at a time, and sometimes I think that's what she's done to me. I didn't even realize there were pieces of myself missing until it was too late.

Then there's the other thing on my mind...Enoch and his roommates. How'd he come to live with his father and nephew? He's not the sort of person who plays well with others. He's too driven, too fastidious. It's impossible for me to imagine the man I knew living with a teenager. I don't want to be interested, but I am.

Is it morally wrong of me to want to boot Enoch from my life, and Asheville, when I'd be giving them the boot too?

I call Nicole to talk about it after a glass of rosé and a chocolate bar, my go-to cheer-up method, fail to banish images of her tripping a teenager or feeding an old man spoiled carrots. I mean...what the hell is she doing over there anyway?

She ignores the call and instantly responds by text message.

Nicole: *Only call me if you're dying. Are you dying?*
Me: *No, but I'm getting cold feet.*
Nicole: *You know what else has cold feet? A corpse.*
Me: *Is that a death threat?*
Nicole: *No, but it would be a pretty cool one, huh?*
Me: *I didn't know Enoch was living with his dad and his nephew. Don't mess with them. They've done nothing wrong.*
Me: *Nothing wrong to me, at any rate.*

They are related to Enoch, after all, so who's to say they've done no wrong to anyone?

Nicole: *I'm going to HELP them, Grace, just like I'm going to help you. It's Enoch who needs to worry.*

This pacifies me, slightly, although I'm starting to realize that what Nicole means by *help* doesn't necessarily fit other people's definition of the word. I sip down the rest of my wine and sit watching *Bridgerton*, but my mind keeps skipping back to Enoch. What could have possibly induced him to take custody of his nephew if his half sister is still alive? Why did he come to Asheville in the first place?

It still feels too coincidental to be a coincidence, but I don't have a large enough ego to think he did it just to fuck with me, or because he thinks we have unfinished business. After all, he said he and a couple of other guys have opened an Asheville branch of Parker Brand Management. Surely even Enoch, even my *father*, wouldn't do such a thing just to poke at me. And yet, I can't help but think it's an offensive move of some kind.

Although I haven't heard from my father for years, I *am* subscribed to the Parker Brand Management newsletter. Not by choice, mind you. I cancelled the subscription, twice, but those emails still find their way to me.

I think it's my father's way of showing me he's still watching. Or maybe that he still disapproves of me and thinks I'm unworthy of the name I rejected.

Before I know it, the show's credits are rolling, and I didn't even absorb a single line of dialogue. My wine is gone.

Without really meaning to, I text Enoch.

Me: *Why are your father and nephew living with you?*
Enoch: *Hello, Gracie. I see you kept my card.*

Goddammit. I grit my teeth. So *this* is why he hid his number when he texted me the other day. He wanted to find out if I'd saved his card despite saying otherwise.

Teeth still clamped together tightly enough to hurt my jaw, I type, *You know what they say about keeping your enemies close.*

Enoch: *Is that an invitation?*
Me: *Forget it.*

I cast my phone aside with a huff. It's only morbid curiosity that has me picking it up again after it vibrates.

Enoch: *My sister relinquished custody of my nephew. I can only assume my father came to Asheville with us because of FOMO. He certainly isn't helpful around the house.*
Enoch: *So you can be properly judgmental of me for making that comment, I should mention that he suffered an injury at work a few years ago and hasn't been able to work since.*
Me: *No workman's comp?*

Enoch: *They said it was his negligence.*

My mouth drops open, and I'm flooded with righteous indignation.

Me: *That's ridiculous!*
Enoch: *They were right. He was on a night shift, and he was taking some-thing to stay awake.*

I'm shocked he's telling me this much. I want to know more. I'm desperate to ask why his half sister would ask him to finish raising her son, but it's none of my business, and I don't want him to think I want to know.

Yes, I see the irony there.

Enoch: *Any other questions, Gracie?*
Me: *Yes. Dozens.*
Enoch: *Why don't you make a list and send it my way?*
Me: *You'd answer?*

The very thought shocks me. He's never been the sort to play his cards—they're held so tightly to his suit jacket, they're practically sewn up in the pocket.

Enoch: *Nah, but it'd allow me to ignore them in order.*
Me: *You're impossible.*
Enoch: *I prefer improbable. Has Vera asked you to research any other niche sex things?*
Me: *Yes, I'm watching porn as I write this.*
Enoch: *Making it would be better practice.*

It's a sign that there's something very wrong with me that I'm smiling as I push my phone away again.

* * *

The next morning dawns bright and sunny. It's the kind of day where it feels like anything can happen—as if you've stepped into a happy book, the way I used to pretend I could when I was a kid.

That's a good sign, right?

The fairy-tale feeling wanes by the time I get to Vera's house, though, because within five minutes the following things unfold: I step into a mess Pumpkin left by the front door, which is so putrid I can't actually tell which end it came out of; Vera asks me to clean it and give Pumpkin a bath; and in chasing Pumpkin to the bathtub—barefoot for obvious reasons—I slip on a rug and fall on my face.

This is going to be a disaster.

In fact, Vera is cold and distant all morning, to the point where I'm wondering if I should ask what I did to offend her. She gives me a very long list of tasks, most of them pointless busy work, from reorganizing her bookshelves so the books are in reverse rainbow order to laundering and folding Pumpkin's spring outfits since she's *certain the weather will warm soon* now that February's almost over.

How is this the same woman who used to send me her manuscripts chapter by chapter, who's told me dozens of times that she simply couldn't do without me, and who cried after drinking too much sake in Japan last year because she misses her mother?

That woman has been a second mother to me. She's filled the void inside of me left by the loss of the mother I only remember as a feeling, not a person. She's encouraged my dream in a way my father never did.

Of course, there's the other side of Vera too, the one that Andy always likes to bring up. She can be callous with other people's feelings, almost as if she doesn't realize other people *have* feelings. Example. Vera spent several months last year dating a twenty-two-year-old model and a successful surgeon, neither of whom knew about the other, and then made me break up with the model for her.

He cried on my shoulder—literally—and I had to spend half an hour assuring him he was beautiful (he was).

Doesn't matter. I need to talk to her.

So after I finish folding a tutu covered in hot dogs in buns, I steel my nerves, imagining I'm someone fiercer—someone like Andy or Nicole, who have teeth designed for something other than gnawing plants—and show myself into Vera's office.

Despite her no knocking rule, she squawks and slams the lid of her laptop shut when I walk in, shooting me a dirty look from her desk. Maybe she just doesn't like to damage the mystique—for years she used only a typewriter, and I was the one who transferred her manuscripts to word processing, word by painful word, but recently she made the switch to the twenty-first century. She made me swear on one of her valuable editions of *Pride and Prejudice* not to tell anyone.

Is it a sign that that very edition was damaged by Pumpkin's pee?

"What is it, Grace?" Vera asks coldly, her eyes cool and distant. "Can't you see I'm busy?"

Part of me wants to turn away, to slink out of the room like a child who's done something wrong, but I hear Enoch in my head again—*you let everyone walk all over you*—and Andy—*that woman's not going to help you.* I need to know.

I approach the desk, and Vera's gaze turns even colder, casting an Arctic chill on my skin. "I said I'm busy."

"I'll only take a minute of your time," I say, not jumping to soothe her like I usually would. She calls it her artistic temperament, the way she sometimes jumps down people's throats.

She watches me as I lower into the fuzzy chair across from her, and even though my heart is pounding in my chest, telling me to *run, run, run*, I keep my composure. "I wanted to talk to you about my book, Vera. It's been a few weeks now. Did you have the opportunity to read it?"

She works her lips to the side as she studies me. There's something in her eyes, but I can't read the look. If I were asked to describe it in writing, I'd choose the word *elusive*.

"Yes, I've been meaning to speak with you about that, dear."

Thump, thump, thump. My heart is a rabbit, leaping about in my chest.

She makes a face. "The thing is, darling girl, some people aren't meant to be writers. You have a real talent for editing, for making other people shine, but you don't have any shine of your own." She taps a nail against her desk, her expression a little wry. If she knows she's twisting my heart and wrenching it out of my chest, it doesn't show.

Or maybe she's enjoying it, whispers a voice inside of me.

"Oh," I say softly. "But you read it?"

Her lips pull down farther. "I did. The writing is tolerably good, but I think it would be a shame for you to try submitting it to any agents. There's the connection to me, you know, and I wouldn't—"

"You'd be embarrassed."

"Now, I didn't say that," she says, tapping her fingers again. "But. Even so."

"I see," I tell her.

I want to believe Andy. I want to think Vera's just jealous, but why would she be? Even if she thinks the book is good, she's written almost seventy of her own, all of which have been bestsellers to some degree or other. Any small success of mine would do nothing to diminish hers.

"Well," I say, clearing my throat of emotion, "would you like me to read anything for you? It's been a while."

"Thank you for offering," she says, pursing her lips, "but I'd like to keep the projects I'm working on now strictly confidential. You'll be the first to read them, of course—I depend on you to give me some of that shine—but they're not ready for other people's eyes."

Something twists inside of me, and I'm angry without knowing why, without having a real outlet for that anger. I'm tempted to quit, but I didn't give myself a plan B. I don't have anything else lined up.

My mother made sure I was taken care of. I have money—enough of it that I don't need to work—but I'm the kind of person who can't not work. I guess I'm like my father in that way. I need a purpose to drive me, and Vera's just yanked mine away.

You've published short stories under a pseudonym, that voice in my head reminds me. *They're not as good as* Between the Stacks, *but your editors liked them. They asked for more. Your friends loved the book other than the ending.*

I guess my dream is not so eager to die.

"I'll go see to my list," I say. There's a hot press of tears behind my eyes, but I won't let them fall. I know she'd see it as a weakness. Maybe even a victory. "Wouldn't want to miss a speck of dust."

She studies me, her gaze shrewd, and for the first time, I find myself wondering if Vera actually *likes* me. There's something detached in the way she's looking at me—as if I'm a bug she might or might not crush with her shoe. "I'm not sure I appreciate your tone, Grace. There are any number of young women out there who would be beside themselves with gratitude to have your position. Wonderful benefits. International vacations. Exposure to beautiful people. First look at my manuscripts."

"I know."

She continues to look at me like that for several seconds before saying, "I tell you what. Why don't you take next Monday off? We'll probably both want a lie-in after the photo shoot."

"Thank you," I say stiffly, since she's clearly expecting it.

I leave the office and shut the door behind me. There's no sign of Pumpkin, so she's probably off destroying something priceless. Now that I'm away from Vera, now that there's at least a shut door between us—the wood a heavy mahogany—those tears are reasserting themselves.

I'll go to the scullery. (Yes, this house has one.) Vera never goes there, so I can tuck myself away for a good cry before I take up that list of chores. At least the duties she's laid out for me are mindless. The day will be done before I have a chance to think about it too much, and then I can meet up with Marnie and Andy.

I make my way there, barely paying attention to my surroundings—one hallway and then another, through the little-traveled back statue room—and then slam into a solid chest. I take a step back, stunned by the impact, and by the feeling of static electricity that accompanies it.

"Gracie." It's Enoch, dressed in a charcoal-gray suit with a green tie that matches his eyes.

Not him. I can't deal with him right now. I *can't*.

"Gracie," he repeats, his tone intense.

"What are you doing?" I blurt. "No one comes to the back statue room."

"Do they favor the front one?" he asks, but he's not smiling as he says it. His hand traces up my cheek and finds the tears that have started streaming down my face.

"What? Do you want to drink them to exult in your victory?" I ask.

His expression is horrified. To be fair, it was an aggressive question. It's just...someone said that in the book I read in between bouts of sleeplessness last night. I guess it stuck in my head.

"Is that what you think? You think I *want* you to cry?" He looks around, then pulls me to the side, behind an enormous statue of Dumpling, Vera's previous dog—an enormous black Newfoundland. There's a stately pillar behind it, the kind of thing that belongs in a Grecian temple rather than a private home. It strikes me with no small amount of amusement that Pumpkin is trailing Enoch like a loving lap dog.

He's not going to like you back, Pumpkin.

"*What did she do?*" Enoch's hand is still on my arm, the points of contact sending tingles of sensation through me like I'm one of those lightning balls.

He's being good to me, finally, and for some reason that stokes the anger buried inside my chest.

"What right do *you* have to act like you care?" I ask through my teeth. "You've made it very clear what you think of me."

His expression sobers and he lets his hand drop. "The world's not painted in black and white, Gracie. Everything's brushed in different shades of gray. Including me. Including *you*."

"I'm not surprised you think so," I say. "It gives you an excuse to take whatever you want and rationalize it away. You're not going to rationalize away what you did to me." I make the mistake of reaching out to push his chest. It's solid, with no give. It feels delectable. I let my hand drop. "I let you in, and you *betrayed* me."

Some anger lights in his eyes, making them a lighter green, as if they glow from within. I'm caught within that gaze, pinned like a butterfly, and I realize this is the harm of Enoch. He could still pin me to a board—or a bed—with such little effort, and if he knew, if I *let* him know, he would destroy me. My will is as thin and flammable as paper when it comes to this man, despite everything, including my contempt for him.

His nostrils flare. "You think I take everything I want?"

"Don't you?" Suddenly I'm breathing heavily, like the air has turned heavy and thick. Like we're breathing in liquid.

He takes my hands in one of his, so large it easily encompasses them, and the air leaves my lungs when he pins them to the pillar, as if he heard my innermost thoughts, as if this is him staking his claim on that butterfly. There's an instant when I could pull away, when I know he would let me, but I don't. Then, his eyes blazing into me, he kisses me.

His lips are hot on mine, claiming and fierce. *Familiar.*

I should push him away. I *should*. But it's only a surprised instant before I'm parting my lips and inviting him in, his tongue weaving with mine as he pushes me against that pillar. It feels molten and hot and wicked, and it fills me with a kind of wanting that's surely too big for one woman. It feels like I'll choke on it. His hard body is crowding me, his silky tie pressing into me, making me wish he'd pull it off and tie my hands. That he'd rip my clothes off and take me here in the back of Vera's house.

It's the kind of thing that happens in my fantasies. Maybe that's why I pull one of my hands free...but only to guide *his* hand beneath the waistband of my leggings.

He takes the permission greedily, hissing into my mouth when he finds me wet. While his other hand still holds me to the pillar, pinned in place for him, his mouth moves over mine, and he circles my clit and curls two fingers up into me, finding a spot that makes my knees so weak I'd tumble if he weren't pressed into me. So big and strong. So much of him. But it's not enough. I press harder into his mouth, my hips bucking against him, my tongue fighting with his. I want my other hand back, but only so I can pull him closer. Only so I can wrap it around his dick.

I feel myself heading for the edge. Yes, I'm about to come in my boss's house, pressed to one of her pointless decorative pillars, behind a *dog* statue, and at this particular moment I don't care. It feels good. It feels like living. Pumpkin paws at my leg, but I barely notice her. Every molecule of my body is focused on what Enoch's doing to me—on what he's making me feel.

He pulls back his head slightly, and I nip his lip in protest, but it only makes him smile.

"You're about to come for me, Gracie, I can feel it. You're about to come on my hand."

His smug tone pisses me off, but I want to finish. I want it badly enough that I settle for bucking into him, keeping silent. I won't admit with words that I want him.

Then he pulls his hands out of my leggings, right when I'm on the edge of a pleasure that was practically blinding in its intensity, and lifts his fingers to his mouth. Keeping his eyes on mine, his one hand still holding mine to the pillar, he sticks them in his mouth and licks them clean.

Then he releases me. He...he's stepping away.

"How *dare* you," I accuse, my breathy voice betraying me to my own ears. My body is an ache made human. I was so close. So achingly close. I push Enoch's hard chest, moving him not an inch. "Why would you do something like that?"

He gives me a look I can't fully untwist. "You told me I take what I want. This is me, proving you wrong."

And then he walks away from me, Pumpkin trotting at his heels, leaving me more confused than I've ever felt in my life.

I RUN HARDER, my body straining, sweat dripping down my face and neck and chest, but it's not enough. I stop the treadmill and wipe off with a towel before heading over to the weights, choosing ones that will punish my body.

Not enough. Not enough.

My mind keeps going to Grace, to the way she looked at me when I pinned her arms to that pillar, her eyes hooded behind those librarian glasses, her red lips slightly parted, her body bowing toward me in invitation. To the way she pushed my hand into her pants and the feeling of her sweet pussy clenching around my fingers.

I'm an asshole for not giving her what she wanted. For trying to prove a point even though I'm not altogether sure what the point was other than that I want her and I can't have her.

If she didn't hate me before, she certainly does now, but it's better if she hates me. It's easier. Because I seem to have trouble staying away from her, so she'll need to be the one who stays away from me.

After half an hour, I give up and head to the showers. It's late by the time I head home, past seven, so I'm surprised to see Dana's car still in the driveway. She was supposed to leave at five. Still, maybe she decided to stay late to get to know Remi. I can hardly fault her for that.

But when I open the door, there's a weird smell in the house, like a dumpster burped. Did Dad or Remi get sick? Is that why Dana stuck around?

But I only have half a second to worry, because a creature gallops around the corner and jumps up on me, its front paws practically as high as my armpits. It's ugly, with brown hair that's long and short in patches and an underbite that distorts its face. Within seconds, it's licking my face.

It takes me a beat to process a few things: This is a dog. It's in my house. It's the source of the garbage smell.

"Uncle Knock, you met Udolpho!" Remi says, following the nightmare dog. He has something in his hands, but I don't register what it is because the dog is still propped up on me. I cringe a little as I push it off. It instantly sticks its head into my crotch, sniffing. I push it away.

"What?" I ask. Not exactly my most eloquent, but it's been a hell of a day.

Twenty seconds later, Dana and my father enter the room, Dana with a glint in her eye.

It strikes me that Remi and my father are carrying mugs of hot cocoa. What gives? My dad is not a hot cocoa sort of man, not unless there's bourbon in it, but surely his new companion wouldn't be giving him bourbon...

"So you met our new friend," Dana says ruefully. "He showed up at your doorstep after Remi came home from school. Can you believe it? He scratched a couple of times, and we had to let him in. There's no tag, but I have a friend who works at a dog shelter. I'm sure she'll be happy to check for a microchip."

"Good—so you can take him?" I ask. The house has already been tainted with the garbage smell, and I can see that some of his fur has brushed off on the couch, but it'll be easy enough for her to clean up after him when she comes in tomorrow.

Dana gives a significant look to Remi, whose face has fallen. For some ungodly reason, he's set his cocoa down so he can pet the beast, which looks large enough that it could give him rides. I know what Dana's trying to communicate, and revulsion courses through me at the thought.

"It's not a good idea for us to have a dog, bud," I tell Remi. "This isn't a house for pets. It's too small."

It's a logical argument, and I expect him to go for it. After all, there's only sixteen hundred square feet to work with, split between the three of us, and now we have Dana around during the day. The last thing we need is a dog to add to the chaos, particularly one like this, big and bumbling and smelly.

But Remi looks downcast, something I've seen enough of lately, and I have the not-exactly-novel feeling of being an asshole, a crusher of dreams, a betrayer of hopes.

"I could get you some free supplies to get you started," Dana says, shrugging a shoulder. "Some bowls, a leash, that kind of thing. Like I said, I know a woman who runs a shelter."

I shoot her a *not helping* look, but she doesn't respond.

"Wouldn't your friend be able to put him up?" I ask through my teeth.

She makes a face and tilts her head. Bites her lip. "Udolpho looks like the kind of dog who'd be put down at a shelter, to be honest. I'd give him twenty-four hours. Maybe less if he's a barker."

Fuck. Remi looks like someone just gave *him* a death sentence, not the mangy dog.

"Wouldn't be so bad to have a dog around here," my dad offers, taking a sip of the cocoa-maybe bourbon before he continues. "You always had a dog growing up."

We did, when he lived with us. But he moved out when I was nine, and my mother never had any animals in the house after that.

No messes, no unpredictability—everything orderly, just the way she and I liked it.

But there's a longing in my dad's expression too. Shit. Lately, he and Remi haven't seemed excited by anything, other than Remi showing some interest in this weekend's photo shoot.

I cast a glance at the dog just as a string of foul slobber falls from its mouth to the hardwood floor.

"I'm not walking this thing," I say, gesturing to him.

"His name's Udolpho," Dana supplies unhelpfully. It's on the edge of my tongue to ask who came up with that godawful name, but for all I know it was my nephew.

"You won't have to," Remi blurts, his hand still buried in the dog's coat. He really shouldn't touch him before we give him a bath. "I'll do everything."

I'm reluctant.

No, I'm beyond reluctant, but I've skimmed a few books on parenting a teenager over the last few months, and all of them encourage me to give Remi responsibilities and encourage him toward independence. His therapist suggested the same thing the last time I spoke with her.

Maybe this isn't such a bad idea.

Actually, from the way my nephew is looking at me, I don't have much of a choice.

"Okay," I say. "He can stay for now. But we're going to bring him in to the shelter to see if he has a microchip," I add. Even as I say it, I know it's a lost cause. If someone "lost" Udolpho, I'm pretty damn sure they did it on purpose. He's not some gold-ribbon puppy someone's weeping into their granola about. "We need to give him a bath though." I wrinkle my nose. "Maybe two."

"We already did," Dana says, smiling beatifically.

"So this is the way he naturally smells?"

My father huffs a laugh and lowers into his armchair, which, true to Dana's word, she has not cleaned.

Actually, come to think of it, the house doesn't look as immaculate as it should, all things considered. Maybe it's just the incursion of the dog, but there are hair particles on the floor, and I see a smudge on the wall next to the door. A Parcheesi set has been left out on the coffee table between my father's chair and the couch, and there are two partially drunk glasses of water sitting on it without coasters.

I certainly couldn't eat off the floor, like that lawyer lady claimed.

"You didn't smell much better when you were a half-pint," my dad says, shifting my attention to him.

Remi and Dana both laugh, and suddenly it feels like I'm on the outside looking in on their happy trio, and even though I didn't want to live with Remi and my dad, and I feel like this whole situation was forced on me, I can't deny there's a little pang in my chest.

Still. I don't want a dog, especially not *this* dog. My mother used to say they tracked in dirt and shed fur, and this is Exhibit-Fucking-A that she was right.

Gracie would keep the dog.

Hell, she would probably knit it a welcome mat and bedazzle its water bowl. She'd give it hugs and cuddles and make it feel like a rockstar just for being born.

Maybe that's why I feel the rest of my objections crack like spider-webbed glass. I don't like the way Gracie sees me. I don't want to be that man anymore, the one who takes but doesn't give. This is something I can give to my dad and Remi.

I don't want to come off as a total pushover, though, especially with a new employee, so I nod to Dana. "Can I talk to you for a moment?"

"I don't see any reason for that," my father says, surprising me. Why the hell does he have an opinion about this? He was resistant to hiring her, annoyed by her presence until she offered to play Parcheesi with him.

"Dana *needs* to get home," Remi agrees, his hands still on the sloppy dog's coat. The animal looks up and gives him a wet kiss that makes me cringe. "She only stayed this late to help with Udolpho."

Yes, I'm sure she did. Intuition pricks at me that something's up with Dana, but I can't put my finger on what that might be. Besides, it's quite obvious that both Remi and my father love her, and wasn't that the whole point in hiring her?

"We'll talk in the morning, if that's okay," Dana says, patting my arm.

There's something firm in her voice, something that tells me no isn't an answer she'll accept, and for some reason, I'm reluctant to push her. Maybe it's because I feel like I'm on uncertain footing here, in my own house.

The dog gives a sad little yip as she moves toward the door, and I barely restrain the impulse to tell Dana to take him with her, please, for the love of God.

"Goodbye, friends," she says, although her gaze only takes in Remi and my father, not me. Then she finally looks my way and adds, "I brought the suits you need for the trip to the dry cleaner. They'll be ready right before you leave. Guaranteed."

At least she did something useful.

I nod firmly, not smiling, because I've lost control of this moment so utterly I need to express my dissatisfaction in some way.

When she leaves, shutting the door behind her, my gaze settles on Udolpho. "I guess he'll need dog food."

"There's no need for that right now," Remi says, still petting the beast. "She gave Udolpho some rice and beans. We already ate too. Dana said she was going to save something for you in the refrigerator."

My father has already opted out of our conversation, turning on a rerun of *Frasier* on the TV with a grunt that says he's going to be out here all night unless I argue him into his bedroom.

I don't have the energy.

I leave them in the living room and make my way to the kitchen, but when I look inside the refrigerator, the only food waiting for me is a Tupperware of rice and beans so small it wouldn't feed a toddler.

I didn't ask Dana to cook them dinner. I didn't expect her to. But it's a little strange she'd go out of her way to say she left food for me, when *this* is what she left. It pisses me off, adding to the fire in my gut over the mess she left despite having been hired as a maid.

I swallow it down and make a couple of sandwiches.

I'm still eating when Remi comes in to sit across from me. Udolpho slides under the table remarkably easily for a dog of his size —and immediately nuzzles his head into my crotch.

"Jesus," I say, pushing back. "Bad dog."

"He didn't mean to," Remi says. His eyes look so big in his face, reminding me of when he was a toddler who used to follow me around with nothing but admiration. Not that he doesn't respect me now, but our relationship has changed. I guess it was bound to. "He's a dog. We have to teach him what he can and can't do."

"I know." I set the rest of my sandwich back on my plate, no longer hungry. "He really scratched at our door?"

"Yeah, it was nuts!" He's grinning, but the joy in his expression wavers. "Until that happened, it was kind of a shit day, Uncle Knock." He makes a face. "Jeremy emptied his lunch tray on me, and I had to wear my gym clothes all day."

"That's not okay, Remi," I say, instantly pissed. "What did the school do about this?"

He raises his eyebrows. "Snitches get stitches. I told them it was an accident."

"I'm going to have a talk with your principal."

"Please don't," he says, adjusting his glasses. "Seriously. It'll pass if I ignore them."

I don't agree with him, and I hate the thought of that little shit Jeremy giving him hell. But I also don't want to take away his agency by talking to the principal without his knowledge and consent. For all I know, he's right, and it would only make things worse.

So what the hell am I supposed to do? It's clear that I have to do something.

The dog leans in for another sniff, making my skin itch, but I pet his ears. If he's making Remi this happy, then maybe he's all right.

"You tell me if that kid keeps bothering you."

My nephew gives a slight nod.

"I mean it, Remi. This is not okay."

"I know it's not," he says, one corner of his mouth tipping up in a move that reminds me of myself. "But there are plenty of things in life that aren't okay. Let's not pretend otherwise."

Later, in my office, I notice that a few things have been moved around—a paperweight an old client gave me is in the wrong spot, and a red pen has been added to the cup of black ones. My filing cabinet looks like it's been shifted slightly.

There's a weird prickle of *things are not as they should be*, but I decide to let it go. After all, I have a weird dog prancing around the house—*of course* things aren't as they should be, and my mind is more reactive right now because of how I left things with Gracie.

The thought brings a memory of Gracie leaned up against that pillar, her face and the peaks of her breasts flushed, her lips swollen and red, her eyes glimmering with want...and also dislike. Because if she wants me it's against her better judgment and even inclination. It's against reason.

I had no right to take what I wanted, and I damn well know it. I showed myself to be exactly the man she thinks I am. When I saw her crying, I should have bought her coffee or a stiff drink and asked her what had happened. The last thing I should have done was kiss her like that, as if I had some right to claim her. It doesn't matter that it felt good—better than anything else has, for years.

Fuck. I trace my fingers across the mahogany surface of the desk, grateful that *that*, at least, looks the way I left it.

I need to apologize, don't I?

I should have apologized, *really* apologized, years ago, but the dark truth about the part I'd played had made it feel pointless. Or as if I'd be unburdening myself but burdening her.

Even so, I find myself pulling out my phone.

I craft the apology—*I'm sorry Grace, I'm "an asshole molded convincingly to look like a person,"* I write, pulling the quote from *The Wind in Her Hair*, and send it.

I squint at the phone. There's no *Delivered* or *Read* notification.

Fuck, she blocked me.

Fuck.

I pound a fist on the desk, which is a stupid thing to do, since it's made of hard wood, and clench my jaw against the pain. Still, pain can be grounding. It can be *learned from*. Opening a door between me and Gracie would be a mistake. Sure, I wanted to come here to see how she was doing, to help her if I could. To make amends. But that doesn't mean she can be mine.

Teeth gritted, I pull out the bourbon I keep in the bottom drawer of my filing cabinet, but I don't bother with a glass. I just take a swig from the bottle, something that would horrify my mother.

And, with Gracie on my mind, her cheeks wet with tears, her eyes glimmering and full of pain, I finish it.

ten

ENOCH

GRACIE LOOKS at me as she pulls down the top of her dress, one strap and then the other, revealing a blue lace bra that matches her eyes. It's not a memory, because she has glasses on, and the Gracie of before never wore them.

"Is this really happening?" I ask, reaching forward to trace her bare arms and skim my fingers across the swell of her breasts.

"No," she answers, her chest shaking with silent laughter. "It's a dream, you idiot."

Huh. Even Gracie in my dreams thinks poorly of me.

Still, waste not, want not. I can have her here, if nowhere else. I go to kiss her, but she pulls back and lifts my hand, her eyes meeting mine as she sucks my finger into her mouth, curling her tongue around it.

"Are you getting ready for my cock?" I ask. In the way of dreams, I'm naked suddenly, and I reach down and stroke myself.

Except instead of responding, she takes two more of my fingers into her mouth, and why is her tongue suddenly so long, her mouth so full of spit?

My eyes pop open, and I see the lumbering dog, Udolpho, lapping at my hand as if it's a beefsteak. I jolt away, a movement

94

that jars my head and makes me register the hangover hammering at my skull.

And there goes my erection.

Shit. I should not have finished that bottle last night.

Then again, there are a lot of things I shouldn't have done.

"Go away," I croak out. He ambles closer, sniffing at me, which is when I realize it smells terrible in here, much worse than it did last night.

I stagger to my feet, only to step in...

"Fuck," I shout, and the dog wags his tail excitedly, which is when I look down and see I'm not the only one who's stepped in his mess. His paws are covered in it, and he's been padding around my chair, spreading the mess. "Fuck," I repeat with feeling. My head feels like it's been carved out like a pumpkin, the insides scooped into a strainer, but I'm going to have to clean this mess up. It won't wait until Dana shows up, because judging by the darkness of the room, it's still not morning.

Can I wipe my foot on printer paper? The dog's still wagging his tail, like he wants to be praised for covering my floor in liquid feces.

I hear shuffling in the other room, and my dad appears in the doorway. His room is in the back of the house, so I'm guessing I'm not the only one who fell asleep in my chair tonight. At least it worked out to my advantage this time. His annoyance shifts to amusement as he takes in my plight, and I realize I must look ridiculous, my shit foot raised off the floor, my other planted on the wood, as if I'm playing a ridiculous game of Twister. The dog's footprints encircle me in a literal circle of shit.

"Burning the midnight oil, huh?" my father says, chuckling.

"Yes, very funny," I say, each of the words taxing me to my breaking point. "I've got a pounding headache, Dad, and a foot covered in shit. Can you save the mockery for later?"

"Would you?" he asks.

It's a fair point, but right now I'm not feeling particularly fair. "Dad," I grind out, "would you—"

He waves his injured hand at me. "Oh, I'm just fucking with you. Let me go get you a towel." But the dog chooses that moment to bustle up to him, spreading his shit footprints farther across the room and onto the Persian rug—an expensive gift from a former client. Fucking fantastic.

Dad pats him. "Let's get you a bath, buddy."

"My foot!" I say, and my father gives another unconcerned toss of his hand.

He disappears with the nightmare dog, and I'm pretty sure he's abandoned me—that he's disappeared as completely as my mother ensured he did when I was kid, his things packed and gone in record time—when he comes back and throws a towel at me with a shit-eating grin on his face. "Maybe next time try sleeping in your bed."

Yeah, yeah, very funny.

Then he repeats another favorite phrase of mine. "Make sure you recycle the bottle." His nod indicates the empty bottle of bourbon on the floor.

It's an excruciating hour of cleaning, done with a head that still feels like a carved pumpkin, followed by a shower that does little to refresh me, and by the time I tumble into my bed and choke down some Tylenol and a metric ton of water, it's almost time to wake up.

When my alarm clock goes off, it's immediately obvious that my self-treatment in the middle of the night did nothing to improve my hangover.

I almost roll over and go back to sleep, but that would be undisciplined. Besides, I really do want to have a conversation with Dana when she arrives. The dissatisfaction I felt last night has boiled into anger. This is her fault, somehow. All of it.

Well, not the situation with Grace, obviously, but it feels good to have someone to blame for some of my misfortunes when the orchestrator of the rest is so obviously myself.

I struggle through my morning routine, and by the time I enter the kitchen, Dana has arrived. She's sitting at the table with my dad while Remi makes breakfast.

There's a pile of dog stuff near the table, a bed, a bowl, a leash, and a bag of food, so I guess Udolpho will be staying. The dog's standing next to Remi as if glued to his leg—or riveted to the bacon he's preparing in the frying pan—but he rushes to my side, tail wagging, and immediately gets reddish-brown hair all over the pants of my suit.

Through gritted teeth, I say, "Dana, it's time for that talk."

"Don't be rude," my father says. "Remi's making breakfast. Why don't you sit down and join us?"

Dana studies me with a pinched expression, then nods to herself. "You have a hangover. I can always tell." Her eyes sparkle. "Was it bourbon? I'm guessing it was bourbon."

What the fuck?

"How'd you—" But I cut myself off. It doesn't matter, and I don't want to talk about my hangover in front of Remi, who needs at least one adult in his life to be a good example, even if I feel like I'm failing to live up to that standard. "I need to talk to you. *Before* breakfast."

She snaps her fingers and gets to her feet. "You know what? I have the perfect hangover cure. Let me whip it up for you. It'll be no trouble at all."

"That's okay," I stay stiffly. "I'm not hungover."

She casts a knowing glance between me and Remi, then winks at me. "So I'll just make you a breakfast smoothie."

I'm starting to harbor genuine dislike for this woman, but if the task will shut her up, maybe it's worthwhile. Who knows. Maybe whatever "smoothie" she whips up will actually help ease the pounding in my head.

"Fine," I say like a sullen child, lowering into the chair next to my father. I try—and fail—to brush the hair off my pants. "You'll bring the dog to the shelter to get him checked for a microchip?" I ask, hanging on to that last bit of hope.

"Oh, I will." She glances back and smiles at my father. "Your dad said he'd go with me. But I showed my friend a picture, and she said she wouldn't hold out much hope."

It's on the edge of my tongue to ask why she didn't just bring the dog there last night if she went to the shelter anyway to get the bowls and whatnot, but Remi's posture seems rigid, and I can tell he doesn't like my mode of inquiry. He wants this dog.

I glance at the clock. Seven twenty. I have to be at the new office at eight to receive a delivery. I'm running out of time. There won't be an opportunity to talk to Dana alone, so I decide I'll have to do it in front of my dad and Remi.

"I noticed a few things needed picking up around the house last night," I say. "Isn't that part of your job description?"

My dad grunts. "Your mother raised you better."

I bite back, *You certainly didn't.*

Dana stops whatever she's doing and turns to look at me, her expression as sweet as spun sugar. "No, he's right, Richard," she says, shocking me. Who calls my father Richard? I can count on one hand. To everyone who knows him, he's Rich. Or Dick when he's especially salty. "I didn't do my duties. I'll admit that everything spun out of control after poor Udolpho showed up, needing our help."

Udolpho wags his tail, as if he already knows his name, which is ridiculous, being that he's a dog, and he only came by the name yesterday...

Right?

I mean, if he had a name, he'd have a collar also, and I saw no collar when I arrived home.

"Who named the dog?" I ask as Dana runs the blender.

"What?" she shouts, the combination of her loud voice and the whirring of the blender like an axe slamming into my already pained skull. "I can't hear you!"

If the noise is bothering my dad and Remi, it doesn't show. Remi has finished preparing the bacon and eggs and plated them—three plates, but when he brings them to the table, the third goes in front of an empty chair, not me. I look at him in question, and he gestures to Dana. "I thought she was making you her miracle hangover cure for breakfast."

"I don't have a hangover," I repeat lamely.

He rolls his eyes at me. "I wasn't born yesterday, Uncle Knock." His nose wrinkles. "You smell like alcohol."

I'm tempted to ask him why his sense of smell is refined enough to pick up the scent of alcohol and not his new best friend Udolpho, but instead ask, "How do you know what alcohol smells like?"

Another eyeroll. "I'm sixteen, not six."

I don't much like that response. Is his experience with alcohol limited to seeing his parents drunk, or is he drinking? Is this something we need to talk about? Is—

Dana sets a thick-looking red concoction on the table in front of me.

"What's in there?" I ask suspiciously.

She laughs as if I've said something incredibly amusing. "It's not poison. It has a bit of a kick, but it'll cure you of that hangover."

"Who named the dog?" I repeat.

"I did," she says with a sharp grin that does nothing to soothe my prickled nerves. "I always had a thing for *The Mysteries of Udolpho.*"

The dog responds to the name again, wagging his tail. My mind darts back to the things in my office, slightly out of place. I want to accuse Dana of something, but I'm not quite sure what. Besides, my father and Remi have made it clear whose side they're on—namely, not mine—and I'm not sure I can deal with this situation with the scooped-out feeling in my head.

So I take a tentative sip of the drink. To my surprise, it tastes pretty good, fruity but kind of spicy, so I drink more of it.

Shockingly, my head already feels clearer. I glance at Dana in surprise as I keep drinking. She's eating the plate of food put in front of her, and he and my dad are chowing down too. Someone must have put food in Udolpho's bowl, because he's crunching on some dry pellets.

My gaze takes in the word on his bowl—*Udolpho*.

Would she have had time to do that last night?

I'm so distracted by it that I finish the glass without even realizing it.

Pushing it aside, I say, "What was in that, anyway?"

"Bit of this, bit of that," she says with another disconcerting wink. Then she touches a finger to her lips. "I should have warned you, though. It has some side effects."

"Like what?" I bark.

My dad gives me another disapproving look, as if he's not every bit the grumpy curmudgeon he's silently accusing me of being.

Dana moves her hand again, and I notice a tattoo beneath her wedding ring. It doesn't seem in keeping with her overall wholesome image, but I'm starting to realize there's nothing typical about this woman. "Well, let's just say you'll want to be close to a bathroom for the rest of the day."

eleven

GRACE

"THIS WHOLE THING IS MOOT," I say, studying Nicole and Damien in the booth across from me in Summer Nights. It's Wednesday, the evening after Pillargate.

Marnie is sitting at the bar next to the Santa-esque regular, Reggie, giving me some space to talk to my fairy godmothers, but I get a worried glance from her every few minutes. She and Andy know about my meeting with Vera. About Pillargate. About *everything*. Andy would be here too, probably sitting beside me as my self-appointed advocate, but her grandmother is sick. "I'm going to quit."

"What does *moot* mean?" Nicole says, studying her phone. She started poring over it the minute I sat down, as if she can't be bothered to talk to me.

"You know what *moot* means," Damien tells her, smiling slyly. "Like that time you tried to fairy-godmother that woman whose husband was cheating on her, but she'd already thrown every piece of his clothing out of the second floor window and run off with her gardener. That point was moot."

"Very funny," she says wryly, but I don't miss the way her lips have lifted.

"I'm going to quit," I repeat. "So there's no need for us to send Enoch away. He can stay and rot with Vera for all I care."

Nicole looks up with an excited glimmer in her eyes that tells me I definitely went too far.

It's just...my head has been a very unquiet place for the last thirty-ish hours—immune to comforts like sunshine and chocolate, wine and *Bridgerton* and romance novels. Nothing has helped settle me. With just a few simple touches, Enoch upended my world... again. He proved to me what part of me already knew.

I've dated several men over the past six years. Seven in fact. Some lasted a few weeks, others a month or two. One, Ray, lasted a year. But Andy coined them my seven shades of vanilla, and Marnie, who's more polite, has told me she thinks I play it safe.

They're right. Because none of those other men could make me wet in a matter of seconds. None of them could make me forget myself so much that I'd push his hand down my pants in my boss's house—in a place that wasn't even all that private, truth be told. Only Enoch has ever done that to me. And the only reason he did it was to make an asinine point. He doesn't have any interest in claiming me for real, even if such a thing were possible. He only wants me the way he wants everything—so he can find a neat little place for me. A display case or a treasure chest, hidden away, like the pretty things I used to gather as a kid.

I want to be wanted for real, the way Nicole and Damien clearly want each other, the way Marnie, leaning across the bar to press a kiss to Griffin's nose, clearly wants him—and vice versa. I don't want someone to want me only so he can have me.

Besides, I haven't forgotten who Enoch works for...and how he got the job. I can never forget that.

Then there's Vera. She was so cold to me yesterday, so dismissive. If she's right about my book, what's the point in working for her any longer? I'll never be a writer, so I'll have to take a step back, pull up my big-girl panties, and figure out what the hell else I'm going to do with my life.

Or you can refuse to let her decide whether you're any good. That's what Marnie and Andy told me to do last night, in a talk that came perilously close to being a lecture.

Either way, there's no point in me hanging around to dust and clean up after Pumpkin.

"Anyway," I say, tugging on the ends of my hair. "Moot. I guess you guys can move on to your next client. I'm sorry to have wasted your time."

Nicole snorts and ruffles a hand through her short pink hair. "Yeah, sorry, you can't fire us. You can't fire people you're not paying."

"Can I start paying you so I can then fire you?"

"That'd also be a no."

Frustration boils inside of me, fed by the anger I've been stuffing down for the past couple of days. "You're not making this easy."

"Is that what you want, *Gracie*?" she asks, pushing her drink away as if it's disgusted her. "Something easy? If so, I've overestimated you. There's nothing worthwhile about things that are easy. Everything important in life has to be worked for in some way or another."

"Nice TED Talk." Damien nudges her with his shoulder. "What she means to say is that she's having too much fun to stop."

"What have you been doing?" I ask, leaning forward, interested without quite wanting to be.

She presses into Damien. "I want *you* to have fun too, and that requires Gracie hanging on at least through the weekend."

His face creases into the kind of grin that could sail a thousand ships. "I *always* have fun with you."

Their energy and connection felt inspirational the other day, but now it just feels like salt in my wound.

"Guys? Right here. Across the table from you. What've you been doing, Nicole? And what's the plan for this weekend?"

Nicole turns to me, but not before kissing Damien so thoroughly it leaves me blushing. "Well, technically, I got fired today," she tells me. "Or I should say Dana did. But don't worry, your guy will be begging to have me back by morning."

"Wait, what happened?"

She waves a hand as if to say it was nothing. "He got a teensy bit upset because I gave him a hangover cure without telling him there were side effects."

My eyes bulge. "The same one you said would put me in the bathroom all day?"

She nods through her laughter. "Similar. And I arranged for a mangy stray to show up at his door. Naturally, his nephew and father wanted to take it in."

"Oh my God," I say, getting into this in spite of myself. "You got Enoch a dog?"

Despite having seen him with Pumpkin, I can't imagine him with a dog. He's so polished, so perfect, so controlled. How did he react?

"One that sheds. A lot." She shrugs. "And apparently rice and beans doesn't agree with him. Who knew?"

Damien, silently laughing, puts an arm around her and tugs her close, and again, I feel a tugging on my heartstrings. A sore patch in my heart that wants what they so clearly have.

Maybe that's why I say something stupid.

"He kissed me," I blurt.

This time Nicole's the one who leans forward, her eyes gleaming. "Six years ago? Because if so, you're only telling us what we already know and it's fake news."

"Yesterday." I give my hair another little tug.

"Why do you keep doing that?" she asks.

"Nerves."

"Well, stop. It's distracting. You've been doing it more than usual lately."

I scoff at her. "If it were easy to stop, then I would."

She gives a shrug. "So he kissed you and now you want to quit?" She makes a face. "Nah, I don't buy it. It was more than a kiss, wasn't it?"

"Yes," I say, if only because it'll make this conversation go faster. "But I didn't sleep with him."

"If you want to quit and you didn't even get lucky, whatever happened was either really fucking good or really fucking bad. Which?"

I want to tell her that Enoch Laskin means nothing to me—that I'm neither attracted to him nor interested in him—but I find it hard to lie to Nicole. There's something about her that invites or maybe insists on truthfulness.

"Somewhere in the middle," I mumble. I'm thrown back to yesterday, to the feeling of Enoch pinning me against that pillar, his body hard and sure against mine, his hand inside of me. A mixture of anger and attraction fire up inside of me. "He teased me but didn't—"

My gaze shoots to Damien, who lifts up his hand as if to apologize for the male half of the species. "Only an asshole wouldn't make a woman come."

"Anyway," I say, my mouth firming. "I can't be around him."

Nicole's mouth twists to the side, and she gives a slight nod. I'd be reassured, but somehow I get the impression she's agreeing with herself and not me.

"You need to fuck him."

Damien does some of that silent laughing again, and I'm pretty sure I'm gaping.

"Why on earth would I do that?" I ask. "The whole purpose of all of this is to make him go away. He needs to go away."

Before he finds out about the book...

Before he drives me crazy...

Before I forget all the reasons I need to stay away from him...

"Because you have a serious lady boner for him," she says with feeling, "and if I'm picking up what you're putting down, you haven't had a good lay in years. You need to enjoy a few trips to Pound Town before you send this horse out to pasture."

"That is a very confusing mixture of metaphors." I tug on my hair again and then scowl, either at myself or Nicole, because I caught myself doing it. "And no, absolutely not."

"Think about it," she says as she pops a pretzel from the bowl in the center of the table. "But we're not quitting, and neither are you. Not yet. I have a feeling some interesting revelations are about to come to light."

Her words arrest something in me. "Do you know something I don't?" I want to reach into her head and steal it.

She laughs. "I know a lot of things you don't, but I assume you're talking about the Suit." She lifts her eyebrows. "I *do* know a few things, and I'm pretty sure they'd be of interest to you. But if you quit on us now, you'll never find out."

My heart quickens, because I don't miss the implications. She found something in Enoch's house, possibly something related to me, and she won't tell me what is unless I stay the course for a while longer.

"You're diabolical."

"Thank you," she says with a grin. "Now, what else aren't you telling us? Because from what I can gather, you've been in that shitty, dead-end job for years. However much that kiss rocked your world"—she wiggles her eyebrows up and down, as if to suggest that something else would rock my world even more—"that's not why you're suddenly willing to give up. So what happened? Give it to us straight, Cinderella."

"Cinderella?"

Damien gives me a lazy grin. "I came up with that one. Dog named Pumpkin. Boss who makes you clean up after her."

"Good, right?" Nicole says.

"She's my least favorite Disney princess," I say, then a sigh leaks out of me. Because I kind of *am* like Cinderella, aren't I?

When I parted ways with my father, I was determined to take control of my life, and in many ways I did. I found my own apartment. I made a family of friends. I wrote several short stories and a book, for God's sake. But I also let Vera draw me in with her promises and the glow of everything she was and had accomplished.

I find myself telling them more about the book. About how Marnie and Andy liked it but Vera told me I had no light—only an ability to make others burn brighter.

After I finish, Nicole watches me for a long moment before reverting to the fairy-tale conversation. "Seriously, you prefer Sleeping Beauty or Snow White to Cinderella? All they did was fucking sleep."

She has a point.

"What about Mulan or Belle?"

"Mulan's not a princess, and let's be real, Belle was down to bone a literal beast. There's no way she was pleased when he transformed into a prince," she says, surprisingly knowledgeable about Disney. "She's a total furry."

"You're definitely a Cinderella," Damien offers.

"I feel like we're losing the thread of this conversation."

"Yes, you are," Nicole says pointedly. "For someone who does every last thing that sea witch commands, you're being remarkably uncooperative with us. Why did you keep this a secret?"

I'm tempted to call her out for mixing fairy tales, but it's beside the point and I know it. The thing is, I'm afraid Vera's right. I'm also afraid that I can't escape her... She has this hold on me, like she's a wolf, and I'm a pup she has by the scruff of its neck. Maybe it's because I've always wanted to be like her—successful and owning it —but it feels like it runs deeper.

"I don't know," I manage to say.

"Well, no need to worry," Nicole says, tapping the table. "Damien is good at making women talk."

I gape at her, and she waves a hand in dismissal. "Oh, don't look at me like that. I'd never let another woman touch him, but he talks a good game, and it makes other people spill their secrets. We've got this. If she's lying, we'll find out. Now scram, Cinderella. We've got business to attend to."

Judging by the way she's slowly moved into Damien's lap, his hand possessively on her hip, I'm guessing the only business they have planned is sex in the bathroom, but I don't object. I'm happy to leave. Talking to them has sucked something out of me...and yet, I also feel different than I did half an hour ago. I feel hopeful.

Before I go, I turn toward Nicole. "Do you know why Enoch's nephew lives with him?"

She makes a face. "The kid's mother is a piece of shit. She let her husband kick him out because he's gay."

Something loosens inside of me, and it takes me a few seconds, until I've turned away and am walking toward the bar, to realize why. I like that this allows me to think Enoch has some redeeming qualities. Maybe it's because he's the only man who's ever had that paperclip hold on my heart, and I want to think I'm not stupid enough to fall for someone like my father.

Marnie gestures me forward. "Well, what did they say?" she asks as I claim the seat between her and Reggie. He turns toward us as if he's part of the conversation.

"Nicole tricked Enoch into adopting a big, messy dog and poisoned him with a hangover cure that made him spend half the day in the bathroom. So, yeah, she got fired."

Reggie snorts and then starts choking on a gulp of beer. I'm about to jump out of my seat and start hammering his back for worry he accidentally aspirated a bar pretzel, when he finally stops. "Ain't the first time that's happened to me," he says through more chuckles. "Seems like every damn time I recommend someone for a job, they lose it within a week."

"We'll keep that in mind the next time you recommend someone," Marnie says dryly.

"Well, she seems confident she can get him to hire her back." I cast a glance at Marnie, wanting her to tell me...I don't know. I guess I want to hear someone I trust say that everything's going to be okay. "I told them about Vera and my book. They want me to wait until at least after the weekend to quit. They say they have *plans*."

Leaning in toward me, possibly to prevent Reggie from further involvement in our conversation, she says, "Let them do their thing." She waves a hand at Griffin, who flashes her the Vulcan symbol—their own personal form of foreplay. "They might have unusual methods, but they get results. You need results."

I think again of Enoch, of the hot press of him. It occurs to me that if he had a hangover today it was because he drank to excess last night. Did he do it because of me? Did the kiss upset him?

Excite him?

Because I spent the whole night sleepless, caught in a snarl of emotions, of need and anger and grief. Of fear.

"I don't know if I can see Enoch again after...well....after..."

"After he kissed you until your knees turned weak?" Marnie asks. There's speculation in her eyes, but she doesn't push me like Andy might. It's not her way.

"Did he at least catch you after he made your knees go weak?" Reggie asks. He strokes his Santa beard thoughtfully. "He should have at least caught you."

"It was...against a pillar," I say, stammering halfway through because I have no idea why I'm actually answering him, let alone so honestly.

He nods thoughtfully. "Smooth."

Marnie holds in her laughter, mostly. "Are you worried it'll be awkward?"

I consider it for a moment. No, not really. I don't care about awkwardness, and his wounded feelings shouldn't be my concern either. I'm worried I'll kiss him again. Because even if I have very good reasons for disliking Enoch Laskin, there's no denying I *want* him.

"How's Sinclair doing?" I ask. I start to grab the ends of my hair, then stop myself.

Marnie sighs. "I think she's seriously losing it. She took a Play with Clay class yesterday, wearing a blue wig from Nicole. *Blue.* I mean, blue is cool, but she's not really a blue-wig kind of woman."

"Did the class do anything for her?" Maybe I should take a clay class. Maybe, all this time, I've been thinking I want and need to be a writer, but there's a clay artist living inside of me, waiting to be unlocked. A clay flower arrangement takes life in my head before I mentally veto it. The blossoms would be too heavy for the stems.

"She made an *interesting* vase for Griff as a peace offering. You know, because they didn't use to get along. I think it's supposed to be shaped like a light saber, but it kind of looks like—"

"A dong," Reggie says, cutting her off with a laugh. "I saw the picture. That was a dong, clear as day."

"Never change, Reggie," Marnie says.

We talk a little longer, Reggie and Griffin interjecting, and I'm not remotely surprised to see Nicole and Damien emerge from the back before I go. There's an air of satisfaction emanating from them, and I feel a stab of jealousy.

Later, back at home, I pull out my phone and scowl at it, as if it's a person who let me down. Should I unblock Enoch? Should I text him?

Maybe, but I have no idea what I'd say. Nicole thinks I should give in to the way he makes me feel—hot and cold at the same time, fizzy with life, heavy with need—but I could never do that...

I'm spinning the phone around, thinking of Enoch and that pillar, daydreaming about him stripping off his tie and wrapping it around my hands, the way he did that night back in business school before he lowered down and put his mouth to me, when a notification pops up on my screen.

It immediately erases all thoughts of Enoch, of Vera, of everything.

It's an email from my father, and not just one of those newsletters I never subscribed to.

Hand shaking, I click into it.

Grace,

It's time we have a conversation. I'll be in Asheville in two weeks' time. We'll meet that Saturday at our Asheville office. 4:00 p.m.

Your father

He doesn't provide the address, and although it's probable it's listed online, I know him better than to think that's why. It's a power move.

ENOCH

"I'M *SO* sorry for the misunderstanding," Dana says, although I can see in her eyes she's not sorry at all. No, she seems to take delight in my misery.

Fuck. I'm being melodramatic, but being poisoned will do that to a man. Admittedly, her tonic took away my headache, but at a cost no sane person would willingly accept. I almost shit my pants in a meeting yesterday, which wouldn't have been a good confidence builder.

Firing her was a no-brainer. Everything in my house was covered in dog fuzz, and although I did manage to get home without thoroughly shaming myself, I couldn't leave the bathroom for more than ten minutes at a time. To make matters worse, Udolpho has separation anxiety, and for some godforsaken reason he's decided I'm his secondary person, the primary position going to my nephew, who was at school all day. So I was either in the bathroom or sitting on the couch with Udolpho practically parked on my lap despite the fact that he has to weigh a good seventy pounds and is by no one's definition a lap dog. All the while, Dana was sitting with my father, playing casual games of Parcheesi or watching TV reruns, doing jack shit around the house. After two hours of this cycle of misery, I exploded and told her to get the fuck out, promising that if anyone ever asked for a reference, I'd tell them that she'd poisoned me and made my house a disaster area.

If I'd thought that would help me escape said cycle of misery, I was mistaken, because every time I left the bathroom after that my father was waiting for me with a scowl and a lecture about manners and/or a guilt trip about Remi, whom he claims is very attached to Dana despite having known her for so little time.

Still, I wouldn't have yielded. No fucking way would I have yielded. Except she'd already brought my three best suits to the dry cleaner, and I had no idea *which* dry cleaner. She'd also never gotten around to bringing Udolpho to her friend at the shelter, and it's possible, although certainly not probable, that the friend will locate an insane family who somehow misses the ridiculous creature.

Besides, Remi actually seemed near tears yesterday evening. I guess Dana had promised him that her husband would help him with his bully problem.

"I think it might really make a difference, Uncle Knock," he said.

When I asked why he'd let Dana's husband help but not me, he gave me a long look as if to say, *Look at you. The only thing you can help me with is getting bullied more.*

If that's not a kick in the nuts, I don't know what is.

Still, I undertook the distasteful task of asking her to come back.

When I called her, she said brightly, "I was expecting to hear from you," which obviously pissed me off, but I eked out an apology anyway. "There, that wasn't so hard, was it?" she asked, and now here she is.

It *was* hard.

I work my jaw, trying not to let my dislike show. "Yes. Well, I'm glad you could come on such short notice." As if anyone else would offer her a job. The people who gave her references must have been hired for the gig. I make a mental note to follow up on that theory later, not that it matters. I need her to stay on until I get back, at least.

"Of course," she says, beaming at my father and Remi, who are eating a breakfast Remi made for just the two of them. "I love spending time with my favorite guys."

Udolpho makes a sound that might have been a bark if he didn't have jacked-up vocal cords.

"Oh, you're one of my favorites too," she says, giving his head a scratch.

"You just met all of them on Monday," I say, unable to hold in my pique. "Are they truly supposed to believe you're their favorites?"

"So literal," she says airily. "We're going to have a wonderful time while you're away."

I'll probably come back to discover she's opened a home for abandoned pets in my house. There's another throb of misgiving, of wondering if my judgment has let me down yet again, but she brought my suits back this morning and she's promised to swing Udolpho by the shelter after work today. That's good, right?

Besides, Remi should have another adult around in case of emergencies. My father could handle most situations, but he needs more help than he'd ever admit. Dana stays.

You could have asked Gracie for help, a voice whispers in my head.

The voice is a fucking sentimental idiot, of course, because Gracie hates me enough to block me on her phone. There's no way she'd do me any favors—or if she did, it would only be because she felt obligated to help an older man, a young boy, and a dog. If she were to help, I wouldn't want it to be out of obligation. I'd want—

You're an idiot.

I am, so I settle for nodding in response to Dana's obvious dig. "Yes, I'm sure you will."

"I still get to go to the photo shoot this weekend, don't I, Uncle Knock?" Remi asks.

God help me, I'd get out of it if I could. The last thing I feel like doing is sitting around and watching while Vera tries on a progression of outfits and "interviews" the models who show up for the open call.

"Yes," I say through tight lips. "Of course, bud."

"A photo shoot, huh?" Dana asks with a grin. "How fancy."

"It's for that author lady," my father says, "Vera Valence."

From the lack of surprise on Dana's face, it's obvious my father's been telling her any number of things about Vera. Good God. Who knew he had a Chatty Cathy buried inside of him, waiting for someone to lure it out?

"Very fancy," she says, her eyes sparkling. "She going to take a photo of you, Richard?"

My father laughs gruffly. "She's more likely to ask Sunshine here to take off his shirt. All the time he spends at the gym, you can tell he's just waiting for someone to ask."

I roll my eyes. "There will be no shirts removed."

"Famous last words," Dana says with a wink.

"What does *that* mean?" I ask. If there's a slightly aggressive edge to it, I can't help myself.

"She's just joking, Uncle Knock," Remi says, giving me a wary look, like he's afraid I'm going to have a temper tantrum and fire Dana on the spot. Tempting.

"All right," I say. "Well. Time for me to go. I'll let you know when I get in." I feel a little pinch of awkwardness, but Remi must have gotten over his annoyance at me enough to say goodbye. He gets up and gives me a hug, the kind of squeeze he used to give me when he was little. I must be still fucked up from that tonic—*from the kiss with Grace*—because I feel choked up. He still trusts me. I haven't messed that up yet. My dad gives me a nod, which I return, and Dana salutes me, her eyes bright with amusement.

"Bye-bye, oh, Captain, my captain."

I decide to ignore her. Udolpho follows me as I bring my bag to the door, and he gives a little whimper as I open it and stow my things outside of it. No one in the kitchen can see and misinterpret —they've all returned to their breakfasts—so I give his ears a rub. "Behave," I tell him. "No more rice and beans."

He licks me.

I grimace.

We part ways amicably enough, and I load my things into the car, careful to hang up my suits.

After I arrive at the airport and go through security, I call Vera. We didn't speak yesterday—for obvious reasons—but she still hasn't sent me the mystery manuscript she was talking up the other day. She answers on the first ring, sounding a little manic, as if maybe she hasn't been getting a lot of sleep either, and confirms that she has finished the manuscript and is sending it to my device as we speak.

"It's the one, Enoch," she says. "This is the one that's going to be made into a film. I know it."

"I'll read it on the flight," I say. My money's still on *The Wind in Her Hair*, although I'll admit I'm partial to it because of Gracie. I'd like to be able to tell her that I've paved the road to getting her favorite book made into a movie. It could be a peace offering or a declaration that I don't totally fuck *everything* up—just the things that matter.

"Call me the instant you land," Vera blurts, and I make a promise that I have little intention of keeping. I can just as easily text her about the book.

Once on the plane, I white-knuckle the armrests through takeoff —losing control isn't easy for me; relinquishing it to an unknown pilot and a tin tube is even harder—and then acquire a single bourbon from the flight attendant and pull out my iPad. I ignore the woman sitting beside me, the small child next to her.

My first impression is that the book is well written—as good as *The Wind in Her Hair* and much less schlocky than Vera's newer stuff. If there weren't distinct Vera touches here and there—*that brash boy*, *his turgid member*, and *her insides quivered like a kaleidoscope of butterflies had been unleashed* are all phrases I've read in at least two different Vera Valence books—I'd wonder if it were even hers.

My second reaction is dawning horror. Because I *know* this story. I *fucking lived it*, and reading it is bringing everything I've buried up to the surface.

The characters, Renee and Dean, are rivals in business school who are assigned to run a fake business together. Just. Like. Gracie and me. Some of the conversations might as well have been airlifted from our past.

The two of us had taken an instant dislike to each other. Part of it was pride on my part—she looked the part of the good little rich girl, raised with a silver spoon pressed between those pouty lips. I had three suits that I'd worked over the summers to afford and a bunch of dress shirts and ties to make it look like I wasn't poor as fuck. Part of my problem with her was that she didn't seem to give a shit about being in business school, but she was good—smarter than I was, easily, with instincts that were just as good if less cutthroat. It pissed me off that she had what I wanted without having strived and bled for it. That she didn't even care about having it. It *infuriated* me that I wanted to strip off her pencil skirt and take her over one of the desks.

Later, she'd confessed that she'd thought I was a carbon copy of the prep-school assholes she'd grown up with, so apparently my act was solid.

We were the top two students in our program, always pitted against each other, although we didn't need much pitting.

We weren't thrilled to work with each other, but our professor— Professor Newman, who reminded me of Newman from *Seinfeld*, my father's favorite show—forced the issue.

"I'll be interested to see what you two come up with together," he'd said with a smug look. "It'll either be terrible or great. No in- between."

"What if we kill each other?" Gracie asked, deadpan. "Will you hold yourself responsible?"

He laughed.

I gave her the evil eye.

We kept fighting at first because it was what we knew best. The race of one-upmanship. Of trying to be the best and prove to the other that we were worthy.

It didn't take long for me to realize she deserved everything she had. It came easily to her, but she tried hard too. She poured herself into everything she did, as if each task had equal merit.

It's all there, on my device, although it's from one point of view: hers.

Fuck. I rub my chest as I keep reading, my mind racing. Did Gracie give our story to Vera? It's hard to imagine, although according to what Vera's said she hasn't shown this manuscript to Gracie—or anyone else. Is that because she doesn't want Gracie knowing she turned her personal experiences into a novel?

Vera can't have realized I was the man Gracie was talking about. Otherwise she would have given me a wink or a nod or something. I suspect she wouldn't have been able to help herself.

I keep reading in a daze, pausing only to ask for another bourbon after I finish the first.

Then I get to *that night*. It's different, but it's us. *It's us.*

Renee works in the library, and she lets Dean in after-hours so they can work on their project. It doesn't start well because Dean's a dick (some things don't change in fiction).

"Why do you hate me so much?" she asked.

He laughed bitterly. "I don't hate you. It would be easier if I did."

"What would be?"

He doesn't tell her, of course, because *I* didn't tell her. No, I pulled out a flask, just like Dean does, and offered it to her.

"Let's not talk about the program," he said.

"So what are we supposed to talk about?" She made a face. "The weather? It has been unseasonably cold lately."

He laughed. "Why do people feel the need to comment on the weather? We're both experiencing it, aren't we? If it's snowing, we can both see it. Conversation done."

"So no weather talk." She mimed striking it off a list, hoping she could get him to laugh again, grateful when she did. "What about politics?"

"Nope. Definite vibe killer."

"So no school, weather, or politics. Where does that leave us? Do we have to talk about our families?"

His laugh was humorless this time, but he loosened his tie, probably the only time she'd seen him do that. "No, I definitely don't want to talk about them."

Good. She didn't want to do that either. It wasn't easy being the only daughter of a verified genius. Less so when he seemed to be disappointed with everything she did—each moment a test she was failing.

My conscience—yes, I do have one, buried down deep—stabs me.

I hate him.

My fingers tighten their curl around the iPad as I keep reading.

Dean and Renee get a little tipsy. They talk about the ways they've screwed with each other—the time Renee bought a version of his favorite suit and wore it to class, or when Dean found one of her vision boards online and made tongue-and-cheek comments on all of the photos. They drink some more.

In the book, Dean's the one who kisses Renee first.

Grace is the one who kissed me first.

I wanted her. I fucking *wanted* her.

But she was off-limits. My competitor.

Supposed to be, anyway.

I keep reading, my eyebrows hiking up as Renee confesses to Dean that she's always loved romance novels. She tells him it's her dream to write them.

"Don't you know shit like that doesn't happen in real life?" Dean asked with a snort.

"I do," she said. "But I wish it would. Life would be a lot better if it did."

A corner of his mouth lifted. "If unicorns farted rainbows and men walked around shirtless?"

"The latter, sure, but I was talking about the grand gestures. The passion. Getting carried away in public places and falling in love when every last circumstance seems set against it." She felt herself flushing a little. She tended to get carried away when she talked about romance. It was her thing. Her escape.

Her dream.

He looked at her for a long moment, a new warmth kindling in his eyes. Who would have thought that Dean Larchmont, of all people, would look at her that way? She certainly hadn't imagined it. She'd caught him looking at her before, but never like this. Never in a way that so obviously wasn't distaste.

"Okay," he said, holding out his hand. She took it, her heart hammering, and his touch seemed to electrify her.

"What are we doing?"

"We're going to make ridiculous shit happen in real life," he said with a wicked grin.

"Is that a promise?"

"Damn straight."

I know what happens next. Dean secures her arms to one of the pillars with his tie...

I remember wrapping it around her wrists while she watched me, her eyes wide and hungry, her smile a bit naughty, like she enjoyed that we were doing this in the library, out in the open, where anyone could see us. We were away from windows, of course, and the building was locked up, but someone could have come in anyway, and we both knew it.

I felt like more of a man than I ever had before or since. Because she was trusting me with herself. It was fucking hot, having her tied up to that pillar, waiting for me to *do something*.

"Is this ridiculous enough for you?" I'd asked once I finished the knot.

"It's too PG," she said breathlessly, her breasts pressing against her white button-down shirt.

"We can fix that." I started to unbutton her shirt, and she made a hiss as I lowered my head to her breasts, kissing at the crux of her bra, then tugging it aside the way I'd been dreaming about for years and claiming her nipple with my mouth and tongue. She bucked toward me, flexing her arms as if she wanted to break free. To do what? Push me closer?

I attended to the other one with my fingers before switching, wanting to show both of them a proper amount of worship. Then I finished unbuttoning her shirt and kissed my way down to the waist of her pencil skirt. I stared up at her as I reached back to unclasp and unzip it, soaking in the sight of her looking at me, her eyes hooded with the same lust pounding through my veins and my cock.

There were stacks of books behind her, behind me. It somehow made the moment more erotic, more taboo.

"You've got me, Suit. What *are* you going to do with me?" she taunted.

If I could've gotten any harder, that would've done it. I pushed down her skirt and panties, greeted with the sweetest sight known to man, and for a second I just stared at her, hands trussed up with my tie, breasts on display in a white bra.

"What would happen in one of your romance books, Gracie?" I

asked, rolling a slow circle around her clit and watching the way her body bucked against the pillar. "Should I sing you a sonnet?"

"A sonnet's a poem, you dick," she said, arcing her head back as I ran my fingers along her folds, touching her wetness. I liked feeling the evidence of what I'd done to her, knowing I wasn't the only one who was being driven crazy. "And no, I'd prefer for you to get to work. I was under the impression you had a better work ethic than this."

But her voice hitched as she said it, because I was pressing my palm against her clit, my fingers pulsing inside of her.

"Let me guess," I said. "You have better use for my mouth than useless talking."

"Yes," she said on a sigh. "Yes."

"I need to hear you say it."

"I want your mouth on me," she said, her cheeks flushing.

"Tell me to tongue-fuck your pussy," I said. Maybe I said it because I wanted a reaction from her.

To my surprise, her back straightened and her voice took on its own kind of command. "Tongue-fuck my pussy, Enoch."

"Your wish is my command," I said, lowering to take her clit in my mouth as I kept working her with my fingers. She was so responsive to me, so beautiful, and she tasted like honey and musk and salt, and I couldn't get enough.

I shifted my positioning so my tongue was between her folds, my fingers pulsing against her clit—making good on my promise while she writhed and made delicious sounds of distress and pleasure, her pussy clenching around me as I switched on and off in turns, mouth and hand, mouth and hand.

I felt like a god among men when she called out my name— *Enoch*, not the Suit.

Then I think of the other day—of how I brought her to the brink and pulled back.

You dick.

I'm aroused. I'm upset. I'm pissed. I'm...pleased. I can't remember the last time I felt so many things at once, when most of my life passes by without a blip—organized event A leading into organized event B, one strategy flowing into the next.

One thought overrides the rest. I know Gracie didn't tell Vera Valence any of this shit. She wouldn't have. That can only mean one thing....

I slam the bourbon back, earning me a dirty look from the woman who's sitting next to me. Her son is making a drawing in red crayon that seems to be of a couple of dead trolls, so she has bigger concerns.

Then her eyes fall to my iPad. I'm at the part where Dean tells Renee she has a sweet little pussy and she can ask him to taste it whenever she wants, wherever she wants. The woman's eyes fly wide, and she edges closer to the other side of her seat, nearer her son, and says, "Oscar, we're going to play the eyes-closed game."

"No, Mom," he whines. "I'm drawing a picture of you and Dad."

Yup, definitely bigger concerns.

I shift my iPad out of her view and keep reading.

Renee takes Dean home. She doesn't tell him she's a virgin until he breaks her barrier and takes that from her too. They spill their souls to each other. She tells him about her father, the asshole. Dean's shocked to find out who he is, but he's not shocked in the same way I was.

He knew her father only by reputation. I'd already met John Parker by then.

Dean encourages her to pursue her dream, even if her important father thinks romance is on par with reality television. Because she's *good*. Because she never really wanted to travel the road that was paved for her. Because her dreams aren't smaller just because they're different.

The heartbreak Renee feels when she finds out Dean took a job with her father, a position that had been slated for her, slices into my heart. Because Renee thinks Dean seduced her and pumped her for information solely because he wanted that job. She thinks his heart never opened to her.

It's not true.

But I can tell Renee's not the only one who believes it.

I'll have to talk to her about that. And about the book, obviously, because now I know without question that Gracie did write that book she'd dreamed of...

It's about us.

And Vera Valence is trying to steal it.

thirteen

GRACE

I HAVEN'T ANSWERED my father's email, but the knowledge of it sitting there in my inbox is picking away at my brain.

What does he want from me?

Is this all part of some extremely long long game?

"Does this look like an orange?" Marnie asks me, nodding to her work in progress.

"No, it looks like a ball of clay." Mine isn't any better. In fact, I've paid so little attention to what I'm doing that my orange is more of a square.

It's Friday evening. Sinclair rented out the local Play with Clay for a "girls' night"—her words. We're supposed to be making clay fruit for centerpieces.

Despite her indifference to Sinclair, Andy came anyway and filled her plastic wine glass to the brim. Her fake fruit actually looks like fruit. It's pretty damn impressive, actually.

Nicole's here too, drinking some kind of mixed drink she brought in a travel tumbler emblazoned with the words *This isn't coffee* and offering unasked-for critiques on our work. She's spending an extra-long time on her banana.

My gaze darts to Sinclair. Her beautiful brow is knit with consternation as she studies her lumpy fruit, the banana not too far off from Nicole's, although I'm pretty sure Sinclair actually wants hers to look like fruit and not male genitalia. The teacher, a woman with apple cheeks, dark hair, and incredibly cool pink-framed glasses, has been standing next to her for the entire lesson. I guess when you have a celebrity client—which Sinclair obviously is despite the blue wig she's wearing—you give them your full attention and leave everyone else to flounder.

Marnie sighs loudly. "She wants it to be perfect. She expects to be good at everything. It's an unfortunate side effect of being good at most things, so I've never had to experience it."

"You're good at lots of things," I say. "If we were drawing, you'd have an expert bowl of fruit, only they'd probably have faces and be swearing at each other." Marnie runs a small graphic design business called Sweet Nothings. She makes cards, chore wheels, and the like—all with her snarky sense of humor on full display.

"Where do you get off being so good at this?" Marnie asks Andy.

She snorts. "I'm a daycare teacher. Play-Doh is basically a lifestyle for me."

"Aren't you going to compliment my banana?" Nicole asks, lifting it up. "I'm injured." It's very distinctly a dick, probably Damien's dick.

"Are you going to display that on your kitchen table, Nicole?" Andy waggles her eyebrows.

"No," she answers, waving it around a bit, giving it a curve Damien's hopefully doesn't have in real life. "This beauty's going over my fireplace. I want everyone to see how lucky I am."

Yup, definitely Damien's dick.

"A remarkable talent," I hear the teacher tell Sinclair.

Sinclair looks at her dubiously, but she's heard this sort of thing from every sycophant around her for years, so I'm guessing she's primed to believe it. This time tomorrow, she'll probably own fifty different kinds of clay and a kiln to bake them in.

Nicole slaps down the clay dick and joins them. "Don't listen to her, Sin. She's blowing smoke up your ass."

"I would *never*," the teacher says, her tone scandalized. "It's against my professional integrity to lie about art."

"Oh, is there a code of ethics for making clay sculptures?" Nicole asks.

I'd like to see where this goes, but my phone chooses that moment to ring. My heart rate escalates as I pull it out and look at the screen. Unknown number. Is it my father?

I've told my friends about his message. Andy's stance is that he and I have done a perfectly good job of ignoring each other for years and there's no need for us to stop now. Marnie, who grew up with a narcissistic mother, is more troubled. She knows that my father isn't the kind of person who'll back off unless he wants to. Disowning me was a strategy that didn't pan out the way he was hoping. This is a new strategy. We just don't know what it means yet.

I look up and meet her worried gaze.

"Unknown number. Are you going to answer?" she asks. In the background, I can hear Nicole bickering with the teacher, but my gaze is now locked on the phone as it stops ringing and starts up again.

"Who is that?" Andy asks, setting down the apple she's working on. Her attention is half on me, half on the scene at the other table.

"I'll be right back," I tell them through lips that suddenly feel numb.

This is what my father does to me. He turns me into a statue. Into a person drained of blood.

You've been reading too many paranormal romances again, Grace.

I grab my coat and put it on over stiff, awkward limbs. Once I'm outside on the sidewalk, I stand close the building and answer my phone, which had stopped ringing and started up again for a third time. The caller is impatient, which suggests it's him. My father is the kind of person who expects you to answer the instant you're summoned.

Even if he's gone six years without talking to you.

"Hello?" I say, instantly annoyed with myself for making it a question. I'm not the little girl I was, the one who almost gave up her life to make him happy.

"I need to talk to you, Gracie," Enoch says, and the sound of his voice is a surprising balm. My blood starts flowing again. My heart beating. My vampire fate has been averted. Why hearing from Enoch should be a comfort I couldn't say, except at least he isn't my father.

"When someone blocks you, it typically means they don't want to talk to you."

He's silent for a beat, and then he says, "There's nothing typical about you."

I'm not sure how to respond to that. Truthfully, it's one of the things I've been yearning to hear. Particularly from him. Finally, I tug my hair—dammit—and say, "Well, you're talking now, aren't you? What do you want?"

"First, to apologize," he says, his voice gruff. "I was a dick."

"When?" I ask, feigning surprise. "On which occasion?"

"You know on which occasion, Gracie. I was a dick for touching you when I shouldn't have. I was an unpardonable dick for not letting you come."

"You were," I confirm. "I'm shocked to get an apology from you, but thank you for admitting you were wrong. And second?" It amuses me the way he uses lists. Another sign of Enoch's attempts to control the world around him.

"Second...we can talk about in person."

There's an electric intensity to his voice, pressing into me the way his lips did. A shudder travels through me, and I almost drop the phone. "Why?"

"Trust me," he says gruffly.

"I don't."

His laugh is slightly bitter, but he doesn't disagree with me or try to persuade me with a sweet lie. "I know. You've made that perfectly clear. I guess...trust that it's important. I'll be back on Sunday."

"We have Vera's photo shoot."

"I know," he says with a groan. "I'm flying in on a red-eye so I can be there."

"We'll talk afterward, then."

"Meet me at Duck Park beforehand. The open call starts at twelve, so let's say eleven. I have something important to tell you. A couple of important things, actually." He pauses, then adds, "It can't wait, Gracie."

Duck Park is a private park on Vera's property, where a little cabin overlooks a pond with ducks. Frankly, it's one of the places she goes to mess around with models and other men who've served as inspiration. Andy has a less than charitable nickname for it that rhymes with *duck*.

Maybe that's why Enoch knows about it.

I give the internal voice a mental swat. I don't actually believe there's anything going on between them, although I suspect Vera's tried. He probably knows about the spot because she gave him a tour—the same as she does for anyone who visits her property, myself included. Duck Park isn't only used for...well, you know. She's held the occasional event in the cottage, and sometimes she asks me to bring Pumpkin there so the little dog can chase the ducks. I usually try to shoo them away first, because Pumpkin would absolutely bring a duckling down for the thrill of it.

"Is this about my father?" I ask, my heart beating hard. "Because I just got an email from him. He's going to be in town in two weeks. He asked me to meet him at the Asheville office."

"Fuck," he says. I can distinctly hear a thump on the other end of the line, like maybe he punched the wall. Sure enough, his next

"Fuck" sounds pained. "No," he finally says. "It's not about him. But we need to talk about him too."

My mind shifts to Nicole, to the thing she learned but wouldn't tell me. I can't imagine there's anything that could rebrand what Enoch did, but the stupid part of me, the romantic who knows there's no one who's affected me like him, hopes.

"Okay." It's the perfect place to cut our conversation short, but I find myself saying. "Did you pitch them the book?"

He makes a strangled sound. "Yeah. There are more meetings tomorrow."

"Isn't tomorrow Saturday?"

"Have I made you doubt the days of the week?" He doesn't pause for my response, though, just sighs and says, "We're wining and dining a couple of people. You'll meet with me?"

Maybe this is another attempt to get to Sinclair, to convince her that she needs Parker Brand Management. But there's the possibility I can get answers, and I'm as hungry for them as I am covetous of shiny things. So I sigh, and say, "I'll be there. No need to borrow your hook-up's phone again or whatever. I'll unblock you."

There's a flash of discomfort inside me, as if someone stirred my insides with a spoon. I'm not even sure why I said it, though a little voice whispers, *Maybe you wanted him to tell you he's alone.*

I guess I'd just like to think he's not unaffected by what happened between us the other day, in spite of what he did.

"I'm not with a woman," he says with no hesitation. "I'm at my hotel. I'm calling you from their phone."

My mind's a traitor because I can't help but imagine him sitting on a crisp white bed, wearing a suit. Dark blue or maybe charcoal.

"What color suit are you wearing today?" I blurt out before I can help myself.

"You're asking what I'm wearing, Gracie?" he asks, his voice husky. "I was going to use that line."

"I have on a large winter coat," I say. "It's *very* sexy."

Am I...flirting with him? What the hell is wrong with me anyway?

The feeling of his lips on me must have ignited my memories. Although, I'll be honest, they've never been very far away. Because when I sat down to right my book, it was a like a catharsis, pouring out all the things that had passed between us, putting words to the passion he'd lit inside of me. With him, it's a blaze; with the others, it was all matches.

I stuff the feelings down. Bury them. Turn the key. But I already feel something pressing on the door, trying to wedge it open.

"I'm going to the gym," Enoch says. "I'm not wearing a suit. Sorry. You're outside?"

"Yes," I say, my mouth suddenly dry from the thought of him in his gym clothes. I haven't told anyone, but I kept the photo he sent me the other week. "You interrupted my Play with Clay class."

He laughs, though this time with genuine amusement. "Well, in that case, you're welcome."

"I'm surprised you didn't ask if I'm making a bust of you."

"Well, are you?"

I don't know what possesses me, but I say, "I guess you'll have to wait to find out."

"Duck Park. Eleven a.m.," he repeats, his tone officious.

"I don't have the memory of a goldfish," I say, annoyed. "I'll be there."

"That's good, Gracie." He pauses, as if thinking twice about whatever he's about to say, then adds, "Be careful around Vera. We'll figure out a strategy for dealing with your father."

With that, he hangs up.

What the fuck? My mind pings between his warning about Vera to the way he used "we" so freely, between being pleased that he wants us to work together and pissed that he thinks he gets to make that decision.

I'm tempted to call him back, to insist he tell me what he knows *now*, but he's fixated on talking in person, and maybe he's right. Maybe I've been going about things the wrong way, leaving Nicole and Damien to do my dirty work. This will give Enoch and me a chance to have it out. I can air the grievances he knows I have, give him the chance to explain himself...

Except what explanation could he possibly give me?

I return to the room feeling unmoored, as if I'm a balloon whose string is grazing over a kid's hand.

"This is a perfect peach," the teacher is saying officiously, waving it in front of Nicole's nose. "Very few people could make a peach this perfect, especially with such minimal training. This woman has *true talent*. Why, in all my years of teaching, I've never seen such a peach. A person could bite into it without realizing it's clay. It's practically a health hazard."

Sinclair blushes, something that probably happens only on blood moons. "It's a tomato. You know who I am, don't you?" A hand lifts to the blue wig that does very little to conceal her identity. When you have a face like hers, you get noticed. Especially if you've been emblazoned on the sides of buses.

"What? Who?" the woman squawks unconvincingly.

"You had me on the verge of buying a kiln," Sinclair says flatly. "Of paying for studio space."

She pauses, giving the woman a chance to redeem herself, but although her mouth opens, nothing comes out.

"I won't be coming here anymore," Sinclair says. "And if you say anything to the press, I'll tell them exactly what I think about the lessons you offer. We're leaving now."

Her tone is withering, and Marnie starts gathering her lumpy fruit, her eyes wide. It won't do her any good since we don't have a kiln to fire them, but I'll tell her later. Nicole shrugs and returns to her station to gather her dick. Andy, whose fruit truly *is* a health hazard, perfect enough to be unwittingly eaten, leaves it. She's obviously done this sort of thing before and realizes it's a no-go without the kiln. Mine stays at its station too, but I glug my wine before collecting my purse. It gives me burst of acid warmth that's better, at least, than that unmoored feeling.

"I knew it was a tomato," the teacher blusters to Sinclair, trying to turn things around. "It's a *genius* tomato. I was testing your friend." She gestures wildly at Nicole.

"No, you weren't," Sinclair says, and there's something sad in the way she says it. I feel a throb of sympathy for her. She's rich and beautiful. She's *famous*. But how many people have lied to or misled her? How many people can she actually trust?

The teacher's mouth purses into an aggrieved pout. "What would a tomato be doing in a fruit basket anyway?"

Nicole laughs, slinging her free arm around Sinclair's shoulder. The other is holding the clay cock. "You must have skipped a crucial day in Biology. A tomato's a fruit."

"You're an awful woman," the teacher says, her cheeks now as bright as the frames of her glasses.

Nicole tilts her head and lifts a finger. "I get that a lot."

We all bustle out of the door, which is slammed shut after us.

Sinclair sighs and looks up and down the sidewalk before lifting the large hood of her coat over the blue wig. "Sorry about that, ladies. I thought... Well, never mind. I'll see you later."

Right now, seeing her like this, I feel *bad* for her. So I say, "I could use a drink—anyone else?"

"How about some Bloody Marys?" Nicole asks with a grin. "I'm feeling partial toward tomatoes."

I glance at Sinclair, thinking she'll probably be pissed—salt in wounds and all that—but she bursts out laughing. It's spontaneous and joyful, and I see Andy give a small shrug, as if to acknowledge that maybe people *can* grow. The Sinclair we used to know wouldn't have laughed at a joke in which she made an appearance in the punch line.

"You're right about one thing," Marnie says. "Let's go to the bar." She looks to her sister for a nod, and Sinclair gives it.

Andy indicates her acceptance, and I say, "Yes, please."

Marnie lifts her uncooked clay fruit, purses her mouth to a side, and then her eyes light up at the sight of a nearby trashcan. She's about to toss them in, when she turns to Sinclair and asks, "Want to do the honors, Clair?"

Her answer is to grab a nondescript round thing and throw it in.

Or try.

Athletics is clearly not a strong suit either.

She grabs the next one and lobs it hard, plenty of anger behind this one, and a rat scurries out of the trashcan, making everyone other than Nicole jump. Next comes a banana—except this one gets lobbed into the broad back of a passerby.

"Oh, shit," Nicole says.

The guy turns around. He's big and bulky, the sort of man who spends most of his time in a gym. His hair is almost as dark as Enoch's, but his eyes are a soft brown that doesn't seem to match his physique. He bends and picks up the flaccid clay banana and shakes it at Sinclair. "Did you just throw a clay dildo at me?"

"*Excuse* me?"

"A. Clay. Dildo," he repeats, shaking it. The top slumps to the side, like a dick that's gone soft.

"You're insulting my sister's banana," she says, her cheeks pink.

"And *you* were throwing it away."

"This was very clearly an unfortunate accident," Marnie says. "We're sorry to have inconvenienced you, sir."

A laugh rumbles through him as he tosses the banana.

"She's not sorry," he says, nodding to Sinclair.

He's being hard on her, but to be fair, she doesn't *look* very sorry.

"I'm not sorry," she admits. "You're very rude. Maybe people should throw clay dildos at you more often."

She looks hopefully at Nicole, who shakes her head. "Nope, I'm keeping my clay dick."

For a second, the guy looks like he's going to smile. Maybe because she admitted Marnie's artwork looked more like a dick than a fruit, but his expression slips into sullen. "*I'm* very rude?"

"Can anything good come out of prolonging this?" Andy asks, giving him a dark glare. "When kids throw things at each other at the playground, it doesn't last this long. It was a mistake. She's not sorry because she's kind of an ass. You're making a big deal out of it because *you're* an ass. End of story."

He shrugs and shakes his head, but he must be one of those last word people, because he tells Sinclair, "You keep looking for a fight, someone's going to give it to you. Be more careful."

When he leaves, Sinclair gives his back the finger, prompting Nicole to cackle.

The whole clay thing must have thrown Sinclair for a loop. I honestly didn't think she had it in her.

The bar's fairly busy, which isn't a surprise given it's Friday, it's cold, and we're not the only ones in a drinking mood, but the corner near Reggie is always miraculously empty. It's better for us to sit at the bar anyway, where Sinclair's face will only be directed toward us or Griffin.

We sit next to Reggie like a line of ducklings, Marnie next to him, Sinclair next to Marnie, me next to Sinclair, then Andy and Nicole, who slings her clay dick onto the bar with zero self-consciousness.

"How was Play with Clay?" Griffin asks. His gaze dips to Nicole's work of art, but he's known her too long to be surprised.

"A round of Bloody Mary's, Griff," Sinclair says.

The corners of his mouth lift up. "That good, huh?"

"Let's just say I'm not going to switch art mediums any time soon," Marnie says, reaching over the bar for his collar and pulling him down for a kiss. The heat between them is the real deal—the blaze, not the sparks made by matches.

My mind skips to that photo of Enoch at the gym, dressed in his shorts and shirt, his muscles thick and stacked—the kind that invite you to take a bite.

I know that I'll be pulling it up on my phone when I get home—pulling it up and getting out my vibrator. Maybe Nicole is right, and I should enjoy him while he's here—the way you sometimes need to gorge yourself on chocolate and ice cream and whipped calories even though you know they're not good for your body long term.

Maybe—

Sinclair turns to us with a grim look on her face. "I just wanted to thank you guys for bearing with me. I know I've been a little erratic with the activities recently."

Marnie watches her for a second, then says, "Have you been looking at scripts?"

Sinclair sighs and scratches beneath her wig, another thing I never imagined her doing. "My agent's sent over a few projects." Her expression tightens as much as her most recent Botox injections will allow. "They're for mothers. Mothers of *teenagers*. I've gone from college to motherhood." Her jaw works. "The fucked up thing is that I actually *could* have a teenage kid. I mean, I would have needed to be a teenage mom, but even so."

"Well, shit," Nicole says as Griffin reappears with the drinks. "I'll drink to that."

Sinclair agrees with the sentiment, judging by the way she glugs her drink. A Bloody Mary's not really a glugging drink, but I guess if you're in a glugging mood, any old thing will do.

Marnie gives me a pointed glance, and I know what she's thinking—Sinclair's brand is in trouble. *Sinclair* is in trouble, looking everywhere for something fulfilling and ending up with nothing but a bunch of jacked-up clay tomatoes.

The only reason Marnie hasn't suggested that she work with Enoch is loyalty to me. I give her a slight nod—an *I'll talk to him* nod.

Because I *will* be talking to Enoch, and depending on what he says, maybe I'll help him too.

Sinclair heaves an unhappy sigh. Her gaze finds Marnie again. "I've been a shitty sister to you and Drew," she says, then waves a hand when Marnie opens her mouth to make a weak objection. "I know I have. It's just...I'm a thirty-two-year-old woman, and I don't know who I am." Her voice wavers a bit as she says it, and I feel another stab of pity for this woman who, on the surface, has it all.

"You're at least thirty percent less of a jerk than you used to be, so you have that going for you," Andy says.

Nicole pounds the bottom of her drink on the bar. "I'll tell you who you are: you're Sinclair Fucking Jones. Don't you let anyone make you forget it."

Well, the half a dozen people who just overheard her at the bar certainly aren't about to forget it. But the look on Nicole's face suggests she doesn't care about them—just the woman sitting next to me.

Reggie glances at us with sleepy eyes. "Did anyone get me a Bloody Mary?"

It's only later, after we've finished the first round, that Nicole turns to me and says conversationally, "So, did you know Enoch corresponded with your dad *before* you graduated business school?"

What the actual hell?

fourteen

ENOCH

YOU NEED to make them want what you're selling.

You need to make them hungry for it.

I was taught it's best not to bring up what you really want to discuss at a dinner meeting until at least the halfway mark. You allude to it. You describe the wrapping paper down to the stripes, but you don't tell them what's in the package—not until they're salivating for it.

Which is why we make it to coffee and dessert before Frank, Vera's film agent, and I bring up *The Wind in Her Hair*. I'm making a real case for it—a swan song—complete with my plan that the movie can be filmed in Western North Carolina, like *The Hunger Games*, to further boost my new branding for Vera. Then I drop the hint that perhaps a locally grown actress could fill lead role, accompanied by a wink and a nod and a, "Hell, I even know her sister."

It's all true. Sort of.

The Vera I'm talking up *is* a local success story, a pillar of the community. The kind of woman who sells books *and* movies.

Even when they're not hers.

I rub my chest, trying to silence that voice, which keeps reminding me that John Parker isn't the only one undeserving of wealth and power. My mind's been a fucking mess, a tangle that no amount of reorganization can fix, ever since I spoke to Gracie. I hate the thought of him snaking back into her life. Trying to force his will.

I knew he was up to something when he asked me to woo Vera.

I did it anyway, because he has leverage on me. Because, fucking idiot that I am, I wanted to see Gracie. And I wanted to be nearby in case he tried to pull something.

Did he open an Asheville branch of the company to try backing Gracie into accepting a role there? Did he send me there purposefully, in the hopes that our competition from business school would reignite and she'd take a job with him to spite me?

Whatever it is, I can't let him win. I won't.

Then something strange happens. I noticed a loose thread on my suit earlier, but I just rolled my eyes at the incompetence of Dana's alleyway dry cleaner and tucked it in. Now, though, moving my arm suddenly, I can feel the seam tearing. What the fuck?

Trying to ignore it, I continue. "Women across the country already have Pinterest boards with their preferred actors for the characters. There's a built-in audience. They'll want midnight showings. Some of them will show up in costumes. We can circulate the pictures to help build buzz."

Frank laughs jovially. "Let's make sure we give 'em skimpy costumes, then, huh? I'd like to see some tits and ass in those pictures."

Frank's a pig. A dick. But I laugh with him, because the producer we're meeting with, Emil Davis, is laughing so hard his eyes are crinkling.

You're a hypocrite, my inner critic suggests conversationally.

Then: *You're going to have to tell Gracie everything. She'll never trust you unless you do.*

That's when I notice the white gaping through the now obvious opening at the shoulder in my suit jacket.

What the fuck?

I try to adjust it so the hole's not visible...and my sleeve falls off. Tumbles onto the floor like it's a napkin from someone's lap and not something that used to be connected to my clothes.

Shock rolls through me. Then alarm.

Emil tilts his head, studying me. "Everything okay, Enoch?"

I nod, trying to pretend that my suits fall apart on business meetings on the daily and there's nothing particularly strange about this one doing so. Then I take off what's left of my jacket. "New dry cleaner," I say. "They must have done something screwy."

Emil clucks his tongue. "I used someone new once and they tried to give me someone else's suit. Three sizes too small."

I laugh on cue, but the rogue sleeve drops onto the floor. I swivel to pick it up...and feel a tearing in my pants.

Sweet fuck, are they going to fall apart too?

Sweat beads on my brow. I do like to make meetings a show, but usually the show isn't *me*.

"Excuse me," I say. "I'll be right back." I don't really have a plan, other than I'd prefer not to have my entire suit fall apart in front of Emil and Fred. From the feel of my pants, I can already tell there's a tear down the center of the back.

Can I wrap the suit jacket around my waist like some kid from the eighties? But could I even get it to wrap around my waist if it only has one sleeve? I could try, for sure, but I've already made a spectacle of myself.

I've only made it two steps before our server hustles up to me. "Sir, please come with me."

Do they have a room for borrowed suits? She leads me into the hallway that branches toward the bathrooms. Looking at me with her mouth pressed in a hard line, she says, "Sir, I won't say this is the first time this has happened, nor do I dare assume it will be the last, but we don't allow strippers to do their business in the dining room. That's a hard rule. This is a *respectable* establishment."

My mouth gapes open. "Stripper? My suit started falling apart at dinner, I—"

"When someone's suit starts falling apart at the seams at dessert, there's usually a reason for that." She gives me a look as if to say she wasn't born yesterday. "*Because it was designed to.* It's attached together with Velcro, isn't it?"

"I'm not a stripper," I say, my voice too adamant. Both Emil and Fred glance toward the hallway—Emil laughing so hard he's liable to piss himself, and shit, so are half a dozen other people. "Someone messed with my suit."

The server gives me a *likely story* look, as if she's heard that excuse a dozen times.

Dana.

How many times am I going to have to fire that woman?

And what did I ever do to her to make her hate me?

* * *

The server and manager apologized to me.

Emil bought me a bottle of bourbon that's probably going to explode in my checked bag and told me he's never laughed harder in his life.

I consider calling Dana and firing her over the phone, but she could hang up on me. I want to talk to her in person so I can get to the bottom of why she's been fucking with me. Because there's no longer any question that she has been. Something's been off from the beginning. The knowing looks between her and that woman at Bear's Buns, the over-the-top references that don't at all fit the woman I'd come to know, the slight microaggressions. Udolpho. The hangover cure. And now my suit.

I spend the flight home dreaming how satisfying it will feel to fire Dana in person—permanently this time. It's helpful because it keeps me from dwelling on what I need to tell Gracie.

She'll resent you.

She already does, of course, except for occasional slip-ups. This will only shore up her will. That's for the best. Still. When I slip into sleep, we're Renee and Dean, we're in her bed, and her hands are gripping my shoulders as I drive into her. She says his name, though, not mine.

I get home in the morning, exhausted and in ill humor. Udolpho jumps on me the moment I walk through the door, making me drop my bag, which causes the bourbon to explode.

"You sneaking alcohol around now, Sunshine?" my father asks. There's some genuine concern behind the question, like he worries I'm trailing in his footsteps, only going for downers rather than uppers, and it makes my jaw flex.

"No," I say flatly. "It was a gift from a producer." I glance down at Udolpho, who's now licking the knee of my pants for some godforsaken reason. "I'm guessing Dana didn't find his owners."

Honestly, given all the other shit she's pulled, I wouldn't be surprised if she'd plucked him from his owners expressly to mess with me.

"No," Remi says, ruffling his ears. Looking up at me, he adds, "You know, he slept in your bed the whole time you were gone. I think he missed you."

The dog gives me a dopey open-mouthed look and then licks the leg of my pants again.

I barely restrain a groan. With the way this dog sheds, my entire bed is going to be covered in little orangish hairs. "And Dana didn't do anything else, did she? I'm not going to find new ferrets in there or some kind of pet fungus?"

My father studies me for a minute. "No, son, although she did clean your room yesterday. Must've taken what you said to heart."

Doubtful. More like she was screwing with more of my stuff.

Remi looks away, maybe because he senses, quite rightly, that I don't like his new friend.

"When do we need to be ready for your little shindig?" my father adds.

Oh, fuck.

I'd forgotten about inviting him and Remi to the photo shoot, but my nephew's staring at me with hopeful eyes, and I don't want to be the person who tells him he can't have something he wants, especially when it's something I can so easily give him.

I need to tell them I'm firing Dana, but I'll wait until after the photo shoot. Maybe Remi's excitement over Vera will help temper his disappointment.

"I have to go in early," I say, smoothing my hair. "How about you meet me there at one? The open call for models will be almost over by then. That'll be boring."

"The whole thing will be boring," my father says. "Is there going to be a buffet? Remi was going to tuck into lunch here, but I figured there'd be a buffet."

"There'll be food," I say with a smirk. They'll probably be the only ones eating it, but there *will* be food. I know because I heard Vera tell Gracie to arrange for it. My mouth firms with dislike. That woman. She's been treating Gracie like an indentured servant, all while she steals her book out from under her.

Worse, she thought she could get away with it by changing a few details, adding that Vera Valence "polish" and big-ticket happy ending. I could tell the ending was all her. There was none of Gracie's sunshine, none of her passion.

Did she think Gracie would just roll over and take it?

"Did someone piss in your cornflakes?" my dad asks, snorting.

"No, someone messed with my wo—suit."

I rub my mouth, trying to regain something like equanimity, because I almost just called Grace Donnelly my woman.

I spend the next half hour cleaning up my bag, showering, and getting dressed. I don't wear a suit. For all I know, Dana fucked with all of them while I was gone, and I'd prefer not to find myself suddenly naked at Vera's photo shoot. Something tells me it would be taken as an invitation.

Nerves prickle at me. My mouth is dry.

I have to do it.

Like a Band-Aid, I can hear my mother saying. *Better to take all the hurt at once.*

Like when she decided my father needed to move out, then insisted all of his things had to be gathered and gone in one night.

It didn't hurt less that way, but it *did* hurt slower—the kind of hurt you don't fully register until it's too late to really do anything about it. The kind that sticks with you.

The way Gracie has stuck with me all these years.

On the edge of my nerves is something like…excitement. Because I haven't seen her since that kiss, and even though she won't be kissing me today, part of me is still hoping. The stupid part of me, namely my dick.

Still, Gracie wrote me into her book. That means what we shared meant something to her. Maybe it still does.

When I get to Duck Park, she's already there, sitting on the bench just beside the front windows of the cottage. They're slightly open, maybe to air it out for Vera, should she decide one of the models from the cold call is worth her time. It's eleven a.m., and the day is chilly despite the sunshine. Gracie looks beautiful in her black coat, her light hair burnished gold in the sun, her lips a pop of red that demand to be notice and appreciated. To be *kissed.* She's left her glasses at home today. It doesn't surprise me one bit that she's throwing corn into the pond, and the ducks are coming to her like she's a goddamn Disney princess.

Villains don't deserve the princess.

I park next to her car and go to her, my heart racing.

"Hello, Enoch," she calls out, but there's something detached and cold about it, like she's closed herself off from me since that phone call the other night. Maybe she has. Her coat, I notice, is zipped right up to the point of her chin.

I try to convince myself that's a good thing.

"It's nice out here," I say, sitting next to her.

"Leave it to you to prefer cold weather." She studies me, taking in my pants and sweater. "No suit? Did you personality swap with someone in Los Angeles?"

"That's a story for later," I say. Maybe I *will* tell her about being accused of being a stripper. For some reason, it doesn't bother me when Gracie laughs at me, but I came here to say something, and I'm damn well going to do it. "I need to tell you something. Well, a couple of things "

She tilts her head, revealing a flash of her long neck, and I have an errant desire to bite the soft flesh and mark her. "Good," she says, "because I have some things to say too."

"What I have to tell you...it's about your father."

She flinches, her lips parting.

Just say it.

"When we were assigned to work together on our final project, your father asked to meet with me." I swallow, feeling her gaze drill into me, dislike varnished back into place. "He told me he had an open associate's position and he planned on hiring one of the top two people in our program. Me—"

"Or me," she says in a whisper. "You never said."

I lift a hand. "I'm not making excuses for myself, Gracie. I'm stating facts. I didn't know John Parker was your father. You'd changed your name to Donnelly, and he made damn sure not to bring it up. He asked me to send him regular updates about the project. What ideas we'd each come up with, that kind of thing."

Her expression shores up, but she lifts a hand to her hair, tugging, something I've seen her do for years whenever she's nervous. I quell the need to tug her fingers away, to kiss them. "And I suppose you told him I was worthless. That I was a silly little woman who didn't do my part."

"No," I snap, because it's important for her to understand this. "Did I make myself look good? Absolutely. I was under the impression that he was also getting updates from you—that we both knew we were in competition with each other. I figured it was my job to make myself look good, yours to make *you* look good. I didn't know he was your father until that night." I swear under my breath. "That's when I figured out what he'd been up to. Having me spy on you without fucking realizing it."

"But you still told me to talk to him about wanting to write," she says, her tone hard. "You told me not to take the job."

"Because you did want to write. You *do*." I turn toward her on the bench. "Gracie, you and I aren't as different as you've been telling yourself. We both need passion to push us along. We need *purpose*. It would have killed you to take that job. Maybe not at first, but it would have changed you. It would have taken away your joy."

Like one of those Band-Aid wounds. Quick and painful, then a slow burn of processing the hurt.

"Convenient," she says, but her tone's brittle, like some of the anger is residual and she's not sure what to do with it. "You expect me to believe you weren't motivated by self-interest?"

"No," I say, "I'm only telling you all of this because you have a right to know. And because he's trying to manipulate you again."

"Why didn't you tell me then?" she asks flatly. "I had just as much of a right to know then."

"Because he's your father," I say. "Because it was a shitty thing for him to do, and I knew he'd already hurt you. I didn't want to make the cut any deeper."

"But you *did*," she says, her eyes shining. "You agreed to work with him, after all of that. After he cut me off like I was nothing."

"I did," I say, "and I don't have an excuse for that. He offered it, and I wanted it. I didn't have much hope of getting a job like that from anyone else, Gracie." I pause. Shore up my will. "You know as well as I do that success in this field depends on who you know. I didn't come from money. My mother and I lived in a shit apartment, and she was always struggling to make ends meet. My dad...he sent us money to help out when he could, but he worked a night job in a factory. I didn't know anyone who had influence or pull. It was on me to make things happen."

She looks like I just pulled a rug out from under her. "Why didn't you tell me any of this before?"

She's hurt, I realize, and she has every right to be. I did tell her things about myself that weekend. I told her about my dream, about my mother, who'd always supported and pushed me. About my difficult relationships with my father and my half sister. About my need to prove myself. But I didn't tell her this.

"I didn't tell anybody. I saw business school as my chance to become someone else." She doesn't look impressed, which is fair, so I say the words that make my mouth feel full of sawdust, "I was ashamed. You grew up in a mansion. I got a scholarship, and I had to work two jobs every break to afford my clothes."

"Your suits," she says quietly, her eyes glimmering.

"My suits."

"I wish you'd told me." She touches my arm—such a light touch, but I feel it down to the bone. "I wouldn't have cared. The money means nothing to me."

I can't help it. My lips lift, and I say, "Spoken like someone who's always been rich."

She gives a nod, those fingers skimming up and down my arm again, leaving a trail of fire. I want to pull her onto my lap. I want to fuck her on this bench in front of those stupid ducks. I want to claim her as my own. I want her to be my sweetness and light, because I didn't realize how much she was adding to my days, even when I fooled myself into thinking I didn't like her, until she was gone.

I'm caught in a web of my own making, though, and I can't have her.

Because I'm an idiot, I take her hand anyway. I haven't touched her since I brought her to the brink of orgasm the other day, and I need to have my hands on her, even if it's like this. It's a compulsion. She must feel it too, because she lets me.

"It doesn't change anything, Gracie. I still took the job. I knew he was an asshole, but he was a *successful* asshole. Someone I could learn from. I'm not trying to excuse myself. You've always been right about me: I'm a dick. I took that job even though I knew I'd lose you. You were the only person in my life who made me want to be better instead of stronger, but it seemed so important at the time, getting that job...making something of myself. I was a dumb kid. I didn't realize..."

I didn't realize I'd never meet anyone else who made me feel the way you did.

I didn't realize you were the only woman who'd challenge me.

I didn't realize I wouldn't move on.

I clear my throat. "But I didn't have good reasons for doing what I did. It didn't take me long to figure out I'd made a losing bargain."

Because it had closed a door between the two of us. Because John Parker *is* a dick, more so than I'd realized when I made that bargain. He's the kind of man who ruins people with a grin. One of my colleagues quit a couple of years back, wanting to make a go of it on his own, and John Parker smiled and clapped him on the back—and then made damn sure that no one more influential than a TikToker with a thousand followers would hire him.

"So why are you still there?" she asks, her brow furrowing. "You have the experience now. You could find a different job."

In for a penny.

"Yeah. About that. I needed some money, and he fronted it to me. But he asked me to sign a five-year contract. If I try to leave and work somewhere else before the time is up, he'll sink me."

"Why would you agree to that?" she asks, squeezing my hand.

"You don't need to tell me it was fucking stupid. I didn't feel like I had a choice." I pause. But she's my confessor, and it feels surprisingly good to let all of this go. "My father was injured at work, like I told you. His employers blamed him for what happened. They said he'd endangered more people than just himself by working with heavy machinery while he was under the influence. They went after him in court, and he needed a lawyer. A good one. There was a trial, and it ate into my savings fast. Your father wouldn't give me an advance on my salary, but he said he'd give me a bonus if I signed a new contract. There's a strict penalty if I renege—triple the original payout—and you and I both know he'd enforce it." I swallow, because I hate admitting this part. I'm ashamed of it. "He pays me well, but I still don't have that kind of money lying around. My retirement accounts are tied to the contract too."

She tilts her head, her eyes boring into me as if she's peering into my soul and gauging the color. Is it black as pitch? Or is she starting to see the shades of gray that run through it? I hope they're there. I fucking hope so.

"Back then, you didn't seem like you had much respect for your father."

My mouth firms. "He's my father. He wasn't blameless, but if they don't want people taking uppers, they should have better policies. He'd told them he was suffering from exhaustion, but they'd threatened to fire him if he took time off. It was their fault as much as his. He doesn't know about my agreement with John. He doesn't realize how much it cost me to keep him out of jail."

"Oh." Her eyes widen, and she nestles her hand deeper into mine. "*When* did you make this agreement with my father?"

"Three years ago," I say with a humorless smile. My gaze shifts to the pond, where the ducks swim in a neat little row, one clearly in the lead. I feel like one of those small fuckers, forced to follow along. I've always wanted to be the one in front. I still do. My dream is to start my own company, to run it differently than John's, but if he screwed up my old colleague's life, it's nothing on what he'd do to me. Especially if I try to leave before the time's up.

"Which means I have to hang on for at least two more years." I hold on to her hand, caressing the back with my finger because touching her feels fucking awesome. Because I can't stay away. "I can't be with you, Gracie, because you need to stay away from him. Even though Vera is a nightmare, you're more yourself here. You're happier. I should have talked him into assigning this job to someone else, especially since I suspected he had other motives, but..." I shrug. "I wanted to see you. I was hoping you were living your dream. That you had manuscripts stuffed into your drawer or in the pipeline to be published. I'd looked you up, but I couldn't find anything much, other than that you were working with Vera."

"Well, you're living *your* dream. So at least one of us got what they wanted."

I raise my eyebrows. "Does this look like the face of a man who has it all?"

"Yes," she says, finally pulling her hand away. "You put on a good show. Always have. You realize that makes it impossible to trust you."

Resigned, I nod. "There's something else I need to say."

"There's more?"

Looking into her eyes, I say, "I read your book, Gracie. That's why I told you all of this. I realize it's hopeless, but I couldn't let you think I don't care. I did then. I do now."

I LEAP TO MY FEET, horrified. *Embarrassed.* In the last twenty minutes, I've run the gamut of emotions, like my heart has become a spin chart.

First, it trips over what he said. He cares about me? Then *and* now? The surly part of me wants to suggest he has a hell of a way of showing it, but then my brain processes his second revelation.

Enoch read *Between the Stacks*?

How? *Why?*

My mind instantly hops to two dozen places in the manuscript. The description of what we did in the library, in my room…

I spilled my broken heart onto those pages.

He knows he got to you. He knows everything.

"You did what? How? Are you…*spying* on me?"

"No," he says, getting to his feet too. "Obviously not." He says this last bit with a little annoyance, which sparks *my* annoyance. How can he be surprised I'd wonder now that I know he was essentially spying on me in business school, whether he realized what he was doing or not?

"Then how?"

Sighing, he runs a hand through his black hair, rumpling it. It

151

never looks like this—*he* never looks like this, undone and informal. Like a man and not an image. Not the Suit. I feel an ache that goes down to my bones. I'm tired. Exhausted. Wrung out.

"*How?*"

He swears under his breath. Paces one step toward me, one step back. "It's Vera," he says. "She sent it to me on Thursday. She wanted me to pitch it to her film agent and producers as *her* work. She made some changes, Gracie, but I know it's yours. I'd know if I read it anywhere. It's about us."

A feeling of...violation washes over me, sickening. I'm on the verge of retching. Vera was encased in glass in my mind for so long —glass that's held up despite some cracking recently—and he just took a baseball bat to it. Now I see her for who she is. A liar. A thief. A—

"That cunt!" It's Andy's voice—another jolt to the system. Fresh horror coils through me. I'd completely forgotten they were waiting in the cottage. Andy and Marnie. *Sinclair.* They came for moral support after what Nicole told me about Enoch's business-school correspondence with my father. We all got steamed up at Summer Nights, spending half an hour ranting about men being idiots while Griffin brought us free drinks.

And, yes, I see the irony.

"You brought friends?" Enoch says coldly, taking a step away from me. A few minutes ago, he was all warmth and earnestness, wriggling toward my heart again even though I'd stoned it off from him. Even though he had betrayed me, albeit in a lesser way than I'd originally thought. "Didn't take you for the sort who couldn't even go to the bathroom without a buddy."

My mind rewinds through all the things he said to me, things I'm pretty damn sure he wouldn't have said to anyone else. His father. My father. The money. *Shit.* I can't focus. There's too much in my head. "I didn't—"

"What were you going to do?" he asks them, turning toward the window, although I get the distinct impression he's doing it so he doesn't have to look at me. "Throw me in with the ducks?"

This is the Suit again—the polished, funny, *cutting* Enoch.

Everything about this moment feels broken and wrong.

"I wanted her to convince you to go skinny dipping so we could steal your clothes and drive away," Andy says, "but they reminded me it was seasonally inappropriate."

"So what were you going to settle for?" he asks, one corner of his mouth moving up in a facsimile of a smile. "Don't tell me you waited in there just to eavesdrop. Gracie tells me I already have an inflated ego. You wouldn't want to make it any worse."

Marnie shrugs and lifts the water balloon in her hand. "We *did* have a plan." The brown dirt inside is obvious through the translucent siding.

"Dirt bags," he says. "Cute." He does glance at me then. "I guess that's why you were so disappointed I wasn't wearing one of my suits." His eyes are burning. Not with the usual arrogance and confidence, though. No, I've hurt him, and I feel the cut in my own heart.

I had no way of knowing he was thinking this way, *feeling* this way. There's no real reason for guilt, but I feel it anyway. He wanted to protect me, to tell me there were wolves at my door, and I treated him like he was one.

He still did something shitty, a voice in my head reminds me. *He admitted it.*

And yet...he was twenty-four. A kid, like he said, or as good as.

I'm an adult woman, and I should have known better. It's just that Enoch does something to me. The other day, right when I felt myself softening toward him, Nicole told me about his connection with my father. It felt like all of my worst fears had been realized. So, yeah, as we got progressively drunker and they suggested this scheme, I shrugged and said, "Sure, why not? I've been waiting for years to get one of his suits dirty." It made me feel stronger, coming here with them, knowing I wasn't alone. It made me feel like I could confront him without breaking apart. But it's no excuse. It was childish and petty. Stupid.

"Anyway," he says, sticking his hands in his coat pockets. "It looks to me like you have plenty of help, Gracie. You won't need mine. I don't know how Vera planned on getting away with stealing your work, but she seemed confident she would. Since it's obvious you don't trust me, I guess I should tell you that I didn't bring it up the film agent or the producers. I won't be telling your father either." Turning to my friends again, he says, "So, what's it going to be? Will I be target practice today?"

Andy lifts her eyebrows. "Well, you did—"

Marnie gives her a little shove, cutting her off. "Not today," she tells him. "But make better choices. Because we're watching you." Proving she's been spending too much time with Nicole, she points two fingers of her free hand to her eyes before shifting them to him. Then she pulls a face. "Actually, that was a super creepy thing to say. We're not watching you, but we do have Grace's back. So don't mess with her."

He acknowledges this with a nod and spears me with another glance. "If this schoolyard shit is your version of revenge, you better watch your back with your father *and* Vera, Gracie. Because you're playing tic-tac-toe, and they play chess. Think about *that*."

Then, to my bafflement, he approaches the window and presents a business card to Sinclair. "I've been meaning to get in touch with you," he says politely. "I have plans for your brand. Let's meet."

"I can still throw dirt at him, Gracie," Andy says, glowering at him—and at Sinclair, who takes the card with a somewhat baffled look on her face. "It's not too late."

"No," I say, and it comes out choked. Because this is *horrible*. "Enoch," I say, my voice cracking, "she...Vera used to have me type up her manuscripts when she wrote them on a typewriter. She hasn't told anyone she switched to a word processor. What if she claims that *I* stole from *her*?"

He gives me a look that's so absent any emotion, I want to cry. "I think you know the answer to that, Grace. Well, this has been fun, ladies, but I think I'm going to leave all the same. *Enjoy the view.*"

He turns and leaves, and I'm not sure if he was talking about himself—because it *is* a fine view—or the ducks.

Maybe he's all out of ducks when it comes to me. I don't know if he can get over having shared all of that in front of an audience. I should have stopped him, but the whole ridiculous plan had been erased from my mind the instant he started opening up to me. He had taken center stage, something he does all too easily with me.

I slowly lower onto the bench, feeling the hot press of tears behind my eyes. What a mess. Maybe Enoch was a jerk, but he's not the jerk who's out to ruin my life. Vera is. And my father.

I sent the Fairy Godmother Agency after the wrong villain.

* * *

"I still think he sucks," Andy says, throwing a piece of corn across the pond. It hits one of the ducks in the head. My friends came out of the cottage after Enoch left, and we're all sitting on the bench. Well, the three of us are. Sinclair is standing next to us, probably because she's not at the thighs-touching stage of her relationship with anyone but Marnie.

Marnie is in the middle, with Andy and me on either side of her. She nudges Andy's shoulder. "You think every guy sucks."

"Not all of them. Your brother's a nerd, but he's not a jerk."

"What am I going to do?" I say hopelessly, half to myself. "I'm supposed to go to this photo shoot in half an hour. I'm pretty sure Damien plans on showing up, but I have no idea what he intends to do. Enoch's obviously not the enemy here."

"Does that mean I can call him?" Sinclair asks. "For branding help, I mean."

We all ignore her, and Marnie reaches out to squeeze my arm. "You like him, huh?"

"I don't know. I'm in a bit of a mind storm." Some of the things I've accepted as truths for years are floating away on the wind like dandelion fluff.

Enoch could have told me all of this years ago, of course, but he's right—it wouldn't have mattered. He took the job at Parker Brand Management because he wanted it, and even if I'd known about my father's manipulation, I still would have walked away from him.

Then there's Vera. After everything we've shared, I can't believe she'd do this. I don't want to. Yet the proof just walked away from me.

The proof. I drop my hands and look up at my friends, all three staring at me like they're the fates spinning out my future in spider silk. The view in the background really *is* spectacular, ducks gliding past lazily on the water, little decorative rocks surrounding the pond. Suddenly, everything seems ten times better than it did thirty seconds ago.

"He's the proof!"

"Of what?" Marnie asks. "Your dad being an asshole? You can join Clair, Drew, and me in the shitty parent club."

"No, you guys. My book is about Enoch and me. He's the proof. He knows it's mine."

Andy throws a corn missile at another duck before turning to me. "Is he really going to put himself out there for you, Grace? You heard what he said. If he pisses off your dad, your father's going to go nuclear. To be honest, I'll bet your dad would prefer for Vera to put her name to that book than you."

Sinclair clears her throat. "From what you've said about your father, I'll bet he has plenty of stipulations in that contract. Enoch probably has no choice but to fall in line with him."

She says it like someone who knows a thing or two about bad contracts.

Andy makes a face. "Are you going to wait two years for him to tell everyone it's yours? Vera will probably be attending the film premiere of *Between the Stacks* by then. I doubt you'll be walking the red carpet with her unless she brings that dog."

She's right. Considering the past few weeks through this new lens, I can see that Vera has been *trying* to drive me away or at least distract me. She's been sitting in her office, adding her polish to my book while ordering me to reorganize her bookshelves for the umpteenth time or brush Pumpkin's teeth or make Jell-O into a mold resembling the house.

My hands fist.

She *planned* this. It wasn't some impulsive action, and it wasn't born out of desperation. It was done out of greed and malice. Jealousy.

She was my idol. But she's trying to steal not just my book, but my *life*. My story.

"I'm not going to let her get away with this," I seethe through my teeth.

Andy's beaming at me like I'm one of her star pupils. "There's that inner rage that doesn't roll out nearly often enough."

"We'll help you," Sinclair blurts, then looks at Marnie for guidance. "We're going to help her, right?"

"Hey, that's the spirit," Andy says, reaching over and patting her on the back, a little harder than she was ready for, because it looks like she's about to go careening into the pond.

"Of course we're going to help her," Marnie says. "With all of it."

Sinclair seems to firm up, becoming more like the woman I remember from my television screen and less like the lost woman who's been wandering the streets of Asheville in a collection of progressively hipper wigs. "First off, you can't quit. Not yet. As long as you work for her, you have access. I'm not sure how much Marnie told you—" She glances at Marnie, who mouths, *Everything*. Luckily Sinclair seems more amused than annoyed when she adds, "But the director who took over on my old TV show made an art of sexual harassment. I gathered as much evidence as I could because I knew he was going to come gunning for me. That's what you have to do, Grace. You need her to think nothing has changed so she doesn't pull your access."

She's right. Unfortunately, I know how to play pretend. I did it for years with my father. When he was around, I'd pretend not to notice pops of beauty in the world around me—flowers growing up through the sidewalk, golden veins shooting through fabric—because he thought the things I loved were gaudy or inappropriate.

I think back to what Enoch said—I never wanted that other life, and if I'd allowed it to claim me, it would have changed me.

He was right.

Still kind of an asshole, but in all fairness, I guess I've been no better. Someone nice wouldn't have willingly taken part in any of this. These feelings I have toward him—the push-pull, the anger and desire—they've made me into someone else. Or maybe they've just pulled something out of me that's always been there, dormant, and only *he* can tap into.

"I can do that," I say slowly.

"Hey, maybe I can give you an acting lesson," Sinclair says, warming to the subject. "We can do it at my loft after the photo shoot. I'll make drinks."

I could tell her that I don't need one, that I know perfectly well how to act, but she looks excited. It's obvious she needs this, even if I don't.

"*Griffin* will make drinks," Marnie interjects, lifting a finger. "Your drinks are all grain alcohol with a splash of flavored seltzer."

"What's wrong with that?" Sinclair tilts her head. "There are fewer calories that way."

"Just when I was starting to think you're okay," Andy says, shaking her head.

"Let's do it tomorrow evening, if that's all right," I say, giving my hair another tug. "Today's been a lot."

"Great!" Sinclair says. "That'll give me time to prepare. Five thirty?"

We all murmur our agreement.

It's nice, having them here, knowing they're all supporting me—even Sinclair, who's at least partly a jerk. But there's a cold, sucking emptiness inside of me. It's not only because of what Vera did. It's the way Enoch changed just now, as if he were closing himself back up in that suit cocoon. I want to believe he'll help me, but I'm not sure I can. Because to trust him, I have to forgive him all the way—and he'll have to forgive *me*.

I'm going to ask him to help me, though. Because I've spent too long hiding from the things I want, pawing around the edges of them like a dog who doesn't know how to open a package of treats.

A voice inside of me whispers that Enoch's forgiveness isn't the only thing I want from him. I ignore it.

Before I leave for the main house, I text Nicole and Damien.

Me: *Change of plans. We're going to take down Vera Valence.*
Nicole: *Does this mean I don't get to mess with Enoch anymore?*
Damien: *Affirmative, Nicole. What'd she do?*

So I tell them.

sixteen

GRACE

"UGLY," Vera says into my earpiece. *"Dreadfully ugly. No, he'll never do."* From the sound of chewing, she just popped a bonbon into her mouth. They're penis-shaped chocolates she asked me to special order from the Chocolate Fetish for this exact occasion.

She's sitting at a picture window, peering down at me—literally—while I "interview" the people who showed up for the open call at the side of the house.

Gritting my teeth, I tell the young guy—probably a college student in search of a few extra bucks—that we won't be photographing him today. There's nothing "dreadfully ugly" about him, although if you're used to looking at models all day, I suppose the vast majority of people are ugly.

In the past, I might have written off her behavior by telling myself she's overtired or stressed out. I feel like a fool for not seeing what's as obvious as the mole on the poor, rejected college student's face: Vera Valence is not a nice person. This is the seventeenth time she's called someone "dreadfully ugly" since we started this farce half an hour ago, and with half an hour to go, I'm sure we'll have at least ten more. Another ten will be deemed too fat, too thin, or too unremarkable.

Luckily, I didn't have to talk to her for more than two minutes before being sent out here. It went something like this: I arrived two minutes early, she accused me of being late, and then she sent me outside in the cold to wait for the models to start showing up.

Not much longer, I soothe myself. *You're playing a role.*

It chafes like a drying too-small swimsuit. I've tried to ease the discomfort by going over all the things I need to do as an in-house spy. Her computer is the holy grail, of course, but I don't know how I'll get into it.

Besides, what would she have on there? She's not foolish enough to have saved the email I sent her with my manuscript.

I *do* have time-stamped entries on my computer, but I've been writing the book for as long as I've worked for her. She could claim that she gave me the typewritten manuscript in chunks to transcribe at home.

The best way to prove it's mine is to get Enoch to back me, but if he does that, he loses everything.

Except...

What if she's done something else? Something we could use as leverage or to damage her reputation?

No, not we. *I.* Enoch's job is to make her look good. He wouldn't stand in my way, I don't think, but I doubt he'd put everything on the line for me.

I feel that coldness inside again, that emptiness.

"I'm sorry," I say to the young guy. "You don't have the look we're going for."

"You know, it's fucking cold out here," he says, glowering at me. "You shouldn't make people wait outside. It's a shit move."

"Not her decision, *friend,*" snaps a familiar voice, sending a shockwave of awareness through me. I can feel him then, at my back, as if his shape is a black hole sucking me in.

Enoch steps forward, letting his greater height and the bulk he's picked up since business school tell this kid that he'd better listen.

"Yeah, whatever," says the young guy. He goes to step away, but Enoch reaches out and stops him.

"I don't know where you went to charm school," he says, his smile fierce, "but you're supposed to apologize when you wrong someone. Grace here is *just doing her job*."

"I'm sorry," the guy mutters unconvincingly, but Enoch lets him go.

The guy leaves, and Vera hisses into my ear. *"Ugly face does have a nice ass. Maybe we should bring him back and shoot him from behind."* Thankfully, she immediately forgets her request and says, *"Be a dear and convince Enoch to take some photos for me. He's looking even more delicious than usual today, but I do wish he'd worn a suit."*

"Why are you here, Grace?" Enoch asks under his breath, his voice seething. "You're seriously going to keep working for her, knowing what you know?"

Other than earlier, at the pond, I can't remember the last time he called me Grace, just Grace, and I feel weirdly bereft of my nickname. He's definitely angry, but he's still standing up for me. Why?

Vera can talk to me, but she can't hear me, so I murmur, "Keep your friends close and your enemies closer, right?"

"I hope you're planning this through better than you did those dirt bags," he says. I look for traces of wry humor around the edges of his mouth, but there are none. His expression is closed off, cold.

Anxiety grips me, and I touch my hair. He reaches for my hand and slowly lowers it, sending sensation coursing through me. His eyes sear into me, and he opens his mouth as if to say something—

"Hey, they cut in line," someone says as an older man and a young boy with glasses and a dark mop of hair approach us from the back.

"Too old and too young," Vera says disgustedly. *"Much too old and young. Though the old one is rather handsome in a rugged, rumpled sort of way. Collect his information in case I decide to write an ex-boyfriend's-father book."*

"They're here with me," Enoch says in response to the continued grumbling from the would-be models. Several dirty glances are sent his way.

"Is this the kind of guy they're looking for?" says a man with a patchy beard, gesturing to Enoch. "If so, we don't stand a chance."

He's right—or at least he's right about his own lack of prospects. *Looks like he has mange,* I can practically hear Vera say.

"Hear that, Sunshine?" the older man says, coming up and pounding Enoch on the back. "It's your lucky day. Maybe you'll get to take your shirt off after all."

Is this...

"Are you his *father*?" I ask, the words bursting out of me.

"So his mother tells me," the man says, holding his left hand out for a shake. I get a glimpse of his other hand, three fingers severed at the knuckle. "Rich."

"I'm Grace," I say, shaking the proffered hand.

I can feel Enoch watching us, and I have to wonder what he's thinking. Is he annoyed by the necessity to introduce me to his father?

I hadn't known they'd be coming today, but I'm...*fascinated.* I'd ask this man two hundred questions if I could. He looks a bit like Enoch, but he's shorter and broader—as burly as a boxer—and his hair is white. The boy doesn't look much like either of them, except for that thick dark hair, just the slightest bit wavy, and the shape of his eyes.

"I told Vera they were coming," Enoch says. Nodding to his nephew, he adds, "Remi's interested in photography."

"And Vera Valence." The boy gives me a nod of greeting, then glances around with shining eyes. "Is she out here?"

His excitement reminds me of the way I used to feel about Vera. I don't want to tell him that she's crouched behind that window like a pervert, making snide comments about other people's bodies while she pops bonbons and sips wine.

So I settle for, "No, but she'll come out soon."

"You know," Remi says, studying me with serious eyes, "Uncle Knock told me about you. He said you went to school together."

My gaze finds Enoch. "What—"

"*No, not the boy,*" Vera says into my earpiece. "*He looks younger than eighteen. Bad metrics. Don't want to get accused of any funny business.*"

I shake my head at the window, trying to silently communicate that they're here to watch the photo shoot, not participate. I pull out my phone and text her.

Me: *They're Enoch's family. He says he told you they'd be here.*
Vera: *Oh, yes. I was hoping they'd pressure him into posing for a couple of photos. Clothed, of course. ;-)*

God, I really hate her. The blinders have thoroughly been removed.

Enoch's father looks around and whistles. We're set up to one side of the sprawling house, just within view of the fountain in front, just out of view of the tent that we put up for part of the photo shoot. "She can afford all of this on a little slap-and-tickle?"

"A lot of it, actually," I say. His attitude isn't unfamiliar to me, but he said it playfully, without any of my father's cold loathing.

Rich laughs, then says, "We heard there'd be food. Any truth to that, or is Sunshine over here pulling my leg?"

"Sunshine?" I ask, turning to Enoch.

"You like that, Gracie?" he rebuts, raising his eyebrows. "You can call me anything you like."

"Does that mean I get to call you Sunshine too?" Remi asks.

"To you, it's Uncle Sunshine." He gives him a playful nudge, and I feel a blossoming warmth inside of me.

He's not happy with you, I remind myself. *And he still works for Dad.*

But my body's an idiot, apparently, because it doesn't care.

I clear my throat and address Enoch's father. "There's a heated tent around the corner. That's where we'll be starting the photo shoot. The refreshments are in there. Please help yourselves."

A groan goes up from the line as Rich and Remi make their way back to the tent.

"Hey," Patchy Beard says. "The kid with the mole was right. You've been making us wait out here while there's a heated tent with *food*. What gives?"

The two men behind him—one of whom Vera will call *dreadfully, horribly ugly* and another *too generic, pass*—get in on the action, grumbling about the unfair conditions.

I glance at Enoch, remembering what he told me about his plan for Vera's brand: local, friendly, homegrown. This probably isn't a good look. She lives in a mansion much too large for one woman and one dog and treats her would-be employees like cattle. I should have warned him, probably, but I didn't devote a single brain cell to arranging this photo shoot.

Enoch's lips lift into a charming grin that doesn't meet his eyes. Although he's not wearing a suit, this is his suit persona. He's not the same man who made himself vulnerable to me at Duck Park. There's a tingle of unease inside of me, unease and unwilling attraction, because even if I'm more drawn to that version of Enoch, I want both of them equally.

"It's a test of tenacity, friend," he says. "Vera writes about the kind of man who can lift his woman in one arm and move a boulder with the other. She writes about men who could survive twenty degree weather without noticing it. You understand why she'd need that kind of man as a cover model too, don't you? No one wants to promote a false image. Vera's all about real experiences. Real stories."

His gaze shoots to mine for an instant, and annoyance roils through me, chased by a flash of heat. Because he looked at me the same way while he finger-fucked me against that pillar last week. He's baiting me.

Actually, maybe the annoyance is at myself because his tactic is working—on me *and* the men. They're nodding slowly, and I see one of them take off his jacket, a mistake he must immediately regret judging by the speed with which he pulls it back on.

"Besides," Enoch adds graciously. "Everyone who waits is eligible to win the gift package. We have your names from the waivers you submitted before coming."

"What's in the gift package?" Generic asks excitedly, perking up.

The others seem to have rallied too.

I'm a little in awe, a little aggravated, and a little, well, wet.

Enoch puts an arm around my shoulders and says, "Gracie here knows. She's the one who put it together."

He lifts his arm, leaving an empty space where it had been.

"Well?" Patchy Beard presses.

I'm tempted to tell them it's nonexistent or a giant bouquet of Vera's signed books, but Enoch's looking at me with interest—like he wants me to meet his challenge.

"Beer," I say, clearing my throat. "A selection of local beer, a hand-sculpted beer stein from East Fork, and a gift certificate to the Whale. You know, that beer joint in West Asheville. Since she knows you're the kind of men who would prefer shaving with a single razor, she also told me to include shaving supplies and soap from Appalachian Natural Soaps. And, of course, signed copies of her books for the women in your lives."

All local stores, fitting with the image Enoch said we were trying to convey.

I give him an arch look, and I notice his smile is more genuine this time. Damn it, we're flirting, aren't we?

"Wow," Patchy Beard says, rubbing his patchy beard. "They only make that beer stein for Father's Day."

"Exactly," I say. "Limited edition."

"I'd like to get my hands on that gift package."

"Of course you would," I say, shifting my attention to him. "It's very nice. Only the best breweries are represented."

"The next three are a hell no," Vera says into my ear. *"What's the hold up? We've only selected three models so far, and we need at least six if I'm going to re-cover the Naughty Stepbrothers series. Chop-chop!"*

I'm pulling out my phone to type a response to her, when Generic calls out, "Hey, he's cutting in line!"

I look up and gasp, because it's Damien who's stirred them up, walking toward us with the confidence of someone who knows he's a ten. He's wearing a red sweater that perfectly offsets his light brown skin, and his sliced eyebrow adds a hint of danger.

"I heard there was an open call for models?" he says, lifting his eyebrows. There's no indication he notices the line snaking around the building.

"Uh, yes," I say awkwardly. Again, I can feel Enoch watching me. Why? Can he tell that Damien and I know each other?

The window of Vera's office swings open so suddenly it clips Patchy Beard in the face. He yelps and jumps away, knocking into Generic and the third guy.

Vera either doesn't notice or doesn't care. Her attention is fixed on Damien.

"Him," she cries out. *"Him!"*

"Has she been in there the whole time?" Generic asks, sounding annoyed.

"Well," I say to Damien, "it looks like you're one of the chosen ones." I gesture around back. "The tent's that way."

"There are refreshments in there," says Patchy Beard disconsolately.

"Sorry," I tell him, pointing to Generic next and then their buddy. "You three have all been cut. But at least you get a chance at the beer bucket, huh?"

"It comes in a bucket?" Generic asks excitedly.

It does now.

* * *

"Here's your chance to search her computer," Damien says, popping the top of a seltzer. "I'll keep her busy."

"By posing?" I ask. Vera's eating lunch inside the house—even though I ordered only high-quality food for the buffet, she refuses to eat from any shared platters—but after she finishes, she'll come out to the tent and the "fun" will begin. Enoch is sitting with his father at a table across the tent, and his nephew is speaking with the photographer, who seems amused and entertained by his interest. I make a mental note to give the boy a set of signed books before they leave. The other models are on their phones or sipping drinks.

"Yes," Damien says, giving me a broad smile that is slightly mesmerizing. "Among other things. It's like Nicole said. I have my ways."

"Well, make sure she doesn't corner you alone. She has *her* ways."

His laughter is easy. "I'm not afraid of Vera Valence."

"Neither was I until this morning," I say, rubbing my chest. "I have a newfound respect for her ruthlessness."

"He keeps looking at us, you know," Damien says, his gaze still on me. Does he have eyes in the back of his head?

"Enoch?"

"He looks jealous. Do you want him to be jealous?" His eyes glitter with mischief. "I could help you with that, you know."

My gaze whips around to Enoch, and he *is* watching me, his eyes beating into me. There's hot moment of eye contact before he casually looks away, as if it meant nothing.

"I don't know," I say with a sigh. "He's confusing."

Damien's laugh is a deep rumble in his chest. "You've met my wife. The ones who are *confusing* are more interesting, wouldn't you say?"

"But more trouble."

"Absolutely more trouble. But wouldn't life be boring otherwise?" He lifts his eyebrows, drawing my attention again to the one with the slice through it.

I have a feeling we have different definitions of *interesting*.

"I guess," I hedge.

"What's worth having is worth fighting for."

His words, so similar to what Nicole told me the other night, put an uncomfortable twist in my chest. I'm not used to fighting. I was raised *not* to fight—to go along with things, to be a *good* girl. My metamorphosis into Grace Donnelly happened slowly. I changed my name before starting business school because my father knew everyone at UNC, and I deluded myself into thinking it would make things more fair—that any success I managed in the field he'd chosen for me would be because of me. Not because of him.

Then came my big revolution, spurred by Enoch, who encouraged me to tell my father the truth about what I wanted for the first time in my life.

When my father said he would disown me if I persisted in my "delusions" and tried to write "pornography," I didn't fold.

He believed I would. I saw it in his eyes and the smirk on his lips. I heard it in the way his voice rang with certainty. True, my decision was simpler, knowing I had my mother's financial support from beyond the grave, but it wasn't easy. He wasn't much of a father, but he was the only father I'd ever known, the only *parent* I'd ever known.

Here's what my father didn't understand then and probably still doesn't get—I'm not totally dissimilar from him. Some traits, I guess, are genetic. If you push me hard enough, I'll form roots.

Vera enters the tent, and because her green satin dress and

diamond necklace aren't enough of a statement, she claps her hands. "Let the games begin," she says.

Indeed.

ENOCH

"YOU'VE MADE THE KID HAPPY," my dad says, clapping me on the back. He's looking at me with something like approval.

"First time for everything," I say, but I can't deny Remi does seem to be having the time of his life. The photographer, Giorgio, actually let him take a couple of shots with his camera, and now he's watching the man work with something like awe.

"It's not the first time," Dad says. "I questioned you for bringing him here, but you were right. It's been good for him. The dog. Dana. This." He motions to the scene.

I internally cringe at the mention of Dana—another situation in which I'll be shoveling shit for the foreseeable future. "Dad, I have to fire Dana."

He makes a sound that's half laugh, half grunt. "Not surprised to hear you say so. She hasn't cleaned a single thing since she started."

Surprise chases a laugh out of me. "Why'd you want me to hire her back?"

"She's good for the kid and for these old bones. I like that she challenges you. It's good for you, to be around someone who challenges you."

"I've got you, don't I?"

"Stop!" Vera Valence screeches. A model standing at the food table drops a Danish onto his foot. "That's perfect. Perfect! Ten photos at least, Giorgio. *Ten*."

I glance over and see that she's got a model balanced on the toes of one foot, his hands lifted in the air. He's the one she practically went into hysterics over earlier—the guy who seemed a little too affectionate with Gracie. Damien, I heard her call him, like they knew each other. My mouth firms into a line.

"Yeah, you *do* have me," my dad says, reclaiming my attention. "I didn't want to come here just for Remi, Sunshine. I was worried about you. You work too much, and ever since you started that job, something's hardened in you. You've always wanted better things, like your mother, and I've never blamed either of you. But I don't want you to forget to laugh at yourself, kid. If I can teach you one thing, it's that. You're going to make mistakes. You know damn well I've made my fair share. But if you can laugh at yourself, you'll get through them, sure as shit."

"You expect me to believe you came here for me?" I ask, my lips curling up slightly.

"Someone needs to keep you in your place," he says. "I wasn't there as much as I should have been when you were a kid. I let your mother decide on all of that, but at least I can help you now by being a surly old bastard." He pauses, glancing at the scene as Damien balances precariously while the photographer snaps away.

Something loosens in my chest—a place I hadn't consciously realized was holding tight. "You certainly do a good job of it," I say, because that's our way. Then—"Thanks, Dad."

"You know, I noticed the way you look at that woman."

"Who?" I ask. "Vera Valence?"

He laughs. "The blond one. Grace. You said you went to business school with her."

"I did," I say, rubbing my chest, which suddenly feels tight as fuck again. I look for her in the tent, but she's gone. She slid out half an hour ago and hasn't come back.

"Here's another piece of unsolicited advice to chew on: if you've found a woman who winds you into knots, don't let her go."

I feel his eyes on me, his gaze heavy. "There's...history there. I don't know if we can get past it." Not to mention the fact that she dislikes me enough to have recruited her friends to throw literal dirt at me. I'd thought our last conversation had gotten us beyond that point, but then again, I did bring her to the brink of orgasm and leave her unsatisfied. That's probably the kind of sin you can't come back from.

"The best thing to do from history is learn from it."

My smile broadens. "Look at you, spouting wisdom today."

He shrugs. "Had to happen sometime."

"The fountain!" Vera shouts. "We *must* shoot next to the fountain!"

"Hey," Cheese Danish Guy calls out. "Are you going to take photos of any of the rest of us?"

"Yeah," another guy says. "We've been waiting an hour."

She's only taken photos of the new guy, as if she's forgotten the rest of them are there.

"Oh, there'll be plenty of time for all of that," Vera says dismissively.

Something tells me we'll have to give away another couple of beer buckets to keep things friendly.

I'm mentally steeling myself to talk the other models into cooperative moods when Vera comes over to us, flushed. "I've had a *wonderful* idea, Enoch dear."

I have a feeling I might disagree, but I manage a slight head tilt. "Oh?"

"Yes—I'm going to make *Filthy Business* a menage!"

That's one I can figure out without Gracie doing any of her sex research for me.

"Sounds fun," my dad says, prompting her to release a trilling laugh.

"Oh, it will be. Your son is the inspiration for my current work in progress, and now I know, *I know*, that Damien is meant to be the other man." She lifts her fingers to her mouth, clearly delighted with herself. "Two men like you. Oh, the readers will love me. Now, Enoch, don't be a tease. You simply must pose with Damien for the cover!"

My dad looks like he's about to have a heart attack—not out of concern for me but from repressed laughter. Thank God Remi is talking to the photographer again and hasn't heard.

"I won't be doing that, Vera," I say through my teeth. "It's not exactly in keeping with my own image to be on the cover of a romance novel."

"Damien," she shouts, completely ignoring me. "Damien, *come here*, my dear, dear man."

Damien struts over, and I find myself clenching my jaw.

"I've had the most *perfect* idea," she says, then goes on to share her shitty idea with him.

On her third effusion of "brilliant," I interrupt. "You'll have to use one of the other models as the second guy, Vera." I wave to one of them, who's watching the spoke of the tent with glazed eyes, like he fell into a fugue state. "They're all so inspired by you. They want their place in Vera Valence history, and it's like we said—local models, local vision. I'm from Mecklenberg County. It would never work."

"Poppycock," she says. "Same state. We're going to make magic happen, boys."

"I always make magic happen," Damien says, smirking at me.

My temper's on the verge of snapping. Is it my imagination, or is he trying to tell me he knows something I don't?

Has he touched Gracie?

Tasted her?

I struggle with the sudden desire to punch him. Something tells me he'd punch me right back, and then Vera would start giving her photographer shouted directives while he snaps photos of us annihilating each other.

Finally, Damien breaks eye contact. "It would never work with him and me in a menage," he tells Vera. "We're both alphas, and alphas don't share."

Her eyes light up. "Oh, that's good. That's good, good, good." She takes out her phone to make a note. "Of course, when a man says it'll never work, it only makes a woman more eager to prove him wrong. Two alphas, indeed. There's a reason for fiction."

She's going to steal his line. Fancy that.

My mood darkens further. My father's balancing his phone in his injured hand, typing with the other. The thought that he's probably sending this story to one of his buddies does nothing to cheer me up.

I'm glancing around again for Gracie, tense as fuck, when Damien touches my arm. I almost hit him on impulse but reel it in. "As an *alpha*, you should know when not to touch another man," I say, trying to make it sound like a joke. It doesn't.

Vera laughs. "So no crossing swords, huh? Oh, that's a shame. I would have liked to see that."

My father's laughing openly now, and Damien's still smirking.

Fuck. Just...*fuck*.

"What's going on over here?" Remi asks, joining us at the front of the tent. He looks as excited as I felt the first time someone called me the Suit.

"No," I snap.

"No what?" His brow wrinkles.

"I want the photographer to take pictures of your uncle," Vera says loftily, "but—"

"You're going to be on a book cover, Uncle Knock?" Remi asks as if I were just awarded the Medal of Honor. As much as I want him to look up to me, it won't be for this.

Smelling victory, Vera tells Remi, "I'll even name one of my characters after you. What's your name?"

"Remi."

She makes a face. "I'll give him a name that starts with the letter *R*." She turns back to me. "Well?"

An expletive sits on my tongue, but Damien lifts his hands and looks at me. "Let's talk, Enoch. I think I have an idea that'll make us all happy."

I fucking doubt it. Still. Maybe I can find out how he knows Gracie.

Eyes shining, Vera says, "Yes, take all the time you need."

Damien nods with his chin to a little table across the way. I walk over there with him but don't sit. "I'd prefer to stand."

"Funny," he says, "so would I. You know, I think she's disappointed we didn't wander off to cross swords," he adds, gesturing back to Vera.

My father's saying something to her. I'm glad I'm too far away to hear.

"What do you want?" I ask, looking back at him. "Because you definitely want something."

I half expect him to say that he wants Gracie, or maybe that she's *his* and he wants *me* to stay away. I'm not sure how I'd react to that, but I know I wouldn't be able to maintain my cool. It's already cracked in half a dozen places.

"Direct," he says. "I like that."

"So why don't you give it a try?"

"I guess there's a first time for everything," he says, still looking far too pleased with himself. His gaze turns shrewd. "I'm distracting Vera as a favor to our *mutual friend*. If you want to give her a chance to find what she needs in that house, then you'll help me."

It takes a second for his message to get through—

Grace is inside looking for evidence to use against Vera.

She needs more time.

And—

"She told you everything?" I choke out.

She wouldn't have told just anyone... This suggests he's special to her.

Would she have invited me touch her like that if she has a boyfriend?

I can't believe she would. And yet...

I never asked.

"She needs *someone* to help her," Damien says pointedly, giving me a look that suggests I'm a spineless piece of shit.

It's like a second stab in an open wound. He's right. If she went to him, it was because she knew I wouldn't do anything. That I'd be in here waving a couple of pom-poms for the woman who's trying to ruin her.

"She doesn't want my help," I say, rubbing my cheeks. There's a hint of scruff, like maybe I did a crap job of shaving earlier. Then again, I had to do it with Udolpho's nose pressed to the side of my leg, because he wouldn't let me walk more than a few feet from him before we left the house.

"She needs all the help she can get, *friend*," Damien says. "Now, what do you say? Are you ready to take one for the team?"

"How do you know Grace?" I ask.

"It's a long story," he says, being intentionally vague, I can tell.

"I *like* long stories."

"She'll have to be the one to tell you."

She'd have to trust me first, and she just got done telling me— and showing me—that she doesn't. She probably never will.

I swallow down the bitterness. "I'm not much of a team player."

"No," he says. "Neither am I. But I am the kind of person who'll help out a friend in a jam. Are you?"

"What do you want me to do?"

The smile comes back, giving me another urge to punch him. "Nothing objectionable. We're going to pose for some photos."

eighteen

ENOCH

"I GET to look at all of them," I remind the photographer. "And not my face. None of them can show my face."

My father's giving me a dubious look, like he thinks I body-swapped with someone when his back was turned.

Remi's excited, at least. On the downside, he's shooting photos with his phone camera, so there's going to be no end to this, probably.

This is something you can do for Gracie. This is how you show her—

What? That I'm willing to make an absolute fool of myself for her?

The water beats down in the fountain behind Damien and me, the spray hitting our T-shirts, which doesn't make this any more pleasant. Yes, T-shirts. We were ordered to take off our sweaters even though it's no more than forty-five degrees out. My hands are on his shoulders, my back to the camera. To the viewer, I'm either pushing him into the fountain or—

Well, I won't be reading this book.

"Shouldn't there be a woman in there if it's a menage?" my dad asks pleasantly.

"Nah," Vera says. "The men sell. No one cares about the woman."

An interesting sentiment for a woman who writes books primarily for other women, but she's made it pretty clear she doesn't give a shit about anyone but herself.

"We can always Photoshop one in between them later. Actually, that's a good idea. Enoch, take another step back so there's room in between you."

Damien has an amused, slightly smug expression on his face, even though it's become clear he's probably something other than a professional model. My mind races again at the thought of how he came to know Gracie so well.

"Yes," the photographer says excitedly. "Yes, that look of aggression is perfect."

"You're not supposed to show my face," I hiss.

"Oh, you're so literal, Enoch dear," Vera says. "We can feel your aggression from the taut muscles in your tight, delicious body."

My father clears his throat. Remi makes a vomiting sound.

"I've got it," the photographer calls out with satisfaction. "Perfect amount of room to add in a female model if you choose."

"Maybe I'll get a copy of it blown up for my office," Vera says thoughtfully. "Yes, that'll be just the thing. I can take pictures posed in front of it."

I'm in hell.

Maybe I died before coming to Asheville and everything that's happened to me since has been Purgatory.

"Are we done?" I ask.

Damien gives me a censorious look, reminding me that the longer this farce takes, the more time Gracie has to find what she needs.

"We're done with this pose," the photographer confirms.

"I think we should chase each other around the fountain," Damien suggests as I pull my hands away.

Whoever he is, I think I hate him.

"Ooh, yes," Vera exclaims. "An inspired idea. It'll be like the fountain scene in *Bridget Jones's Diary*."

"Wouldn't you prefer to do something original?" I say tightly.

She gives me a sharp look, but I smile back at her—the *you want a make a deal with me* smile that's gotten me places. The tension in her leaks out, and she lifts a hand to fluff her violently red hair. "You're right of course—there's nothing like a Vera Valence original—but they call them classics for a reason, you naughty boy. And any romance reader or writer knows the value of tropes."

A trope is one thing. Stealing someone's story, word for word, is different. Especially since Gracie's story isn't just a flight of fancy. It's *us*.

And you're helping her by frolicking around a fountain? You should be in there looking for evidence.

I'm not sure there's any evidence to find, but someone who likes to get dirty does it often. This won't be a first offense. She's done something else.

That's when it hits me. *The Wind in Her Hair* didn't feel like a Vera Valence book any more than *Between the Stacks* did—there were a few of her key phrases in there, sure, but the writing was different. The *energy* was different. Is she a repeat offender?

Fuck, what if Gracie's looking for the wrong thing?

"I need to talk to Gracie," I tell Damien in an undertone.

"Let her do her thing," he whispers back.

"I have to tell her what to look for."

"You sure you don't just want to escape this photo shoot?"

"Fuck yes, I want to escape this photo shoot," I whisper-hiss back.

He actually laughs, which doesn't make me like him any better. I still don't know what his place is in all of this, but I resent the hell out of it.

"What are you boys whispering about?" Vera says excitedly. "Do you have a surprise for me?"

Damien studies me for a second, shouts, "Think fast, Giorgio," to the photographer, and then shoves me into the fountain. Literally. He catches me so off guard that I lose balance, and my upper half is dunked before I can react. My shirt and face and hair are instantly soaked with water. It's freezing.

"What the fuck?" I ask, pulling myself out and shoving him. He takes a couple of steps back, lifting his hands to signal he's not going to fight me, however much I might want to at this particular moment. I see Giorgio circling around, his face intense as he snaps photo after photo. "Not my face!" I shout.

This situation has completely spiraled out of my control, although now that the shock has eased, I realize why Damien did it. He's giving me an excuse to go into the house—an unnecessarily shitty one, since all I had to say was that I needed to use the rest room or grab a glass of water, but whatever.

I'll take it.

"Brilliant," Vera is saying. "*Brilliant*. My dear. You should walk around with a wet shirt at all times."

"Get inside before you get hypothermia," my dad says, giving her a dirty look.

Remi walks up to me. "Are you okay, Uncle Knock?"

"I'm fine," I say. "But I do need to go in and grab some towels."

"Of course," Vera says, all kindness and consideration now that she has what she wanted.

"I don't want to interrupt the photo shoot," I say. "You carry on, and I'll come back out when I'm ready."

"There are robes in all sizes in the pink powder room," she says. "You do know where that one is, don't you? It's the fourth door on the left if you go in the back way."

"Thank you," I say, starting to shiver.

"Whatever you do, don't let Pumpkin out."

I wave a hand as I make my way to the house, water dripping from me as I go. Vera would probably be more worried about her floors if she weren't looking over Giorgio's shoulder, presumably at my wet-shirt shots. Fantastic.

As I make my way to the house, I pass the cluster of ignored models, the three of them sharing a blunt within a circle of bushes cut to look like cocks.

"What'd they do to you, man?" one of them calls out as I pass. From his dubious expression, he's having second thoughts about sticking around to see if he's remembered.

"What haven't they done?" I quip back as I make my way to the back door.

My teeth are chattering. I need to get to the bathroom—and that robe—before I find Gracie. Now that I'm inside, out of view of Vera and Giorgio, I strip off my shirt and sling it over my shoulder, because having on a soaking wet shirt isn't helping. My skin is pale and covered in goose bumps.

I put a little speed on, and I'm about to reach the door to the bathroom when someone turns the corner, moving fast, and slams into me. I know it's her before I even have time to register her hair color or the familiar shape of her body. Before I notice there are tears on her cheeks, again.

I'm freezing, and she's so, so warm, and I pull Gracie to me without thinking it through, like it's the most natural thing in the world.

ONE MINUTE my mind is full of Vera and my father, and the next my whole world is taken up by Enoch. He's shirtless and wet, and I'm plastered against his cold and very defined chest. He always had a nice body, but it's different now. I suppose he shows the same merciless dedication to working out as he does to being the best in other ways. My palms are pressed to his chest, and I can't help it—I let them slide down slowly, taking in every ridge of muscle.

I'm about to pull away, to apologize, to ask him why he's here, shirtless and *wet*, but he wraps me up in his arms. Even though he's freezing, it feels so good that a sigh escapes me. He was angry earlier —very—but he doesn't hate me. Or if he does, he still can't stay away from me. The distinction should matter, but in this particular moment it doesn't. I need him like a person needs water.

"Gracie," he says, running his hand down my back, sending shockwaves through me. "We've got to st-ttt-op running into each other like this."

"What...?" I start.

He shakes his head and moves me to his side, keeping his arm around me, then opens the door to Vera's pink powder room. Every surface is pink—the floor, the walls, the ceiling. There's a golden hanging rack just inside the door with pink robes in a variety of sizes, kept there for her visitors.

"Fuck," he says with a groan as he slings his wet shirt, which had been over his shoulder, onto a pink bench. "Of cours-ss-e they're pp-pink."

His teeth chatter as he talks, and alarm floods me, crowding out the wanting, the worry, the fear.

"Enoch, what the hell happened?" I ask, but I'm already pulling away and grabbing an extra-large robe from the rack. I bring it to him. But his pants are soaking wet at the waist too. "Your pants," I say, handing him the robe, which he slings over his broad shoulders but leaves open. I lean into his chest, giving him my warmth. Willing his body to soak it in. "You'll have to take them off."

His eyes hood as he eases back and studies me. "You're telling me to ttt-take my pants off?"

"Oh, for God's sake," I say. "Stop being an ass and pull them off."

He laughs. "There you are."

His fingers fumble with his belt buckle, so I reach down and unfasten it for him, my own fingers quivering, although not from cold. He lets me, and his gaze silently soaks me in.

I can feel him grow hard beneath his pants, and I bite my lip. *Do not touch Enoch Laskin's cock. Do not touch Enoch Laskin's cock.*

When I look into his eyes again, he's peering down at me with serious intensity, and a bolt of pure need shoots through me. Despite everything, I've never stopped wanting him. I'm afraid of that feeling, which is the precise reason I've spent the last six years dating every man I could find who was the opposite of him. He unmoors me, unsettles me, drives me crazy.

"You look ridiculous in that robe," I say, but my voice is shaking as much as his was moments ago.

"You were going to take my pants off, Gracie," he says, his voice husky. "It's not like you to leave a job half done."

His teeth are barely chattering anymore, and he'll probably be perfectly fine with the wet pants on so long as he doesn't leave the house, but I don't tell him any of that. I reach down and run my open palm over his dick, straining to escape his pants, and savor the way he hisses in air, like his lungs suddenly need more of it. He's so hard for me, and this evidence that he wants me—that I haven't ruined that, at least—makes warmth and need pulse inside of me.

Moving slowly, I unbutton his pants and then unfasten the zipper, one track at a time.

"I believe in being thorough," I say.

"I know you do," he says through his teeth. "I count on it."

I slide the pants down his waist, and he steps out of them, leaving him in his boxer briefs, his socks and shoes, and the pink robe. Any other man would have looked ridiculous, but he looks just as potent and virile like this, in a fluffy pink robe, as he does in his suits. I want to run my hands and tongue over his abs. I want to consume him. I want—

"Gracie," he says, stopping my hand as I reach for his boxer briefs.

"They're wet too," I say through a dry mouth. "I think they'd better come off."

"Gracie," he repeats, his voice strained. There's something severe about his countenance, like he's a professor telling a student not to be naughty. "I need you to tell me...are you *with* Damien?"

Shock is my first reaction. What did Damien say to make him think so? My next gut reaction is to be offended, although I know I have no right to be. "No, absolutely not. How could you think I'd...if I were?"

"I needed to know," he says, swallowing. "You told him about Vera and the book, and he showed up to help you distract her. I couldn't understand why unless...he..." His jaw works. He pauses, studying my eyes as if I'm a codex that contains all the mysteries to the universe. He's so beautiful it hurts, all dark hair and those luminescent light green eyes. "You hate me, but you still want me."

It's not a question. We both know that last part is true.

"I don't hate you," I say, leaning in to plant a soft kiss on his mouth. He kisses me back but pulls away, giving me a chance to finish speaking. "I've tried—hard—but it never stuck."

"Your friends…"

"I found out that you were in contact with my father in business school, before we… I didn't know the rest. I was pissed at myself for letting you in again. They wanted to be supportive. Sometimes they're too supportive."

Please don't ask me how I knew.

He gives me a smile that doesn't meet his eyes. "Oh. *That.*"

"Honestly, Enoch, I'd forgotten they were there. I forget myself around you."

His mouth twists to the side. "You're not alone in that affliction. Why were you crying when I came in just now?"

I want him to be thinking about my hand on his cock, about his cock inside of me, not about why I was crying.

"We can talk about it later."

He traces my jawline and then my lips. "I'd like to talk about it now." His fingers pad down my cheeks, tracing the paths of my tears.

"You really are going to swallow them, aren't you?" I ask, but neither of us laugh.

"I've never wanted to make you cry," he says, soft but firm. "It's not something I want to be good at."

"Look at you, being an overachiever." Another joke that fails to land. I run my hands over his chest again—still cold but no longer icy. "I looked through Vera's office. I was hoping to find something I could use." Emotion rips through me again, threatening more tears, and I look down. "Enoch, she typed up my book on her typewriter to back up her story."

"Shit," he says, his eyes stormy with anger. He weaves a hand through my hair, tipping my head back slightly so I'm looking at him.

"I went through her email too, and get this—my father reached out to her three months ago. He asked her about what kind of employee I was...and then said he wanted her to fire me. He told her he'd give her free brand management services if she did. She's been icing me out, Enoch. She's been doing all of this deliberately so I'll quit."

He lets his hand drop from my hair. "That asshole. Fuck. Grace, I didn't know about any of that. I swear to God. I *didn't know*."

His reaction surprises me, and then *my* reaction surprises me. "It didn't even occur to me that you might have."

It's as if my words ignited something in him, because suddenly his hand is in my hair again and he's pulling me to him. It's almost violent—and so is the way I push myself into his mouth as he kisses me. I already need more. Being around him and unable to touch him has been a form of torture.

We're not gentle with each other, our mouths and bodies fighting to be closer. The pleasure of having his mouth on mine is almost enough to make my knees buckle. Seconds ago he was chilly, but his kiss is so warm it nearly ignites me. His lips move to my neck, and he bites me lightly as if he's a werewolf marking his mate, then moves his hands up the back of my sweater to the clasp of my bra. It's the work of a moment to unfasten it. His mouth moves down the bare part of my chest, leaving open-mouthed kisses as he makes his way to my breasts. My hand finds his cock through his boxer briefs and strokes up and down as he lifts my breasts out of my sweater and sucks my nipples one at a time, thorough in his attention. I reach into his underwear and greedily tug him out, stroking from base to tip, loving how hard and needy he is for me.

He backs me into the small bench, the one he slung his T-shirt over, and I sit heavily. He edges his big body between my legs, reaching a hand down past the band of my leggings and under my panties. I know what he'll find. I'm as ready for him as he is for me.

He sucks in a breath and tugs at my leggings. I hold myself up on the bench, letting him pull them off. Needing him between my legs. Everywhere.

His hair is a rumpled mess, and I have the satisfaction of having left my own mark on him.

"Gracie," he says, panting as he pulls back slightly. "I...I can't stay away from you." He swallows, his Adam's apple bobbing in his throat, then adds, "Fuck it. I know all the reasons I should, but I don't *want* to. I want you too damn much. I think you're maybe the only woman I'll ever want."

Despite the open robe, he's still bared to me—his chest, his cock straining out of his boxer briefs. It's a sign of trust that puts a lump in my throat. Because he *shouldn't* trust me. He doesn't know about Nicole and Damien, and I'm going to have to tell him. He's a proud man, and I've already tested his pride once today. What will he do when he finds out I've been messing with him—with Nicole as my proxy—for the past two weeks?

Fresh tears push at my eyes. I press my hands to his chest because I might not get another chance to touch him once he knows. How bad would it be if I let myself have him, once, before I tell him?

He runs a hand through his hair. Swears under his breath. "I don't know how long Damien can distract Vera. I came in here because I needed to tell you. *The Wind in Her Hair*. It didn't feel like a Vera book. I think she's done this before."

Fresh horror slices into me. Because that book is the reason that I put Vera on a pedestal and overlooked so many of her shortcomings. I figured she had to be an okay sort of person, deep down, if she'd written a book like that. No one could create such a beautiful story if they had only bile in them. But if he's right, then my understanding of her was built on a lie.

"Oh, Enoch," I say through numb lips.

"I know." He reaches up to cup my cheek, his kindness another stab. "I know."

"How can we find out for sure?"

"Her email correspondence? Maybe the real author's reached out to her?"

"But she could just block their email address. I think she would, right?"

"What about her fan mail?"

I think of those red letters, lined up in a row, all from the same person. I remember Vera's strange response to them...

"You might be on to something," I whisper.

"We'll go look." He pulls his underwear over his straining bulge and closes the robe. Regret hugs me.

"Won't you get blue balls?" I blurt.

He laughs, his face settling into a grin that's so radiant I have the irrational urge to gravitate around it as if it's my sun. "I've been walking around with blue balls for the past two weeks, and this is the first time you've seemed remotely concerned about it."

"Well, you did give me blue lady balls."

"You don't have balls, but I am going to make that up to you. I'm going to make you come twenty times for the one time I stole from you." He glances at the pink heart clock mounted to the wall. "Fuck it," he says, "maybe we do have time. I need to taste you, Gracie. I need to make you writhe with my tongue."

He reaches for me, and I know I should push back. I know I should tell him no, but I need him. I *need* him. He kisses my lips with a hunger that pulls a sigh from me and reaches between my legs again, slipping his hand under my pants. I swallow his growl.

"You're so wet for me, Gracie. Do you want me to make you come?"

"Yes," I say. "Please."

"Good girl." He pushes my pants down to my shoes, the motion almost violent, and the cool air kissing my skin only makes me hotter for him. Need roils through me. I want his mouth on me. I want his dick. I want all of him.

But shit. I can't do this, can I?

I can't let him touch me again until he knows everything. I *won't* do that to him. He opened himself to me earlier, and we can't do... whatever this is until I do the same.

Something flickers in his eyes when I pull my pants back up. Regret? Disappointment?

"What is it?" he asks.

"Enoch, there's something I need to tell you. It's about Damien..."

His expression closes down, and he lowers his hand. Closes his robe. I can feel the wall lifting between us. "Oh?"

But I don't get to finish because the door swings open.

There's a flash of pink hair as Nicole walks into the room.

twenty
ENOCH

I DON'T EVEN HAVE time to process her words—*It's about Damien*—or the burn of jealousy that chases them before Dana Mitchell walks through the door like she belongs here.

"Oh shit," Dana says. Her hair is pink, but it's unmistakably her. "Did I interrupt something? I thought you were alone."

"You," I say, my voice shaky. "What the fuck are *you* doing here?"

Gracie looks pale, shaken, but it strikes me that she's not looking at Dana the way she would an unknown intruder. She *knows* Dana. Moreover, I realize that Dana was talking to her, not me.

"I followed you," Dana tells me. "I couldn't help myself. I'm a stalker, desperately in love with you. I only messed with your suits because I wanted one of them to fall apart in front of me."

"You're fired," I say.

She nods. "That's fair."

I shift my attention to Gracie. "You know her. You..."

My mind skates back over the past two weeks. Udolpho. The way my office looked like it had been picked through. The hangover tonic. My suits.

Gracie. All of it could be traced back to her.

"You sent her to work for me," I say through a lump in my throat. "To fuck with me. You wanted revenge."

The regret in her eyes is a confirmation.

Part of the reason I agreed to come here was because I wanted to make things right with Grace. I was drawn here, despite my better judgment, because I've never gotten over her—I've always wondered what would have happened if I'd let my heart decide and not my head. If I hadn't ranked my career aspirations before every other thing. But she hasn't been thinking that way. She might have written a book about us, but maybe I interpreted that the wrong way too.

Maybe writing it was about exorcising me from her life and memories.

The feeling inside my chest is so awful I'd prefer to never feel anything again. I've spent years in varying states of numb, and this is worse. Knowing that the one woman I've ever cared for thinks so little of me that she'd do anything to drive me away—even hire a stranger to mess with my life. My house. My family.

"You brought this person into my home. Around my *family*," I growl.

Grace is pale and shaking slightly, and the ugly feeling within me only grows.

"Didn't you hear me?" Dana asks. "Total stalker over here. Guilty as charged. I even went through your sock drawer. You have an amazing proportion of matched socks. Color me impressed."

Grace lifts a quivering hand, silencing her. "You're right," she tells me. "Damien and Nicole are private investigators, but they also run the Fairy Godmother Agency. They help women who've been wronged get their lives back. They...they've been helping me. I was about to tell you about them."

"Before you let me fuck you, or after?"

She flinches but doesn't speak.

"Maybe I was wrong about you, Grace," I say. "Maybe you do play chess after all. You're more like your father than I thought."

The hurt on her face isn't a balm to my wounded ego. It makes me feel worse—like my chest has been cracked open, acid poured into it. All the hopes I've let blossom within me wither and die. Gracie might feel the tension between us, the chemistry, but she doesn't want to. She only wants me to leave.

I turn to go, but Nicole presses a palm to my pink robe, stopping me. "You're not a totally hopeless case."

I look down at her, floored. "What the hell are you talking about?"

"You're uptight, and your addiction to suits is borderline weird. But you're not a hopeless case. You let Udolpho stay, and Remi says you pet him when no one's looking. You rehired me the other day because your father and nephew wanted my company, even after I gave you a hangover cure no one's ever grateful for." She nods to Grace. "You've also been trying to help Grace, in your own way. We would have found out about the book, now that Damien has an in, but we're a step ahead of where we would have been without your help."

"You went through my things," I say through cold lips. Realization sets in. "That's how Grace knew about my meetings with her father." A feeling of deep violation stabs at me. This woman was in my *house*. She's sifted through the pieces of me and put them on her own personal scale of justice—and I didn't know any of it was happening.

She gives a slight nod but doesn't say anything.

I glance back at Gracie, but she doesn't say anything either. She's staring at me with a silent entreaty, though for what, I don't know.

"Okay," I say with a slow nod. "You want me out, I'm out."

"I don't—" she starts, then clears her throat. "I don't want that anymore. I thought you were coming back to mess with me, Enoch. To turn my world upside down again. I didn't know…"

What? That I care about her? That I've spent years dreaming about her? That I haven't had a relationship longer than three weeks in the past six years because no one else has ever made me feel the way she did? Like she appreciated me more for who I was than for who I aspired to be. Like I was enough for her as just Enoch, not the Suit.

But I ruined that, and here's the proof that we can't go back.

"It's too late, Grace," I say tightly. "Maybe it was always too late, and it just took me longer to figure it out."

She takes a step toward me. There are tears in her eyes, and it's another stab to the gut to know that I *am* good at putting them there. Maybe it's the only thing I'm good at. "After you talked to me earlier, at the pond, I let Nicole and Damien know that I'd gotten it all wrong. That Vera and my dad are the bad guys. I don't hate you, Enoch," she repeats. "Even when I thought I did, you were never far from my mind. When I wrote my book, I didn't mean for Dean to be you, but I couldn't help myself. Because that was the only time I ever…" She clears her throat. "When you came here and we started talking, it felt like I was right back where I'd started. I didn't want to lose myself again. I couldn't let that happen. You kept asking about Sinclair, and I was worried you were using me…"

"Goodbye, Grace," I say.

"Please don't leave like this," she says, fresh tears tracking down her cheeks. "Enoch, *please.*"

Part of me wants to go to her, even now, and I'm pissed off by the impulse.

If I'm leaving what's left of my hardened heart behind me, then I don't want either of them to know. A man has to keep part of his ego alive, after all.

* * *

I walk outside in my pink robe, not even registering that I left my clothes inside until I get out the door. Fuck it. The robe's warm, and I don't have anyone to impress. Grace thinks the worst of me. Damien is a plant, hired to mess with me and now, I guess, Vera. Vera's a class act, and the other models are all probably too stoned to notice me.

When I walk out, laughter spills out of me because someone—Nicole, probably—let out Pumpkin, and she's chasing one of the models around the fountain while he screams and Giorgio takes photos. Damien's coolly watching the show, talking to my dad and Remi, which makes me bristle. Is he looking for other ways to muck up my day?

Vera shouts, "Be careful! Pumpkin gets dizzy!" as if the model is having a playdate with her. I should probably try to smooth things over, but I'm done here, aren't I?

If I call asking for a reassignment, John Parker will remind me that he owns me. I'd like to tell him to go fuck himself, but I'm not the only person I'd be screwing. Remi depends on me now. So does my dad. They need me to figure this situation out in a way that won't end with the three of us out on the streets. I could tell John that Vera's trying to steal his daughter's book before giving her the boot, but I have to conclude what Vera obviously did—he wouldn't care. Maybe he even knows and encouraged her. If he doesn't want his daughter writing smut, he'd be all for anyone standing in her way. Hell, he'd push them into her path.

I feel the urge to protect Grace. To help her through this. To prove myself to her as a man. But I also meant what I said.

I don't know if this is the kind of thing we can get past. Maybe it's not the kind of thing we *should* get past.

"Is that a cashmere robe?" Remi asks excitedly when he sees me. He reaches out to touch the fabric. "It is," he adds in wonder.

"You getting comfortable, Sunshine?" my father says. "We've been getting quite the show out here."

Damien waves to me. I hold back the urge to shove him. Barely.

"Your wife's inside," I tell him, the words sour to the taste. "I know all about your little game."

"Game?" my father asks in confusion.

"He's married to *Dana*."

Remi's studying us with a timid expression, like he knows I'm wrestling with the need to hit something. Fuck. I don't want him to ever have to worry about that with me. "Everything's fine, Remi."

"I'm not an idiot," he says, peeved.

"I know." He waves a hand at the tableau before us—the man running from the dog, Vera screeching something, Giorgio snapping photos. The fountain. Toward the tent. "None of this is normal." Turning to Damien, he adds, "Why are you here, Mr. Dana?"

Damien laughs as he rubs a hand over his jaw. "My wife's name is Nicole, actually, but sure, I'll answer to Mr. Nicole. I'm here because I'm helping your uncle's friend Grace."

Raw, blistering hurt chokes me. "She's not my fucking fr—"

"Be careful of what you say right now," Damien says. "When you speak in anger, you're likely to say something you'll want to take back later. Grace was hurt, and Nicole and I offered to help her. She accepted. But neither of us got the sense she wanted revenge on *you*. She wanted you to go away because you unsettled her. There were unresolved feelings. My wife figured it would benefit both of you if she could get you to loosen up. That's all she's been trying to do."

"By going through my things?" I seethe. "Fucking up my life?"

"Seems like you did a good enough job of that yourself, friend," he says. "None of this would have happened if you'd been straightforward about your feelings in the first place. What was Grace supposed to think?"

I do push him then, but he doesn't try to retaliate. Shame floods me, and I step back.

"Grace tried to fire us last week," he tells me. "She told us that she was quitting her job. Vera told her that her book was no good. And although Grace didn't give us particulars, something also happened with the two of you."

A screech suggests Pumpkin has caught her quarry. Someone'll definitely have to give that guy a beer bucket, but it won't be me.

"My wife convinced her to change her mind," Damien continues.

"By telling her about my connection with Grace's father," I say with a snort. "Yeah, thank you for that."

"By telling her that our job's not done. And it's not. I think you know as well as I do that Grace needs help to get herself out of this one. She's surrounded by ruthless people—people who would use her without compunction. She needs friends who are just as ruthless."

I laugh at that. "She has them. You. Her other friends. You've all made it very clear that I'm not wanted. She doesn't need me."

"Do you really believe that?" Damien asks.

I look over and see that Remi and my dad are watching me, and while at least a third of this conversation has to be completely nonsensical to them, they seem to have understood enough.

"We've got your back, Uncle Knock," Remi says, and gratitude unfurls in my chest when my father nods.

I don't deserve their unequivocal support, but I need it. I'll take it.

"Enoch?" Vera calls. "Enoch, can you come here? You *do* have a wonderful way of calming Pumpkin."

It's on the edge of my tongue to tell her to fuck off, but I can feel Damien staring at me. I can hear his unspoken message—Grace is still inside that house, with his wife. They're looking for something to use against Vera, and if we don't give them enough time to find it, they won't.

I'm pissed. I'm hurt. But I...I don't want her to lose everything. That book is hers, and I know she bled her heart into it. The heart I broke. Despite what she thinks of me, despite the hurt between us, I'll be goddamned if I let this woman take her book from her.

I'll be goddamned if I let her father do it either.

So I go into Suit mode. Here I am, Enoch Laskin, charmer of yippy dogs and narcissists.

twenty-one

GRACE

"DID THAT GO WELL?" Nicole asks. "I feel like it didn't go well."

"You feel right," I say. All of my nerve endings feel raw and bloody. I hadn't realized how much Enoch was getting to me. How much he was weeding his way back into my heart and my affections, until this very moment. He won't forgive me for this. Hell. Maybe he shouldn't. I *did* unleash a couple of private investigators on him.

"How'd you find me?" I ask.

"There were literally wet footprints leading into this room. It was possible you weren't involved, but either way I was interested in seeing what was going on."

"What did you mean about Enoch's suits?" I ask through numb lips.

"Oh, this is good," she says. "I pulled the seams on all of the suits he asked me to take to the dry cleaner's. I can only hope and assume they fell apart at a very inconvenient time. I mean, I know he's not the bad guy anymore, but it would be pretty damn funny if it happened at a meeting."

"Shit," I say with feeling. But I don't go racing after him—it

199

wouldn't help, and I'm not even sure what I'd say. Maybe he's right. Maybe we were a losing bet from the beginning.

But when we're together it doesn't *feel* like a losing bet—when I'm with him, I feel more myself. I feel braver and bolder and more alive. Tears press at my eyes again, but I fold up his wet clothes, telling myself I'll give them back later, and turn to Nicole. "We need to look through some fan mail."

"That sounds like the kind of thing I'd enjoy," she says. "You think anyone sent their panties?"

"I don't like that word," I say, making a face.

"You don't like that word? You're a romance writer, how do you not like that word? It's like a chocolatier disliking chocolate."

"No, that would be if I disliked the word *cock*."

"Fair enough."

I don't know how much time we'll have left. Enoch will leave, obviously, but Damien's presumably still out there, posing.

"Let's go," I say, finding a shopping bag under the sink and putting his clothes in it.

"You going to give him a special delivery later?" Nicole asks, waggling her eyebrows.

"Just don't," I say. "You heard him. He never wants to see me again."

She shakes her head as she follows me out of the bathroom and into the hallway. "Not the impression I get. You know the guy has a Google alert on you? And he kept the letter you wrote him after he took the job. Get this, he has it in a filing cabinet. You like 'em type A, don't you?"

My chest tightens, and those tears press harder. "Let's just go."

We find the red envelopes, and I tell Nicole about the emails Vera exchanged with my father.

"Did you take photos of them?" she asks.

"I did," I confirm.

"Anything else of interest?"

"Nothing that'll help," I say sullenly. I spent an hour searching, and the most I was able to confirm is that Vera Valence is indeed an awful person. There were sullen messages sent to friends, bashing other, more successful authors. Messages to multiple men, each implying that he's her inspiration, her one and only guy.

Nicole shakes her head, almost admiring. "This woman has some serious balls. If she weren't fucking with other women, I'd almost respect her."

"Yeah, been there. Made that mistake," I say with a sigh. "Let's get out of here." I'm disgusted with all of it—Vera's excesses and lies, my own stupid mistakes. "I need to quit."

Nicole's already shaking her head as we make our way to the door and leave the office. "Nope. Nada. Not happening."

"*Nada* means *nothing*, not *no*," I say sullenly.

"Don't pretend you didn't get the message. You can't quit now. You need to maintain access to Vera and this house. Yes, Damien can get in here now, but you still have influence over her."

"I don't know how much influence I could possibly have," I say with a snort, although it occurs to me that she's saying exactly what Sinclair told me hours ago. "She's planning on abusing me until I quit."

"You have the influence to convince her to throw a big event"— her eyes flash—"a ball, and invite a lot of important, influential people. Such a ball might be a very good venue to make certain accusations public, don't you think?"

"She'll sue me if I say she's trying to steal my book," I tell her. "She prepared. You saw." I'd shown her the typed-up manuscript, neatly stacked. Vera had even gone to the trouble of typing up my original ending. According to Enoch, she'd changed it, so she's gone to extraordinary lengths to back up her story.

"We'll take care of finding proof. Don't you worry about that."

I stop walking and turn the idea over in my mind. Nicole stops too. "Something like that will take a long time to prepare for," I argue.

"You could tell her it'll seem more elite and exclusive if there's less of a build-up. If it's inconvenient for people to come. And, hey, you've got a TV star who'll definitely show."

She would, I'll bet.

Nicole snaps her fingers. "I'm pretty sure we can also get that famous outdoorsman guy to come too. You know, the one with the boring name that only sounds cool with his last name."

"Edgar James?" He's one of Marnie's clients, former star of the reality TV show *Extreme Camping*.

"That's the one."

"Interesting," I say. "I'll take it under advisement. I still think it would take weeks to arrange something like that. I can't work for Vera for weeks." The thought is depressing, and I already feel drained of anything good.

That look Enoch gave me...

"Two of them," Nicole says. "Two weeks." A mischievous smile stretches across her face, making her look like the Cheshire cat. "It should obviously overlap with that meeting your father summoned you to. How's that for sending a message?"

"He'll probably come to the party," I say, touching my throat. "Especially if he's planning on being in Asheville anyway."

"And you need to face him too, Grace. This is going to be epic. Think of an anniversary it lines up with...the release of one of Vera's books, maybe, or the little squash's birthday. Be creative."

She seems too proud of her own plan.

Still, she's not wrong. I've let all of this happen to me, and I'm done letting things happen. It's time to make a stand for myself, my book, and the love story at the heart of it—even if I've lost the very person who inspired me.

"It'll be the tenth anniversary of the box-set release of the Naughty Stepbrothers series," I say numbly.

"Perfect. Everyone's going to want to celebrate that."

"They *were* bestsellers," I say.

When we approach the fountain, my mouth drops open. Enoch and Damien are posing for a photo, each of them holding half of Pumpkin, who seems so docile I have to wonder if Vera's been feeding her CBD. No, maybe she just shares her owner's weakness for aggressively handsome men.

Enoch's still wearing his pink robe.

"I'd buy that calendar, am I right?" Nicole says with a bawdy laugh. "They're wearing too many clothes, but I know Damien's cock so well I could sculpt it."

"I know," I say softly, reaching up to my collarbone. "You have."

Enoch stayed. He stayed, after all of that. He must have done it to buy me more time.

But as soon as he catches sight of us approaching them, he says something to Damien. Damien takes Pumpkin from him, and then Enoch waves to Vera. He claps his nephew on the back, and they walk away with his father. All I can do is watch in mute horror.

I've gotten so much wrong in my life, but this mistake feels like the hardest to bear. I'd assumed that Enoch had changed since business school, but I'd imagined him getting worse—doubling down on his ambition and ruthlessness. But he hasn't. He's a man who put himself on the line for a father he doesn't always get along with, who offered his nephew a home without blinking an eye, who put his career on the line to tell me about Vera's plan.

Who would have given up everything for me if I'd let him.

I've changed too.

I wrote a book.

I forged a family.

I made a life for myself.

In so many ways, I'm a stronger person, but I'm weaker in this: I've trusted the wrong people, or at least some of the wrong people, and now I'm paying the price.

"Who are you?" Vera says as we get closer.

It takes me a second to realize she's talking to Nicole, who's making a beeline for Damien. "I'm his wife," she says, putting a possessive arm around him.

"Oh, that's a pity," Vera says, her expression souring like old milk. She takes Pumpkin from Damien, thereby saving me from the necessity. "Unless..." She taps her lips, looking Nicole up and down. "You *are* pretty enough. Will you pose for a few photographs?"

She preens. "Absolutely."

Why two private investigators would want to be on a book cover is beyond me, but maybe they're hoping it'll never see the light of day. Maybe they presume that I—Cinderella—will be able to take down Vera Valence. I tug my hair before I can stop myself.

"Vera," I say once Giorgio is occupied with taking photographs of Nicole next to the fountain.

"Yes, dear, what is it? You know, you were gone an *awfully* long time. I know I asked you to see to unplugging the toilet in the blue bathroom, but you're taking liberties, hm? Pumpkin got out of the house." Pumpkin takes this prompt to begin licking Vera's mouth. "And while it worked out for the best, with some *delightful* photographs, I don't appreciate your dereliction of duty, especially since I was kind enough to give you tomorrow off. Where are the other models? I could have used you to keep an eye on them."

"Will you be photographing them?" I ask.

She makes a face. "They're not much to look at compared with Damien and Enoch, but I suppose we'll make the most of our time. I can always have Giorgio shoot them from the neck down."

I smelled a strong whiff of pot on the way out of the house, so I suspect their whereabouts are a mystery easily unraveled.

"Vera," I say, "you and Enoch have been doing so much work on your brand and image... I think we should hold an event at your house, something exclusive and on brand. We should make it happen soon to snowball things. Maybe in two weeks? It'll be close to the ten-year anniversary of the release of the box set for the Naughty Stepbrothers. Might be good from a marketing standpoint. You can announce that you're re-covering the series with local models."

"Why, Grace Parker," she says. "That's the first good idea you've had in weeks."

I wonder if she even realizes she called me by the wrong last name.

* * *

"He still took that job with Gracie's father," Andy says. "Ipso facto, Enoch's still the asshole."

I shake my head, smiling wryly. "*I'm* the asshole. He did a shitty thing, but it was years ago and he's apologized for it. I haven't even gotten the chance to properly apologize for the shitty thing I *just* did. I mean, how can you even apologize for something like that?"

"Has it occurred to you that you might *both* be assholes?" Nicole asks. "I mean, I'm definitely an asshole, so no judgment from me." We're sitting around the bar at Summer Nights. There's a busyish crowd, so Sinclair's not around. It's Andy, Marnie, Nicole, Damien, and me, with Griffin stopping by to talk to us whenever he gets a chance.

"Or maybe neither of you are," Damien says, lifting his brow. "Enoch let Giorgio photograph him for hours. He seemed pretty opposed to it before I let him know that you were in the house, trying to find something. Hell, he even stuck around after I threw him into the fountain."

After I tried to seduce him, I mentally correct, only for him to find out I'd hired a maniac to mess with him.

Nicole purses her lips. "That man does still seem to have blue balls for you."

"You need to talk to him," Marnie says. "To tell him all of this."

She bangs the top of the bar, then makes a face because the sound was probably louder than intended. "Put yourself out there, Grace." She glances at Andy, who does a nod-shrug combo, then says, "Andy and I both think you have unresolved feelings toward him. We thought so even before he showed up. It's all there in your book."

"And the guys you've dated," Andy adds, making a sweeping gesture with her hand. "You weren't really trying."

Their words pound into me, joining the drumbeat chorus that's been screaming at me for hours. *Make. This. Right. Make. This. Right. Make. This. Right.*

"But wouldn't it be wrong of me to tell him how I feel when I know he's locked into working with my dad?"

Marnie lifts a hand in a *who knows* gesture. "I'll interject that I made up a fake boyfriend and told everyone his name was Mitchell Mountainbottom, and it worked out pretty well for me."

"You should have held out for Edgar James," Nicole says, shooting a wicked look at Griffin, who has just stopped in front of us.

"Probably," he says with a grin. Marnie leans forward and grabs him by the collar. I have to look away when they kiss, because everything related to romance feels poisoned right now. There's no one else to blame for that: I'm the one who poisoned it.

"If you care about him," Damien says slowly, "then you're in the wrong place."

His words are like a revelation. I'm being cowardly, snuggling up to my friends after a bad day. I'm being like Cinderella—waiting for a man to rescue me.

But I've already told Enoch to go away, both directly and indirectly. I've been telling him for weeks, even though, in my heart of hearts *I don't want him to.*

When I first saw him at this bar, before I realized he was working with Vera, I felt something inside me of awaken—as if a slumbering giant had been poked. I felt how very un-immune I was to Enoch

Laskin even after years of hating him, of trying to leak my feelings out into my book. I tried to push him away, yes, because I looked at him and saw my father. I saw a man who'd break people just to step on their backs. I saw a man who'd make a naive girl fall in love with him, only to turn around and use her to get a job he wanted. I tried to push him away, because with every second I spent near him, I felt my resolve weaken. Because even though he is arrogant and sometimes obnoxious, he's also funny and smart and capable of kindness and loyalty. He's the only man who's made me feel in danger of losing my heart.

Nicole snaps her fingers. "My phone just regained charge. I'll text Richard to find out where Enoch is."

"Text Richard?" I repeat, dumbfounded.

"Yeah, Enoch's dad and I have become pals."

"You think he'd still want to talk to you after this?"

"I'm pretty sure he was on to me the whole time, or at least partly. I *did* admit that I was trying to get Enoch to loosen up because he's in love with my friend and I don't want her to end up with a stuck-up prick."

"He's not," I say, my heart pounding in my chest. My ears buzzing. "Or at least he's not anymore."

Marnie gives me an empathetic look. "If it were that easy to stop caring about someone, would you still care about him after all this time?"

"This all sounds very exciting," Reggie says from his usual corner. "But can someone fill up my beer?"

twenty-two
ENOCH

I TEXT John Parker the minute I leave Vera's house.

I need a new assignment. It's come to my attention that Vera hasn't properly attributed all of her books. If we get into the middle of this, it will be a big mess.

His response lands before I pull into our driveway.

Absolutely not. Stay the course.

I'm surprised by the slight feeling of relief that flutters through me. The realization of why I'm relieved makes me scowl.

I'll have to look for proof that she's a thief, naturally. It's my job. It's not something I'd be doing only to help Gracie.

My father and Remi didn't say much to me in the car, probably guessing—correctly—that I'm in a shit mood and won't have anything nice to say to anyone right now.

"Is Vera a bad person, Uncle Knock?" Remi asks as he gets out.

"Yeah, I think maybe she is," I say. "I'm sorry, bud. I know you were hoping to get some signed books."

He gestures my apology away. "I kind of assume that all celebrities are shitty people. But at least we got to see the photo shoot. Does Grace have to keep working for her?"

"I don't know," I say, rubbing my chest. "Probably for a little while. I guess you were surprised to find out Dana's not really a maid."

"Not that she's not a maid," he says with a shrug. "She wasn't very good at cleaning, but I *am* surprised to find out she and Damien are together. She was always talking up her husband, saying he could help me with bullies, and now I get why."

"Why?" I ask, puzzled and a little annoyed.

"He's swole," he says, gesturing to his arms.

"So am I."

He gives me a dubious look. My dad laughs. Both reactions increase my sense of annoyance.

"You're just doubting me because I'm dressed in this pink robe. Which might not help you with the bullies, admittedly, but if I had a suit on—"

"Uncle Knock, most people my age don't really respect men in suits."

My bad mood increases when we get in the house and discover that Udolpho managed to bang his way out of the back door, which has a crap latch.

I'm not sure why this feels like bad news, other than that Remi's obviously upset, but it does. I don't like the thought of Udolpho wandering around on his own. He's not very smart, and I can imagine him approaching an oncoming car with a wagging tail, thinking he's met his new best friend.

"Call Nicole, Dad," I say, after calming Remi down. "Her friend works for that dog shelter."

I believe that part, at least, since it's obvious Udolpho came from somewhere, and I'm guessing she adopted him for us.

He dials her immediately, then shakes his head. "No answer."

"Okay," I say, pacing the kitchen, trying to think. My mind is sluggish because it's stuck on what happened today, on Gracie. On the pleading in her eyes when she asked me not to leave her.

Udolpho.

"Okay," I repeat. "Here's what's going to happen. Dad, you and Remi will get posters made with his face on them. I assume you have good pictures, Remi?" He nods, and I continue, "Plaster them around the neighborhood and also send the poster to the local dog shelters. All of them. And Remi, post about him on Nextdoor and Facebook. I know there are groups for dog owners."

I know this because I've looked. At first because I was hoping to find someone who'd want to adopt Udolpho, presuming he had no other owners, and then because I was hoping someone would have tips for dealing with separation anxiety.

"I'm going to look for him," I say.

"In that pink robe?" my dad asks.

I look down and laughter spills out of me. Fuck. I'd honestly forgotten I was wearing it.

"After. Definitely after."

* * *

It's dark. I've been out casing the neighborhood for a few hours now, or at least that's what I was accused of by a man who backed off pretty damn quickly as soon as he caught a better look at me. There's no sign of Udolpho. One woman told me she saw an off-leash dog run into a tree trunk earlier, and while that certainly sounds like Udolpho, there's no way of proving it.

Getting him home safely has become a weird kind of need. If I can't save Udolpho, it's going to feel like I can't do *anything* right. I may not have wanted a dog, but he's become my responsibility, and I won't shirk it. I won't let him wander around all night alone, without anyone to tell him he shouldn't run into tree trunks.

It starts raining, but I keep up the search, walking up and down sidewalks, peering into people's garages, calling out his name like a crazy person. The rain gets harder, and soon I'm nearly as soaked as I was earlier. I keep going.

Finally, I hear a whimpering when I call out his name.

"Udolpho?" I shout, my voice nearly swallowed by the rain.

His hulking shape steps out of the trees, slowly at first, then he runs toward me in an awkward loping gait that has me worried for half a second that he got hit by a car, but then I rewind in my head and remember he's always run like this. Then he's on me, his feet on my shoulders, his terrible dog breath wafting onto my face, and I've never been happier to see the fuzzy bastard.

I'm shocked to feel warmth behind my eyes as he licks my face. I get him down and kneel beside him, petting his wet face, looking his body over to make sure he's not injured.

"You fucking scared me," I say, only then realizing it's true. "I thought something had happened to you." He licks my nose, and I laugh, even though it's no less disgusting than it was that first day. "You want me around, bud, don't you?"

The wound in my chest is soothed by the knowledge that this dog I didn't want or choose has somehow decided I'm his person.

My mind summons Gracie. The expression of hurt on her face earlier...and the look she gave me six years ago, when I told her that I'd taken a job with her father.

That look hasn't left me. I've thought about it at crucial moments in my life—when my sister asked me to take Remi. When my father said he wanted to move to Asheville with us. It occurs to me that she's been with me this whole time, making me a better man even if she didn't know it.

"What the fuck am I going to do, Udolpho?" I ask. His response is to dole out another disgusting face lick. At least the rain has slowed to a steady drizzle. "Let's get you home, buddy." I grab his collar and pull out my phone to plug in the address, since I have no idea where my rambling has gotten me, and it's dark as pitch outside, very few streetlights in this neighborhood.

That's when I see her messages.

Grace: *Enoch, I'm coming to help. I know you don't like me very much right now, but I want to help. Please let me help. Nicole's friend told me what to do.*
Grace: *Enoch, where are you? We're worried. Your dad hasn't heard from you for a couple of hours.*
Grace: *Please text your father or Remi. I understand if you don't want to talk to me. Let THEM know you're okay.*
Grace: *I think maybe you're not coming home because you don't want to see me. I'm going to leave, Enoch. Don't worry about me. But please let them know you're okay. And if you're all right with it, they've said they'll tell me.*
Grace: *I'm so sorry.*

I suddenly register that I'm cold, desperately cold, and Udolpho probably is too.

I start to write a response to Gracie, then delete it. I don't know what I want to say yet, and I don't want to say it here, hunched over in the cold.

Instead, I call my dad, one hand still looped through Udolpho's collar in case he gets any grandiose ideas.

"I found him," I say when he answers.

"Found *him?*" he says, his voice sounding hoarse. "We were worried about *you*. You haven't called home in hours, Sunshine. It's past ten. We thought something might have happened to you. Your friend Grace was here. She put up posters with Remi, and she's been driving around talking to our neighbors. She just went home because she got it into her head that you might be avoiding her."

"That's not true," I grind out. "I only just saw her texts."

"She seemed mighty upset, Enoch. You might want to tell her that yourself. Where are you?"

"Hang on a second." I pull the phone away from my face to pull up the Maps app, then laugh bitterly when I see I'm five miles from home.

"It's gonna be a long walk, Dad. I'm five miles away."

"You must be soaking wet," he says. "I'll come get you."

"You don't have to do that."

"Obviously," he says. "Like I said, we've all been worried about you. Don't know that I've ever seen anyone as upset as Grace."

Something tears open inside of me, but it's too early for me to tell whether that's bad or good.

"Thanks, Dad," I say wearily. "I'll send you a pin."

He shows up admirably fast, but by the time he does, I'm shivering again, the cold having caught up with me now that I'm not rampaging through the streets.

He tosses me a dry shirt after I get in the passenger seat, having settled Udolpho in the back. The seats are going to be soaked with rain and stippled with dog hair, obviously, but it's a nightmare I'm happy to put off worrying about until tomorrow.

I look at the slogan on the shirt—*I may be wrong, but it's highly unlikely*—then lift my eyebrows at my father. "A generic white shirt wouldn't do?"

"Not today, nope," he says. "Figured it was my one big chance to back you into wearing your Christmas present."

I'm fucking cold, so I change into it.

"You'll excuse me for saying so, but you need to go talk to that girl."

"She's very much a woman, Dad," I say, looking out the window.

"Semantics. You know exactly what I mean."

"She wanted to get rid of me so badly she hired a stranger to immolate my life," I say, turning toward him in my seat, steaming myself up all over again. "Nicole made us adopt this dog. She gave me that horrible hangover cure. She screwed with my suits. Gracie was behind all of that."

My dad pulls over at the curb, prompting Udolpho to try to pop his head out of the window to see where we are. Of course, the window is closed, and he hits his head. No one will be rewarding him for his intelligence, that's for damn sure.

"Think of what you're saying, son. Yes, Nicole *made* us adopt this dog. This dog you apparently care enough about that you've spent the last several hours out there searching for him in the rain. This dog who's made Remi feel more at home. And, sure, she gave you a shitty hangover cure, if you'll pardon the pun, and I haven't heard about the suits, but I'm sure whatever happened will give me great amusement. Those suits of yours have always been your armor, kid, and you're just as good without it. You want to know something else?"

"I don't have a choice, do I?" I ask, sort of pissed, sort of interested.

"Nicole didn't tell me what she was up to, but she did tell me she was intentionally messing with you to get you to loosen up. And it's worked. She also told me that you were in love with her friend."

I look away but don't say anything.

"I can't pretend to be very good at relationships, Enoch, but if you love this woman, you owe it to yourself to see if you can work things out. She seems like a nice gi—woman. She went out of her way to make Remi feel better. Even brought him a signed set of that Valence woman's books, although I'm not sure he wants them anymore."

"It's not that simple, Dad," I say. "She's John Parker's daughter. He disowned her just before I started working for him. What happened between them...it was partly my fault."

He whistles. "You're lucky she didn't send ten Nicoles after you."

"That's my point," I say, fisting my hands. "I don't know that we can get beyond this. Even if we wanted to, I'm stuck working for her father for another two years."

"People leave their jobs, son. The world won't end if you leave yours."

Frustrations wells inside of me, but a little voice that sounds a lot like Gracie's says, *Tell him. It's not fair to resent him if he doesn't even know.*

I turn in my seat to face him. "He's the one who gave me money to pay the lawyers, Dad. It was a signing bonus for a five-year contract. If I break the contract or do something bad enough to get fired, I'll owe him three times what he gave me. I don't have that kind of money sitting around."

He listens to this with a flat expression, then swears. "Jesus, Enoch, you said you had the money. If you'd told me this, I would have insisted you let it go."

"Let it go?" I say, gesturing wildly. Udolpho gives a forlorn howl. "You would have gone to jail."

"I've always wanted to learn how to print license plates," he says.

"Funny."

Staring at me, he says, "You didn't need to step in and save me, Sunshine. That's supposed to be my job as your father. Somewhere along the way we lost track of that. As far as Grace goes...why don't you see if there's something to save before you go thinking through all the things that could ruin it?"

I shake my head slightly, smiling in spite of myself. "Fuck, when did *you* become wise? The world really is turning on its head."

"You're a good kid, Enoch," he says slowly, looking at me. "I wish I could take more credit for it. I won't say a word against your mother—God knows she raised you right—but you've always taken too much on your shoulders."

"I don't know about that."

"Grace, whatever she's done or said, cares about you. Any fool can see that."

My mind summons up what she said to me when I was leaving Vera's house.

I need to see her. It's been in the back of my mind ever since I saw those messages. Half of me thinks I'm less of a man for it—shouldn't I have more pride? But my pride has never made me happy.

"Can you bring me somewhere, Dad?"

"I'm going to be very disappointed in you if you're asking me to take you on a late-night Taco Bell run."

twenty-three

GRACE

"WHAT IF HE'S DEAD?" I ask, my heart galloping in my chest. "What if he stepped in front of a car chasing that dog Nicole made him adopt? I'd be a murderer. I'd wear a scarlet *M* on my chest for the rest of my life."

"You're spiraling," Marnie says over our Zoom chat.

"Yes, definitely spiraling," Andy agrees, popping a chip.

They both offered to come over, but I told them no. I'm so nervous, I feel uncomfortable in my own skin, and I can't have my friends here, hanging out. It would feel undeserved to take comfort in them right now, knowing that Enoch is wandering around in the rain or maybe...

"He's not dead," Andy says. "I mean, kudos to him for going after the dog, it makes me think he's less of a tool, but yeah, he'll do just fine on the mean streets of Asheville."

"Our crime rate has skyrocketed this year. Skyrocketed!" I say, thinking of Enoch getting bashed over the head or mugged or... "You don't think...you don't think he stayed away because I was at his house, do you?"

"No," Andy says. "He strikes me as a direct sort of person. If he wanted to tell you to go fuck yourself, he'd probably tell you to go

217

fuck yourself. Admittedly, I've had very limited interactions with him, but I try not to let that get in the way of forming impressions about someone."

Marnie tries to pass off a laugh as a cough. "My brother's here," she says. "What was your first impression of Drew?"

"*Nerd*," Andy says, using the inflection from a popular sound bite.

"I heard that," someone calls out from the background on Marnie's end.

"Good—you were supposed to."

A knock lands on my door, loud and crisp. My heart starts racing in my chest.

"Did someone just knock on your door?" Andy asks, leaning toward the camera as if my life is a TV show that just got interesting.

"I've got to go," I say.

"Bye," Marnie says. "Make good decisions!" She grimaces. "I don't know what I mean by that in this case, actually. It's a very complicated situation. But hey, at least he's probably not dead!"

I hang up on them, everything in me is focused on that door.

"But he doesn't know where you live, you idiot," I mutter to myself. I told him about the building, sure, but he wouldn't remember a thing like that.

I grab my pepper spray, just in case—it's highly unlikely a would-be intruder and rapist would knock at my door past ten on a Sunday, but you never know—and open the door a crack.

Enoch lifts his eyebrows. "You plan on using that? It's been a pretty shitty day, so you might as well get it over with."

I throw the can and pull him into the room by the bottom of his shirt. His pants are rain-soaked, and so is his hair. He looks a lot like he did earlier, actually, when I pulled him into the pink powder room.

"Your shirt," I say with a start, noticing the slogan.

"My dad gave it to me." His smile is slight, but it's not nonexistent. I'll take it.

"Enoch, how are you here? I never told you which unit I live in."

"Are you accusing me of stalking now?"

"No," I say, looking down. "I—"

His fingers lift my chin up so I'm looking at him. "I knocked on the two doors before yours. The woman in A invited me inside, and the guy in B threatened to murder me."

"Did you find your dog?" I ask softly, trying to act like my heart isn't in danger of exploding through my chest, like every last nerve ending in my body isn't focused on that small part of my chin that his hand is still touching. He's so gorgeous I can hardly bear it, the lack of his usual composure and polish only making me want him more.

"I did." He swallows. "You came to my house."

I feel myself flushing. "Nicole gave me the address."

He nods as if to say he'd guessed as much. He lowers his hand, and I almost cry out from the loss. "You helped Remi. Why? Because your Candyland heart couldn't take it to hear about a missing dog?"

He's still angry. Of course, he's still angry.

"Yes, but that's not why I did it." I swallow. "I did it because of you. I wanted to help you. I needed to show you—"

His hair drips water onto his shirt.

"Let me get a towel for you. You must be freezing, again. I don't want you to catch cold."

He grabs my arm before I can leave. "I don't want a towel, Gracie." His voice is low, husky. "I want you to finish what you were saying."

"I'm so sorry, Enoch," I say, tears hot behind my eyes again. "I don't know how I can apologize for what I did. It was so stupid and wrong. I just...I worried that I'd find myself right back where I started, and—"

He pulls me to him by my arm, not all that gently, and his lips claim mine. There's no other word for it. Relief and need course through me, taking away any conscious thought beyond this—I want him, and I'm finally going to get him. I don't care about what comes afterward. I *need* him with a fever I've never experienced with anyone else. My hands lift up into his soaking-wet hair, gripping it as I bring him closer.

He slides his hands under my shirt, and they're so much warmer than they have any right to be, so broad and wide they seem to encompass all of me, spreading tingles of pleasure to every place they touch. Our mouths clash and come together, clash and come together, a battle I don't want to win. I don't know how long it goes on. Time has ceased to have meaning. Blood is beating in my ears and between my legs, and every inch of me is alive with sensation. With the need for his mouth and hands, for his cock.

He pulls back slightly, smiling at me, his hands still splayed on the bare skin beneath my top as if to say I'm his. "You going to take my pants off again?"

"They're soaked from the rain," I say, my voice shaking.

"Yes, only you stand between me and hypothermia." He lifts my shirt over my head and drops it to the floor. "I've heard skin-to-skin contact helps."

I'm wearing the same simple bra I had on earlier, the kind of thing you buy in Target, not a lingerie store, but he runs his fingers across the top of it. "Fucking beautiful." Then he bends his head and kisses my flesh, his hands going back to expertly unfasten the clasp. I shrug it off, and his head's already there, kissing my breasts, finding my nipple and sucking, pulling a needy sound from me that I can barely believe came from my mouth.

But he's still wearing that short-sleeved shirt, totally inappropriate for the weather, covered in wet spots from his hair, and I pull back so I can tug it up and over his head.

His chest is a work of art, something you wouldn't expect in a man who wears so many suits. I want to touch every ridge of muscle. I want to lick ice cream off him.

I must have said that last part out loud, because he says, "Fuck, Gracie. I think we can arrange that." But I'm not embarrassed. I don't try to take it back.

"Those pants," I say through my dry mouth. "We'd better get them off."

"Yes, you'd better," he says.

I reach down, my hands shaking like earlier, and undo the button and zipper. He pulls his pants off and then toes out of his shoes and takes off his socks, leaving him in nothing but his boxer briefs, his dick straining against the material, begging for my touch. I don't hold back, reaching in and stroking him. I'm in wonder that, after everything, he still wants me this much. I feel an electric, hurting need, one that can only be fulfilled by having him inside me again.

He moves my hand, eliciting a sound of protest from me—right up until he tugs down my yoga pants and underwear.

"Twenty times, I said. I'd better get started."

He reaches down to touch me, his pupils dilating when he feels how wet I am for him.

"I haven't slept right since I touched you but didn't let you come."

"It was a dirty trick," I say. He's edging me back toward the sofa, a predator coming for his prey. The couch cushions scratch against the backs of my legs, sensitized by his touch, and I lower onto the cushions. He crowds me, standing between my legs.

"Spread them for me," he says, his voice commanding and low. It shivers through me as I spread my legs wide.

"Do you want me to taste you, Gracie?" he asks, looking in my eyes. "You must have liked it if you wrote it into your book."

"You know I liked it." I spread my legs wider in invitation.

He leans down and kisses me deeply, his tongue sparring with mine, then pulls away and kisses down my jaw and neck, pausing to suck in the flesh and bite softly. Getting to his knees, he kisses down my chest, sucking in my nipples one at a time, his hand paying attention to the one not in his mouth, and then continues on down, his hair brushing my flesh as he kisses his way to the apex between my legs.

Looking up at me, he spreads them wider, smiles at me devilishly, and then traces his fingers over my folds before curling two of them inside of me and pulsing. Pleasure spirals through me, pure and almost painful in its intensity. "Do you like the way that feels?" he asks, watching me.

"Yes, *yes.*"

"Do you want something else?" Pleasure spirals up my body in waves, making me almost vibrate with it. No one else has been able to draw it out of him like me—like it's natural, like my body was built for delivering me wave after wave of mind-numbing bliss.

"Yes," I say, weaving my hand into his still-wet hair and pushing it down. I can see the hint of a smile before he lowers his head, swirling his tongue around my clit while he continues to pulse his fingers, move them in and out.

I keep my hand in his hair, needing an anchor while he plays me like I'm an instrument made for his hands.

He shifts, running his tongue down my folds while he rubs circles around my clit, and it's as if the past and present have melded, as if fiction has become fact, and I feel myself tumbling over the edge—

"Enoch, I'm coming," I say, tightening my hand in his hair, and he quickens his tempo, brushing his thumb over my clit as he continues those maddening circles, moving his tongue inside of me, and it's all so much that I buck into his mouth and lose any control I had left. The pleasure crests, and he moves his mouth up to my clit, sucking, before lifting his head to look at me.

"Fuck, you're beautiful." He slides a hand up to my neck, then lets it glide slowly down my body, pausing to trace my breasts. "Gracie, I can't wait anymore. I need…"

I'm dizzy with pleasure, drunk on it. "The bathroom cabinet. I have some condoms."

His expression sours slightly.

"I…I'm not on birth control. It's been a while since…"

"It's not that," he says, leaning in to plant a kiss on my neck. "I don't like thinking of you with anyone else."

I grab his hair, pulling it a little too hard probably. "You think I've liked imagining you with other women? My father keeps subscribing me to his company newsletter. There've been photos of parties."

And photos of Enoch out with their clients.

If I'm being honest with myself, that's why I haven't tried harder to find a way to permanently unsubscribe myself. Those photos of him in his prime, dressed in one of his suits, his eyes laughing, his mouth in a perma-smirk.

The look on his face is satisfied, if anything. "I didn't know. But the reason I'm upset is because it's my own damn fault. All of these years. We could have been together, and we weren't. That's on me."

"Don't think of it that way," I say. "I've grown. You've grown. Who knows what would have happened if things had gone down differently? Maybe you'd still be an arrogant dick and I'd be making flight reservations for my father instead of Vera, with my book locked away in my head."

He studies me for a second, then softly kisses my lips, and the taste of my own arousal on his tongue floods me with new desire.

"Get the condom," I say, pulling away. "I need you too. So bad."

"Did you just tell me you need my cock?" he teases.

"Yes," I say, reaching down to stroke him, gratified that he's still so hard, "but don't get a big head about it."

"Even so, I'd like to hear you say it."

Still holding his cock, stroking it up and down, I look into his eyes and say, "Yes, Enoch Laskin, I want your cock."

He's on his feet in a second, and he shocks me into laughter when he lifts me into a princess hold and carries me with him.

"You don't need to bring me with you," I object even as I snuggle closer to his chest.

"I don't want to let you out of my sight."

My heart thrums and expands. It's almost too much to believe that he's really here—that we didn't ruin what's between us beyond any redemption.

He carries me to the bathroom like he really can't bear to put me down, even for a second, and then sits me down on the sink so he can open the cabinet.

His eyes gleaming, he steps out of his boxer briefs and opens the condom wrapper. Rolls it on. Anticipation has me in its grip.

"I can't wait another fucking second," he says, his voice almost wild with it. He's more beautiful to me than he's ever been—his dark hair still messy, his eyes a light luminescent green. "I need to be inside you."

He lines himself up and enters me, just slightly, the tip of him a delicious tease, before grabbing me by the butt and pulling me to him, fully seating himself. I gasp at the sensation, so full of him, every last inch of my skin attuned to the places where our bodies are touching.

"You feel so damn good, Gracie," he says, his voice husky. He carries me, his cock still inside of me, my legs wrapped around his waist. I rock against him, needing the friction, and it feels so intensely good that I almost come again. When he gets to the couch, he sits down hard. We're facing each other, him inside of me—a wonderful ache stretching me.

He reaches down for my clit, circling and flicking as I ride him. "I want you to pleasure yourself on my cock, Gracie. Tell me what you need."

"I... Rocking against you feels so good. It's hitting that place inside me."

"The one I like to touch," he says, then leans in and kisses my neck, just behind my ear, as he thrusts up to meet me. It makes something catch in my throat that, after all this time, he still knows the things I like. The things that make me moan. Of course, he just had a refresher course if he read *Between the Stacks*. His teeth glance off my ear as I rock against his cock. His fingers are on my clit, his other hand paying homage to my breasts, and I don't think I've ever felt so much at once, like my body has become a writhing fire—the sensations building on each other and driving me higher and higher.

"Enoch," I say, my voice choked. "I'm coming."

His eyes take on a look of purpose, and he works me harder with his hand and his cock as I rock against him, the sensations blasting through me. For a second, the intensity is almost painful, and I have to close my eyes and lean into it, pleasure rippling through and around me.

When I look again, he's watching me with hooded eyes. I kiss him, trying to let him know what he's done for me.

He shifts me so I'm lying on my back on the couch, his body raised over mine, and thrusts in deeper, and even though I just came, twice, I feel another wave of sensation.

"Fuck," he says, sweat beading on his brow. "I can't hold back anymore."

"Don't you dare."

He pulls out and thrusts in harder, and then again, lost to it, his hands on my breasts, his mouth finding mine as he pushes into me, making me breathless. He pulls one of my legs up over his shoulder, allowing him to go deeper, and the pressure is enough to elicit a moan from me. I feel him quiver over me as he comes, saying my name. Saying *Gracie*. And even though I'd thought all possible pleasure had already been pulled from my body, he proves me wrong, because I jump into the abyss with him.

When he collapses on top of me, still inside of me, I feel a moment of pure happiness. Of rightness. As if we were lost for six years, both of us, and finally we've been found.

twenty-four

ENOCH

I FEEL content in a deep way, like the part of me that's always been grasping and striving, insisting on more or better, is finally at peace. But there's something else riding that feeling—fear. Because this could so easily be taken from me.

John Parker will ruin me if I break my contract. He'll ruin me and then spit on me if I break it so I can be with his daughter.

I need to figure it out, because I'm not willing to give her up—not again—but I also don't want my father and Remi to get caught in the crosshairs of my problem.

I watch her, lying on her pillow, her light hair a mess over her face, her lips swollen from mine, and that peaceful feeling swells inside of me. I stayed over last night because it was late and she asked. Because I couldn't bear to be away from her yet. Because this place of hers is so totally her it feels like a safe haven, even if I wouldn't have chosen any of these things. There are bright paintings on the walls, splashes of orange and red and blue, deep-pile rugs that Udolpho would make a nightmare of, beveled mirrors, and a small sculpture in the living room that looks like it was made of reclaimed trash.

Neither of us have to go to work this morning. Vera gave Gracie the day off, and it's a vacation day for me, something I arranged for last week, anticipating that I'd need a break after the quick Los Angeles trip followed by the photo shoot. So Gracie and I stayed up late, talking and fucking and soaking each other in.

I texted my father last night to tell him I wouldn't be coming home, and he responded with a few choice emojis before saying: *I'm glad you're smart enough to know a woman's more important than Taco Bell. I think you've got yourself a good one.*

He's right.

I'll do anything for her. I'll break down bridges. I'll throw John Parker from them. I'll reveal Vera Valence for the fraud she is. I'll—

"Are you staring at me while I sleep?" Gracie murmurs.

"You'd like that, huh?" I say, twirling her hair around my finger. She turns toward me, her breasts peeking out from the covers, the pink tips begging for my mouth. "I know all about Eddie in *Twilight*," I add.

She starts laughing, her breasts bobbing with it. "Eddie?"

"Come on, have you ever met an Edward who didn't go by Ed or Eddie? I don't believe it. Over the course of a hundred years, someone would have given that asshole a nickname."

Still laughing, she says, "When did you read *Twilight*?"

I pull a face. "Remi wanted to listen to the audiobook in the car on the way here."

"It's a two-hour drive from Charlotte. Did you keep listening to it?"

"I was hoping her policeman father was going to haul him away for sniffing her underwear, or whatever, in the middle of the night."

"You didn't think that was going to happen."

I nod my accession to her point. "I figured it would give me something to talk to Remi about. Sometimes it's hard." I swallow, and she reaches over to touch my Adam's apple.

"You even swallow sexy."

"Thank you," I say, giving her a look. "I'll bet you swallow sexy too."

She throws a pillow at me.

"Hey," I say, grabbing it and lifting it like a shield. "It wasn't a request. I was just saying, if the mood should ever strike, I'll bet it would be sexy."

"Uh-huh, sure," she says, but her eyes are bright with mirth. "It must have been hard, taking in your nephew."

"No," I say honestly, sitting up on the bed. "It was the easiest decision I ever made. His stepfather's a dick, and my half sister chose him over her own son. He's a good kid. The *best* kid. I'm not much of a parent to him, but at least he has my dad."

"Give yourself more credit. You're not so bad."

My lips lift at the corners. "I'm glad I've been elevated from abject hatred in your esteem. Now, why don't you come sit on my face?"

Laughter crinkles the corner of her eyes, her whole face glowing with it.

"I have a better idea," she says, flipping the comforter over—it's yellow and ruffled. If you ask me, it looks like a sun threw up, but at the same time...it's fitting.

They don't call me Sunshine for nothing, I guess.

All other thoughts flee my mind because Gracie is coming toward me on her hands and knees. "You don't have to do that," I say as she reaches for my cock. The sensation of her breathing on it brings my morning wood all the way up to attention.

"Obviously," she says, leaning in to plant an open-mouthed kiss on it.

I collect her hair in my fist, pulling gently. "You're gorgeous. I'd watch you while you sleep any day. If you're really attached to the idea, I'll even figure out a way to sparkle in the sun."

She laughs. "Hey, I'm trying to be sexy here."

"You're succeeding."

* * *

When I finally break our mutually agreed–upon silence about the shit storm we're in, we're sitting in the kitchen part of the loft, painted sunshine yellow. Gracie's in the T-shirt I had on last night, and I'm in my boxer briefs.

"Did you and Nicole find anything in Vera's house?"

Her eyes light up. "We did. I completely forgot about it after the photo shoot. Vera made me sweet-talk the leftover models into posing from the neck down because she thought their faces couldn't compete with Damien's. Or *yours*." She runs a hand over my arm, her touch suffusing me with warmth. "He told me what you did for me, Enoch. I can't tell you how much it means to me."

"Yeah, let's not make a big thing about it," I say. "I'm really hoping we ruin her before those photos ever see the light of day. What'd you find?"

She retrieves several red envelopes from her bag, explaining why she thought they might be important, then bites her lip as she studies them. "I'm worried to open them. Isn't that silly?"

"How about I open one too?" I say. "One piece of anthrax-laced hate mail each. We'll be poisoned together."

Her lips tip up slightly. "And I thought I was the one with an overactive imagination."

"Hey, I'm just being romantic."

She hands me one before taking up her own. I regard mine for a moment. There's a California return address but no name on it. I'm feeling a little punch-drunk, or maybe Gracie-drunk, so I tap my envelope to hers before ripping it open.

I'm not sure what I was expecting, although my mind conjured images of letters put together from cut-up magazine articles. Instead, it's a simple handwritten letter.

Dear Vera,

I meant what I said over the phone. I'd like to make The Wind in Her Hair into a film. I have the means to make it happen. What's holding us back?

Victor Biscoff

Interesting. Victor Biscoff is a big fucking deal.

He's notorious for his dislike of email, despite being a film producer, so I'm not surprised by the handwritten follow-up. He's also known for his intensity, which explains why there were several handwritten follow-ups. What *does* surprise me is that Vera didn't mention a single word of this to me before my trip, even when I specifically mentioned *The Wind in Her Hair*. Nor did she or her agent suggest a meeting with Victor.

Gracie looks at me with raised eyebrows. "What does it mean?"

"This is where I get to say my favorite words," I say, although I don't plan on applauding myself. "I was right. It must not be hers, or at least not totally hers."

"But Enoch," she says, "she told you to pitch *my* book."

"Because she thinks she covered her bases with you," I say, my mind whirring. "Maybe she learned from her mistakes. What if the person who wrote *The Wind in Her Hair* was an old assistant or someone she took a writing class with? There'll be a connection somewhere if we look back far enough."

"Well, we know when it was published. That should help."

"It gives us a place to start," I agree.

"I'm an idiot," she says with a groan, her hands fisting. "I can't believe I trusted that woman."

I put my hand over one of hers, smoothing it out into a flattened palm. "A lot of people have trusted her," I say. "A lot of people have looked up to her. We're going to set the record straight."

"About that..." Gracie looks down at the tabletop, tracing the grain in the wood with her free hand. She tells me about the plan she

and Nicole hatched—the ball, the important guest list, her speech...
"I know you don't have a great impression of Nicole, and rightly so, but I think she can help us find more proof. Damien too."

"I'm not sure I like their way of helping," I say flatly, "but I guess we're going to need all the help we can get."

Smiling at me, she turns her hand around so our hands are linked. "You said *we*."

"Damn straight. I'm a part of this now. Don't steal my chance to be involved in potentially illegal activities. My nephew might finally think I'm cool."

Her smile drops. "Enoch, the position you're in with my father. . ."

"Let me worry about that," I say, even though I still don't have even a glimmer of a solution on that front. I can't work with him *and* be with her, especially not if she defies him so publicly. He'll use me to punish her. But I also can't ghost my job. Wherever I go, he'd find me.

Which is why I need to be smarter than him. One step ahead.

But after the nightmare of yesterday that ended in the bliss of last night, I'm not on top of my game.

"Absolutely not," she says, pulling her hand away. "You can't tell me that you're going to help me and then refuse me the opportunity to help you. That's not the way this works."

"Oh yeah?" I say, amused. Touched. "So how does it work?"

"We help each other, obviously."

"Teamwork," I say, winking. "You know that doesn't come naturally to me."

Something stirs in her eyes, and she gets up off her chair and stalks over to me like a goddess. "Teamwork can be taught," she says as she climbs onto my lap. She grinds over my dick, each gyration of her body sending a bolt of need through me.

"God, you're something." I run a hand up under her T-shirt and trace the curves of her breasts.

"*Something* is a very general word."

"Look at you, critiquing my vocabulary."

My phone starts ringing on the table, and my gaze skips to it. It's *him*.

John Parker.

My eyes meet Gracie's, and I can tell she saw it too. "Answer him," she says, but she doesn't stop grinding against me. Fuck.

I pick up the call. "John?"

"Your vacation day is going to be cut short. You're about to get your in with Sinclair."

"Excuse me?"

"Lean in hard on your contact. She'll be open to talking to you after this afternoon."

Gracie grinds a little harder against my dick, moving with little circles of her hips. I fight the urge to toss the phone aside and flip her onto the table. To take her from behind and forget that John Parker exists. But I can't do that. Like I told her, he's playing chess. Constantly. That means I can't stop being vigilant.

The one time I did, I ended up with that contract that's been hanging over my head for years.

It's almost a relief when Gracie gets up and disappears into the other room—her sweet torture had me on the verge of losing my mind.

"What happens this evening?"

"Tune in to *Your Afternoon Delight* at three p.m.," he says, his tone smug. I'm pretty sure Sinclair won't like whatever happens on the show. He's hoping to back her into a deal, just like he backed me into mine. That sets me on edge because Sinclair is Marnie's sister, and it's clear Gracie sees Marnie as family.

"You're not being reassigned," he says, "so don't ask again. But just so we have everything out on the table in a pretty little picnic, tell me which of Vera's books has you so worked up."

I wonder if he's fishing. If so, I won't satisfy him.

"*The Wind in Her Hair*," I say, looking up as Gracie returns with a condom in her hand. Swallowing, I add, "I'm going to make sure there's nothing to it."

She tugs at my underwear, and I lift up, letting her pull them down. I'm an idiot, but I'm an idiot with a hard-on that would dent metal, and I'm not going to stop whatever she has planned.

"Or shut up whoever's making a problem," he counters.

"Or that," I say, feeling a pulse of anger in my chest that's swamped by a different feeling as Gracie rolls the condom over me.

Fuck. She's really doing this.

"Have you seen my daughter?" John asks as she slowly lowers onto my cock, one inch at a time, the feeling so fucking exquisite, I almost crush the phone in my hand.

"Yes," I say. *Right now, in fact. She's riding my dick as we speak.* I clear my throat. "She's at Vera's house a lot. Our paths have crossed."

I put a hand on her hip as she starts moving over me, her inner walls hugging my dick.

"I'm going to bring her on board," he says. "I've given her enough time to change her mind. I have reason to believe she'll be grateful for it."

"Oh?" I say, the word coming out a little breathy as Gracie rocks against me, changing the angle and taking me out and in as she tips her head back, the column of her throat begging for my mouth and teeth. I press my lips to it before leaning back, watching her face as she rides me. She's driving me crazy, and the look on her face says she knows it. That she *likes* it.

"I always get what I want in the end, Enoch," her father says. "This afternoon. You'll see."

He hangs up. I throw the phone onto the table and lift Gracie off me. "You're a naughty girl," I say, running my hands up under the huge T-shirt. "Turn around."

"Are you going to spank me?" she says as she does as requested, planting her palms on the table and pushing out her ass.

Christ, what has she learned working for that Valence woman? Part of me wants to give Vera a medal. Then again, it's been six years since Gracie and I were together. I don't know who she's been with or what experiences she's had.

"Do you want me to?" I ask hoarsely.

"Maybe a little," she says, looking at me over her shoulder. "I've always wondered what it would feel like."

The internal weight I feel lessens, and I palm her ass, looking at her. "You were a very bad girl, Gracie. You were trying to drive me crazy, and it worked." I slap her ass lightly, curling my fingers around toward her pussy.

"God, Enoch. Do it again. The other side."

I slap the other side, curling my fingers around again, then adjust myself and thrust into her sweet heat. Her moan curls around me and drives me to thrust harder.

"Touch yourself while I fuck you," I say, leaning into her ear and then giving the lobe a light nip.

Watching her reach down and touch her clit while I rail her from behind is the best kind of awakening. It's my fairy tale come true. Because for me, fairy tales aren't full of stardust and butterflies, they're full of Gracie—talking to her, touching her, being inside of her. It's hard for me to believe this is real. I spent so long telling myself I didn't need her, and then that it didn't matter because I couldn't have her, but I'm finally ready to be honest with myself.

I love this woman.

In some ways, I think I always have.

"MAYBE I CAN TALK her out of giving me the acting class," I tell Enoch as we take the elevator up to Sinclair's penthouse.

He laughs. "I don't know. I'd like to witness that."

"You don't...resent my friends over the whole dirt-bag thing, do you?"

His lips twitch. "No. I like that they're so loyal to you. Nicole? Yes, I resent the hell out of that woman, and don't expect me to be nice to her."

"Fair," I say, rubbing my throat. It would be fair if he resented me too, but magically he doesn't. We talked everything through last night. I've realized that even when I hated him for choosing my father—and I *did* hate him—I couldn't stop thinking about him. He occupied my mind, my dreams, my fiction. I envisioned him having a paper-clip-grip on my heart, but someone must have applied Gorilla Glue to it because it never fully let go.

This morning I texted my friends to fill them in on my father's warning and let them know Enoch was coming with me. We moved up the timetable for the meeting, which was only inconvenient for Andy since Marnie's a freelancer, Sinclair's not working, and Nicole, who invited herself, is once again her own boss. Andy pretended to come down with a stomach virus, though, so she's going to be there too.

The elevator stops, and Enoch and I exchange a *here goes nothing* look before we get out.

He takes my hand, squeezes it. "Your father's not the only one who knows how to play games," he says. "Depend on it. We'll just have to do it better." He smiles. "And guess what? There's two of us now, and there's only one person your father completely trusts."

"You?" I quip.

"Himself."

"You're right." But my father still looms over our lives like a Disney villain. I try to tell myself that the villain always pays in the end in fairy tales, but that's only true in Hollywood. In the original version of *The Little Mermaid*, the mermaid turns into seafoam at the end. And don't even ask me what happens to Bluebeard's wife... That story gave me nightmares for a solid two weeks when I was a kid.

Sinclair greets us at the door, and although I'm sure she's nervous, you'd never guess from looking at her.

"Thanks for coming," she says, waving us inside. "There's a tray of amuses-bouches on the dining room table. Please help yourselves."

I glance over, and Andy, who's standing by the table with Marnie, shakes her head frantically and slices a hand across her throat.

Don't try the amuses-bouches, duly noted.

According to Marnie, cooking classes are the latest way in which Sinclair is trying to find herself, only instead of starting at the beginning and working her way up, she's tried to learn "elevated" recipes for entertaining.

The penthouse is frankly gorgeous, not that one would expect anything less from a celebrity temporarily living in a small city. There are floor-to-ceiling windows that look out over the mountains, hardwood floors, and sculpted wooden arches on the high ceilings. I know from a past visit that there's even a stained-glass window in the bathroom. The floors are covered in colorful rugs. It's the kind of place that seems naturally inclined to make a person happy just by being here, but Sinclair's obviously not happy.

Something tells me she'll be even less happy after whatever happens on *Your Afternoon Delight*.

Nicole turns around on the couch, facing us, and Enoch groans.

"Hey, Gracie," she says. "Hey, *boss*."

"You're fired," he tells her.

"Yeah, that's fair," she responds with a grin. "Your dad said you found the dog?"

He gives a stiff nod, his jaw working.

She tilts her head, observing him. "You know, Udolpho's been through a lot. He might have a brain the size of a pea, but he's not half bad. For people who are into dogs."

"That's exactly why you shouldn't have used him as a pawn," Enoch says in a dark tone.

Nicole shrugs. "I knew you'd let him stay. Your dad told me you used to have dogs when you were a kid. Said you begged your mother to let the family dog sleep in your bed."

I glance at Enoch as she peels back this other layer of him. I wonder if it will always be like this—one layer peeled off after another.

"If I could fire you again, I would," he scoffs. "You ruined three of my best suits."

"You look better like this," Nicole says.

Enoch hasn't been home yet, so he's wearing the *I may be wrong, but it's highly unlikely* T-shirt again. I can see why she'd say so. He seems more vulnerable this way, more touchable. Even now, while she's pushing all of his buttons.

"I didn't ask for a style critique," he says.

"That comes for free. Besides, my friend's going to fix your suits."

He barks a laugh. "You think I'd trust your friend with my suits?"

"You did a few days ago. He's the one who messed with the seams."

"You just got fired for a third time."

"Fourth," Nicole corrects. "You fired me for the first time after I gave you the hangover cure."

"Okay." He nods. "That was the fourth, and this is the fifth."

Nicole laughs at this, then says, "You know what? You're not half bad."

He glowers at her. "The feeling is not mutual."

Turning her attention to me, Nicole says, "Edgar James says he'll come to Vera's ball. You're welcome."

"Hey," Marnie calls out from behind me. "I'm the one who arranged that."

"It was my idea," Nicole says. "So you're both welcome."

Sinclair, who's walking up with a silver tray topped with two drinks in short martini glasses with elaborate garnishes, nearly drops the tray. "Edgar James is coming?"

"That the guy from *Extreme Camping*?" Enoch asks.

"That's the one," Marnie says, but her gaze is on her sister. "Are you *interested* in him, Clair?"

She shrugs disaffectedly. "I've seen a few episodes of the show when it was on Discovery."

He doesn't seem like he'd be her type. I've never met him, but according to Marnie, he's quiet and intense, obsessed with the outdoors and getting his hands dirty. Then again, there's no controlling who you're drawn to. That's the beauty—and curse—of romance. Actually, the romantic in me is swooning a bit at the image of the two of them together—Edgar James all gruff and outdoorsy, Sinclair so perfectly groomed she probably notices if one of her nails is a millimeter longer than the rest.

"Your sister can hook you up," Nicole says, with a wink and a nod. "Get you some outdoorsman dick."

"Classy," Enoch says, but his expression is contemplative. He reaches down as if to adjust his tie, then smiles ruefully to himself because he's not wearing one.

"Never pretended to be," Nicole says with a yawn.

"It could work," he adds.

"Getting her dick?" I sputter.

"*Dating* him—or pretending to—could work for her image." He shifts his attention to Sinclair. "You'd be telling people you're not the prissy Hollywood type. That you don't mind getting your hands dirty."

"Except she kind of does," Marnie says, pulling her mouth to that side. After that one gardening class, Sinclair gave everything she'd purchased for her new hobby—multiple sets of gardening gloves, Vera Wang pots, and at least thirty exotic plants—to her brother and sister. Andy and I came over a few weeks ago to help pot them, but apparently only a third have survived.

"Maybe she'd make an exception for Edgar James." Andy, who's wandered over to join our discussion, waggles her eyebrows. I notice she left her amuses-bouches on the table.

"You think?" Sinclair asks, her gaze stuck on Enoch.

"It would be a good look for him too," he says. His eyes dart to me for a second before returning to her. "He's on Parker Brand Management's recruitment list. He almost drowned a few months ago, *on camera*, and his career took a hit. Not a good look for an outdoorsman."

"That's fucked up," Marnie says. "If he weren't an outdoorsman, he *would* have drowned. Accidents can happen to anyone."

"No one said public perception was fair," Enoch says, lifting his hands. "The court of public opinion is quick to execute. *You* know that."

I'm not surprised he knows about Marnie's brush with infamy. Most people do. Still, it's a little weird to hear him talk about it when

I'm not the one who told him. It's an unwelcome reminder of the years we've spent at odds with each other.

"True," Marnie acknowledges.

"If he starts dating a Hollywood actress, suddenly he's a god again." He nods to Sinclair. "And if you're seen as outdoorsy and adventurous, there's less of a chance you'll be inundated with soft roles you don't want."

"You said you're a brand manager?" Sinclair says with interest.

"I am." His gaze drifts to me. "But I'm not taking new clients right now."

"You just gave me your card yesterday."

"Yes," he says, putting an arm around me and drawing me closer. Warmth unfurls inside of me. "A lot has happened since then. I can give you some advice though."

"Yes, he loves telling people what to do," Nicole interjects.

"I do, yes. Especially my employees. You just got fired a sixth time."

She laughs and starts scrolling on her phone.

If Sinclair has questions, she doesn't ask them. All she does is blurt, "Thanks," then jut the silver tray at us with enough force that some of the liquid splashes onto the tray. One of the garnishes wiggles threateningly but stays put.

Marnie gives me a thumbs-up. "I brought those over from the bar."

"But I did the garnishes," Sinclair says with a smile. She's a good enough actress that her eyes aren't empty of it, but it still feels fake. Her mind is working over what Enoch told her—and over whatever is going to happen today on the talk show. "I watched a few YouTube videos on cocktail garnishes. I figured maybe I could help Griffin out at the bar a few times for fun. You can't eat them though. Don't try to eat them." She glances at Andy as she says this.

"Yes," Andy says, her tone dry. "I made the mistake of thinking the food served to me would be edible."

"They're pretty," I tell Sinclair.

She could never help out at Griffin's bar, of course. This is another of her pipe dreams, like the plants. The clay. Half of the people there would recognize her. Maybe more than half. There'd probably be a mob situation.

I cast a glance at Enoch. Sinclair really *could* use his help...

It's a sign of loyalty to me that he's not trying to poach her for my father. Bringing in Sinclair and Edgar James as clients would be a huge coup for him. My father is capable of being generous to those who please him. Enoch would probably get a big bonus—more if he's right about the fake-dating thing.

But Enoch and I both know we can't be together if he's working for my father, and that's not the only reason we need to get him out. From what he's told me, he's wanted to escape Parker Brand Management for a while. Although he loves his career, working for someone like my father, whose moral compass isn't so much broken as nonexistent, is toxic.

My mind's already working on that problem, although I have a feeling he won't like the solution I have to suggest. But maybe...

Sinclair glances at the clock as she tucks the silver tray under her arm. "We'll start the acting class after the show." She taps the side of her head. "I've been giving this some thought, though, and the best advice I have for you is to bury your own thoughts and desires and needs while you're playing a role."

"Fuck," Andy says. "Stop making me feel bad for you."

"I'm *very* happy and fulfilled," Sinclair snaps. Turning back to us, she adds, "Help yourselves to the amuses-bouches."

"Thank you," Enoch says. "I just ate, but Gracie mentioned in the elevator that she was starving."

He gives me a wicked look, and I'm torn between being amused and annoyed.

"Help yourself," she says with a wave. "Please."

I head toward the table, trailed by Andy and Marnie, leaving

Enoch with Sinclair and Nicole on the couch, scrolling through her phone. As I go, I hear Enoch ask Sinclair if she knows who the show's "mystery guest" will be.

She doesn't.

The table is immaculately set up, with more of the pretty silver trays, each behind a small calligraphed sign. There are matching plates, which I recognize from a local pottery store, and silk napkins. The food looks like something that would be served at a school cafeteria.

Andy makes some more *this food will kill you* gestures, which I ignore as I select the least offensive-looking item.

"Your funeral," she whispers.

I tip my head toward Sinclair, who's regarding me with a hopeful expression. Then I take a small bite of the tomato tart. My mind instantly conjures an image of a couple of British judges talking about soggy bottoms.

Marnie waves us over to the other side of the penthouse. "Want a tour?"

I've been here before, and from what I understand there are only two bedrooms, most of the space open and breezy, but it's obvious Marnie's more interested in getting us alone for a chat than in showing us Sinclair's bedsheets—even though I'm sure they're nice, exactly the sort a person would fawn over if he or she were impressed by bedsheets.

"I'm coming too," Nicole says, popping up from the couch like a groundhog. I glance over, and Enoch's deep in conversation with Sinclair. He's in professional mode—his smile charming, his posture that of a man who doesn't possess a single doubt in himself. Then he glances at me and winks, and my heart goes gooey.

Part of me hates that he affects me this much—that he makes my highs so high, my lows so low—but more of me savors it.

In fact, my mind has been working overtime all day, picking at the end of my book. Reweaving it into the kind of happily-ever-after any real romance book deserves.

It's what I want for myself. Why would I give my alter ego anything less?

"You're mooning," Marnie says, grinning at me. "I've never seen you like this."

"Certainly not about Roy," Andy says.

"Ray," I correct. "And no, the seven shades of vanilla have nothing on Enoch."

Andy chokes out a laugh. "I got you to say it!"

"What's he going to do about your dad?" Nicole asks.

"Did they tell you about the contract he signed?" I return.

"We have no secrets," she says.

I'm not so sure about that, but when I look to Marnie, she gives a little nod.

"If he breaks the terms of the contract, he'll owe my dad three hundred thousand dollars, on the spot. We also assume my father will try to ruin him. He does it to anyone who leaves his company— we've both seen it happen. I had an uncle Tommy, who worked with my dad for ten years when I was a kid. He was my godfather. Then Uncle Tommy went to work somewhere else, and I never saw him again. The man's ruthless."

"And your plan?" Nicole asks.

"I'm working on it," I say. "Where's Damien?"

"He's with Vera." She laughs. "Admit it, I'm not the only one who wants to read Vera's menage romance inspired by Enoch and Damien." She lifts a finger. "After we destroy her, obviously."

"*After* is the key word," Marnie says. "We can laugh about it afterward. But that's not why I wanted to get you guys alone."

"You lured us here under false pretenses?" Nicole asks, her eyes shining with approval. "You've really come a long way."

"I'm glad I can impress you with my dishonesty. But feel free to admire Sinclair's paintings while we're in here. You'd really make her day."

Nicole glances at the walls. One of the paintings is clearly intended to be a bowl of fruit, only there are two round fruits and a banana, which makes it look like...

"Shit," she says. "We better figure out a way to keep her acting career alive, huh?"

Andy laughs, but Marnie looks worried.

"What is it?" I ask, touching her arm. I set my drink down on a side table, and Marnie's eyes instantly round.

"Oh shit, you'd better pick that up. That's an antique. Someone from *90210* used to own it."

"*90210?*"

"Well," she glances at the door, "don't tell Sinclair, but she's not exactly an A-list celebrity. She wouldn't be able to buy something Bette Davis used to own."

I pick up the drink, but the huge garnish falls, and although I'm quick to snatch it up, a splash of color is left behind.

We all stare at it, then Nicole moves one of the awards sitting on the dresser to that spot. "Problem solved. Now, tell us what's robbed you of your sense of humor, Marnie."

"Sinclair's agent dropped her this morning. She wouldn't say why, but she must have gotten a hint about whatever's happening on this talk show. It's going to be bad. I'm worried about Clair."

Nicole perks up. "Do you know who the guest star is?"

"I think I might." She looks around as if worried a camera might be hanging from the ceiling. "If I'm right...it's our mother."

"IT WASN'T THAT BAD," Gracie says, trying to smile.

No, the show was a catastrophe.

A plague on Sinclair Jones and anyone who might be interested in making her employable.

A fucking dream for a brand manager, because there's nothing so satisfying as turning a person's career around.

The interview started with Sinclair's mother and former manager saying, "I don't like to say a bad word about my own daughter, but..." and she went on to make dozens of accusations, including that her daughter had actually been fired from her former show, *Sisters of Sin*, for erratic behavior.

Not true, according to Sinclair and her friends, but not easily disprovable, since it would suit the director to pretend it's accurate.

She also claimed that Sinclair has a drug habit. In her fantasyland version of the truth, Sinclair moved to Asheville because Marnie's boyfriend, Griffin, who went to jail briefly for drug possession—"He was covering for his dad!" Marnie shouted at the TV—is her new supplier. She says she's desperate to get a message to her daughter but her other children have essentially been holding Sinclair hostage.

Finally, she denied circulating the viral video of Marnie. According to her, Marnie did it herself in order to gain attention.

Now that it's over, Marnie looks like she wants to murder someone. I'm pretty sure I know who's first on her list.

"Did you watch what the rest of us watched?" Andy asks. "I'm all about being positive, Gracie, but there's a difference between positive and unrealistic."

"She just declared war," I say, my eyes on Sinclair. She's sitting at the edge of her chair, her posture perfect, her face void of any emotion. The only crack in her composed appearance is in the fiery look in her eyes. Good, she'll need that. "What are you going to do next?"

"Meet her on the battlefield."

"Maybe we should just put a hit on her," Nicole says from where she's standing by the dining room table. She pops an amuse-bouche into her mouth and instantly cringes.

Serves her right. I hope it packs the same kick as the "cure" she gave me.

"It's tempting, right?" Marnie says, then pauses. "I'm joking... I'm going to assume you're joking too."

Nicole makes an off-handed gesture. "At least ninety percent. But Griffin's going to lose his shit over this."

"He should," I say. "She's out to ruin his reputation too. Same for you and your brother." I nod to Marnie.

"That's not going to happen," Sinclair says tightly. "What do I do?"

She's asking *me*. This is where I could swoop and tell her that Parker Brand Management is going to wrap this shit up in a pretty package and tie a goddamn bow around it. With sparkles. She'd go for it. I can tell from the look on her face. Hell, I knew before that from the garnishes, the amuses-bouches, and the misshapen clay centerpiece. This is a woman who loves acting. She quit her show, the next big thing hasn't materialized yet, and she's trying to fill the void with every other damn thing under the sun.

But I can't give Sinclair Jones to John on one of those silver platters she must have bought in bulk.

I can give her advice, for free, but I can't be her brand manager unless she gives me a three-hundred-thousand-dollar down payment.

A glance at Gracie says she's hoping I can solve this mess for her friend, and dammit, I need to. For *her*.

"I should make a rebuttal, right?" Sinclair says.

"Yes," I say slowly, "but not how you're thinking."

I get to my feet, reaching for my tie before I remember I'm not wearing one, and settle for stuffing my hands into my pockets. I pace a few steps.

"Are you *leaving*?" Andy asks.

Gracie hushes her. "He's thinking."

She gives me a knowing look, like she thinks I'm about to pull a miracle out of my ass. There's some heat behind the look, promising me I'm going to like what happens if I manage said miracle.

"You've basically gone off the grid since you got here," I say to Sinclair. Not a question. I've looked. She gave an interview to a reporter from Charlotte after quitting her show. She told him why she'd fired her momager—namely, her mother's decision to circulate that embarrassing tape of Marnie for personal gain—but it just became a she said–she said kind of situation. "That was a mistake. For all anyone knows, she's right. You could be living in a hovel or your sister's closet. Your rebuttal should be to bring your fans into your life. Show them this place." I wave around the apartment. "Let them know what you've been working on. The clay. The garnishes. They'll admire you for your struggle."

"Struggle?" she says in question. She obviously believes she's been more successful at these pastimes than evidence would suggest, not that I'm surprised. She's a celebrity—she's not used to being smacked with reality checks.

"They'll love you if you show them your vulnerable side. Your mother will end up looking like a cold bitch for slinging accusations at you while you're over here trying to live your best life. Trying to master clay and failing. Trying to master cooking and ending up with something out of *Nailed It!* She'll look like a liar when you show them Marnie and Griffin at the bar. Or hangouts with your brother and sister."

"You guys don't like the amuses-bouches?" she asks, looking around at the others. She seems a little crestfallen, but I'm not going to apologize. I need to get through to her. If that requires me to be blunt, so be it.

Her sister crinkles her nose and shakes her head. Andy says, "Nope," popping the *p*, "and I really wish you'd stop calling them that."

Nicole doesn't respond at all, back on her phone.

When it's her turn to answer, Gracie smiles at Sinclair and says, "You made really pretty signs for them."

It's such a Gracie answer, all I can do is grin at her. She's so adorable it makes my head hurt, but I know she has a killer instinct buried beneath her sweetness. She knows I'm right.

"'Your signs are pretty' is nice-people speak for the food *suhhhh-hcks*," Nicole says, proof that she's listening after all.

"You could have just told me," Sinclair says, firming her lips. "I don't like it when people lie to me."

"And you don't like it when they tell the truth either," I say. "If you're going to survive in this business, you need to develop a sixth sense for when people are lying to you. Yours is dull. You'll want to work on honing that."

She seems pissed off, but she gives a slight nod. "Okay. I can look like an idiot on camera. It'll be like playing another role."

Andy swallows a laugh. She's obviously a tough customer.

I pace a little more, back and forth, then snap my fingers and point at Sinclair. "And if Edgar James and his people are on board to sell a relationship between you two, we can craft a whole narrative for it. You can tell your fans you have a crush on him and he's working with your sister. They'll egg you on. You can ask him to go to Vera's ball with you. The whole thing will be a fucking PR dream for both of you. His team would be foolish to say no. Hell, you might get lucky enough to have someone script a Lifetime movie about your romance."

"Or a book," Gracie says with a small smile.

My blood is pulsing faster through my veins, and I feel the high of having developed a kickass strategy for someone. Actually, it's the first time I've felt this way about my job in a long time. Maybe because it's not for him—it's for *her*.

Not Sinclair Jones, but my sunshine girl, beaming at me like I'm not the asshole who fucked up her life.

"He's right," she says. "It's perfect."

I mime taking a bow.

Someone flings an amuse-bouche at me.

"That was Nicole, wasn't it?" I growl.

Andy lifts a hand. "I couldn't be satisfied until I threw *something* at you," she says. "Things may have turned out okay, but you *did* make Gracie sad."

"I know," I say, feeling the burn of it in my chest. My eyes go to Gracie, who's looking at me like *I'm* sunshine. "But I'm going to do everything in my power to make up for it."

"It's a good plan," Marnie tells her sister. "I'll talk to Edgar about it, but Enoch's right—I don't see why he wouldn't go for it. It would be good for both of you."

I smile at Gracie. "I wonder if he goes by Eddie?"

"God, I hope not," Sinclair says. "That would really take the luster off, wouldn't it?"

But even though she's probably still pissed at me for telling her the truth, there's something different about her now, like she's a knife honed for battle.

God, I love what I do.

I catch Nicole giving me a sidelong glance, and I give her the finger.

She laughs, the psychopath.

"Something else you need to be aware of," I tell Sinclair. "Your presence has just been announced to the world. People may have noticed you around town—some of them probably even wrote about it on blogs or talked about it on TikTok—but they're going to be hungry for you now. You won't be able to go anywhere without getting spotted by someone. You may want to get a bodyguard."

"Oh, I don't want to do that," Sinclair says. She glances at her sister and then their friends. "Wouldn't that make me seem less approachable?"

"Maybe," I say, "but you might find it necessary. Start looking at local ads. Be prepared. The last thing you want is an entourage of fans and hecklers following you around everywhere you go. You want to look comfortable here."

"No," she says sadly. "I want to *be* comfortable here."

It's on the edge of my tongue to tell her there's no difference, but my gaze lands on Gracie again. Even when I told myself I disliked her, back when we were in school together, my eyes always sought out her bright hair, in front of me in class, or those sexy pencil skirts she used to wear—the same way they keep seeking out glimpses of her now. Her leggings. The slope of her chin. Her neck. Her breasts. All of her, like they can't get enough.

I've always looked like I belong.

I've always acted like I belong.

But only with her—and with Remi and my dad, when I let myself—do I *feel* like I belong.

"COME INSIDE," I tell Gracie. No one mentioned the original plan for the acting class after my talk with Sinclair, for which Gracie was extremely grateful. Sinclair said she had a lot of thinking to do, and we all took the hint and left, Gracie driving me back home to the house I share with my dad and Remi. I called my father earlier, mostly to assure him I wasn't dead, and he said Udolpho slept in my bed all night, his head on my pillow. It would be touching, maybe, if it didn't mean my whole pillow must now be covered in hair and slobber. Still, there's no denying I'm stuck with Udolpho now. Looking for him last night bonded us in a way I've never felt connected with an animal.

Gracie bites her lip. "I was here yesterday. They both probably think I'm crazy." She looks away. "I was a little...upset."

I turn her face toward me. "You don't have to apologize for being worried about me. Not to be a dick, but it makes me feel pretty goddamn great that you were worried about me. When I left Vera's yesterday, I figured you wouldn't care if I got flattened by a semi."

"That's never been true," she says, batting my hand away.

"Not even right after I told you I'd accepted the job?"

She gives a half smile, as if she's reluctant about it. "Okay, maybe then."

I lean in and kiss her, reminding myself that things have changed between us. They're changing still. But I'm going to figure out a way to make all of this work. Because I have to, and if there's a greater motivator than need, I'm not sure what it is.

"There's a very strong chance they will end up liking you more than they do me. My dad thinks I'm a tool at least fifty percent of the time, and Remi keeps puncturing my ego by telling me I'm not hip."

"You know what?" she says wryly. "They're both right. For some reason, I like you anyway."

"Good. I'm not going to try to talk you out of it."

I reach for my door handle, but she stops me by touching my arm. I glance back, and she runs her fingers up and down my arm, a simple caress that reminds me of the way she looked at me in Sinclair's apartment—like I'm a fucking god of branding. It turns me on more than it should, given we're parked in front of my house and my dad and nephew and stalker dog are probably all home by now. "Thank you for that. For helping Sinclair. You didn't need to do it."

"I know," I say. "And I'd be lying if I said I didn't do it for you, but I like strategizing for people, Gracie. It was no hardship."

"I know," she says. "We need to talk about my dad."

"Not yet. Give me some time to strategize."

To raise three hundred thousand dollars.

"We're going to talk about it," she says.

"Agreed," I tell her. "But let me look into my options first."

Her expression says she doesn't like it, but she doesn't object. Probably because she doesn't have a magical solution to our problem either. Ideally, I'd like to start my own company, but there's that three hundred grand to think of—plus the start-up fees—and that's presuming I'd be able to survive whatever screw-you campaign John Parker sends my way. Because if he felt compelled to ruin a man just for leaving his job—two weeks' notice and every-thing—he'll want to grind me into powder and snort it.

"In the meantime, I need to pretend it's business like usual," I continue. "I'll tell him that I'm making in-roads toward recruiting Sinclair as a client. I'll make sure to be seen having lunch with her or something so he believes it, but he won't like it when she starts gaining traction on her own. It'll make him suspicious."

"Will he identify it as one of your strategies?" she asks.

"I don't think so," I say. "It's a strategy that fits her and her particular situation, but it's not the kind of thing I've set up for anyone else." I grin at her. "I must be spending too much time around romance writers, because the fake-romance thing came to me on the spot."

"It was brilliant," she says, her eyes shining. "It's the kind of story everyone's going to want to follow."

"Are you going to write about it, Gracie?" I ask, my voice a little husky because I'm thinking about what she wrote about us.

"Maybe," she says, "but first I have to finish our story."

"I thought it was finished," I say. But even as I say it, I remember that the ending felt a little rushed and very Vera.

"Not my version of it."

"Are you going to give us a happy ending?"

She smiles at me, but it's not without a touch of sadness. "I hope so."

"So do I," I say, tucking a lock of hair behind her ear. "Because I'm particular, in case you haven't noticed, and I'll accept nothing less."

"Oh, I've noticed." She leans in and kisses me, sweet and soft, and I'm tempted to put the car in drive and leave—to go somewhere far away, where none of our troubles can reach us. But it's just a fantasy, and I'd no sooner leave my dad, Remi, and yes, Udolpho, than she would leave her book in Vera Valence's clutches.

When we go inside, I'm immediately love-bombed by Udolpho,

who pulls his usual shoulder-tackle move before sniffing my crotch and then moving on to Gracie, wagging his tail at a discordant tempo the whole time.

"This is your dog?" she asks, laughing as she gets down to pet his ears. He twitches spasmodically, like she's hitting a good spot.

Fuck, I can't lie to myself, I appreciate the sight of them together. Gracie getting down low to give him ear pets, Udolpho looking every bit as stupid and good-natured as he is. There's a warm feeling inside of me—like the burn you get from a good bourbon.

"Yeah," I say, my voice suddenly thick. "I guess he is."

"You finally back, son?" my dad calls from the kitchen.

I'm prepared for him to make an inappropriate comment, but not for what actually happens—Damien steps into the living room from the kitchen, followed by Remi, who's clearly met a hero he is capable of worshipping.

"What are you doing here?" I blurt.

"Hey," Damien says, lifting his hands with his palms facing me. "I thought we bonded after modeling together for two hours in the freezing cold yesterday. If that's not a bonding experience, I don't know what is."

"You're married to Nicole."

It comes out as an accusation—which, I guess, it is.

"I don't deny it."

"He's helping me with my situation at school," Remi says, sounding much too excited about it.

"We'll see," I say.

"He is, Uncle Knock," he insists. "He said the best way to get to a bully is through his parents. Turns out you and Damien aren't the only ones who've got some embarrassing photos."

"The last thing I need to be caught up in now is blackmail," I say, giving Damien a dark look.

Admittedly, it has occurred to me that blackmail would be an ideal way out of my John Parker problem—if I had anything on him.

Unfortunately, I'm not sure there's anything to be had. He's done terrible things, many of which I know about, but none of them were illegal, and in our profession, ruthlessness isn't viewed as a bad thing. I'd probably give his career a boost if I let people know what a shit he is.

Damien lifts his hands in a keep-the-peace gesture. "Remi wasn't named personally. Neither were you. But the dad'll be watching that kid so closely, he won't be able to shoplift a stick of gum."

I give a slight nod because I don't object all that much. If the guy was enough of a dumbass to do something shady and get photographed doing it, maybe he deserves to be blackmailed. Maybe it'll make him do the job of a parent. "Thanks. I guess."

My dad appears next to them, and he gives me a cat-that-got-the-cream look, as if he wants to claim all responsibility for me and Gracie getting together.

Fuck, I'll give it to him. I'm not the only Laskin who likes being right.

I nod back to him, then say, "Let's have some tea. Would everyone like some tea?" I'm tempted to dis-include Damien from the offer, but Gracie's right—we need all the help we can get, and according to Nicole, Damien spent part of the day at Vera's house. It's possible he knows something useful.

"You're going to make us tea?" Gracie asks, looking delighted. I reach for her jacket, and she gives it to me, then watches as I hang it on one of the hooks by the door. I'm still in the dumb slogan shirt, no coat.

"I need a drink," I admit. "Desperately. But I try not to drink around Remi."

Remi snorts. "Then why'd you have such a bad hangover before you left for LA?"

"That happened after you went to sleep. All rules are off once you're asleep."

"I'd love some tea," Gracie says.

I hold out a hand to her, and she takes it, beaming at me, and I'm struck again by how much has changed in twenty-four hours. In six years.

I can't lose her. I *won't.*

Once everyone's in the kitchen, I make some tea in a teapot Vera gave me as a welcome gift a few weeks ago. Not my cup of tea, if you'll forgive the shitty pun, but I smiled and nodded and oohed and ahed and figured it would never once leave my cupboard. As reluctant as I am to use a gift from Vera, I'm glad I have something to offer Gracie.

The tea blend that came with the pot is called Happy Thoughts, which is both lame and exactly the kind of detail likely to make her smile, so I show her the bag, and sure enough, she grins at me.

"Who are you, and what have you done with my son?" my dad asks.

"Very funny," I say as I fill the electric kettle and set it to boil.

"You went to business school with Uncle Knock," Remi says. "Was he always like this?"

"No," Gracie says, watching me. "He's gotten better with age."

"I'm not sure whether that's an insult or a compliment," I rebut, "but I'm choosing to interpret it as a compliment."

"That's your right."

"I knew I liked you," my father tells her. It's a simple comment, probably thoughtlessly given, but it makes me happy in a way I don't feel compelled to reflect on. I measure out the tea, then pour in the water and bring over the little cups and saucers that go with it. On impulse—because I want things to be nice for her, goddammit— I bring out the honey.

"I'm seeing a whole new side to you," she says.

"So am I," I agree.

"I'm seeing a whole new teapot," Remi says.

"It's been in the cabinet for weeks, smartass," I say, then tousle his hair before sitting down next to Gracie. My father's across from her, Remi's across from me, and Damien's on the outside, as if ready to take off at a moment's notice. I pour her tea first, then serve the rest of us.

"So," I say to Damien. "Did you find anything at Vera's?"

He gives a slow nod. "Records of her previous employees. Nicole and I will look into that first."

I touch Gracie's arm. "This is good. This will help."

"It would help more if we could narrow the search," Damien says.

"I think we might be able to help you there." I tell him about the letters from Victor and our theory—now almost confirmed—that *The Wind in Her Hair* isn't a Vera Valence original.

"Okay," he says. "We can work with that."

I notice Remi is playing with his teacup instead of drinking what's inside of it. There's a glum look on his face, and I remember that he had a thing for a Vera Valence books. He's obviously upset by this, and he's not the sort of person who'd feel glum because he's disappointed his new collection of signed books might not be worth very much if we succeed in revealing her.

"I'm sorry, bud," I tell him. "I know it's a letdown when people aren't who you want them to be."

"I'm not upset about her," he says, giving the teacup a little push. "She's dead in the eyes. I knew inside of five minutes she wasn't a good person. I'm upset for whoever really wrote *The Wind in Her Hair*. And for *you*, Gracie." His eyes go wide. "Am I allowed to call you that? Or should I call you Miss Gracie or something else?"

"You go ahead and call me Gracie," she says—and it strikes me that *her* eyes go all the way down to her soul, to her warm, tender heart.

"It's not fair when someone takes credit for someone else's work," Remi continues. "It's like bullying. I guess I'm just disappointed it doesn't stop at high school."

I'm proud of him because he's a good person too. A deserving person. I need to figure out a way to escape John Parker—not just for me, not just for Gracie, but also for my nephew.

"You're right, Remi," I say. "But we're going to stop her."

If it ruins me, then at least I'll have taken a stand for what's right.

"Yes," Gracie says, placing a hand on my thigh. "*We* will."

"Anyone up for a round of Parcheesi?" my father says.

He seems surprised when we all agree, and we spend the rest of the afternoon playing Parcheesi together, three rounds.

"Nicole's going to be pissed that she missed this," Damien says, but he doesn't suggest calling her, and I don't invite him to.

I'm still salty about being accused of being a stripper, I guess.

We order pizza, and Remi tells us about his photography project for school. Apparently, Giorgio volunteered to help him.

After dinner, Damien takes off, my father takes up his usual evening position in his armchair, the TV blaring, and Remi leaves to go to the movies with a friend. Gracie demurs about going home, but I shake my head. "I need you to stay with me tonight."

"Oh, you need me to?" she asks, her lips lifting.

"Yes. Desperately. I like having you here."

"I like being here. You're not worried about Remi seeing me in the morning?" She gives her hair a slight tug. "I guess I can sneak out in the middle of the night."

"There will be no sneaking out," I say, capturing her hand and bringing it to my lips. I kiss her knuckles, then look up at her. "He's a teenager. We don't need to protect his innocence."

"My father..." she starts.

"Lives in Charlotte," I supply. "And the other guys in the office aren't coming over for tea. I don't like to mix my personal life with business."

She laughs at that, giving me a pointed look that says we're the ultimate mixture of business and pleasure and always have been.

"I never said I wasn't a hypocrite," I tell her, releasing her hand and cradling her face. "I think you like me that way."

"Against my better judgement, yes."

"Good. Make sure you keep your better judgment out of the picture, then."

"But what if—"

I stop her with a kiss because I know what she's thinking. I can see it in her eyes.

"Please don't say *what if it doesn't work out*," I say, pulling back. "I figure we've been there, done that. I'm going to move hell and earth to make this work, because I won't lose you again." My throat is suddenly dry. I want to tell her that I love her. That she's been with me all of these years, even though miles separated us. I want to tell her that she's it for me, but I can't get the words out. So instead, I pick her up the same way I did yesterday, and I carry her to my room and make love to her.

It's slow this time and sweet, and she lifts my hand up to cover her mouth as she moans my name.

It's maybe the best day of my life.

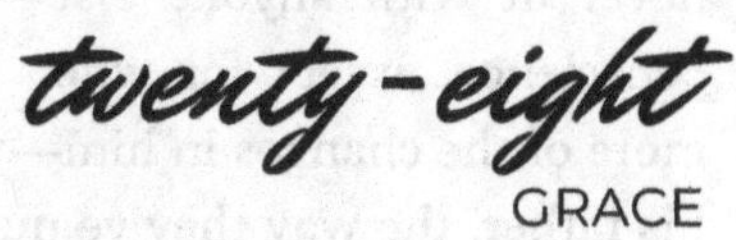

"DO you think he'll do it?" Vera asks me, practically dancing on her feet at the thought.

"You're asking me if I think Damien will agree to jump out of a cake at the ball?" I tilt my head. "Honestly, I don't know. Maybe? They'll need to make the cake bigger if there's going to be a six-foot-three man in it."

The plan was always to have someone jump out of the cake, but she's vacillated on who it should be—this Monday, she said it should be the singer we hired as entertainment, but the woman immediately objected. On Tuesday, she thought *she* should jump out of the cake. It didn't take her long to realize it was a bad idea, however, on account of her dress. On Wednesday, she suggested we hire an exotic dancer, and when I pointed out there would be reporters present, she suggested that one of *them* might want to do it. Now, we've moved on to Damien, and suddenly it can be no one but him.

It's Thursday, almost two weeks since Enoch came to my apartment soaked in rain. The ball is on Saturday.

"Will you ask?" she says. "I don't want there to be any awkwardness between us if he has to say no. You don't care about things like that, but I'm *very* sensitive. It's my artist's temperament."

"So you've told me," I mutter.

She gives me a sharp look. "What's gotten into you, Grace? You've been different lately."

I should hope so. I'm *happy*. Enoch and I fit together in a way I've never fit with anyone else—he's my cutting knife, and I'm his conscience...except for when it's the other way around. I've seen more of the changes in him—the way he's stepped up for Remi and his father, the way they've pulled sweetness out of him, even if it's reluctant. The way he is with Udolpho, even though he still insists he never wanted "that damn dog."

We've spent every night together, at his house or my apartment. My place is more private of course—we can ravage each other on every surface, and we have—but I love that he wants me to spend time with his family. It shows how much he's grown.

Enoch's still ambitious, of course—I see it in the plan he formed for Sinclair, in the daily update calls they have even though he's still working full-time for Vera and for other Parker clients. We often work together, him on his laptop, me on mine—writing.

Enoch's plan is *working*. A couple of weeks ago, people were talking about Sinclair, the washed-up starlet and maybe drug addict, and the brother and sister who are enabling her. Now they're talking about the hilarious videos Enoch has helped her make, which show her "drug bordello," aka the penthouse; her pushers, Marnie, Drew, and Griffin; and her addiction—to taking crafting classes and failing at them. She talked openly about her struggle to find passions in addition to acting. Part of the reason she's been hopping from one hobby to another is that she never got a chance to explore her interests when she was a kid. Her mother had started bringing her to auditions before she could walk. She also admitted to having a crush on Edgar James, and blushed so convincingly when she said it that I'm guessing it's at least half-true.

She was sensitive, funny. *Human.*

People love this side of her.

Better yet, Marnie reached out to Edgar James, and his team is very open to Enoch's idea about a fake romance. They're in the middle of making a deal for another reality TV show for him, and Sinclair's involvement might cinch it. She wouldn't be on the show, beyond a few guest appearances, but it would up the show's profile without relegating her to the reality-TV dungeon.

Enoch is brilliant at this...which is one of the only burrs in my happiness.

He *needs* his career. He's talented, ambitious, driven. I can't take that from him.

He says he's working on a plan to curb my dad, but as talented and smart as he is, I don't see how he can raise three hundred thousand dollars this quickly. He sold his apartment in Charlotte for a good price, but he'll need to pay off his mortgage after closing. It won't be enough. His retirement accounts are untouchable, tied to the contract.

It goes without saying that my father is losing patience. He told Enoch to bring in Sinclair Jones, and suddenly she's become marketable on her own.

When the news comes out about Edgar James, I'm certain he'll see Enoch's fingerprints on it. They're going to the ball together, which means the truth is going to come out *soon.*

If time were an hour glass, we'd be down to the last grains.

My father called me after he received his invitation to the ball, written out in calligraphy by Sinclair, who'd offered to help with the invitations after I complimented her signs.

I answered, because if I'm going to defy him and expose Vera, I need to at least be able to survive a conversation with him.

"I got your invitation in the mail," he'd said. "What's the meaning of this? We have a meeting that day."

We hadn't spoken in six years, although I can't say his "greeting" came as a surprise. In his mind, people exist only to serve him or be boosted by him, so they can in turn boost his reputation. If he had a different side when my mother was alive, I'll never know.

"Hi, Dad," I said. "It's a big celebration for Vera. I'm her assistant, and you run her brand management company. We should both be there. We can talk at the ball."

"I told you to meet me at the office."

"You did, but neither of us can miss this celebration."

I wonder if he's pissed that Vera isn't fulfilling her side of the agreement—free brand management in exchange for selling me out. Probably. At the same time, he's a logical man. I suspect he'd make the same call: get his assistant to make the arrangements for a big party before cutting her loose.

The last several days have been a whirlwind of ordering ice sculptures—one of a nude man, the other a nude woman; neither of them, thankfully, anyone I know—arranging for a horse-drawn carriage that will give guests joy rides to Duck Pond to show off the splendor of Vera's property, hiring half a dozen sketch artists to make drawings of everyone in their finery, and arranging for a couple of local restaurants to feed everyone a menu of delicacies inspired by Vera's books. That such a thing could be achieved in such a short period of time is proof, I suppose, that money may not be able to buy happiness, but it can certainly get you anything else you want.

To be honest, I've enjoyed making the preparations, despite the kernel of dread rooted in the back of my mind, telling me that I might be arranging a celebration that will end with me losing everything, from my boyfriend to my shoes to my dignity.

My book.

The guest list isn't enormous, as such things go, but there will be over a hundred people, which is a considerable number given we've had less than two weeks to prepare.

My father didn't know any of that, though. Nor would he have cared. "We'll meet on Sunday too," he insisted. "Just me and you."

Then he hung up without another word. "Your wish is my command," I said sarcastically to my cell phone, which had no real opinion on the matter.

I, on the other hand, have plenty of opinions.

I want to *give* Enoch the money to pay my dad off.

He'd be free to start his own business then, and even though my father could probably get him successfully blackballed in some ways, it wouldn't stick. Sinclair would hire him in a heartbeat, and I suspect Edgar James would too.

I know he'd never accept a handout. His pride would refuse the possibility. And while both Edgar and Sinclair would be willing to pay a retainer, I'll bet, there will be start-up costs for his business. It would never be enough.

I think I've figured out how to frame my idea, but I haven't brought it up yet. I need to, obviously, because I can practically feel those last grains of sand falling...

Pumpkin paws anxiously at my leg, reminding me that I haven't responded to Vera.

Maybe it's Stockholm Syndrome, but I'm going to miss the little dog.

Or maybe I just pity her—yesterday Vera had her own face shaved into Pumpkin's fur. I can already imagine the emails she's going to get from PETA.

"Not even listening to me," Vera says, clucking her tongue. I open my mouth to speak, but she gives a wave of her hand. "You're on your period, aren't you?"

"Yes," I say, trying to keep the bite out of my tone. "Yes, that's exactly it. I'm sorry I'm distracted."

She frowns at me. "Well, you should probably stay away from Pumpkin. You know she's very sensitive to the presence of hormonal women."

I lean down to pet Pumpkin. She nips my finger.

"It's your hormones," Vera says, then picks up Pumpkin and snuggles her into her cleavage. Pumpkin tries to bat her way free, leaving a welt, but Vera just clucks her tongue. "Naughty Grace. Let's get you somewhere safe."

She brings Pumpkin to the door, then sees her out, shutting it behind her.

"The design came out well, though, didn't it?" Vera asks me. "People are going to get such a kick out of seeing my face on her."

I could point out that no one needs to see her face on her dog, on account of she'll be there, but I know better.

I glance up at the enormous photo of Enoch and Damien she had mocked up for her office. "And that? Will you be displaying it to preview the new book?"

She gives it a contemplative look, her gaze lingering on Enoch's ass for longer than I'd like, and I feel my hands tightening into fists. "You know, I'm not sure that book will come out next, but it's not a bad idea. It'll be my first menage. This makes it even more important for Damien to jump out of the cake. See to it."

"Oh." I perk up, unable to help myself. "You might be publishing something else first?"

A couple more days, Gracie. Mind your Ps and Qs.

Her expression sharpens. "Maybe, Gracie. It's not like you to be so pushy. You go give Damien a call. I'll be *very* displeased if it doesn't work out."

A couple more days.

"What's so secretive about it?" I ask, unable to help myself. "You've never kept quiet about one of your books before."

"I've been writing this one for a long time," she tells me. "Since we first started working together. There's a lot you don't know about me."

It's said loftily, as if someone with my pea-brained intellect and lack of sparkle couldn't possibly understand her brilliant mind.

"Well, I can't wait to hear about it," I say with forced cheer. "Are you going to make an announcement at the ball?"

Her gaze turns shrewd, focused on some distant sight only she can see. "Maybe," she says softly. "Maybe I will." Turning back to me, she gives a big smile that doesn't fill the eyes Remi described as empty. "Now scram. Make sure they're making the vanilla-crème cake—you know it's the only one I like."

"I doubt anyone's going to eat it," I say, "if someone's jumping out of it."

"Vanille crème," she snaps.

I'm already dialing up Damien as I shut her office door behind me. "Vera wants you to jump out of a vanilla-crème cake at the ball."

"I prefer chocolate cake," he says, seeming unfussed about the whole cake-jumping thing. Then again, if I've learned anything about him and Nicole over the past few weeks, it's that they're up for anything—the more ludicrous, the better.

"She prefers vanilla crème."

"Sure," he says, "sounds fun. You and Enoch have to meet us this evening. We've found something."

"What?"

He and Nicole have been busy. They tracked down the assistant who worked for Vera when *The Wind in Her Hair* was published. She's now a cosmetologist. She told them Vera's a bitch, which tracks, but Vera stole her boyfriend, not her book.

The assistant before her, May Rollins, passed away in a car accident a few years ago.

"May's sister, Jenny," he says. "She's agreed to talk to us. Off the record. Says she signed an NDA with Vera."

"This is it," I say, my heart suddenly burning a hole through my chest. "This is it, huh?"

Part of me had foolishly hoped it wasn't true, if only because I know the pain of seeing someone else's name on my book...

I hate that Vera got away with it.

I won't let her do that again. Not to me. Not to anyone else.

"I think so," he says, "but if she won't go on the record, then it's not solid. We may still need to rely on Lover Boy's testimony."

Enoch has already said he'll back me, although I'm hoping we can avoid it. He needs more time to extricate himself from my father.

"When?" I ask, my voice shaky.

"Five thirty. I'll text you where to meet us. We'll drive to Jenny's place together."

"I'll tell Enoch."

The address comes through seconds after I hang up.

Enoch's probably at lunch with Sinclair, so I settle for texting him: *Meeting with Damien and Nicole and May's sister. 5:30. She signed an NDA with Vera, Enoch.*

When he doesn't answer, I call Vera's favorite bakery. I tell them they can name their price for increasing the size of the cake—and also remind them we'll be filming the "performance" for Vera's Instagram. They don't hesitate to agree. The price hike is absurd, but they'll be losing sleep over this, and Vera won't care.

I return to her office. She slams the lid of her laptop shut and glowers at me. "You came in without knocking again?"

I could point out that she's spent years telling me not to knock, but instead I tell her that the cake plans are a go. She accepts the price change without flinching. "And you've written down all of the plans in our Google Doc?"

"Yes," I say. "With the phone numbers."

She gives a slow nod, then points to the seating area in the corner of her office. "Come, Grace. Sit with me a minute."

My heart pounds faster in my chest.

"Okay," I say, acting cool and unaffected.

I've barely perched in the chair across from the red loveseat before she gets going. "You know, we've had some good times, Grace," she says, folding her hands in her lap. "This arrangement of ours has suited us well. God knows I've done everything I can to make it work because of how fond I am of you, but you've developed an attitude problem over the last several weeks, and it just won't do." She gives me a look that she probably thinks is sympathetic. "Maybe it's my fault for holding you back. You really are good at lending other people your shine, dear. Perhaps you can be an editor. Or an agent. Anyway, you'll figure it out. I've decided to let you go, Grace."

That's it?

That's all she's got for me?

Fire floods my veins and rages in my stomach, so much so I'm surprised smoke isn't issuing from my nose. I get to my feet in a single, fluid movement. This woman... I know what cake flavors she likes and doesn't, I know her dog's special diet, I know that she cried after being dumped by Paolo, a Brazilian model and the only man who's ever broken up with her. I know that she'd wanted to be a writer, or so she told me, ever since she first discovered gothic novels in the sixth grade. I know what her face looks like when she's peeved, hungry, unhappy, jubilant. And yet, she'd steal my book, the work of my heart, and then send me away like I'm no more to her than one of the models she's seduced with lies.

I should take it gracefully. I should tell her that it's okay, that she's right, that she's *always* right. I should keep up the ruse because we're so close I can taste it. But those flames of rage won't let me. "Fuck you, Vera," I say. "I know what you did."

"What?" she says, her hand reaching up to her necklace. One I bought for her for Christmas last year. "Grace, your language. You could take this with dignity."

More rage springs to life inside of me. "I know what you did," I seethe. "What you're trying to do. I saw the typewritten manuscript in your office. I'm not good enough, huh? I have no shine of my own. You must like it well enough if you want to call it yours."

Something closes down in her, the glimpse of vulnerability

papered over. "I don't have any idea what you're talking about. You're acting like, well, a *maniac*. I had hoped you'd be reasonable."

"You're trying to steal my book, Vera. At least admit it."

Emotion flashes through her eyes—fear, slivered through with regret, although maybe it's my own mind putting it there. Then she purses her lips, like I'm a troublesome child she's been tricked into babysitting. "If anyone's stolen anything around here, it's *you*, stealing from *me*. Don't think I didn't notice the missing Vera Wang pumps."

I showed her that Pumpkin had ruined one before I threw them both away. This is another attempt to gaslight me, to fool me into thinking I'm the one in the wrong.

"I realize it was a disappointment for you to discover that your book is unpublishable," she says tightly, "but you have no excuse to take your disappointment out on me. Why, I was too kind to say so, but the whole thing is a rip-off of *my* story. My top-secret story. Which means you've been looking through my things, haven't you?"

There it is. The accusation. The needles slide under my fingernails.

"Does my father know about what you're doing, Vera?" I ask.

I don't want to care, but for some reason I do. For some reason, it matters. I guess, for my mother's sake, I want to believe there's something redeemable about him, even though I know better.

"Your father?" she asks. "Why, I've never met him."

I'm not sure why I thought anything different would come out of this conversation.

It's just...I hoped that she'd be honest. That she would be a human being. That our relationship wasn't all fake and one-sided and there's a part of her that cares about me. Or cares enough to warn me away from the father who's hurt me. But there's one person Vera Valence cares about, and it's not me.

"You're lying. You're a good actress."

"This is most irregular," she adds, shaking her head sadly. "I'll give you an hour to gather your things."

An hour. Six years of my life, and she's giving me an hour.

Not that it matters.

There's so much of me in this place—the chaise lounge I picked out for Pumpkin, the carpet whose color complements the framed cover of *The Wind in Her Hair* that hangs behind her desk. The curtains I selected because she couldn't decide on a decorating scheme. But none of it is mine.

"Don't worry about it," I say. "I'm going."

I could insist on taking the typewritten manuscript with me, but I suspect she'd wrestle it out of my hands. She'd likely record the whole thing to make me look nuts.

So I turn around and leave.

"Grace?" she says from behind me.

I turn to look at her, thinking that maybe, at least, I'll get an apology. A *job well done, mostly. Sorry it ended like this. You* do *have your own shine.*

Something.

She lifts her chin. "Don't let the door hit you on the ass on your way out."

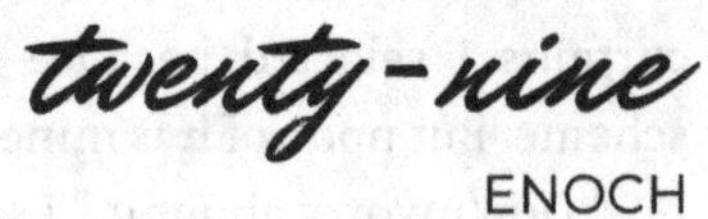

ENOCH

Me: *That's great, Gracie.*
Me: *I just had lunch with Sinclair, and it looks like everything's a go for the ball. Get this, Edgar James is going to ride up to the house on a fucking horse, and she'll be behind him in her ball gown.*
Me: *Who's going to tell her that her dress is going to smell like horse all night?*
Me: *Not it.*

Fifteen minutes later...

Me: *Why aren't you answering your phone? Is everything okay?*

A KNOCK LANDS on my office door.

"Yes?" I say, still looking down at my phone. It's probably my assistant, David, asking for permission to go to the restroom, which he does several times a day despite my having assured him that such requests are unnecessary.

The door opens, and something about the *way* it opens prompts me to look up.

It's not David.

John has Grace's eyes, but I've never seen them widen with wonder or joy. There are plenty of other expressions I've learned to recognize, however, like the one he's wearing now. He's about to ruin someone's day, and he's happy about it.

I'm pretty sure it's my day that's about to be ruined.

"John," I say, getting up. "I thought you weren't coming in until Saturday."

"Yes, there's been a change of plans," he says. He leaves the door open and takes a seat in one of the two chairs in front of my desk. If I were more naïve and knew him less, I'd think he left the door open because he doesn't plan on tearing me a new asshole. Knowing him, he left it open because he intends to do exactly that and wants everyone to witness it.

He's all about doling out lessons, John Parker.

"Oh?" I decide on impulse to stay standing. Might as well go down strong.

Damien's been looking into John for me, but he called me yesterday to tell me what I'd long suspected—John's an asshole, but he hasn't broken enough rules to bite him in the ass. He doesn't even have a single parking or speeding ticket.

So this is it.

I'm not ready. I sold my apartment in Charlotte, but the closing's not for another three weeks. The proceeds will help a lot, but I had a limited amount of equity sunk into it. It's not enough. Even if it were, I'd still need to make enough to pay the rent for our Asheville house. My dad's Social Security checks won't cover it. My sister offered me monthly payments to take Remi in, but I told her to go fuck herself, and I'm not about to go crawling back to ask her for favors.

If I can't pay my debts, my only recourse will be to declare bankruptcy, something that would be beyond a gut punch. All of this struggle, these years of striving...

Then there's the question of what comes next.

What self-respecting person would hire a brand manager who declared bankruptcy and can't take care of his own family? Even if I figure out a way to avoid bankruptcy, I'd still be asking them to take a chance on a man who's been stripped of everything, with no money or resources and a reputation that's in the shitter.

At least you'll have some self-respect, a voice whispers in my head. *At least you'll be your own man.*

And you'll have Gracie.

"You've been holding out on me, Enoch," John says, spreading out his legs and getting comfortable, telling me this is his room and I've only been borrowing it.

He probably wants me to step in, to babble and beg, to plead. I'm not going to give him the satisfaction. I look at him, keeping my expression blank.

"Sinclair Jones."

"I had lunch with her today," I say. "I think she'll bite."

"Are you fucking her, Enoch?" he asks. "Is that how this started? Did you throw everything away for a pretty face and a pair of fake tits?"

"The only thing I've slipped her is a sales pitch," I say flatly. Inside, I'm relieved. This means he doesn't know about me and Gracie. He probably thinks I care about her as little as he obviously does, a thought that makes me want to break him. Not his body, though. Physical violence isn't the way to curb a man like him. No, I'd like to strip away his top clients, one by one, until all that's left is the realization that he's lost the only thing he ever cared about, and he chose the wrong fucking thing.

I don't want to make that mistake. I won't.

"But not a sales pitch for Parker Brand Management, huh?" he asks.

"You'll have to be clearer, sir," I say. "I'm a little hard of understanding."

"I heard from Edgar James's team today. You can imagine my

confusion when they told me that the fake relationship with Sinclair Jones was a go."

Shit. Here I am, a victim of my own success.

I'd asked them to contact me directly, but I *did* give them my card. Rookie mistake. They probably tried me, didn't get through, and went straight to the top.

"Like I said, I've been working her."

"And Edgar James," he says, drumming his fingers on top of the desk. "Do you think I'm a fucking idiot, Enoch?"

"No," I say honestly. "I do not."

"You're acting like you do. Or maybe you're the idiot."

"That's a distinct possibility."

He wants me to grovel. I probably should. Not. Going. To. Happen.

"You did good work," he says, propping his ankle up on his knee and leaning back.

"I did," I agree.

"I told James's people that there was no agreement unless he signs with Parker Brand Management."

"And?"

He leans forward and speaks in a seething undertone, "What do you think they said, you little shit?"

My heart starts beating faster in my chest. "I abhor guessing games."

"They said they would only work directly with *you*, as you well know."

I didn't, actually, but their interactions have solely been with me, so I'm not altogether surprised to hear it. Gratified, though.

"And?" I say again.

"You're the best man I have, Enoch. But you're nothing to me if I can't trust you. I think I'll give your job to my daughter. You want to try landing clients like Sinclair and Edgar Jones while you hustle to pay off your debt, you be my guest. I'll enjoy watching you fail.

They'll come back to me, the way people always do, and they'll beg to be on my roster. You're done."

I want to ask him how much time I have before he throws those wheels into motion, but I don't want to give him the satisfaction. My face is blank, stoic, an empty slate.

"Needless to say, you've given me ample grounds to fire you. *You* have broken our contract, not me. I'm a generous man, though. I'll give you until Monday to pay your debt. After that, I'll sue you for breach of contract." Then he rises from his chair. "You have ten minutes to clean up your things. I've told Daniel to set a timer."

David is peering through the door from his position at his desk, his face drawn and his eyes frightened. "Sorry," he mouths.

I give him a slight nod.

"Okay," I tell John. "Is that it? It would seem I have some work to do."

He laughs then. It seems genuine, although who could tell. "Yes, you do. You know, I'm almost inclined to like you, Enoch. You remind me of myself as a young man. I'd wish you well if you weren't a thorn in my foot. Instead, I'm going to have to pluck you out and throw you away with the rest of the trash."

"Good talk," I say.

Then I grab my bag and phone. That's all that's mine. I never brought anything personal here, not a single photo or anything. *Personal effects can sway someone's impression of you,* John Parker told me once. *Don't give more away than you have to. Keep them guessing.*

Valuable advice, that.

"I'll see myself out."

"You'll be hearing from my lawyers."

"I look forward to it," I say, leaving my office. I salute David, then give a jaunty wave to the other two managers. "Good luck," I tell them. "You're going to need it."

And just like that, I'm unemployed and in the hole for three hundred thousand.

The condo won't help me. The buyer might be willing to move closing up, but surely not to *this weekend*.

Once I'm outside, I walk for a while—aimless, though I try not to look that way—then take out my phone to call the Realtor.

There's one message from Grace: *Can you come over? I need you.*

* * *

"I got fired," Gracie says the moment she opens the door for me.

Her eyes are red, like she's been crying.

The situation is so absurd, I have to laugh, even though we now have no reasonable excuse to crash the party where we were supposed to make our stand.

"Why are you laughing?" she asks, giving my arm a fake punch.

I loosen my tie and shut the door behind me. Taking off my jacket, I sling it over the back of the couch. "I'm laughing because I got fired too. What are the fucking odds?"

The anger drains from her face, and she looks at me with horror. "Enoch, what happened?"

"I knew I was playing with fire," I say, gripping the back of the couch with white knuckles. "I got burned. Edgar James's people got in touch with your dad directly. They said they'd only work with me, and he basically challenged me to try to get Edgar and Sinclair as clients once they find out I'm three hundred grand in the hole."

"The apartment?" she asks, her voice wavering.

"I just got off the phone with the real estate agent. The buyers won't move up closing."

"Enoch." She touches my hand, her fingers quivering. "You need—"

"I need *you*," I say, turning and pulling her to me. I kiss her hard, pouring myself into it, because I'm lost and it's only with her that I feel found.

She kisses me back with equal fervor, her soft little mouth

opening to me, her tongue moving with mine. Her hand moves up into my hair, bringing me closer, and I lift her and prop her up on the back of the couch. Her legs curl around me, and I'm so hard for her that I can almost forget what a fucking mess I've landed myself in. She reaches up and tugs the knot of my tie loose, then unwinds it and removes it from around my neck.

I pull back a little. "Are you asking for something, Gracie?"

"My hands," she says, "tie them up."

Maybe she wants me to do it because I'll have no call to wear suits anymore and she'll miss them. A dark part of me wonders if she's saying goodbye, though. I've become more of a liability than a help. I might as well be a great big red sign saying *Run*.

"You want me to tie you up and fuck you?" I ask, a little more brutal than I meant to be. She's the only sweetness I have, and part of me resents her for it.

"Yes, Enoch," she says, not looking away, her eyes boring into mine. Her legs tighten around me, rubbing her core against my hard dick. "I want you to tie me up and fuck me. I *need* you to."

My need for her, for this escape, is stronger than the dark feelings. I kiss her again, sucking down what she's offering—the sweet taste of her and the benediction of her touch. My tie is still gripped in her hand, her red nails a pop of color against it, and my cock gets a little harder, if possible, at the sight.

I ease back. She keeps her legs splayed open for me.

I go to the bathroom for a condom, grab two, and return to her. She got down from the couch and took her dress off. I watch as she reaches back for the clasp of her bra.

"No," I bark, feeling out of control—driven by desire and some other emotion I can't name. "Let me."

She drops her hand to the side and tips her head up. I set the condoms on top of the couch and reach for her. She kisses me as I reach back and unclasp her bra. I tug it off and throw it on the ground, then grab the tie, which she left slung over the back of the couch. She watches me, lips slightly parted, while I tie her wrists together behind her. She's so beautiful, I can hardly stand it.

"Aren't you going to get undressed?" she asks.

"Not yet."

I pull down her underwear, letting them drop to the floor, and reach down to touch her. She's so wet for me, a sigh escapes my lips.

Gripping her hands behind her back, I kiss her hard, working her clit with my other hand and then thrusting two fingers into her, curling them toward the spot that drives her wild. She kisses me back like she's just as hungry and desperate.

I can't wait anymore. I need to be inside her with a hunger I don't totally understand. "Turn around," I say, my voice gruff, almost a stranger's voice.

She does, and the sight of her like this, completely bare, her hands tied behind her back with my tie, while I'm still in my shirt and pants, undoes me. I unfasten my belt and pants, pushing them down, and put on a condom. I wrap an arm around her upper body as she leans into the couch, keeping her steady, and with my other hand I work her clit until she leans back into me. Then I grab the end of the tie and thrust into her.

"Enoch, oh my God," she says.

I thrust into her again and again, but I can't get at her clit at this angle. Not while I'm holding the tie. I don't want to let go of the fucking tie. So I pull out—even though my cock does not like any plan that doesn't involve riding this out instantly—and carry her to her room and lay her down on the bed.

"Put a couple of pillows under your stomach." I grab them from the top of the bed, piling them on top of each other, then set out another for her head.

"Take off your clothes," she says.

It's an order, and I don't question it. I unbutton my shirt and pull it off, then tug my pants the rest of the way off and pull off my shoes and socks. When I finish, she's waiting for me, her ass up in the air, her hands tied behind her back, her head resting on the pillow.

"You're so beautiful," I say.

"I'm yours."

I palm her ass and then reach around to touch her. She bucks against me, and I thrust into her as I take up the tie, pulling it taut. It feels incredible, but it's not enough. I need to be closer to her. I *need* her. So after a few thrusts, I pull out again and get onto the bed beside her. She rolls over toward me without saying anything, and I unfasten the tie and throw it to the floor. Tears well in her eyes, and panic steals over me as I wipe them away.

"Shit. Did I do something wrong, Gracie?"

"No, it's just, I didn't realize until right now...but this is how I need you too. Just like this."

It hits me like a slap in the face. I was angry, and I thought I wanted to fuck it out. She needed me to make love to her. I need it too. That's why it wasn't quite right even though it felt awesome.

I kiss her, and she reaches down to guide me home. We make love like that, facing each other on our sides, our mouths locked together, our hands wrapped around each other. And it's like that we finally fall apart—together.

After, we lie together for a long moment.

After, I run my hands through her hair, over her body, trying to soak her in.

Finally, I look at the clock on the wall. "It's almost time. We need to go meet Damien and Nicole."

She kisses me, then gets up. Goes to her drawers and tucks her body out of sight in a bra and underwear. A T-shirt. Jeans. Is it natural to be jealous of clothes?

I get up to. Pull on my underwear and pants. Buckle the belt.

"I have a plan," she tells me.

"I'm glad one of us does," I quip.

"Put on your shirt."

I lift my eyebrows. "So this is a *put on your shirt* kind of conversation? I'm not sure I'm going to like it."

"I'm not sure you are either," she says, doing one of those hair tugs.

I put on my shirt, and she leaves the room. When I come out, she has a glass of water for each of us set out on the table.

"Sit down," she says.

I do. My heart's pounding, and that foreboding feeling from earlier tells me this is it—she's not going to want me anymore now that I'm in the hole. I know better, but there's a part of me that still thinks affluence is the only way I can be a success.

She sits across from me.

"What is this, Gracie?" I ask.

"I have the money. I'm going to give it to you."

"*Gracie*," I start. "I can't take your money. This is... It would be hundreds of thousands of dollars. You've got to understand...I can't just..."

"It's not a gift, it's an investment," she says firmly. As she says this, she's every bit a Parker, her expression severe, almost as if she's daring me to say no. "An investment into your new business. *Laskin Brand Management.*"

My heart pounds like I've been running miles at the gym. "It would be a hell of an investment. When he gets through with me, I'll be vapor. No one will want to work with me."

"Not if you start out with two clients like Sinclair and Edgar."

"I don't think this is a good idea."

She swallows. "How about this? If you don't want to take an investment from me without my direct involvement, we'll run it together."

"Your writing..."

"I wrote my book while working full time." She gives me a Mona Lisa smile, half sad, half happy. "I can write another one the same way."

"That's not right," I say. "You'd be giving your dream up for mine."

"Like you did for me today?"

I get to my feet and pace a few steps, my head spinning. Pounding. Then I sit and pull my hair, urging the thoughts to settle.

Finally, I look up at her, taking in her countenance—no nonsense but with so much warmth behind it.

"I love you," I say.

Her eyes brighten for a split second, but then sorrow chases out the light. "Why do I sense a but?"

"Because you're highly intelligent. I can't let you do this for me."

"It's not just for you," she says, obviously frustrated. "It's for *us*."

"It's a lot of money."

"I *have* a lot of money."

Her words hammer into me. I knew her mother left her something. She'd told me as much six years ago. But she's acting like three hundred thousand would be a drop in the bucket. Part of me feels...lesser. When I was young, I spent so much time pretending to be someone I wasn't, learning to look rich. To act rich. To wear the confidence of someone who'd never had to eat mac and cheese several weeks in a row because his parents were both temporarily out of work. *You can manifest whatever you want to be*, my mother had always told me, and for some godforsaken reason I'd believed her, even though it clearly hadn't worked *for* her.

And now Gracie's telling me this doesn't have to be hard, that all I have to do is let her step in and take care of me.

Even though it wasn't her fault or her choice to inherit her mother's money—however much of it there is—I can't help but quail from the idea of the money. From money that didn't come from my work or hers or probably even her mother's. *Family money*, people would call it.

Everything in me squirms from the idea of accepting her offer, even if she's framing it as a loan and not a handout.

Then there's the possibility that I might take this security blanket from her and lose it. Three hundred thousand fucking dollars might not break her bank, but it will never feel inconsequential to me. If I take her money and fail to make something out of it, that'll be it for us, because even if she could forgive me, I'd never be able to forgive myself. I'd always be the losing bet, the poser.

"I'm not accepting a handout, Gracie. Even from you. Whatever you want to call it, that's what it is."

She gets to her feet, her eyes suddenly alight with anger. "You just told me you love me, Enoch. I love you too. I have the power to help you. Are you going to take that power away from me? Why? Because of stubborn pride?"

My head is a mess, and I can't process all of this. Not even the warm burn of hearing the woman I love tell me that she feels the same way. "Maybe I'll accept a loan until the closing for the loft."

There, a compromise.

"We both know that won't be enough for you to cover the whole sum you owe my father," she says, meeting my gaze and holding it. "And even if it did, it wouldn't cover start-up costs. Let's do this. Together."

"It's not that easy," I tell her.

"But it is," she says. "It really is. Don't let him destroy you, or us, again. Don't do that. *Please*."

"You don't understand."

"No," she says, her tone soft but forceful. "Why don't you break it down for me?"

"I told you I didn't grow up with money. This is a big deal for me." I'm half-pissed at her for pushing me, half-pissed at myself for not giving in. Do I really have a choice? I don't want to leave Gracie or lose my career. She's giving me a way to have everything I want, only...

"You'd feel like less of a man if you take money from your

woman?" She's taunting almost, as if we're back in the thick of thinking we hate each other.

"Damn it, *yes.*"

"I'm not going to watch my father ruin you when I can help you. I can't stand by and do that. I won't."

An alarm goes off on her phone, and she glances up at me. "I need to go meet Nicole and Damien."

"*You* need to?" I ask, feeling the words like a gut punch.

"Take some time to think about this, Enoch," she says, the anger leaking out of her. She sounds sad now. Vulnerable. Like she was opening herself to me and asking me to do the same, and instead I turned away. Shit. That's not what I wanted.

"Okay," I say, my voice cracking a little. "I love you, Gracie."

"I love you too," she says. Coming to me. Kissing me.

But I hear the message behind her words: *sometimes love isn't enough.*

thirty

GRACE

"YOU WHAT?"

"Yeah, you heard me right," Nicole says. "I'm Vera's new assistant."

"But…"

"You'll be amazed what a fake resume can do for a girl. I'm also pretty sure she wants to bone my husband like she did to poor…" She snaps her fingers. "What was the name of that woman who worked for her after May? Anyway, we can get you and Enoch inside for the ball. No problem."

It's a beautiful solution to a problem that was weighing on me, but I can't appreciate it as much as I should. It still feels like a black hole has been ripped into my chest. Enoch left my apartment before I did, promising he'd think about it, but I could tell he'd already built a brick wall against the suggestion.

"That's good," I say. We're standing outside the address that Damien sent me. It's an arts-and-crafts house, two stories, painted a bright turquoise with a red pop of a door. Is this their house? I can't deny I'm curious. On another day, I'd think of an excuse to go inside. Today, I can't think beyond my problem with Enoch.

"Where's Enoch?" Damien asks, which rips the hole in my chest wider.

"He's not going to make it." I clear my throat, then tell them the quick version of what happened today. Mainly, that I wasn't the only one who got fired and Enoch has refused my offer to invest in his business, including my counter offer of working on it *with* him.

"I'll talk to him," Damien offers at once.

Nicole gives him a look. "Shouldn't I talk to him? *You're* the rich one. You're the Grace in this situation. Surely he'd want to talk to the scrappy underdog."

He lifts his eyebrows. "And you're also the one who destroyed his favorite suits."

She pushes her lips out. "I guess I see your point."

He pulls his phone and types off a text message.

"Ready to go?" Nicole asks me. "We figured it would be better for us to go there together. United front."

Damien's phone beeps, and he frowns down at the screen.

"Go on," he tells us. "I'm going to meet Enoch at the bar."

Nicole makes a face at him, then turns to me. "So, it'll be a smaller united front. Who knows, maybe Jade has a thing for girl power."

"I think her name is Jenny."

"Good talk. Can you drive?"

That's how I wind up on a mini road trip with Nicole...because she'd neglected to mention that Jenny lives forty-five minutes away.

"You don't need to worry about Lover Boy," she says, popping a pretzel from a snack bag in her purse. My stomach growls loudly, reminding me that I skipped lunch.

"Want some?" She pulls out the bag and hands it to me. "I take them from the bar."

Of course she does. Then again, she and Damien invested in the bar, like I want to invest in Enoch's business. I guess it's her right to take some pretzels.

I take one and eat it, mostly to be polite, but then I realize how famished I am and keep popping them into my mouth.

When I hand back the mostly empty bag, I say, "Why? Why don't I need to worry?"

"First," she says, ticking off a finger, "he's crazy about you. I recognized that even before we stopped seeing him as public enemy number one. Second, Damien has a way of convincing people to see sense. It usually involves copious amounts of alcohol. So Enoch's in good hands."

"I don't find that comforting," I mumble.

She shrugs and turns on the radio. "I tried."

She spends the rest of the ride singing along, off-pitch, while I think about Enoch and the money and my father, and by the time I park on the curb outside of Jenny's house, my nerves have been rubbed raw.

It's a tidy green bungalow with new windows and a sculpted garden out front.

"What's our strategy?" I ask, regretting that I hadn't asked twenty minutes ago, during her third rendition of "You're the One That I Want."

"We get her to talk," she says, leaving the car and approaching the house with the confidence of someone who has an actual plan.

Without any other real options, I follow her.

Jenny opens the door before we knock, which suggests she might be as nervous about this meeting as I am. She has dark hair, almost black, and pretty dark eyes. She looks up and down the street, like she's worried Vera might have followed us, then gestures for us to come inside.

Once we step over the threshold, we make introductions. Or, rather, I do, and Nicole peers intrusively into the house.

"Where's Damien?" Jenny asks softly. "He's the one I spoke with on the phone."

"He's getting her boyfriend drunk," Nicole says, waving at me. "Couldn't be avoided. This is what they call the ole bait and switch."

Jenny's obviously taken aback by this, but she waves us into the sitting room instead of pushing us out into the growing dark. "Sit, please."

We lower onto the fat, leather-stuffed couch, and she sits in the chair across from us, whose cushion is decorated with a Regency man and woman. It's a nice touch, and I can't help but wonder if May, her sister who loved romance, might have bought it. The thought carries a pang of regret. *The Wind in Her Hair* is the book that inspired me to write, and if May really wrote it, or most of it, then I'll never meet the person who created it.

"Did you know a major producer wants to make a movie out of *The Wind in Her Hair?*" Nicole says with no preliminaries. "Vera won't meet with him. I'm guessing that's because she'd have to *share.*"

Jenny lifts her fingers to her lips. "A movie?"

"A movie," Nicole confirms. She waves to the TV. "Wouldn't May have liked to see her story on the screen?"

"May hated movies."

"Did she like money?" Nicole asks.

I frown at her, then turn to Jenny. "Was it really May's story?"

"I told Damien," Jenny says, playing with the arm of the chair. "I can only talk to you off the record."

I nod. "Off the record. Was it May's story?"

Jenny's lips press together. "Yes. Vera 'helped' May write it. You can see how that ended."

Something pinches inside of me. "She stole my book too, Jenny. Or she's trying."

"Then I'm sorry I can't do more to help you," she says. "I hate Vera Valence, but the money I get from her pays my mortgage."

"How much more would you get if you got the full royalties?" Nicole asks, lifting her eyebrows. "No offense, Jenny—this house is nice enough, but it's a real dump compared with Vera Valence's mansion. She's got color-themed bathrooms. I shit you not, her dog has a bedroom. Don't you want to be rich enough that you can give a dog a damn bedroom?"

"I don't have a dog," Jenny says, but I can tell Nicole's getting through to her.

"Better yet," Nicole says. "You can give a bedroom to a fictional dog. A stuffed animal! Who doesn't want to be that kind of rich?"

"You might be leaning in too hard on the whole dog thing," I whisper.

Jenny's fingers are pressed to her throat now. "I signed an NDA," she says. "May signed a settlement. She didn't feel she had a choice. The book that was published was different from the one she'd written." She pauses. "I'll never get the full royalties."

"What about the film rights?" Nicole asks, giving her a wicked smile. "I'm guessing there's a reason Vera didn't want those studio bucks. You know...you don't need to go on the record about anything. All you need to do is show us her agreement with your sister. Or the NDA! I'd settle for the NDA." She winks. "No one needs to know how we found it."

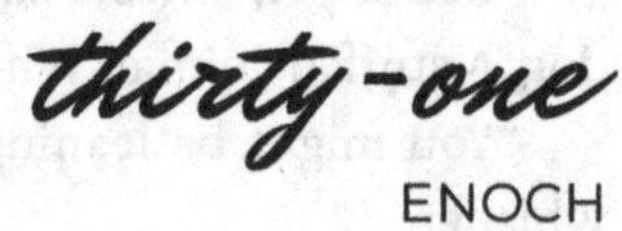

"WOULD you give her the money if you had it?" Damien asks me.

We're at Summer Nights—the first place I saw Gracie again after being separated from her for six years. It feels strangely appropriate to be here tonight.

I take a slug of my bourbon. "Of course."

"Damn sexist of you not to want to take a woman's money," says an old timer, sitting around the corner from us. It's obvious he's been hanging on our every last word. He has a white beard and a red sweater, like he's a Christmas Santa who forgot it's March.

"It's not sexist," I say tightly, but Damien's giving me a wry look, and fuck, *is it* sexist?

If I had the money, I'd invest it in Gracie, no question. "I'd do anything for her."

Damien's eyebrows shoot farther up. "This is what she's asking you to do."

"It's a handout," I say. "Don't you see that? I can't take a handout. We've never taken handouts." My mother was insistent on it.

"My grandmother left me money," Damien says contemplatively. "A lot of it. Nicole likes to take on these little pet projects—"

"Like tormenting me?"

"Like helping Gracie regain control of her life. You're"—he shrugs—"collateral damage."

"Thanks."

"Worked out okay for you, didn't it?" he asks, lifting out his drink.

I must be going crazy, because I clink my glass against his.

"Like I was saying," he continues. "She likes to take on these pet projects. They don't bring in any money. It's something we can afford to do because my grandmother took care of us. Did we do anything to deserve it? Nothing, other than be kind to someone we loved."

"You're saying it doesn't matter if I'm a bad investment."

"I'm saying she doesn't care," he corrects. "She doesn't want to see you ruined. Would you love her if she were the kind of person who'd watch you and your father and your nephew get thrown out on the street when she could prevent it?"

"No," I say thickly, "I guess not. But that's not going to happen. I have a contingency plan."

"Do you?" he asks doubtfully.

"Half of one. I wasn't ready for John to act this soon."

"Even if you raised the money, would you have enough resources to start up your own business?"

We both know the answer, so I don't bother to give it to him.

"Did it ever occur to you that she might see your business as a sound investment? That she believes in you?"

I grip the side of the bar. "She offered to work with me if I wasn't comfortable taking the money as an investment. I'm not going to let her give up her dream for mine."

"She wouldn't have to if you'd take the goddamn loan."

I look down, uncomfortable with how logical he's sounding.

"You know, let's be honest here," Damien continues. "She may feel at fault since John's her father, but it's your own shitty decision-making that's landed you in this bind."

A corner of my mouth hitches up. "You try making a deal with the devil."

"I have," he says with a laugh. "My father's a real peach too, so I feel for Grace. Nicole's the one who helped me break his hold on me."

"Oh?"

Santa Claus edges closer. Damien doesn't seem terribly troubled by his presence, so I don't comment on it.

"Yeah. He managed to get legal and medical control over my grandmother. Wouldn't let me see her unless I playacted the part of the obedient son. Nicole helped me get my grandmother out. My point is that everyone needs help, Enoch, and if you're prepared to give it, you also need to be prepared to receive it."

"That Nicole sure is something," Santa Claus says with a grin. "She could sell oil to a snake."

"I think you got that one wrong, bud," Damien says, slinging back his drink.

I narrow my gaze at the bearded stranger. "Your voice is familiar."

His face lights up, and he snaps his fingers and points at me. "Dana's father's best friend," he says. "One of my best performances."

"You cried," I say, flummoxed. I knew all of "Dana's" references were probably fake, but his was easily the most convincing.

"When life's been nothing but a constant disappointment, friend, it's easy to summon a few crocodile tears." He winks, but fuck, it's a depressing sentiment. Is this what I'll become if I refuse Gracie's help? A mainstay at a bar, with no friends but the ones alcohol has bought me? Maybe it's an unfair sentiment—I know literally nothing about this man—but that's where my mind brings me.

Someone sits down beside me, on the other side from Damien,

and I turn to see Marnie. Her cheeks are flushed, and she seems winded. She also looks upset.

"You okay?" I ask.

"What did you do?" she says, her tone accusatory, as she leans her elbows on the bar.

"You'll need to be more specific."

"You're supposed to be with Gracie, but you're here. What did you do?"

I rub my chest. "We had a disagreement." I pause, then add, "We both got fired today."

"But Nicole got hired as Vera's new assistant," Damien interjects, "so all is right in the world."

Marnie's eyebrows wing up. "Shit. Did you get fired because of Clair?"

I give a slight shrug. "Edgar James's people, but it was my own fault. I knew I was crossing a line. Several, actually."

"They called her this afternoon, you know. The ball is a trial run to see if people think they have enough chemistry to buy the relationship."

"They will," I say, running a finger over the rim of my glass. "Your sister likes him. He seems to be more fond of dirt than people, but no one's going to question whether he's interested in her. She's got stage presence."

"They'd both work with you, you know," she says, her gaze beating into me. "If you went out on your own."

"There's a money issue."

"That's what you're fighting with Gracie about," she says. I guess it's not that much of a leap, but I'm still thrown by it.

I shrug, trying to make it look casual. "I was raised not to take handouts."

"You're being a stubborn ass."

"Yes, that seems to be the consensus."

"*And* sexist."

"That's what I said," offers the bearded guy—Reggie, if he used his real name on the reference sheet. He lifts his glass. There's less than an inch of beer left. Marnie doesn't have a drink yet, but she mimes clinking a glass with him.

Griffin moves in, leaning across the bar to kiss Marnie. "Hey, Padawan," he says. I guess they're into *Star Wars*. Then his brow wrinkles. "What's wrong? You have that worried look."

"It's Sinclair," she says. She takes his hand but shifts her gaze to me. "All of this is working, so thank you for that. You're kind of an evil genius at marketing, but you were right about the other thing too. People know where she is now. I'm worried about her. There was... I was over at her apartment just now, and a bouquet of two dozen red roses got delivered to her. From a secret admirer, it says. She doesn't seem that concerned—I guess it happens a lot—but the note wigged me out."

"Can I get a refill over here?" Reggie asks, pushing his chair closer.

Griffin grabs his glass absently and refills it as he listens.

"What'd it say?" I ask.

"*Seeing you is the highlight of my day*. I mean, maybe he meant online, but it made it sound like someone's watching her. I don't like it."

Neither do I. I've seen these situations before, and they can escalate quickly. Caution is the name of the game.

"You might want to make a move on getting that bodyguard," I say, turning my glass around while I think. "Someone local would be best. It's more of a show of strength than anything else—you'll want someone who's built. Tough."

"I've got just the person for you," Reggie says.

"Are you talking about yourself?" I ask. I must be tipsier than I thought because I start laughing and struggle to stop. It's almost a brilliant idea, if only for the photo opps of Sinclair with a menacing Santa.

"No," he says. "But I could stop a stalker. Brute strength isn't the only thing that can take a man to his knees. I could disarm someone with a pen."

Griffin has an amused look on his face that suggests these over-the-top assertions aren't unusual for Reggie and shouldn't be taken at face value.

"How…" I start, wanting to know anyway, then wave the question away. "Never mind. If you weren't talking about yourself, then who?"

"My son, Rafe. He just lost his job at the gym."

"Why'd he lose his job?" I ask at the same time as Damien asks, "You have a *son*, and this is the first you're mentioning it?"

I imagine it takes a lot to surprise Damien, but Santa Claus has managed it.

"I guess the subject never came up," Reggie says, cackling. "His mother doesn't like me much."

I'm tempted to say, *I wonder why*. Instead, I repeat my question.

"He got into an altercation with a client."

I shoot Marnie a look, which she can hopefully interpret as, *Don't let your sister hire this fucking guy.*

"*Why* did he get into an altercation with a client?" Griffin asks as he passes over the beer. So he's not for tarring and feathering the guy before he gets an explanation. Fair enough.

"The man was being inappropriate with one of the female trainers."

"In what way?" I say.

"He wanted to bench-press her. She said no. He grabbed her anyway. Rafe punched him."

"When can we meet him?" Marnie asks.

"I don't know," I say. "This guy recommended Nicole's housekeeping skills. Do we really trust his judgment?"

Reggie lifts a finger. "I said *Dana* takes care of people." The finger starts moving back and forth like a windshield wiper. "I stand by that."

"I have three suits that beg to differ."

"People are worth more than suits," he says.

It's one of those innocuous statements that doesn't mean much on its own but has more weight because of when it's delivered. I nod slowly, then turn to Marnie. "Is your sister open to hiring a bodyguard?"

"She can be persuaded. I'm not going to let her get hurt."

The look she's giving me conveys that Sinclair isn't the only one she'll protect. If I mess up with Gracie, an army of avenging angels will come after me. Marnie might be surprised to hear it, but I'm comforted by the thought.

"How about you?" Damien asks me, giving my arm a nudge. "Can you be persuaded to see the light?"

I swallow. Consider it. Then I say the only thing I'm honestly sure of right now: "I can't lose her again."

"And her book?" Damien says.

"I won't let anyone take it from her."

"Good," he says, rubbing a hand over his chin. "Then this is what we'll do."

"I'm listening."

"We're going to give them a show the likes of which they'll never forget. Marnie, call Sinclair and Edgar James. We need them in on this too."

thirty-two
GRACE

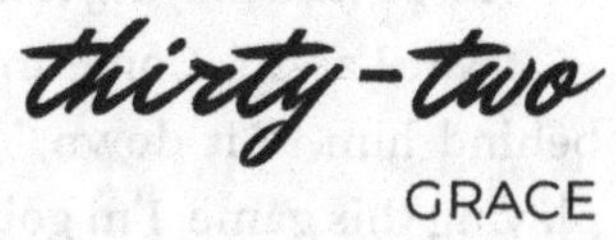

Meeting request from Enoch Laskin. Time: 3:00 p.m., tomorrow. Location: your loft.
Accept?

Me: *What's this about, Enoch?*
Enoch: *It's my understanding that you're supposed to prepare for a meeting with an investor. I was buying some time for myself to do that. But we can move the meeting up if you'd like.*
Me: *Do you mean it?*
Enoch: *It would be in poor taste to use sarcasm in this situation.*

Meeting request accepted.

Enoch: *Let the negotiations begin.*

MY HEART RACES when he knocks on my door. The whole morning has passed impossibly slowly, as if each minute were stretched into an hour. Nothing would make it pass faster, not reading or writing or researching sex acts. Because it feels like my whole future—*our* future—hangs on this meeting.

I swing the door open for him.

He's wearing a suit, of course.

Pin stripes with that green tie that matches his eyes.

I want to pull him in by it and slam the door. I want to lock it.

But he meets my eyes with a playful look and says, "Good afternoon, Ms. Donnelly. Thank you for agreeing to this meeting."

Ah, so he's playing it like that. Anticipation shivers through me.

"Mr. Laskin. Come in." I wave him forward and shut the door behind him. "Sit down," I say, directing him to the table. If we're playing this game, I'm going to play it right.

"Thank you, I will," he says. He lowers into his seat, and I lower into mine, my gaze arrested on him. I want to ask him what happened last night. I want to tell him about Jenny, but first I'm going to let him make his case. Because I know him well enough to know he really did spend the morning preparing for this.

"I'd like to start my presentation by admitting to a character defect, because you should be aware of it if we're going to do business together."

I nod. "Do go on."

His lips twitch slightly. "I'm a stubborn bastard. It can really get in the way of progress sometimes. I have ideas, and I can get locked into them. Sometimes I struggle to shift gears."

"That *is* a flaw," I say. "Especially since I sometimes have trouble standing up for myself and my needs."

"Not with me," he says, his lips tilting up farther.

"Never with you."

"What's one of your preconceived notions?"

He reaches up and undoes his tie, takes it off and hangs it over the back of his chair. Then shrugs out of his jacket. "That I can only feel powerful wearing armor."

"You don't want it for this meeting?" I ask, feeling a tickling of butterflies inside me, like that black hole I felt in my chest hatched them. Everything in me is a great yearning, a tender hope.

"I don't want it around you." He meets my gaze and holds it. "I want you to see me for everything I am, Gracie. I want you to know me for my flaws."

"And your strengths," I insist.

"There are plenty of those for you to consider too," he says, his eyes dancing.

I can't help smiling. "I'm glad I don't need to get used to you having a completely different personality."

"I love you," he says, and the ache of happiness and fear in my chest is hard to breathe through. "I want to make a life with you. I'm sorry if I made you feel differently yesterday."

Tears well in my eyes, but I don't get up and go to him. Not yet. I want him to say whatever he has on his chest.

"If you want to invest in me...if you believe in me enough that you'd do that...I'm the happiest man alive, and I'd be a fool not to accept." He gives a wry smile. "I may prefer to see myself as Prince Charming, swooping down from my horse to save Cinderella, but maybe we can both accept that I'm the scullery maid in this situation." He pauses. "But I don't want you to give up your writing, or your dream, to work with me."

"I won't," I say through a choked throat. "But I do want to help you get started. I want to play a part."

"Ever since I met you," he says, reaching across the table to trace a finger over my hand, "ever since that first day when we shared a class, you've played a part. I didn't know you at first, but I still noticed you. You took up space in my mind. You always have. You always will."

"Oh, Enoch," I say on a gasp. Because those fragile hopes are blooming, and the blossoms are more fantastic than any I've ever seen.

"Maybe someday I'll be able to return the favor. Maybe I'll become a man who's worthy of you. I hope so. But while we're waiting—and it may be a while..." He reaches into his pocket and pulls out a box, passing it to me over the table. "I hope you'll do me the honor of marrying me."

"Enoch, you don't have to..." I begin, those tears starting to fall. "You don't need to do this to take the investment. It—"

He gets to his feet, a storm of emotion on his face, and comes to me. I get up too, and he lifts his hand to my cheeks, tracing my tears. "I don't want to be the man who makes you cry. I want to be the man who makes you moan with pleasure. I want to be the man who fills your heart with happiness. And I need you to know I don't care about the money. I'll accept the investment because you want me to. Because you believe in me, and your belief in me is the best thing that's ever happened to me. But I'm asking you to be my wife because it's what I want most in the world, and I need you to know that going into tomorrow. I need you to know that if I could choose anyone in the world it would be you...and that I'm not going to let anyone fuck with you. Vera. Your father. *Anyone.*"

My heart is so full, I can hardly bear it. More tears track down my cheeks as I lift my trembling hand to his cheek. "Yes...*yes*. I choose you too. I choose us."

He kisses me, the kiss wet from my tears, and somehow it's perfect. It's us. It takes a long moment for him to pull away, and when he does, he says, "You haven't looked at the ring yet." His smile is sly. "You might change your mind."

I open the box and laugh. It's a rose-shaped silver ring Sinclair made in her metal-smithing class.

"She donated it to us," he says, putting an arm around my back. "It's a placeholder. As soon as I can, I'm going to get you such a big fucking rock it's going to hurt your hand to hold it up."

"Let's avoid causing me physical pain."

His smile is radiant. "Well, we can negotiate. Speaking of which, I thought we might make things interesting for our negotiation for the investment?"

"Oh yeah?" I say, pulling him closer. "What were you thinking?"

"One piece of clothing for each point of the contract."

"We're not wearing enough." I laugh and lift up to press a kiss to his mouth.

"That's the whole point."

thirty-three

GRACE

"YOU LOOK LIKE A GODDESS," Andy says. "Are you sure you want to marry this guy? You could totally bag someone else."

"Very funny," I say, but I'm glowing inside. The past twenty-four hours have been a dream come true—I can only hope this evening doesn't slip into a nightmare. There are plenty of things that could go wrong. Enoch and I will be trespassing, for one. For another, it's possible Vera could sue us for libel and our "proof" won't be accepted, or that my father—the master of spin—will figure out a way to refute it. The fact that my book is about my shared history with Enoch should help, but she's had a couple of days now to plan her own attack.

Andy nudges me with her shoulder. "I'm happy for you. You have that sex-love glow going on." She flinches. "Wait a second. You've had sex on every surface in this apartment, haven't you?"

"I plead the fifth," I say, "but I'm a stress cleaner, so you don't have anything to worry about."

"I'm happy for you too," Marnie says. Then she glances at my left hand and grimaces. "Although I'm glad Sinclair didn't stick with the metalsmithing. She doesn't have much of an eye for it, huh?"

We're waiting in my apartment for my pumpkin to arrive—or so

Marnie says. It's a town car, ordered by Nicole for Michelle Mountainbottom. It's a ridiculous fake name, based on the equally ridiculous name Marnie picked for a fake boyfriend before Griffin slid into that role.

With a dark brown wig from Nicole, Andy's makeup skills, contact lenses, and a ball gown, I'm pretty sure I'll be allowed into the party. Better yet, Nicole's arranged it so Sinclair and Edgar will arrive directly before me. On horseback. Vera will be so busy fawning over them, she'll completely miss my arrival.

Or at least that's the plan.

"Hey," Marnie says. "Presuming all goes well, who are you going to pick for Nicole and Damien to help next?"

The bell rings—the vibration loud enough that I can feel it in my body. "I have some ideas about that," I tell her, "but we can talk about it later. It's time."

"Don't mind us," Andy says. "We're just going to stay here, stress-eat your food, and watch the livestream on the TV."

On a suggestion from Enoch, which I backed, the whole event will be livestreamed on Vera's Instagram account. One of Nicole's friends was hired to do the filming. If all goes well, everyone will learn the truth about Vera Valence.

"Have fun," I tell them.

"After-party at the bar?" Marnie says. "Griffin feels left out." She shrugs. "Reggie too. He seemed very invested in all of this the other night."

"Of course."

I grab my clutch and head down the stairs. To an outsider, I might look like a princess, dolled up in a blue satin dress that I *adore*, with a clutch and heels studded with crystals, but I feel like a badass. Strong. Capable. More than equal to the task before me.

Enoch will be arriving separately, with Damien in charge of sneaking him in.

There's a uniformed man waiting for me at the foot of the stairs leading up to my building. "Michelle..." He clears his throat. "Mountainbottom?"

"Yep, that's me," I say.

He opens the back door of the car parked at the curb, and I climb in.

"Interesting name, that," he says as he starts driving.

"Thank you," I say, although no one would be naïve enough to see it as a compliment. He fills the rest of the drive with conversation about Vera's house, which we agree is huge, the speed with which this event was planned—*you're telling me*, and the stories he's heard about Vera.

None of them are good.

I hold my breath when we reach the gate, but the guard barely glances inside before waving us through.

Sure enough, there's a horse in front of us, a woman in a breathtaking ball gown on the back. Her train is flying behind her, over the horse's tail.

"Well, I'll be," the driver says with a whistle. "She know that dress is going to end up smelling like horse?"

"I don't know," I say, "but maybe it's worth it. She looks beautiful."

I feel my heart swell, my inner romantic swooning at the sight of them—Edgar so strong and severe, and Sinclair so softly beautiful, like a fairy-tale princess awakened by a kiss. Maybe, now that my first story has come to a close, a second one is tugging at me. On impulse, I grab my camera and start filming them, figuring I can pass the video along to Sinclair or Enoch later.

If tonight's a trial run for them, it's a hell of a trial.

Then the horse starts expelling waste, great hunks of it falling to the ground at its feet as it moves, and I lift a hand to my mouth in alarm.

Her *dress*.

The driver laughs good-naturedly as we both watch Sinclair

turn and yank it up—too late, judging by the expression of abject horror on her face. It's dark, but I ordered little lanterns to be strung up along the path to add to the magical experience of arriving.

Something tells me the experience will now be less magical. My camera is still focused on Sinclair and Edgar, my mouth slightly open.

"Could have seen that coming from a mile away," the driver says with a chuckle. "Good for Instagram, bad for li— Whoa!"

Edgar James just leaned back with a pocket knife that he must've had concealed on his person and cut off the offending piece of the gown, tossing it to the side of the path.

"Okay, gotta give it to him," he says. "That was pretty smooth."

I turn off the recording, feeling a swell of satisfaction. This will be good for all of them—Enoch, Sinclair, Edgar. It's a lucky break, and I'm just superstitious enough to hope it means I'm about to get another one.

The horse comes to a stop in front of the mansion, and the valet, who reaches up to help Edgar, is ignored. He gets down as easily as descending from a truck, then reaches up and sweeps Sinclair down in her dress, which is a little messed up from the knife but at least not covered in horse excrement.

"God, they look good together," I mutter.

"She'd look good with anyone," the driver responds.

The valet takes the reins Edgar handed him, eyes them dubiously, then walks off. Someone should have probably warned him about the whole horse scheme.

Vera sweeps out of the house in her gold lamé dress, ordered especially for this event, and fawns over the two of them. I bite my lip as another figure emerges behind her. My father. A third person follows them out, carrying a cell phone on a stick. I can only assume this is the "videographer."

I duck down in the back of the car.

My father texted me yesterday, in the middle of my very lengthy "negotiation" session with Enoch.

Him: *Vera tells me she had to let you go.*
Him: *I'm assuming our Sunday meeting will suit?*

I didn't respond. It occurs to me now that he probably told her to move up her *let's fire Grace* plan as punishment for putting off our meeting.

What a dick.

"Miss, are you okay?" the driver asks.

Someone opens the back door, and I gasp before recognizing Nicole. She's wearing a golden dress that would probably have gotten her fired if she were really working for Vera—Vera does not take kindly to other people wearing the same color as her, and for an assistant to do so is more than a fireable offense. In fact, she'd probably put Nicole in front of a firing squad if she could.

"Keep driving," Nicole says.

"Who are you?" the driver asks. His eyes go wide. "Am I being held up?"

"Shit, is everyone in this place melodramatic?" She rolls her eyes. "My friend here needs to use the back entrance. She's someone *important*." She puts plenty of inflection on that word, suggesting I'm the kind of person who could make trouble if my whims aren't catered to.

"Won't it look funny if the car goes by without anyone getting out?" I ask in an undertone.

"Not to knock Andy's makeup skills or my wig, but I'm pretty sure your own father would recognize you if you got out in front of him."

"Keep driving, please," I tell the driver, raising my voice.

"I *knew* Michelle Mountainbottom was a made-up name."

"Yes, you caught me," I say. "Can you please go around back?"

He keeps glancing in the rearview mirror, probably trying to place me and failing, but he does as requested, circling around to the back entrance. There are a couple of people milling about in the back—I had those lanterns hung up across the property, and this is going to be the meeting point later for those who want to take carriage rides to Duck Park—but no one pays us any mind.

"You have a good evening, ladies."

I thank him, give him a sizable tip, and we get out.

"Is Enoch here yet?" I ask Nicole, nervous.

"He's in position," she says with a grin, handing me a folder. I take it. "You ready to kick some ass?"

"You know what? I think I am."

* * *

The ball is beautiful, like something out of a fairy tale. Gilded birdcages full of fairy lights hang from the ceiling, there are servers in red walking around with glasses of champagne and tiny appetizers—not made by Sinclair—and people in ball gowns and suits and tuxedos. The covers of Vera's biggest books have been blown up and arranged throughout the room, although pride of placement has been given to the enormous portrait of her hanging in the great room, across from the entrance.

A string band in the corner of the room is playing sedate love songs, like we're on an elevator ride that will never end. The singer won't arrive until later.

The photo of Damien and Enoch, I'm amused to see, is on display, despite my father having fired Enoch.

Nicole gives me a *here we go* look as someone carts out an enormous cake, depositing it directly below the portrait of Vera. Sinclair, who's supposed to introduce Vera for her big speech, steps forward, and there's a bit of shuffling before one of the red-suited staffers steps forward with a microphone. Something tells me that was supposed to be Nicole's job, but she's obviously decided it's time to quit.

Edgar James is watching Sinclair, although it's hard to tell what he's thinking. He's handsome in a grave, severe way.

Vera and my father step forward, standing directly across from Sinclair. I edge farther into the shadows to her left.

"Hi, everyone," Sinclair says. "I'm so privileged to be here today to introduce my good friend."

Nicole snorts. I nudge her.

The string band begins a rendition of "Cry Me a River."

I smile. That's a Nicole touch if ever there were one.

"Now, most of us know Vera as the author and creator of so many beautiful stories, from *The Wind in Her Hair*"—someone wolf whistles—"to her newest project, inspired by a couple of local friends." She indicates the enormous photo of Damien and Enoch. My father's eyes narrow as he studies it. Enoch's facing away from the camera, but for someone who knows him well, it could really be no one else. "We're all so privileged to be here tonight, at this beautiful event. Coming here with my date"—she nods to Edgar James—"I feel like I'm embarking on my own fairy tale. But this isn't about me. And it's not about Vera Valence. Because she's not the person who most of you think she is."

There are several gasps from the audience.

Vera drops her champagne glass, and my father steps back in distaste. Pumpkin, who was standing at their feet, sees an opportunity and takes a flying leap at the cake.

As she lands on it, the furry portrait of Vera on her side is on full display.

"Pumpkin, no," Vera shrieks. "*What's happening?*"

Enoch must have taken that as his signal, because he bursts out of the cake, making Vera shriek and my father mutter an obscenity. Cake flies everywhere, and guests back up to avoid soiling their dresses and suits. My father stalks off, presumably to find a guard to do his dirty work, and I push forward to stand next to Enoch.

"Oh, they've come to destroy me!" Vera shouts. "Someone help!"

"Give them the chance to speak," Sinclair says. There's cake on her dress—a white splash of frosting on her cheek, but she stands strong and finishes. "I think you'll be interested in what they have to say. This is my friend, Grace Donnelly, and her *fiancé*, Enoch Laskin. Vera Valence tried to steal their story." She lifts a perfectly manicured finger. "And it's not the first time."

Even though nothing is really going to plan, she's *perfect*—radiant and confident, trustworthy.

Either Sinclair warned Edgar what was going to happen or otherwise he's always like this, because he doesn't seem remotely shaken.

She hands me the microphone. "Hello," I say, suddenly feeling at a loss. I have the folder, yes, I have my truth, but what if no one believes me? What if we're pulled away by guards before we have the chance to tell our story? Enoch takes my hand. He's sticky and covered in cake, and he's the most beautiful sight I've ever seen. Pumpkin settles in at his feet, lying down as if she's found her home. Smart girl.

"*Pumpkin, heel!*" Vera shouts.

And suddenly it's not hard at all.

"I've worked for Vera Valence for six years. Like many of you, she was my idol. I wanted to be an author, like she is, and *The Wind in Her Hair* was my favorite book. It felt like a dream come true when she hired me. Even more so when she promised to mentor me after I finished my book. It took me a long time to write it," I say, feeling choked up. Enoch squeezes my hand, and I glance at him, drawing in his strength and love.

"She's a liar," Vera calls out.

"It didn't take her a long time?" someone asks in confusion.

"It's *mine.*" Then Vera's racing toward me with her nails extended, as if she plans to claw me to death.

"Oh shit," shouts someone from the crowd.

Enoch immediately steps in front of me.

Then Vera slips on a large piece of cake—vanilla crème—and falls to the ground. Edgar James is waiting for her when she gets up. "I can't let you touch her, ma'am," he says firmly.

"I'm not a ma'am," she shouts.

Enoch turns toward me. Presses my left hand to his chest. "Finish," he says. "Tell them."

Then he steps aside, and my heart is full as I say, "It took me a long time because it was based on my personal life." I take his hand and lift it. "On him."

Vera lets out a shriek. If a word was embedded in it, I don't know what it was.

"Enoch and I were together in business school, briefly, before circumstances broke us apart. I wrote him into my book because even though I was angry with him, I couldn't stop thinking about him. Since fate's a funny thing, he ended up working with Vera too, as her brand manager." I steal a glance at him, finding his focus entirely on me. The chaos in the room doesn't seem to register. "And she sent him my manuscript, claiming it was hers. She even asked him to pitch it to her film agent and producers." Loud murmuring fills the room. Vera's making incoherent sounds. "But he read it and knew it was mine. She'd changed the ending, you see, but he was there with me. He *knew.*"

"They were Gracie's words," Enoch adds, leaning in to the microphone. "The things that happened to her characters happened to us. The fight they had is the same one that tore us apart. The only thing Vera changed was the ending. There's no way in hell she wrote that book."

"You misunderstood," Vera shouts. "I sent you the wrong file!"

But from the grumblings in the room, it's obvious few people are on her side. Pumpkin laps up cake from Enoch's shoes, showing off the furry portrait of Vera's face again.

"The ending had been changed," Enoch says flatly. "Gracie found a typewritten version of her original manuscript in your office. You intended to claim you'd hired her to transcribe it. Do you deny it?"

"Yes! She set me up," she wails. "What kind of a brand manager are you, anyway?"

"A bad one," my father says, walking up with two bulky security men.

"An honest one," Edgar James says with a nod. "You have my business."

"And mine," Sinclair says.

Someone shouts from the crowd. "You said it wasn't the first book she'd stolen?"

I lift the folder in my hand. "*The Wind in Her Hair* was conceived of by a woman named May Rollins. She also wrote the first draft. May used to work for Vera just like I did. I leave it to you to decide why Vera signed this contract with May after the book was published...and why May received thirty-five percent of Vera's royalties for it. I have the agreement here."

"Get them out of here," my father sneers to the guards, who come toward us. "This little spectacle has gone on for long enough. You should be ashamed of yourselves."

"No," I say, "you should be ashamed of *yourself*. You disowned your own daughter because she wanted to write romance novels, and yet here you are working with a romance novelist. Letting her get away with stealing other people's work. *My* work."

"These are scurrilous accusations," he says, his face getting red. "You broke in there, and—"

"Actually, they seem pretty reasonable," says a woman standing close to him, her hair in a perfect chignon that has a spot of cake perched atop it. "You missed most of what they said."

"Come with me," the first of the guards says as they reach us.

"You don't mind if I call you Dad, do you?" Enoch asks my father. "Gracie and I are getting married."

If his face was red before, now it's purple. "You convinced my daughter to marry you? Maybe you're less foolish than I thought. But you—"

"I've been in love with your daughter for six years, you pompous asshole. Taking a job with you was the stupidest goddamn thing I ever did."

He looks like he wants to punch my father, but I tug him back. Even though he's strong, he can't get past two security guards, and my father is exactly the sort of person to get litigious about a punch, however well-deserved.

"We'll send you the check, Dad," I say. "I'll even have a courier bring it by. I'm sorry to say you won't be invited to the wedding. You understand. We'll need to cut costs."

The security guards look confused, but they still have a job to do, and they take a step forward.

Enoch lifts his free hand, the other holding mine. "You'll get no argument from us. We have a car waiting outside."

Something tells me Damien's sitting behind the wheel.

"It's so romantic," someone says. "Just like a fairy tale."

"Yes," I say to Enoch, smiling as we're led out by security. "It is, isn't it?"

"Wait for us," Sinclair shouts, coming toward us with Edgar James.

"What about Peony?" he asks.

I can only presume he's talking about the horse.

Enoch and I exchange a look and start laughing as we sweep through the front door of Vera Valence's house one final time. The last thing I see is Pumpkin giving me a dejected look before the door closes on that chapter of my life.

I'm ready for the next one.

ENOCH

"THIS IS OVER THE TOP. I don't need a bodyguard," Sinclair says, her mouth pressed in a firm line. "I've spent most of my life in a gilded cage. I don't need some man following me around everywhere."

"You *do* have some man following you around," I say, "and since the police don't seem overly interested in finding him, you definitely need a bodyguard."

"*See*, I told you," Marnie says, pointing at her sister. "Drew did too. But I knew you'd listen to Enoch." We're all gathered around the bar at Summer Nights. It's closed to the public, because Reggie was adamant that the interview take place here.

Gracie casts a glance at me, a smile playing at her lips. It must be the *I knew you'd listen to Enoch* part that's amused her.

"You like listening to me too," I say with a smirk.

"Sometimes," she admits. "You know, you have Udolpho hair all over your jacket. It's really undermining your whole power play."

I groan. "That's what I get for wearing black."

She reaches over to brush it off, and I capture her hand on my chest.

Andy throws a pretzel at us from the bowl on the bar. "You guys are too cute for my well-being."

"Funny," I say. "That's exactly what my dad told us at breakfast this morning."

Dad and Remi are over-the-moon excited about our engagement. My mother is too, although she's always been more reserved than Dad.

I told Gracie it's because they prefer her to me, but she rebutted that they like the me I am with her better than the me I was without her. It's a fair point. I do too. She's moved some things into the house, and we're using her loft as an office for Level Up Brand Management, a name Remi came up with after reading a Remi-friendly version of Gracie's book. He's already seeing a therapist. I don't want him to have to double up on sessions to talk through reading sex scenes inspired by his uncle.

"It's like you leveled up from enemies to lovers," Remi had said excitedly after finishing the book.

"Did I forget to remove a section that should have been removed?"

"No," he said with a laugh. "It's a trope, Uncle Knock. You know about tropes." He makes a face. "You worked for Vera Valence."

Worked being the operative word.

Vera's spread word that she's in a rehab clinic.

When my dad heard that, he snorted, in typical fashion, and said, "There's no rehab for being a bitch," which made Gracie laugh so hard she spat out her tea.

The bonus of all of this is that Remi seems to have transferred his hero worship from Vera to a more deserving recipient: my future wife. Two more deserving recipients, actually. Despite them having fulfilled their role as Grace's "fairy godmothers," Damien still comes over to hang out now and then. Sometimes we play basketball with Remi, which I'm very bad at and therefore do not like very much. Sometimes we all just talk. Nicole comes with him occasionally, and

I bite my tongue. She *did* buy me new suits to replace the ones she ruined—after insisting that I recount the story of my business meeting striptease half a dozen times. She also likes playing Parcheesi with my dad, and since I'd rather not play Parcheesi most of the time, I'm happy to let her do it.

Nearly two weeks have passed since the party at Vera's house. Two weeks during which the public interest in Sinclair—in all of us, really—has been at an all-time high. Gracie found a literary agent on the spot, and between the video of Edgar James saving Sinclair from her soiled dress and the one of him backing her up in the shitshow at Vera's, everyone in Asheville, and probably the country at large, is convinced they're a couple. Most people can't get enough of them, which is to my benefit since Level Up Brand Management currently has two clients: Edgar James and Sinclair Jones. The reality show is a done deal, set to begin filming soon.

Gracie gave her father the money, but he didn't undergo a personality swap overnight. He's done his damnedest to turn his contacts against me. However, he's not looking so good right now. He's the man who publicly defended Vera Valence, even after she tried to steal his daughter's book.

Needless to say, my clients are important to me because they're my *only* clients. I'm determined to earn the trust that the woman I love has put in me. Which means I'm not going to sit back and watch Sinclair be stupid about this. After she was publicly seen with Edgar, she received a flurry of messages from a secret admirer, presumably the same guy who sent the roses. Some were wheedling, others angry.

They're all trouble.

If you ask me, she needs a bodyguard yesterday. The only reason we haven't pressed the issue before now is because Sinclair went back to Los Angeles to pack up her apartment. She's decided to stay in Asheville long term, with the plan that she'll fly to other locations for filming as necessary. Right now, the only thing she has lined up is Edgar's show. She's hoping a few guest appearances will lead to more daring roles.

"Returning to the whole possible-stalker scenario," Sinclair says. "We don't even know that it's one person." She's speaking in an undertone, like she already knows she's lost the argument. Then she turns toward me on her seat. "Won't it look bad for Edgar's image if his girlfriend has a big beefy guy following her around everywhere?" I can tell from her expression that she thinks she's made a golden point.

"Not at all," I say, taking a sip of my drink. "It'll look like he cares about protecting you from a stalker, since he spends half his time climbing trees."

"Besides, he's not *actually* your boyfriend," Andy says. "You remember that part, right?"

I'm not actually sure why she's here, except that she and Marnie and Gracie are sometimes a package deal.

"It could become real," Griffin says, grinning at Marnie from behind the bar. "Stranger things have happened."

There's movement at the door. Sinclair's back stiffens, but it's just Damien and Nicole coming in.

"Are they here yet?" Damien asks.

"I'm not hiding them behind the bar," Griffin says with a grin.

"Huh," Nicole says, "it's weird to see Reggie's stool without him on it. You think he'd have a heart attack if I keep it warm for him?"

"Yes," Damien says, "and he's about to show up with his jacked son, so let's not try it."

"Do any of us know for sure that this guy actually exists?" I ask as they claim a couple of stools.

Gracie laughs. Damien tilts his head as if he's taking it under serious consideration. "Huh. I guess not," he says after a moment. "Anyone seen a picture?"

There's a chorus of nos.

"Anyway, let's not get distracted," Nicole says. "It's time, Gracie."

"Time for what?" I ask, but Gracie doesn't look confused.

"They're going to help you, Sinclair," she says. "You're their next Fairy Godmother Agency client."

"But I don't need help," Sinclair says. She gestures to me. "I have Enoch."

"Stop," Gracie says, nudging me with her shoulder. "You're going to make him even more arrogant, and then he'll be impossible."

"Improbable." I grin at her and put my hand on her leg.

"Impossible," she repeats but doesn't push my hand away.

I'll take it.

"Did you know about this?" Sinclair asks Marnie.

"We've talked about it," she admits. "You've still been hopping from craft to craft like they're designer drugs."

"Plenty of people have hobbies," Sinclair says with annoyance.

"Usually not a different one every week," Andy offers.

"This is all beside the point," Nicole says. "The point is that you *do* need help. You have a stalker!" She seems entirely too excited about it. "We get to do real investigative work for this one, Damien."

"Shouldn't the police be doing that?" Marnie asks with a frown.

"You know what they said. They can't act until something happens," I say, annoyed. "How messed up is that?"

"Well, you have nothing to worry about," Nicole tells Sinclair. "You have us."

She doesn't seem appeased.

"Besides," Nicole says, "you have a fake boyfriend. We have a high success rate in making fake boyfriends real."

"I'm literally the only person you've managed that trick with," Griffin says from behind the bar, where he's been silently pouring everyone drinks, listening. He does that a lot—soaks in what's going on and builds on conversations without people always noticing he's doing it. "And I think it had a lot more to do with Marnie than your supposed expertise."

"You are totally getting laid tonight," Nicole says.

"Was that in question?" Marnie asks.

"I need to think about this," Sinclair says. "I don't know how I feel about having people poking around in my life."

Gracie, who just took a sip of her drink, sputters on it.

"What?"

Marnie and Andy are laughing with her now, and Damien's mouth is crooked with amusement.

"It's just...you literally just signed up to be an occasional guest star on Edgar James's reality show. Isn't that the definition of people poking around in your life?"

She rolls her eyes. "It's a reality TV show. Everyone knows that's not reality." Her gaze shifts to the clock. "Can we call it? I'm going to go out on a limb and say that Reggie made this guy up."

"Who, me?" We all flinch at Reggie's voice.

"Christ. When did you develop cat-like reflexes?" Nicole asks, watching him take a seat on his usual stool, as if there's nothing particularly special or notable about this day. As if we haven't all been waiting for him.

"You do have a son, don't you?" Griffin asks. "Because you talked about him for about an hour the other night, and I'm seriously worried about your mental well-being if that was all fake."

"He's parking the car, smartass," Reggie says. "Now, pour me a drink."

He shrugs and does. The rest of us watch the door as if it's a kettle of water we're hoping will boil. Footfalls approach the door. I squeeze Gracie's leg and wink at her.

"Holy shit," Andy says. "I really doubted this man's existence."

Then the door opens, and in walks a big, muscular guy with dark hair and Reggie's light brown eyes. Rafe looks the part, sure enough.

"*You*," Sinclair seethes.

"You," he says pleasantly.

"I feel like there's some history here I'm missing," I comment.

Gracie's silently laughing, and through it she explains, "She threw a clay banana at him."

"It looked like a dick," Rafe interjects.

"No, *mine* looked like a dick," Nicole says. "Marnie's looked like a misshapen banana."

"Did you know who I was all along?" Sinclair asks, her gaze focused on Rafe.

"No," he says. "I don't watch TV. But when my father told me about this job, I looked you up."

Sinclair turns to me. "This is never going to work." Her gaze seeks Marnie out. "Marnie? This is completely unnecessary." When she doesn't get the response she wanted, she looks to me.

I consider for a moment, then say, "It's a good thing if you two don't get along. Then no one's going to confuse who they should pay attention to—you and Edgar or you and Rafe."

Her laughter is brittle. "No one would make the mistake of thinking I'd be interested in *him*."

If Rafe cares, it doesn't show. "I'm looking for a job," he says. "If my job's to watch Clay over here, then you can bet your ass no one will be throwing clay at *her*."

"We're dealing with a possible stalker situation," I tell him. "Are you equipped to deal with that?"

"Someone's following you, Clay?" he asks, looking at her.

"Maybe." But it's obvious she's still reluctant to believe it. That's a problem. The realness of the issue is not contingent on her belief in it.

"What would you do if someone took a shot at her?" I ask.

"Isn't that a little overdramatic?" Sinclair says.

"I'd do my damn job and push her out of the way." Rafe lifts his shirt, revealing a scar on his abdomen. "Wouldn't be the first time I took a bullet for someone."

"You've done this before?" Sinclair asks, interested despite herself.

"Didn't say that," he says. "What I said is that I've taken a bullet for someone. I'd do it again if I needed to."

"Even if you don't like me?"

"I do my job."

The way she purses her lips suggests she isn't pleased with his answer, but she gives a slight nod. "Okay."

"Oh, thank God," Marnie says. "I thought you were going to require much more arm twisting. I was going to bring Drew onto the committee."

Andy makes a sound of disbelief. "You honestly thought Drew would be more convincing than us?"

Gracie gives me a significant look, then gets up.

"Give us a second, guys," I say, getting up and following her.

Nicole catcalls us, but I'm pleased to ignore her as I follow Gracie into the hallway leading to the bathrooms. She stops when we're out of sight of the others. "You felt it too," she says, looking at me with raised eyebrows.

"What?" I ask, a grin playing on my lips.

"Enemies to lovers," she says, grabbing the bottom of my shirt and pulling me close. "They have *chemistry*."

My smiles gets wider. "You see chemistry everywhere, Gracie. Two weeks ago, you saw plenty of it between Sinclair and Edgar James."

"I *could* be accused of being a romantic," she says with a small smile.

"Oh, no, I'd never sling around such scurrilous accusations," I respond.

"No, never." She leans in, her face inches from mine.

"Whatever happens, it'll be interesting," I say. "Life's always interesting with you, Gracie Donnelly."

Then I kiss her as if my suit's about to fall apart.

ANGELA CASELLA is a romcom fanatic. Writing them, reading them, watching them—she's greedy, and she does it all. She writes the Fairy Godmother Agency series solo, and she's lucky enough to collaborate with Denise Grover Swank on multiple series.

She lives in Asheville, NC. Her hobbies include herding her daughter toward less dangerous activities, the aforementioned romcom addiction, and dreaming of having someone else clean her house.

Visit her website at www.angelacasella.com or Angela and Denise's shared website at www.arcdgs.com.